Praise for C
Mediev

"*Claire Delacroix is a shining star of the romance genre. Cleverly original, emotional and fast-paced, full of twists and turns, her books will sweep you off your feet!*"
—Julianne Maclean, USA Today bestselling author

"*A beguiling medieval romance...readers will devour this rich and compulsively readable tale.*"
—Publishers' Weekly on **The Rogue**

"*When you open a book by Claire Delacroix, you open a treasure chest of words, rare and exquisite!*"
—Rendezvous

"*An engaging tale of lost love found.*"
—Booklist on **The Rogue**

"*Enthralling and compelling!*"
—TheBestReviews on **The Scoundrel**

"*A delightful romp through medieval times in a game of cat and mouse...The Scoundrel is an enjoyable read, mixed with passion, humor and an unexpected plot that kept me turning the pages.*"
—Romance Junkies

"*[Claire] Delacroix's satisfying tale leaves the reader hungry for the next offering.*"
—Booklist on **The Warrior**

"***The Beauty Bride** is a book that captures you from the first page...a magical and inspiring story. Four hearts!*"
—Pink Heart Reviews

"*A lyrical medieval-era romance!*"
—Publishers Weekly on **The Beauty Bride**

THE
CRUSADER'S
BRIDE

THE
CHAMPIONS
OF
ST. EUPHEMIA

CLAIRE
DELACROIX

The Crusader's Bride
Claire Delacroix

૨⬥

Printing History:
Deborah A. Cooke trade paperback edition
July 2015
ISBN#978-1-927477-51-9

This work has been published in a simultaneous digital edition.

૨⬥

Dear Reader;

Welcome to a new medieval adventure! Beginning a new series is always exciting for me, and this one is particularly so. I love the medieval era and particularly the twelfth century, so it's been wonderful to revisit this period. I've also been thinking for a while about a linked series following a company of knights on a quest, with each knight finding not just adventure but true love along the way. This series begins in Jerusalem, where our knights are given the task of delivering a precious relic to Paris. We journey with them to Venice and then to Paris, the supposed end of their mission. While this is the end of Gaston's part in the mission, it's not the end of the story for the other knights. One knight, Wulfe, will continue in pursuit of the villain, to see justice done. Another knight, Fergus, will secretly take custody of the treasure to see it secured near his home in Scotland.

These stories also intersect and overlap, a structure that intrigues me. For example, Gaston meets and marries Ysmaine in Jerusalem, at the beginning of the quest and the beginning of book #1, **The Crusader's Bride**. *We also meet Christina in this first book, shortly after Wulfe meets her, but we don't witness the adventure that compels them to become reluctant allies. That night is the beginning of* **The Crusader's Heart**, *book #2 in the series. Similarly, neither Gaston nor Ysmaine know what the squires are arguing about, much less why Bartholomew settles the dispute, but we'll learn more about that in a subsequent story. I'm quite enjoying the challenge of showing discussions and incidents from different points of view and hope you enjoy it, too. By the end of* **The Crusader's Vow**, *book #4, all of your questions should be answered!*

I had originally planned for these stories to be linked novellas, but Gaston and Ysmaine insisted that their story be a full length book. So it is and so will the others be. These books will be published at three month intervals, so you can expect Wulfe's book in October 2015, Bartholomew's in January 2016 and Fergus' in April 2016. The additional books are available for pre-order at some portals now.

And finally, a confession: I've taken some poetic license with this series, with two details in particular. Saint Euphemia was a virgin and a martyr who died in AD 303 in Chalcedon. Her relics were subsequently scattered. It was rumored that the Templars possessed the precious relic of her head, and there are accounts in the trials of the Templars (from later centuries) of them worshiping a head. Although there is no absolute evidence that this head was that of Euphemia—and that relic has not been located—I decided to make it so. Also, the tunnel in Acre does exist and was discovered only recently. It is believed to have been built by the Templars and to date from the years after Acre was reclaimed from the Saracens. I decided, for the sake of Gaston and Ysmaine, that it might have been under construction before the city was lost.

In other news, my historical romances are being produced in audio editions. Right now, all of the Jewels of Kinfairlie series is available in audio, as well as **The Rogue**. The True Love Brides are in production and all four titles should be available in audio by the end of 2015. Then we'll go back and finish the Rogues of Ravensmuir. As well as going back, the audio editions are going forward: The Champions of Saint Euphemia will be starting in audio production this fall, with the goal of having each book available in audio just a few months after the initial release.

Until next time, I hope you are well and have plenty of good books to read.

All my best,

THE CRUSADER'S VOW (April 2016)

Short Stories
BEGUILED

Apocalyptic Romances:
The Prometheus Project:
FALLEN
GUARDIAN
REBEL
ABYSS

❧

Deborah Cooke Books

Contemporary Romance:
The Coxwells:
THIRD TIME LUCKY
DOUBLE TROUBLE
ONE MORE TIME
ALL OR NOTHING

Paranormal Romance:
Dragonfire:
KISS OF FIRE
KISS OF FURY
KISS OF FATE
WINTER KISS
WHISPER KISS
DARKFIRE KISS
FLASHFIRE
EMBER'S KISS
THE DRAGON LEGION NOVELLAS
SERPENT'S KISS
FIRESTORM FOREVER

Paranormal Young Adult:
The Dragon Diaries:
FLYING BLIND
WINGING IT
BLAZING THE TRAIL

❧

THE
CRUSADER'S
BRIDE

THE
CHAMPIONS
OF
ST. EUPHEMIA

CLAIRE
DELACROIX

NEW YORK TIMES BESTSELLING AUTHOR

Friday, May 15, 1187

Feast Day of Saint Dympna and Saint Britwyn of Beverley.

❧

Prologue

Jerusalem

Gaston de Châmont-sur-Maine read the missive from his brother's wife again, unable to believe that he had understood the words correctly the first time. That Bayard should have died so suddenly and at such a young age was incomprehensible to Gaston.

That his older brother was not laughing as he rode to hunt was beyond belief.

But Marie's meaning could not be doubted. It was there, before his own eyes. Bayard was dead, and he, Gaston, was now Baron de Châmont-sur-Maine. He touched the red wax seal, embedded with the mark of his family's house, impressed with the signet ring that he had only to ride home to claim.

Châmont-sur-Maine was his.

Gaston would have preferred that Bayard yet lived. His older brother had taken the responsibility of Châmont-sur-Maine with ease and grace, with a charm that Gaston did not share. Gaston was a fighting man, a man accustomed to a simple life. Indeed, as a knight sworn to the Order of the Temple, he should not have held this missive himself. Any correspondence addressed to him or any other brother was delivered to the Grand Master, who chose whether or not to have the missive read aloud to the intended recipient.

Gaston had thought it might be a jest at his expense when Gerard de Ridefort had read this missive aloud in the common room the day before. So great was his astonishment that the Grand Master had read Marie's words twice, permitted Gaston to examine the seal, then had finally surrendered it to Gaston with characteristic impatience.

Gerard had then ordered Gaston to compile all reports of

Saracen movements, before Gaston could submit his request to leave the order. A knight pledged to the Temple could not disobey an order from a superior, so he had to fulfill Gerard's edict before returning home.

It might be a blessing, though, to have a few weeks to plan for his journey. The change to his life would be significant, after all.

Gaston looked around the stables of the Knights Templar, situated in the Temple in the Holy City itself, amazed that he would leave this place to become a baron of the realm. He stood in the stall assigned to his own destrier, Fantôme, even as that steed nuzzled in the hay, and read the missive again. His squires had been dispatched to take a meal in the kitchens, and he had come to this place to consider the abrupt change in his fortunes. The son of his father's third wife, and his father's third son, Gaston had never expected to be a secular lord. That was why he had joined the Templars.

He ached that good fortune came at such a price, and that he would never hear Bayard's bold laughter again. Gaston wished he found it harder to believe that a man so vital could draw breath no longer, but he had seen lives dispatched with such frequency in this place that he took little for granted any longer.

Bayard was gone.

As always, the extensive stables of the Templars were bustling with activity. Even though many had gone to the evening meal, still knights returned from errands and from duty, their horses slick with perspiration. Others were preparing to ride out, their steeds stamping with impatience to run. Some great destriers were being brushed down while others were saddled up. The floor was thick with squires, hastening to do the bidding of their knights, and the air was filled with jokes and commands. He could smell the hay in the stables and hear the clang of anvil on steel from the smithy as repairs were made to armor and armament. Fantôme nibbled Gaston's hair playfully from behind and he rubbed the beast's nose with affection.

Gaston had pledged to the Templars eighteen years before, when he himself had been a youth, and had never expected to leave the order. Well, not while he breathed. Bayard was a mere seven years older than Gaston. He was—or had been—hale and vigorous. Was it strange that Marie had not specified how Bayard had died?

Or had Gaston become too suspicious over the years?

The fact remained that Bayard had only two daughters. His will decreed that Châmont-sur-Maine pass to Gaston instead of his own children.

It was a profoundly sensible choice, and one that no neighbor would argue. Bayard had always been the one who ensured that all continued on a steady course. It was interesting that the dispute in the Latin Kingdoms over the succession was so similar—save that Amalric, unlike Bayard, had put no plan in writing. The daughters of the former King of Jerusalem were locked in a dispute over which of their husbands should gain the crown. The Christians bickered, while Saladin planned his vengeance.

Gaston was keenly aware of the differences between himself and his brother. He was accustomed to war and battle, to the company of men and the good care of horses, to calling the bluff of an adversary, and to settling disputes with a blade. He knew little of running an estate, although he had witnessed his fair share of politics and intrigue. He fingered the letter again, astounded at the opportunity, knowing he could not deny it, yet strangely uncertain of what lay ahead.

His life had been disciplined, governed by the rule of the order for so long that he could not imagine living otherwise. He would ride to hunt at whim, feast in his own hall upon fine fare, garb himself as he chose, and sleep in the same bed every night. It was impossible to associate his brother's life with himself, and Gaston doubted he would accustom himself readily to the change.

There was no choice, though. It was his responsibility to accept this legacy, and Gaston understood duty. He also was a practical man.

He would have to father a son to ensure Châmont-sur-Maine's future and for that, he would need a wife. A bastard son or one got on a mistress would undo Bayard's planning. Gaston must ensure he had a legitimate heir.

If not two.

He read the missive again, his gaze lingering on a detail he had skimmed over earlier for he had been more concerned with Bayard's death. Marie confided that her oldest daughter, Azalaïs, had been wedded this very year, and to Millard de St. Roux. The timing could not be accident or coincidence. Gaston knew Millard well enough for that man was but a year younger than himself.

A younger son, like himself.

A man without a holding or a future, and one who had earned his way with his blade.

Why had Marie told him of this? To imply that the lordship would be assumed by Millard in his absence? Or to warn him of a feud to come?

It was clear that if Gaston wished to claim what was his by right and by law, he would have to return home soon, and with a wife.

If not a son.

Gaston tucked the missive into his tabard, eyeing the activity that surrounded him. He would find a bride and embark upon the task of making sons. He had seen three and thirty summers, and Bayard's death made him taste his own mortality. There was not a moment to waste in securing the future.

As much as he might feel trepidation, Gaston could not regret that he would no longer have to follow Gerard de Ridefort's command. He instinctively distrusted those who followed their impulse and were impetuous as Gerard tended to be. The astonishing losses of Templar knights at Cresson this same month showed the merit of that man's leadership, and Gaston did not imagine for a moment that the Saracen leader Saladin meant to leave matters as they stood.

Here was his opportunity to change his own circumstance, and he would take it.

Indeed, if he meant to return alive to Châmont-sur-Maine and ensure the future of his family holding—as was now his responsibility above all others—he had best complete his current assignment and leave the order as soon as possible.

But where would a man who had long been pledged to chastity and celibacy find a wife? Gaston had no sisters or aunts intent upon finding him a match, nor any friends or fellow knights who maintained connections with women. The rule precluded that.

Christian women on pilgrimage oft prayed at the Church of the Holy Sepulchre. It seemed reasonable to Gaston to begin his search there. His expectations of a bride were minimal. She would have to be of noble blood, unwed, and both young and vigorous enough to bear him multiple sons. It would not be all bad if he found her attractive, for that would make rendering the marital debt more pleasant.

Beyond that, Gaston expected little of a wife. He hoped to find a practical woman, for he knew naught of courtship or even of conversing with women. He imagined that his inheritance would offer sufficient inducement to the kind of woman he sought.

Gaston de Châmont-sur-Maine left the stables with purpose, certain that all could be arranged sensibly and quickly.

This optimism was only possible because Gaston knew so little of women in general, and of Ysmaine de Valeroy in particular.

That situation would not last.

Saturday, July 4, 1187

Feast Day of Saint Odo of Canterbury.

❧

Claire Delacroix

Chapter One

Ysmaine de Valeroy knelt in the Church of the Holy Sepulchre and prayed yet again. She prayed with a fervor unusual to her, her heart in her entreaty as it had never been before. Indeed, there had been a time when she had been outspoken and rebellious, not devout at all. Two short marriages had compelled her to change her ways.

It was not easy. She had tried to atone for her sins, though she feared she had little aptitude for penance. She had donated every item of value she owned. She had given alms and made offerings. She had undertaken a pilgrimage to this most holy of shrines, and she had walked most of the way, letting her maid Radegunde ride the mare. She was certain she had lit a thousand candles, many for her husbands' souls, many for her own. The leather of her shoes was worn through. Her clothes had faded and were filled with dust. She had been hungry for so long that she had become accustomed to the feel of a hollow belly.

But still the challenges mounted before her.

Perhaps she was simply doomed.

Perhaps she was cursed because she did not believe in her guilt. Perhaps she should accept that it was her responsibility that her husbands had died, instead of believing it a trick of fate.

But Ysmaine could not. There was the mark of her stubborn pride again.

It was not uncommon for a young bride to bury an old spouse, and only slightly less uncommon for an aged man to become overly excited at the prospect of consummating his nuptials. One did hear tales of men dying on their wedding night, so the death of Ysmaine's first spouse had been unfortunate, but not that remarkable.

At least to those other than Ysmaine. She would never forget

Claire Delacroix

being trapped beneath Richard's corpse for the duration of the night, feeling his body grow cold even as she was helpless to shift his considerable weight. She would never forget the indignity of being released by four servants the following morning, nor the smell of that bed. She had not known whether to consider herself fortunate or not that Richard had not commenced upon the deed, the anticipation alone having overwhelmed him. To have lain naked beneath a man all the night long yet still be a virgin incited curiosity, if not more.

The whispers had begun then, though she and her family had turned a deaf ear to them. Ysmaine did not believe that her bold nature invited such punishment. She did not believe that her merry manner required discipline by any authority. She simply regretted that her father's good intentions had not borne fruit.

Her father had not been deterred, although his second match had been less brilliant.

All had known Henrik to be fond of his wine, so some were not surprised that he stumbled upon the stairs on his nuptial night and fell to his death without reaching the bed where Ysmaine awaited his amorous attention.

Others, though, began to whisper that Ysmaine had pledged her chastity to God, or worse, that she was a witch determined to never let a man between her thighs. The tales had grown over the Yule, taking on a vehemence that had confounded her father's every effort to make a third match.

He had not even been able to find matches for her younger sisters.

Believing the fault was her own and that the remedy must be her responsibility, Ysmaine had resolved to depart on a pilgrimage. There could be no half-measures with a curse of such magnitude so she had decided to go to Jerusalem itself. Her parents had initially protested, for her mother had been fearful of Ysmaine traveling so far. Seeing his daughter's resolve and his wife's fears, Ysmaine's father had dispatched her with a party of defenders and much gold coin to ensure her safe passage.

Perhaps too much gold coin.

But a fortnight from home, Ysmaine and Radegunde had been robbed by the men hired to defend them. Ysmaine had been certain it was but a test, and that if she could make it to Jerusalem, all would be well. They had been compelled to beg for charity and sell every trinket remaining to them, but they had reached the Holy City.

And now, cruelest of cruelties, Radegunde lay sick with fever. Sweet, faithful Radegunde, the maid compelled to join her mistress on pilgrimage, the maid driven on by her mistress's insistence, would pay the price of Ysmaine's curse.

There was no coin for the apothecary's cure.

There was nothing left to sell to raise the coin.

And Ysmaine feared it was her fault. She wept at her own failures even as she prayed for divine intervention. There was no more lowly sinner than she, and no one less likely to deserve compassion, yet Ysmaine hoped for it all the same. She knelt before the altar of the Virgin, for she expected no mercy from men. Mary the intercessor was her only hope. Surely Mary would see the repentance in Ysmaine's heart and have mercy.

Just spare Radegunde, Ysmaine prayed. *Just let me help her, and I will never desire any other thing in all my days.* She was dizzy with hunger, her hands clenched tightly before herself as she prayed with all her might. She cared naught for her own discomfort. If Radegunde died, Ysmaine feared her own soul would be lost forever.

At the very least, she would go mad with guilt.

Despite her concentration on her prayer, Ysmaine was aware that someone watched her. Surely not another predator? A shiver ran down her spine, and she completed her entreaty, then raised her head to look.

It was a knight.

A Templar.

Ysmaine was slightly relieved, for all knew such men to be honorable.

The knight stood to one side of the chapel, his gaze fixed upon her, his arms folded across his chest. He made no effort to hide his interest in her. There was something appealing about a man who had no desire to disguise his deeds. Ysmaine noted that the others in the chapel were aware of his perusal, and only then understood the space around her on this day.

People believed him to be her protector.

Was he?

His surplice was white, graced with the red cross of the Templar order, and it fell to his knees. He was tall and broad of shoulder, his eyes narrowed with a skepticism Ysmaine had seen often on the faces of those who served. The knights in the Holy Land seemed more hardened in comparison to those fighting men she had encountered at home, to the point of appearing emotionless and cold. She was certain they had witnessed much of the weakness of mortal men, and perhaps observing such shortcomings in this holy place pained them.

This one's scrutiny was disconcerting, though. His hair was as dark as ebony and his face was tanned from the sun. His chain mail gleamed, the mark of an attentive squire, and his boots were dark. There were leather gloves tucked into his belt, and both a knife and sword were in scabbards hanging from it. A mail coif had fallen back on his neck. He appeared to be ready to ride to war at any moment, and Ysmaine wondered how close his destrier was.

She felt a flush rise over her cheeks at his steady perusal and wondered if he thought her a thief. The Knights Templar guarded the sacred shrines, after all, and accompanied pilgrims on the treacherous length of road between the ports and Jerusalem itself.

She stood, genuflected, then made to return to Radegunde, hoping against hope that her prayers had made some difference. There was little else she could do. How she hated the powerlessness of her situation, this new inability to reach into her purse for a coin to make matters better. It was humbling.

Ysmaine would not surrender, no matter how dire all appeared to be. She was the daughter of a line of aristocrats with valiant hearts. Somehow, she would find a way to make all come aright. Somehow, she would dispel this curse, see Radegunde healed, and return home with a scheme for her younger sisters to wed well. The challenges before her were daunting when gathered into a list, but Ysmaine had been born with a will of iron.

Only now, she could see that she would have need of it. Her pride would be her salvation, not her curse.

She started when she heard a step beside her, then glanced down to see a silver penny offered on a man's lined palm. She looked up to find the Templar beside her, his gaze watchful and more potent with proximity. His eyes were a startling blue that made her think of twilight skies at home. A lump rose in her throat, for she was not certain she would ever see that holding or those beloved faces again.

"You mistake my trade, sir," she said stiffly. She averted her gaze, her heart thumping, and hastened out of the church.

He followed her, undeterred, his heavy footfalls audible. He stepped into her path, compelling her to confront him, and offered the coin again. He was taller than she had realized, tall enough that he towered over her. His eyes were yet narrowed, but his expression was not unkind.

"I give alms in a sacred place," he insisted, his voice a low rumble that was uncommonly pleasing. He offered the coin again. "But I would forgo the complication of making my offering through the priests."

Ysmaine found she could not look away from this intent knight. His accent was familiar, and she seized the excuse to study him, wondering whether they had once met. She did not recognize him, though. "Why?" she asked, thinking he might confess to being the son of one of her father's neighbors.

"You are hungry," he said, his tone practical. "It is not uncommon for pilgrims to arrive in this place with no coin left to their names." He took her hand in his, his touch both warm and gentle.

She knew it was only because she was so surprised by his move that he managed to capture her hand. The warmth of his hand folded around hers, making her feel small and delicate, though she was a comparatively tall woman.

He pressed that silver penny into her palm with a heavy fingertip as she watched his hands, his determination evident. "I believe it is the task of men to make a difference in this world, while they yet can. Fortify yourself." He curled her fingers over the coin, then released her, stepping back out of her path, still observing her.

Ysmaine opened her hand, halfway thinking this gift would have disappeared. It might be a mirage, a trick of hunger and of the heat. But the coin was still there, nestled coolly in her own palm. Salvation glinted silver in the sunlight, and even when she blinked, it remained.

"You cannot do this," she protested. "Alms must be given to the church, then dispensed..."

"I can give my charity where I so choose," he corrected, interrupting her with a confidence that she had once shared.

Ysmaine heard her father's warning in her thoughts. *Any offer that appears too good to be true must* not *be true.* Doubtless this gift had a price, and she could guess what it would be. Ysmaine was not prepared to surrender her sole surviving asset, not for one silver penny. She stretched out her hand. "I cannot accept such a gift."

"Why not?" The knight seemed genuinely curious, as if it had not occurred to him that she might decline.

Ysmaine saw no reason to mince words. "Because you will have expectations of me, and I tell you now that I will not fulfill them for a single penny, nor for even a king's ransom."

His smile flashed, softening his features unexpectedly. "I do have an expectation, 'tis true, but not the one you anticipate."

His smile weakened her resolve, which frightened her. Ysmaine pushed the coin toward him again. "I cannot accept your charity."

The knight shook his head. "Yet I will not accept its return." He indicated the people all around them with a smooth gesture. "Drop the coin, if you like. Another will seize it, upon that you can rely."

Ysmaine knew he was right, and a measure of her former boldness returned to her. What harm could come of asking him for the truth? "What expectation do you have of me, then?" she asked, lifting her chin. "Is it too much to ask for the sum of the tale?"

"Indeed not. I have the same expectation of you as of any other person to whom I would surrender a coin." He leaned closer and dropped his voice low, his eyes glinting as if they shared a secret. "That how you spend it will reveal the truth of your nature."

Ysmaine was intrigued by this confession. "Why should you care?"

He arched a dark brow. "I am curious." She sensed that there was yet more than he admitted, but the longer she held the coin, the less readily she could surrender it. He spread his hands, his eyes twinkling in a way that lightened Ysmaine's heart. "And this curiosity is my burden to bear."

"Are you frequently curious?" she asked, unable to stop herself.

"Does it matter?"

"Only that curiosity at this price at frequent intervals could see you in my place. You should take care not to expend too much coin on your burden."

His smile was quick, as if she had surprised him, and faded all too soon. He looked ten years younger when he smiled. "I show marked care with coin, my lady," he assured her, his salute making her heart skip. "You need not fear otherwise."

"Why me?"

"You have come daily to pray for intercession. I would grant your request."

"You noticed."

"I did." There was a shrewdness in his expression then. "In these lands, in my trade, a man who fails to be observant does not survive overlong."

It was easy to believe that this knight had cheated death and deceit, for she doubted he missed any detail. Even as she spoke with him, she was aware that his gaze swept over the area at regular intervals. She did not doubt that he could provide a full description of each person who had arrived and departed while he was there.

Ysmaine looked down at the coin. If this was divine intercession, she would not spurn it. She squared her shoulders and looked up at her benefactor. "Will you tell me where I can find the best apothecary?"

The knight was visibly surprised. "Are you ill?"

"My maid lies abed with a fever." Ysmaine shook her head at her own role in this. "It would be beyond unkind for her to die, a foul reward for her loyalty and devotion."

"But you are hungry." If he had been watchful before, he was doubly so with this revelation.

"And Radegunde is in need of a cure." Ysmaine spoke firmly even as she met his gaze. "If any should die on this pilgrimage, it should be me." He looked startled by her vehemence, but Ysmaine continued. "You are of the Temple. You must abide in this city. Tell me, sir, where I can find the best apothecary, I beg of you."

He nodded once, and she had the sense that he was satisfied with her reply. "Better," he said in that rumbling low voice. "I shall take you there." His fingertips were beneath her elbow then, his touch helpful but chivalrous.

He fairly cut a path through the crowd, his stature and the mark of his order making the people in the street fall back to let him pass. Ysmaine felt a heady sense that she no longer battled against her fate alone and was grateful. Even if this man was her ally solely in obtaining an apothecary's potion, it was more, far more, than she had come to expect of the world.

It was only as they walked that she noted his slight limp. But then, he was a knight and a crusader. Of course, he had been injured. If a limp was the worst of it, he had been more fortunate than many others. She admired that he did not slow his pace or look for sympathy. It said much good of his nature, in her opinion, that he simply carried on without complaint.

Perhaps the injury to his leg was why he knew the best apothecary.

Ysmaine wondered what exactly was wrong with his leg, and if the apothecaries in this city were as competent as those she had known at home. If not, she might be able to suggest some means of relief to this unexpected benefactor. Her grandmother had taught her a few remedies and it seemed only fitting that she offer advice in return for his aid.

Assuming, of course, that he truly took her to an apothecary. Ysmaine reminded herself to be skeptical until his intent was proven and hastened alongside the knight to a destination unknown.

ॐ

Gaston had noticed the noblewoman several days before. She was slender and feminine, undoubtedly more slender than once for her cheeks showed that she had recently lost weight. He could see that her hair was as gold as sunlight beneath her veil and her thickly lashed eyes were a fine clear green. The striking combination was one to which he was particularly susceptible, never mind when the woman in question was as pretty as this lady.

Word had come that Saladin had crossed the Jordan River the day before, and Gaston feared the portent of that. Reginald of Châtillon might have provoked the Saracen leader for the last time. That man, as Lord of Karak by the Dead Sea, had a dangerous habit of attacking Saracen pilgrims on their way to their holy city of Mecca and plundering their wealth. Each time Reginald swore a treaty with Saladin, he broke it again. The previous year, he had broken an oath and captured a caravan with one of the sultan's own sisters. Saladin had vowed to kill Reginald with his own hand. Gaston knew enough of Saladin from his own past duties as a negotiator to fear that the retaliation would be swift and sure.

And so it had been. In March, Saladin had marched toward Karak to defend pilgrims and laid waste to Reginald's territories. Instead of uniting in their own defense, the Christians were at odds over who should claim the throne of Jerusalem. Reginald had allied with Gerard de Ridefort, Master of the Temple, and others to enthrone Sibylla, the older daughter of the previous king Amalric. Sibylla, in her turn, had crowned her husband, Guy de Lusignan, king of Jerusalem. Raymond of Tripoli, however, supported a rival king, Humphrey of Toron, the husband of Amalric's younger daughter, Isabella.

In the spring, the Masters of the Temple and the Hospital had ridden to Tiberias to negotiate with Raymond, hoping to persuade him to accept Guy as king. Raymond, however, had hoped to win Saladin's support for his side, so had allowed Saladin's troops to pass through his lands at Tiberias to avenge the caravan attacks made by Reginald. Although Raymond declared he had warned the Christians, the Grand Master of the Temple insisted they had not known of the safe passage granted to Saladin's forces. The two forces had engaged at the springs of Cresson on the first of May. The Christians had been soundly defeated, with forty knights and Roger de Moulins, Master of the Hospitaliers, killed.

Although Raymond had pled his own innocence and returned to Jerusalem with the retreating Master of the Temple, prepared to support Guy as king, Gerard de Ridefort was not alone in believing him to be a traitor. And so, the Christians were distracted while Gaston gathered impressions of a Saracen force mustering just beyond their borders. Hard details were difficult to obtain, but he knew this region and these personalities well enough to anticipate that Saladin's reckoning had begun.

The King of Jerusalem had ridden out to confront Saladin, the Grand Masters of both the Temple and the Hospital accompanying him. The majority of the Templar knights in Jerusalem had joined the party, and triumph was expected. After all, the Christians had mustered a force of thousands, both knights and foot soldiers. The fortification at La Saphorie was a perfect site to defend, and also the location of a spring sufficiently reliable to ensure that such an army had enough water. Gaston, his departure eminent and his vows dissolved, had been left behind as one of the few knights in the Temple. He was not the only one who expected to have departed by their inevitable return.

At this point, there was little that could be accomplished with diplomacy.

If Saladin had crossed the Jordon, he would come eventually to Jerusalem. It was time to leave the Holy City, if Gaston meant to do so.

It was time to choose a bride, and he would have this one.

The lady was a pilgrim, and he admired how diligently she came to pray. He found her in the Church of the Holy Sepulchre several times a day, always kneeling penitent before the altar of the Virgin. She did not follow the pilgrim's path to pray at the Holy Sepulchre itself, much less the Way of the Cross from the Chapel of the Repose, and her routine did not vary.

Gaston admired her resolve. He was more likely to trust people who were constant and consistent, as well as those who did not accept defeat readily.

Her kirtle had once been crimson, a costly hue, but had faded to a pale rose. He could see the true color along the seams. The embroidery on the hem had been golden and rich, but now was brown and dusty. He was no good judge of women's clothing but he recalled his father's enumerations of the expenses of a wife well enough.

This woman's cloak, too, had once been richest purple, another costly dyestuff, and looked as if the fur lining had been cut out of it. Perhaps she had sold it en route to finance her journey. She held up her chin and did not cast her eyes downward, a mark of her aristocratic status that could not be disguised by grime.

He liked her humility, and that she traveled as a true pilgrim. He admired the vigor of her faith and the strength of her devotion to Mary. He respected that she held her chin high, though clearly she faced many challenges. She wore no wedding ring, but kept her head covered, even when she left the church. She had been married then, but was no longer. There was something about her that snared his attention, a blend of vulnerability and strength, perhaps.

By this, the third day he had seen her, Gaston was resolved that she was a logical choice of bride.

When she rose from her prayers and wavered, apparently so hungry as to be faint, he knew it was time to speak to her.

Within moments, she had surprised him thrice: by her conviction that he sought a whore's favors; by her apparent resolve to decline the coin she so clearly needed; and finally by her request for an apothecary. She thought of her maid before herself, which was both rare and admirable.

Indeed, a clever and compassionate wife would suit Gaston well.

She walked beside him, as tall as a queen, her manner making people step back to give way. It was past midday and the sun was hot, dust rising from the streets as they walked. Throngs of pilgrims made their way to the Church of the Holy Sepulchre, though he and his lady companion walked against the tide. The Street of Palms was thick with pilgrims and vendors selling dried palms. On either side of the street, vendors hawked their wares, shouting the advantages of their goods over the human sea of those come to worship. The lady seemed to draw a little closer to him as the vendors took note of them, that coin locked in her grasp even as she ducked the entreaties on all sides.

Gaston suspected he would not miss these congested routes once he left the city. Indeed, it would be good to ride over verdant hills again and he knew that his destrier would not miss the heat. The climate was hard upon the great warhorses, and even though his had been bred in this region, he would be glad to take Fantôme to France. It was time for his destrier to graze at pasture, a reward for his years of good service.

Home. How curious that he had not thought of Châmont-sur-Maine as home until so recently. Home had been at the Temple, either here in Jerusalem or in Paris.

Gaston escorted the lady, as he had vowed, to the best apothecary in the Street of Herbs. He knew he was not the only one to breathe in relief once they stepped into the darkness of the shop. It smelled of dried herbs and the fire from a brazier. One glimpse of the insignia on his tabard and they were ushered into the back room where the old woman held court amid her roots and potions.

She had dark eyes and golden skin, and her hair had once been dark as well. Now it was lined with silver, and her eyes were narrowed, her face lined. Fatima had seen much and suffered fools poorly. Her skill was exceptional, though, and her sons allowed her to do some trade with Gentiles, for the coin made their life simpler.

Gaston and the knights of the Temple were among those preferred clients. It was not until they stood before Fatima and his companion caught her breath that Gaston realized he might have erred.

"She is an infidel," the lady protested, speaking both in French and under her breath. Gaston feared that this noblewoman might share the views of so many of his brethren.

He had no chance to comment, though. Fatima straightened, fixing Gaston's companion with a stern eye. "Who exactly is the infidel?" she demanded in perfect French, then scoffed.

The lady glanced up at Gaston in confusion, and he doubted she had even spoken to a Saracen before.

"Our lives are mingled in this place," he said mildly. "And together we fare better than alone."

Her lips parted, then tightened.

"The knowledge of the Saracens, my lady, is much admired in matters of medicine." Gaston wondered if she would believe him, or whether she would trust him. "And Fatima's skill is exceptional. You did ask for the best apothecary in Jerusalem."

Fatima nodded, his endorsement restoring her good humor. She nodded at him, indicating his hip. "Better?"

He shrugged. "No worse, which is a blessing in itself."

"You are not sufficiently kind to yourself," Fatima began her usual scolding, but Gaston lifted a hand.

"On this day, the lady has need of your skills." He was well aware that his companion listened to this exchange.

The noblewoman squared her shoulders again, then inclined her head to the older woman. "I apologize for my rudeness. My mistaken belief that you would not understand me does not excuse my poor manners. I was simply surprised."

Gaston was relieved by this speech, and Fatima nodded. "And

you have need of me," she noted, her gaze flicking over the woman by Gaston's side. "What ails you?"

"My maid has a fever."

"When did it begin? How long has it endured? Tell me all of it." The older woman bowed her head and closed her eyes to listen, nodding at intervals as the noblewoman provided details. Gaston was impressed that she was so thorough and observant.

When his lady companion fell silent, Fatima blew through her lips. "It is as so oft befalls the Franj here," she murmured, shaking her head as if his fellows should have the wits to stay home. "But worse."

The noblewoman caught her breath in fear.

But Fatima reached without hesitation for a number of herbs, crumbling them into a mortar. Her confidence and her rhythmic movements seemed to reassure his companion. Roots were added and all ground together with the pestle, the pungent scent of the herbs rising to tease Gaston's nostrils. "You noted her symptoms well," Fatima said as she mixed, her gaze flicking to the noblewoman.

"My grandmother knew much of the useful plants. She taught me some of her cures, so I would have some such skills to take to my husband's household, but mostly, she advised me how to look."

"So that a more skilled healer could aid you." Fatima nodded. "This is more wise than sharing the cure."

The noblewoman smiled. "She said as much herself." The two women exchanged a glance, understanding each other, then Fatima hummed as she continued to assemble the ingredients. Gaston and the noblewoman stood silently together, waiting.

Fatima then—as was her wont—suddenly glanced up and put out her hand, palm up.

Some signs were universal.

The noblewoman put Gaston's silver penny on Fatima's palm without hesitation. Fatima bit it, nodded at the quality of the silver, then glanced at Gaston as if she understood its origin. She said naught, but poured the dry combination of herbs into a crockery cup and offered it to the noblewoman. "Four times you will give it, one quarter of this each time heated in wine. On the morrow, you will return and tell me how she fares."

Claire Delacroix

The lady shook her head. "This will have to suffice. I have no more coin and I would not beg more charity..."

"You have paid for a cure and will have it. You need bring no more coin on the morrow." The older woman's dark eyes glinted and she smiled. "Even an infidel can keep a bargain such as that."

"I thank you, Fatima," Gaston said with a bow.

She let the coin flash before it disappeared. "And I thank you, Franji. Take your ease in the evening, instead of striding about the Temple, and your hip will welcome the change."

"It is not always my choice, Fatima," Gaston acknowledged, well aware that the noblewoman listened avidly. He liked the idea of a wife who could help to ensure the health and welfare of those sworn to his service. They said their farewells and left the shop, the street seeming more hot and congested than it had been before.

The noblewoman let Gaston guide her back to the street, then halted to confront him. "I thank you for your assistance..."

"You have need of a meal yet," he interrupted.

Her eyes flashed in a most beguiling manner. "I will not be further indebted to you..."

He interrupted her flatly. "My lady, no healing can occur when a body is so weakened by lack of food, and you know it as well as I do. Your maid must be as hungry as you are. In the Street of Cookery, which is close by, we will find hot soup."

She licked her lips in anticipation, probably not even aware that she did as much, her hunger undermining her argument. "But..."

Gaston shook his head. "I can well afford a pot of soup. I will carry it back to your lodgings for you, so it is not spilled." Indeed, she was so unsteady on her feet that he scarce trusted her with the herbal remedy, though he already suspected that she would fight him for possession of it.

She had a will of iron, this one, which he also liked.

"Nay." The lady did not move and her lips set with resolve. "You cannot take responsibility for me so readily as that. I am not a stray hound to be gathered up, with no understanding of your intention..."

He set one heavy finger against her lips and her eyes widened at his bold touch even as she fell silent. Gaston saw no reason to argue with her, and indeed, he suspected that his sensible plan

24

would meet with her approval. She seemed a most practical woman.

"I mean to make you my lady wife, and that cannot be done if you are faint with hunger." He saw her astonishment, knowing that he had fully captured her attention. "As my betrothed, you are rightly my responsibility, and the expenditure of some measure of coin to ensure your welfare, as well as that of your maid, is of little concern." Gaston turned to walk to the Street of Cookery, fully confident that the lady would follow.

He smiled when he heard her footstep behind him, for he was right.

Chapter Two

Wed?

Did the Templars accept madmen into their service?

Ysmaine hastened after the knight who had shown her such kindness, noting that he neither slowed his pace nor apparently doubted that she would pursue him. He moved quickly, despite that limp.

"You cannot mean to do as much," she protested when she was just behind him again. He turned, placing his hand beneath her elbow again and guiding her beside him. His grace and his manners were admirable, even if his notions were odd.

"Why ever not?"

"You wear the insignia of the Templars, an order of warrior monks. Surely that means you are pledged to poverty, chastity, and obedience?"

"My days as a Templar knight have come to an end," he said, his tone matter-of-fact. "My older brother has died, leaving me heir to our family holding." She glanced up to find him staring down at her, and her heart leapt when their gazes collided. "I return to France to claim my due, thus I have need of a bride."

"But you know naught of me!"

"I know one truth of your nature. You thought of your maid's health before your own hunger. Such consideration and selflessness is admirable."

Ysmaine was momentarily speechless. He led her into another street, this one familiar to her. It was crowded with vendors of all manner of foodstuffs, the air redolent with the mingled scents of fresh baking, smoked fish, roasting meat, and savory soups. She had avoided this street fastidiously, and her belly growled loudly in complaint at those tempting scents. Again, the crowds parted to make way for her powerful companion, and Ysmaine found it a relief to not to have to shove her way through this congestion.

"That is what you wanted in exchange for the coin," she said, realizing that little was an accident with this man. "To glimpse my nature."

"Indeed. And I admire what you showed to me."

"But you know naught of my family..."

"Your garb is faded but it was not cheaply won."

"I could have stolen it."

"You carry yourself as one born to privilege."

"You do not know my name, and I do not know yours."

"That can be readily resolved." He halted in the midst of the bustling street to bend low over her hand. "Gaston de Châmont-sur-Maine at your service, my lady."

Châmont-sur-Maine. Ysmaine had heard of that holding. It was near Angers, its lord an ally to the duke himself. This knight was Angevin then, which explained why his speech did not sound accented to her. Angers was the key to France, standing on the border of Brittany, where Ysmaine had grown up.

She had come all this way, only to meet a husband whose holding was close to her own home. And a rich holding, too.

Her father would be pleased.

If this Gaston did not lie.

"Surely you jest," Ysmaine protested.

His gaze hardened slightly. "My name is no jest, my lady."

"Of course not," she said with haste. "I simply know of that holding."

His eyes narrowed. "Indeed?"

"I am Ysmaine de Valeroy."

Gaston blinked. "When I was earning my spurs, Amaury de Valeroy wed Richildis...

His words proved that he knew something of the area, at least. "My parents," Ysmaine supplied with a smile. "I am eldest of six daughters."

He winced at that, then frowned. "How is it that you are here with only a maid in your service?"

"I wished to undertake a pilgrimage. My parents agreed with reluctance, and only when a man long in their service agreed to accompany me. I knew Thibaud all of my life, and my father trusted him fully."

"You speak of him as if he were lost."

Ysmaine's tears fell with her confession, for she felt great guilt at this loss. "We were betrayed by the other men hired for our party. Thibaud was killed, and we were robbed."

Gaston's gaze was searching, his eyes bright. "You could have returned home," he suggested gently.

Ysmaine shook her head. "I thought it a test, sir. I thought my fortune could only be changed by completing my pilgrimage and overcoming adversity." She bit her lip, then admitted the worst of it. "I am said to be stubborn, sir."

The corner of his mouth lifted in welcome amusement. "Yet that trait has served you well. You persevered and it seems your conviction has proven true." He might have led her onward, but Ysmaine gripped his fingers.

"Know that I cannot wed you, sir."

Gaston's scowl was fierce. "Why ever not? Are you pledged to another?"

"I have wed twice, sir, and been widowed twice. No man survives his nuptial night with me, it appears, and you, sir, have been too kind to deserve such a fate."

He smiled fully then, the expression lighting his eyes and softening his features so that Ysmaine's breath was fair stolen away. "Is that your sole objection, my lady?"

"It is not inconsequential..."

"And I have not survived eighteen years in service to the Templars because I can be so readily dispatched from this world as that." His lips touched the back of her hand again then he straightened, his gesture more proprietary when he captured her elbow in his hand once more. "We shall wed," he concluded, as if it were beyond dispute.

Ysmaine might have argued with him again, but she doubted it would make any difference to his view. He was determined, she would give him that. And she *had* warned him. If Gaston de Châmont-sur-Maine was resolved to aid her, even knowing the truth of her curse, perhaps it was divine intervention at work.

Perhaps her fortune *had* changed.

"Eighteen years?" she dared to ask, feeling her old confidence begin to muster anew. "You must have been young, indeed."

"A mere youth of fifteen summers, but tall for my age." He

raised his brows before she could ask. "And too fierce an opponent for my cousin. My uncle dubbed me young to be rid of me." He showed no emotion in this confidence and truly, Ysmaine wondered whether it troubled him to have been so hastened on his way. She knew that boys were sent to their uncles to be trained as knights, but she had never heard of one being granted his spurs before he turned sixteen.

"You do not resent your uncle's choice?" she dared to ask.

"If once I did, those days are gone. I joined the Templars, lived well, fought honorably and learned much. There is no cause for complaint in that."

Ysmaine liked that he showed no bitterness. Indeed, he was almost dismissive of her concern, entering a stall to acquire soup. She watched through her lashes as he negotiated for a pot of soup, and allowed herself to admire him. Of all the men she had wed, he was the youngest, the most hale, and the most handsome. He was possessed of honor and seemed most temperate. Mary had answered her prayers, to be sure.

Perhaps she should pray for his survival of their nuptial night.

❧

Gaston returned to the Temple, his optimism restored.

Ysmaine would suit him well.

He entered the stables with a light step, startled despite himself at how quiet they were. He and Ysmaine would be gone before the stables were busy again.

He considered the practicalities. There were ships leaving regularly from the three crusader ports, Jaffa, Acre, and Tyre. Jaffa was nigh overwhelmed by departing pilgrims, he had learned, and also the road was clogged with those who were compelled to walk. Gaston was reviewing the relative merit of the other two ports, when Bartholomew raced around the corner and seized Gaston's tabard.

"My lord!" His squire's hair was tousled and his eyes were wide. Gaston was struck in that moment by the realization that the boy he had taken under his care as squire had become a man. Bartholomew must have seen twenty-three summers, but Gaston still thought of him as the stubborn urchin who had insisted upon carrying his helm when Gaston had ridden out from the Temple in Paris. It had quickly become clear to Gaston that the boy had no home or kin, so he had trained him as his own squire rather than leave him to starve.

Now Bartholomew was a man, and they both would return to France.

"The preceptor seeks you, sir."

"Brother Terricus can wait a few moments," Gaston said mildly, but the younger man shook his head.

"I do not think so. He declares the matter to be of great urgency. I was bidden to find you immediately."

Gaston was concerned. Little was truly urgent in the daily routine of the order, and Terricus was not quick to alarm. "Where is he?" he asked, quickening his step.

"In the chapel." As was characteristic of Bartholomew, he provided Gaston with all the information he knew, even as they strode toward the chapel. "A messenger arrived from Nazareth, his steed in a lather, not moments ago. I have never seen Brother Terricus so white as after he read that missive."

Gaston's heart sank. Had some dark fate befallen the company of Templars ridden to war with the king? He strode more quickly, and Bartholomew, even without an injured leg, was compelled to run to keep up with him.

"He wished to know if you were prepared to leave as yet, and when I said you were nearly so, he bade me fetch you."

Gaston suspected then that not only were the tidings poor, but that Terricus would dispatch him with a message for one of the priories in Europe. They turned the last corner before the chapel to find a fair-haired knight waiting there, the red cross on his white tabard revealing that he, too, was sworn to the order. The knight was as tall as Gaston, tanned from the sun and had a scar upon his cheek. Gaston did not know him but instinctively disliked him. It was not the stranger's hardened manner that irked him, but his obvious impatience. He was slapping his leather gauntlets across his palm, pacing, while two boys watched with wide eyes. Gaston could only conclude that they were his squires and that the new arrival was a demanding master.

It was not this knight's place to be intolerant of waiting on a superior.

"I am here before you," the other knight said with crisp authority, giving Gaston a hard look. "The preceptor will see me first."

Gaston bristled.

"I suspect you are mistaken," he replied, his tone milder than his mood. "For the preceptor sent for me." Gaston made to step past the other knight and reached for the door, only to have the stranger seize his forearm.

"I said I was here before you," that man insisted. "And dispatched to the Grand Master himself. Are common courtesies not observed in the Jerusalem priory any longer?"

Gaston lifted that man's hand from his sleeve with distaste. "They are, which is why a summoned brother shall take precedence. The Grand Master has ridden to war, leaving the preceptor in command."

The knight's eyes flashed and he opened his mouth to argue, proving that his was a stubborn nature. The door to the chapel was opened abruptly in that moment, sparing Gaston the need to dispute the matter. The preceptor himself stood before them, no surprise in his dark eyes when he glanced between the two knights. Gaston assumed he had heard their conversation through the door and expected to be chastised.

Brother Terricus was clearly concerned, for his manner was as different from his usual steady calm as might have been possible. "Who are you?" he demanded of the stranger. "And who dispatched you to the Grand Master?"

This was not the messenger who had arrived so recently, then.

The stranger bowed his head. "I am Brother Wulfe, from the Gaza priory. I have been sent to add my blade to the battle..."

Terricus interrupted him crisply. "You are too late."

Wulfe's shock was clear, and Gaston had trouble hiding his own surprise that Terricus spoke with such finality. "I would have you both join me in prayer," he continued, his gaze flicking between the two men. "Immediately. And Bartholomew, you will join us as well." Without awaiting a reply, Terricus strode to the altar.

Prayer? That was the last action Gaston would have undertaken before bad tidings, but he bit his tongue. What had Terricus learned? This Wulfe inhaled sharply in disapproval, and

Gaston was amused that they had even one perspective in common.

After the two knights and squire followed the preceptor into the small chapel, Terricus glanced back to nod at Bartholomew. The younger man secured the door behind them. The chapel was empty, save for the four of them. It was quiet in the space, the lack of windows and the thick walls ensuring that sounds from outside the chapel were muted. Terricus dropped to his knees, pointing to the floor on either side, as Gaston understood.

They could hear no one, and no one would be able to hear them.

His scalp prickled, and he feared whatever Terricus had learned. Gaston fell to his knees on the left of the preceptor, folded his hands before himself, and bowed his head as if in prayer. Brother Wulfe did the same on the preceptor's right, and Bartholomew knelt beside Gaston.

"The fortress of Tiberias was besieged two days ago," Terricus murmured.

"But it is doughty," Wulfe protested, earning a sharp glance from the preceptor.

"Saladin himself led the forces and refused a payment of tribute to cease his attack. A tower was mined and when it fell, they breached the walls and took the fortress."

Gaston winced, guessing that there was more to be told.

"And Raymond of Tripoli?" Wulfe demanded. "Was he killed defending his holding?"

Terricus spared him a glance. "He left his lady in charge of the keep's defense when he rode to Jerusalem to muster troops with the king."

Wulfe's lips tightened. "He should have left a knight in command."

"It is said that Eschiva is as fierce in battle as any man, and truly the holding comes to Raymond through her lineage," Terricus said. "All the same, the numbers are reported to be such that no commander could have held out against this assault."

"Not if they came prepared to mine beneath the towers," Gaston agreed, thinking of what he knew of the Saracen leader. It was no accident that this attack had occurred when Raymond was away.

This was vengeance.

"He avenges the party that was given safe passage by Raymond, but then attacked at Cresson," he said beneath his breath.

"Do not attribute honor to infidels," Wulfe chided. "They have none!"

Gaston held his tongue, knowing otherwise.

Terricus eyed him for a moment, then continued. "She was defending the citadel when she dispatched the messenger, but he said there was word that Saladin's troops mined that tower as well."

"It must have fallen by now," Wulfe muttered, his agitation clear. "Two days!"

"Did Raymond ride to her defense?" Gaston asked, wondering whether this attack had been a lure.

Terricus shook his head. "The tidings are that he advised against defending Tiberias. He was prepared to lose it, rather than have the Christian forces leave the fortification at La Saphorie."

"He would sacrifice his own holding?" Wulfe was outraged.

Gaston was more outraged that Raymond would sacrifice his wife, but said naught on that matter. "He believed that Saladin desired to draw them out of their strong position," Gaston speculated instead. "He saw the lure."

Terricus nodded. "They argued, two nights ago, according to the messenger. King Guy chose to lead the Christians out, in defense of Tiberias."

Gaston caught his breath. "Folly," he whispered. Wulfe looked sharply at him over the head of Terricus. "Water," he reminded the knight. "La Saphorie was chosen because of the abundance of water there. If they abandon it, they will be done."

"But they must know this," Wulfe argued.

Gaston bit back his protest, thinking of the impetuous nature of Gerard de Ridefort, combined with that of King Guy. It appeared that Saladin taunted them, knowing their respective characters, and that they took the bait.

"I must send word to the priory in Paris of these events." Terricus spoke with resolve, and Gaston was surprised that he would send a missive so soon as this.

"But you know only half the tale," Wulfe protested.

"I fear I can guess its end," Terricus said. "I pray that I am mistaken, but still will send word when I can."

Gaston blinked at the realization that the preceptor believed Jerusalem itself would be lost. Surely, it could not be so dire as that? Surely their stronghold in the Holy City would not be compromised?

But Terricus spoke with resolve. "You must take the missive for me, Gaston. You are the only one prepared to depart." His voice dropped lower. "You are the only one not of the order whom I would trust with such a quest."

He was the only one who could be spared. Gaston understood and was glad of the assignment.

Before he could nod understanding, Terricus removed a sealed scroll of parchment from his sleeve, where it had been hidden, and offered it to him covertly. Gaston took it quickly, slipping it into his own sleeve, then gave every appearance of continuing to pray.

"And you, Brother Wulfe, will accompany him."

Gaston remained silent with an effort.

Wulfe did not. "I answer to the master at Gaza, who dispatched me to Jerusalem to kill Saracens in defense of the Jerusalem priory..."

"And now you kneel in that very priory—" Terricus interrupted with finality "—which makes you subject to my command."

"I will not be a messenger when there is a war to be fought!"

"You will act as couriers, both of you," Terricus said with force. "For I have commanded as much and no Templar defies an order."

Wulfe was seething, but he responded with what Gaston imagined was the closest he could come to subservience. "Aye, sir."

"While the letter is the official reason for your journey, I entrust you with a quest far more important." Terricus took a breath, as if bracing himself for a confession he did not wish to make, and spoke so softly that Gaston had to strain to hear the words. "I have removed the treasure from the crypt."

Gaston's heart stopped, and he heard Bartholomew inhale sharply. The Templars were known to have a remarkable treasure secreted in the Jerusalem priory. He had seen items from that hoard, but never the whole of it. He had only heard rumors of the greatest prize in their possession. The import of this choice shook him as little else might have done.

"You expect Jerusalem to fall," he whispered, wanting Terricus to correct him.

"How can it not?" Terricus asked, fury in his tone. "We are too few and they are too many. If they win this battle, the slaughter will be fierce. There can be no recovery in the short term, not with nigh every man summoned to follow the King of Jerusalem. We will lose the Temple." He took a steadying breath, carrying on before either knight could argue. "The best we may be able to hope is that a new influx of troops, a new crusade, will allow us to recapture the Holy City after it is lost, *if* it is lost. I must see my responsibilities served, in anticipation of failure. I dare not delay, lest any choice be stolen from me in future days." He looked at Gaston. "The success of this quest lies with you, Gaston."

It would be Gaston's last mission for the order, and perhaps the one that ensured the survival of the organization he so loved. Still, he could not believe that matters would become so dire. Surely Terricus was but cautious, or overly fearful.

But an order was an order, however mistaken it might prove to be.

"I will do my best, Brother Terricus."

"No man can ask for more of another." Terricus took a breath. "You are ordered directly to accompany Gaston, Brother Wulfe, and you will cede to his authority in all matters on the journey you undertake. Officially, you are the one to carry the missive to Paris, and you simply travel with Gaston for security."

Wulfe scoffed slightly under his breath, and Gaston felt the other knight's gaze slide over him in assessment. "Then I should be the one to carry the missive."

"You will do as you have been instructed," Terricus said.

"Of course, sir," Wulfe said, his tone hard.

"Officially, Gaston has left the order, but I still grant him command of this party."

"People will see the truth immediately," Wulfe argued. "No Templar takes orders from a secular knight."

"Surely you can understand that you will appear to lead, while following my direction," Gaston said with a mildness he did not feel.

Wulfe's lips pinched so tightly that they were nigh invisible. Only the fierce glare of the preceptor ensured his silence.

"The parcel entrusted to you has been sealed and will be opened only by the Master of the Temple in Paris. This is for the security of all of you, as well as for the contents themselves."

"Aye, sir," both knights replied in unison. Gaston wondered if Wulfe was as curious as he as to the specific item entrusted to them—but a pledge was a pledge. Perhaps it would be shown to them in the Paris Temple.

"You will accompanied by others, to make the party larger and less readily assailed. This will be presented as a matter of practicality and convenience."

"Others?" Wulfe asked.

"Another knight leaves the order as scheduled, to attend his own nuptials in Scotland."

"Brother Fergus?" Gaston asked, suspecting it could be only that man.

"The very man," Terricus agreed. "He awaits your instruction in the stables even now, with his baggage."

Terricus gave this last word an emphasis so slight that none but a man who was holding his gaze—and one who knew him well—would have noted.

Baggage.

Fergus had been entrusted with the treasure.

Gaston nodded as Terricus continued. "Plus two pilgrims have requested protection."

"Pilgrims!" Wulfe muttered but Brother Terricus lifted a finger.

"I remind you, Brother Wulfe, that it is our sworn task to defend pilgrims. Everard de Montmorency returns home in the hope of speaking with his dying father one last time, and the merchant, Joscelin de Provins, doubtless flees while he can."

Gaston nodded. Everard was familiar to him, as a regular visitor to the king's court, although he did not know the merchant.

"You will depart on the morrow, as if your riding forth is routine," Terricus continued softly. "Though it is anything but. I would not have you arouse suspicion as to the truth of your quest."

"Of course, sir," Gaston agreed. No man rode at night in these lands, for to do so invited not just curiosity but the assault of bandits.

There was but one more detail to resolve. He would have to speak to the priest about wedding him to Ysmaine before their departure.

He should speak to Terricus about even bringing a woman into the Temple. Gaston felt torn between his loyalties for the first time in years. He would have preferred to have collected Ysmaine immediately, but no woman could remain overnight within the Temple. He assured himself that the nuns would have secured their portals by this hour and that the city was safe for this night. He felt protective toward his bride and wished he could have ensured her welfare himself.

Had he and Terricus been alone, he would have asked for counsel, but he was well aware of Wulfe listening.

Terricus crossed himself and rose to his feet, bowing before the altar. "Go with God," he said beneath his breath. "That He may see fit to save us all."

But what was the treasure? Which of the prizes from the crypt would they carry?

How much force could he use to defend it?

Terricus appeared unlikely to confide such details, so Gaston hoped that Fergus knew more. Bartholomew hastened to the door to the chapel as the preceptor retreated from the altar. The squire bowed there as he opened the portal. A small crowd of men had gathered in the corridor while they were sequestered, making it impossible to ask more questions.

He would seek Terricus out later, to ask about the exchange of vows.

First, all had to be made ready for their departure.

Gaston stood in his turn, crossing himself before he glanced at his unwilling companion knight. "You must be hungry after your journey," he said, speaking as if nothing untoward had been said. "Now that you have prayed, I will show you to the dormitory and the hall."

Wulfe's eyes narrowed. "I thought..."

Gaston flicked a glance at the curious onlookers in the corridor.

Wulfe followed his look and nodded, almost imperceptibly. "I should appreciate your assistance," he said with a bow. "This priory is far larger than the one I know."

"Come and refresh yourself, brother." Gaston indicated the portal and let Wulfe precede him.

"I would meet the others in the departing party, with your assistance," Wulfe said, his tone commanding. "The better that we can ensure all is prepared for the morning."

Gaston's thoughts flew with his own plans. He had to confer with Fergus as to the defense of the treasure, as well as pack for his own departure. He had to speak with the priest and brother Terricus again. He would have to take Ysmaine to Fatima in the morning and hoped her maid was sufficiently recovered for a journey so soon as this. His schedule might have changed and his plans been modified, but he would not leave Jerusalem without his bride.

Indeed, if the Saracens meant to attack Jerusalem, Gaston might offer the lady's sole chance of survival.

Sunday, July 5, 1187

Feast Day of Saint Fragan and Saint Gwen of England.

❧

Chapter Three

There was nothing like a hot meal in one's belly to restore one's confidence in the future. Ysmaine could not believe the difference in her own perspective and the health of her maid. She had managed to find accommodation in their dormitory for herself and Radegunde, and she liked the tranquility of their cloister. The sound of the bells punctuated each day and the sweep of the nuns' linen kirtles on the stone whispered softly when they moved.

Indeed, she felt blessed that evening as she had not in years. Ysmaine gave the potion to Radegunde, in small portions just as the apothecary had decreed, marveling all the while that the Virgin had been so good to her.

Nay, she had to give credit to Gaston. Mary might have ensured he noticed Ysmaine, but the knight had done all the rest.

And Ysmaine would be wedded again. The notion made something deep within her flutter, though whether it was fear or excitement, she could not say. She grimaced that this knight should be so poorly rewarded for his goodness, that he should die on his nuptial night like her other husbands. But there was no chance of changing his choice, for he clearly thought her fears to be groundless.

Ysmaine hoped in her heart that he *did* survive. There was an integrity about Gaston that she already admired, and she suspected that unlike her other two spouses, he was a man she could come to love.

Despite her initial reservations, she could see that Gaston had taken her to a skilled apothecary, just as he had vowed. Between the soup and the potion, Radegunde was markedly improved by the evening, and Ysmaine was relieved. The maid's brow cooled steadily, and she had opened her eyes twice, sparing a weak smile for Ysmaine that thrilled her to her marrow. She sat beside the younger woman, bathed her skin with cool cloths and gave her more of the potion when she could. She was encouraged by the way the maid's breathing became easier.

The girl would live.

The bells of the chapel of Mary Latina were ringing for the midnight mass, the portal secured against the world and the Benedictine nuns gathering for services, when Radegunde awakened. Her gaze was clear, to Ysmaine's delight.

"My lady," Radegunde murmured. "What happened to me?"

"You have been ill, but are much recovered. Will you have some soup? It is yet warm."

The girl sat up with Ysmaine's help and managed to consume more than Ysmaine might have dared to hope. "I should be serving you, my lady."

"You should heal first," Ysmaine said with a smile.

Radegunde nodded, then lay back and fell into an easy sleep. Ysmaine watched her for a long moment, relief filling her heart with joy.

Gaston had made this possible, and she would ensure that he never regretted his choice in aiding her.

Ysmaine knelt beside Radegunde and prayed, thanking Mary for her compassion.

She thanked Mary also for ensuring that Gaston took note of her.

How far did Her Lady's aid extend? Had she ensured that Gaston had need of a bride, in this very moment, as well?

One matter was clear: Ysmaine would be the best wife possible for him, for as long as she was entrusted with that task.

The man deserved no less.

੨ৡ

Bartholomew loitered outside the Benedictine convent where Gaston's betrothed was a guest. The bells were ringing for the first services of the day when the portal was unbarred, and he drew back into the shadows to watch.

To his surprise, the lady herself was the first through the gate. She looked much recovered from the day before and there was purpose in her step as she hastened down the street.

Charged with ensuring her protection in Gaston's absence, Bartholomew followed. He felt no small curiosity, for it seemed the lady had an errand she would complete with haste.

He smiled when she turned the corner to the Street of Herbs, guessing her destination. She returned to Fatima, it was clear. He followed her even so, waiting for a few moments before entering the shop to ensure that she had been admitted to Fatima's presence. He considered the potions and dried herbs available for sale as one of Fatima's brothers watched him and strained his ears for the sound of the women's conversation.

"And?" Fatima demanded.

"She is much improved," the lady replied, her relief clear in her tone. "I thank you with all my heart for your assistance."

"Tell me how she looks this day."

The lady described the change in her maid's coloring, how she had breathed as she slept, how much of the soup she had eaten, how her skin had cooled. She was nigh as observant as Gaston.

"Then she is past the worst of it," Fatima said with satisfaction. "You came in time, after all."

"It was the knight's doing, for I could not have afforded your services myself." The lady's voice dropped. "I have no coin now, either but I would ask you for a small measure of an herb, all the same."

"Which one?"

"Wolf's bane," the lady replied without hesitation. "Do you know it here?"

Fatima's voice dropped. "What need have you of a poison like that?"

"It is for Gaston, for he will be my husband."

Bartholomew nigh dropped the root he was holding. He glanced back toward the street to cover his reaction, pretending someone called to him from there. He bowed to Fatima's brother and ducked out of the shop in haste, marveling at what he had heard.

Why would Gaston's betrothed wish to ensure his demise?

He could not say, but Gaston had mentioned that she was on pilgrimage because she had buried two husbands. Perhaps their deaths had not been so accidental as that. Perhaps she had to atone for more than unluckiness. Bartholomew lingered in the shadows and could not fail to note that when she did leave Fatima's shop moments later, she carried a small sack. It was plain, like those he had oft collected from the apothecary. The lady hung it from her belt, then hid it quickly in the folds of her dress. She hastened back to the cloister.

But wait. She must have purchased whatever she carried, for Fatima gave naught away. Bartholomew felt his eyes narrow. How had a woman bereft of coin on the day before been able to shop on this morn?

Had she lied to Gaston?

❧

Well pleased with the result of her errand and filled with anticipation, Ysmaine hastened back to the hospice in the convent. It said much for Gaston's true nature that Fatima had surrendered the wolf's bane to her once she had learned of its usefulness. She had told Ysmaine of Gaston's injury, which had been the result of a fall from a horse, just as Ysmaine had feared. He had cracked a bone, by Fatima's reckoning, but not remained abed long enough for it to set well. She imagined it would trouble him always, but warned Ysmaine that it was not the sum of the injuries Gaston had sustained. The women had agreed that Ysmaine would need to ensure Gaston took his leisure more frequently than was his wont and had parted well agreed.

The conversation had been a fine way to begin the day, and Ysmaine was encouraged to have found a common understanding with the other woman. Truly, Gaston had opened her eyes to the similarities between them, compelling her to look beyond the differences. Fatima was not so different from the healer on her parents' holding. Ysmaine's grandmother had taught her of making this unguent but in all other matters, Mathilde was consulted. She could readily imagine Mathilde and Fatima comparing remedies and sharing tales.

Her confidence in the goodness of people restored, Ysmaine found her step light and her heart skipping. She smiled at the porter as she ducked into the courtyard, sleep and soup having restored her optimism.

Radegunde was awake, her gaze even more clear, and sitting

up. She had finished the last of the soup and clearly intended to rise from her bed. Ysmaine helped her to do so, beyond glad that the younger woman was able to walk to the latrine on her own and then wash herself. She helped Radegunde comb and braid her thick dark hair, and the maid thanked her profusely.

She looked to be a different woman.

"Your intended has a generous nature, my lady," Radegunde said, her eyes shining. "I am most grateful."

"As am I." Ysmaine gave the maid the small package she had obtained from Fatima. "Will you ensure the safety of this parcel?"

"What is it, my lady?"

"An herb that can be used to ease the pain in my lord husband's hip, should he permit it to be applied. Fatima says he is cursed stubborn."

"As are you, my lady," Radegunde said with twinkling eyes. "He might have met his match."

"He certainly will see improvement in that limp, if I have anything to say of it." Ysmaine surrendered the parcel. "But keep it safe, for if devoured, this herb is poison and will kill."

Radegunde's eyes widened. "Aye, my lady. You can rely upon me."

ॐ

By morning, Gaston found his usual patience wearing thin. He could not imagine how he would endure Wulfe's company all the way to Paris, for he could see already that it chafed the other knight both to be dispatched from the Holy Land when war was afoot and to have only the appearance of command. He had conferred with Fergus about the safekeeping of the treasure. Fergus appeared to be as laconic as ever, save for the bright glint of his eyes, but Gaston knew better than to trust in that appearance. Terricus had chosen a good guardian for the prize.

It was later than he had hoped when he set out to collect Ysmaine.

Her maid would still be weak, so he took one of his palfreys. He hoped with all his heart that both maid and lady were sufficiently strong to endure this journey. It would not be an easy canter through the countryside. They would ride long and hard, over rough terrain and with no regard to the weather.

He supposed he would learn his lady's mettle soon enough.

Bartholomew met him just outside the entry to the Templar stables, his manner agitated. Gaston frowned at the sight of him for he had bidden the younger man to stand watch over the lady. "What is wrong?" he asked. "Is my lady fallen ill?"

"Nay, she returned to Fatima at first light on her own."

Gaston smiled, encouraged that she took such initiative on her own. "Indeed, these are excellent tidings. There is one less errand for me to accomplish this morn." He strode toward the hospice leading the horse, Bartholomew quick behind him. "And did you hear her report? How fares the maid?"

"She is evidently well recovered, and Fatima sounded nigh as pleased as the lady."

"Excellent." Gaston found his pace increasing. He was filled with an uncharacteristic desire to hasten and an equally unfamiliar sense of anticipation.

"But she made a purchase, sir, and I think you should know of it."

"I thought she had no coin," Gaston said. "Fatima must have declined her request."

Bartholomew shook his head. "She left that place with a package."

"It must have been another potion for her maid's cure."

"Nay, sir, she asked for an herb, though I did not hear its name..."

Gaston, although a practical man, had always trusted his intuition. His heart told him that Ysmaine was trustworthy.

He spun to face his squire. "Bartholomew," he chided gently. "I know that we have not spoken much with women these past years, and I am sure you have heard tales aplenty of their wiles. This lady, however, will be my wife, and I will hear no false accusations against her."

"But she asked for an herb..."

Gaston recalled that his intended had appeared to know something of the useful plants the day before. He waved off the squire's doubts. "She and Fatima seemed to possess similar knowledge. They must have simply compared notions of what would best heal the maid."

"But Fatima declared it a poison and the lady said it was for you!"

Gaston fixed the younger man with a resolute glance. "She has no coin, Bartholomew, and Fatima does not grant her cures without fee. If what you believe you overheard is true—" he let his expression convey the fullness of his own opinion "—then she will not have succeeded in that venture."

"But..."

Gaston interrupted the younger man flatly. "Today will be my wedding day, Bartholomew. I will hear naught against my lady from this moment forward." He watched his squire's lips set mutinously. "But if it will ease your fears, I will eat naught that she has prepared for me until you believe in the goodness of her nature. The feat will be easily accomplished as we travel."

"That would ease my concern, sir," Bartholomew said with evident relief.

"And so it shall be done," Gaston concluded. "I bid you say naught to the lady of this matter. It is unpleasant to be suspected, especially when the cause is so light that it may not prove to have merit." He waited until Bartholomew bowed in agreement, then continued on his way.

He found himself filled with a newfound anticipation and realized he was looking forward to his new and secular life.

With Ysmaine by his side.

ঽ&

Ysmaine was helping Radegunde to dress, a transposition of their usual duties that made them both smile, when she heard a woman clear her throat. She turned to find one of the sisters awaiting her attention. That woman touched a fingertip to her lips and gestured to the cloister. Curious, Ysmaine went to the portal and her heart stopped.

Gaston stood in the gateway to the street beyond, his hands folded behind his back and his gaze lowered as he waited. He could not be permitted within the refuge of the convent because of his gender, but he awaited her at the gate. He stood in a patch of sunlight, as if the sun itself would draw attention to his fine form. He had abandoned the white surplice of the order and now wore a tabard of darkest blue. The hue would favor his eyes well, Ysmaine knew. His hair looked blacker than it had and it was damp, curling against his collar, as if he had bathed before coming to her.

God in Heaven, but he was an alluring man.

There was a question in the eyes of the sister, but Ysmaine smiled. "My betrothed," she murmured, feeling the sister's surprise. "He took me to an apothecary yesterday, for Radegunde."

The woman nodded, her gaze filled with unspoken questions. Aye, doubtless she would want to know where this betrothed had been until this point. Likely she believed that Ysmaine had offered a more earthly reward to this knight than her hand in marriage, but Ysmaine did not care. The sister gestured to Radegunde, indicating that she would watch her while Ysmaine spoke to the knight. She smiled and thanked the sister, then made her way to Gaston.

Her heart quickened its pace as she drew near him.

He glanced up at the sound of her footfall and the gleam of admiration in his eye made Ysmaine's mouth go dry. "How fares your maid?" he asked when she reached his side, his hand rising to cup her elbow as he turned her toward the street. She liked that he was direct.

He led her a few steps into the Street of Palms, that avenue between the Church of the Holy Sepulchre and the church of Saint Mary Major that adjoined the convent of the Benedictine nuns. At the far end of the street, toward the Street of the Patriarch, was the Hospital where the other order of knights had their abode. In the opposite direction, toward the Street of Herbs, was the fish market and though trade had barely begun for the day, the scent of fish was strong.

"She is so much better," Ysmaine said, unable to hide her pleasure. "I thank you so much for your aid in this..."

"Good," Gaston said with a resolve that interrupted her thanks. "My squire says you returned to Fatima this morn already."

"I did. I thought to save you the trouble of escorting me there."

His gaze searched hers. "And her counsel?"

"She is most pleased with Radegunde's improvement, and professed her labor was done." Ysmaine smiled but Gaston simply waited, his manner expectant. "What is amiss, sir?"

"Naught, of course."

His squire knew she had been to Fatima. How? He must have followed her to the apothecary's shop. Under his own initiative or at his knight's command? Ysmaine's glance flew past Gaston to the dark-haired man who watched her from the side of the street. He stood by a horse, his colors matching Gaston's own, and regarded her with such open suspicion that she was startled.

Although it irked Ysmaine to have been found wanting by the squire, she respected that her intended was slow to make any accusation. She held her husband's gaze and spoke more mildly than was her impulse. "Does your squire agree with you in that?"

Gaston pursed his lips. "Bartholomew is protective of my interests."

Ysmaine noted that he did not answer her directly. She did not like the suggestion that her husband had dispatched a man to spy upon her, not in the least. "Did you send your squire to follow me, sir?"

"I sent him to ensure your welfare in my absence."

Ysmaine knew that she should be dutiful and obedient and let the matter pass, but such docility truly was not within her. "Sir, I assure you that my husbands would have been of greater value to me had they continued to draw breath. I did not wish either of them dead, and I did not do any deed to hasten the demise of either. I swear this to you."

Gaston lifted her hand in his, his manner somber. Surely he believed her? "Although your trip to Fatima will save us time this morn, I believe that for the duration of our journey, you should not walk alone."

Was this a measure of distrust? Ysmaine could not be certain of Gaston's thoughts when he was so taciturn. "I have walked most of the way from Brittany with only Radegunde, sir," she noted, fearing he meant to see her confined once they reached his holding.

"And by your own account, the journey was not without incident," Gaston countered gently. Ysmaine averted her gaze at the reminder. Gaston bent toward her and dropped his voice low. "You will be my wife and thus my responsibility. I would see your welfare ensured from this day forward, whether you be in my presence or not."

Ysmaine studied him, hoping that all was as simple as he

would have her believe. "Will you tell me in future if a man is left to watch over me?"

"Of course. I would have told you if I had thought of the scheme while in your company." He spoke so readily that Ysmaine believed him. "I sent Bartholomew from the Temple this morning, for I had many duties to attend." Gaston brushed his lips across the back of her hand. "I meant no offense, but I may err in the details of fulfilling my new responsibilities. They have become unfamiliar and I beg your tolerance."

When she looked up, he arched a brow and his eyes twinkled ever so slightly. "You may find me overly cautious in defending those treasures that have come to my hand." His eyes were so dark a blue that Ysmaine's mouth went dry.

If the man intended to charm her, he was more successful at it than she might have expected from a warrior previously sworn to chastity.

"My mother always said that a good match was a partnership, sir," she said, hoping to convince him of the same notion, but Gaston's smile was fleeting.

"Indeed," he acknowledged. "And now, I bring tidings you may not welcome."

Ysmaine guessed the import of his crisp tone. Gaston was a knight, a former Templar, and a fighting man. She recalled the bustle that had filled the Holy City just weeks past and feared what Gaston had learned. "The King of Jerusalem rode to do battle with Saladin," she said, hoping against hope that the battle had gone favorably for the Christians.

In her limited experience, individual battles lasted months and wars could endure for years. To have tidings already, and tidings so dire that Gaston was solemn, could not be a good portent.

Indeed, he leaned close to her. "We must wed this very morn, my lady." There was an urgency in his tone that set Ysmaine's heart to racing.

"Has the king lost?" She could scarce consider it.

"Nay, the battle continues," he said with care, and she knew by the way he averted his gaze that he knew more than he confessed to her. "But I will depart this day for there is a party destined for Paris that we may join. It will be safer to ride in company, and simpler if we are wed first."

"Departing today?" Ysmaine was dismayed only by the timing. "But that is impossible. Radegunde is not sufficiently healed to move..."

"There is no choice," Gaston said flatly. "She will be treated with every courtesy and comfort I can grant her." His gaze was so steely that Ysmaine understood that he saw no other choice.

She and Radegunde could accompany him or be left behind. She could not imagine that their fate would be good in that circumstance. They had one opportunity to return home, because of Gaston.

God in heaven, but she was fortunate to have made an alliance with this man.

❧

"Can you tell me what you know, sir?" Ysmaine wished to know as much of their circumstance as possible, though she feared her intended would not think such matters a woman's concern.

Gaston glanced over the walls and the people in the streets, as if seeking something or someone she could not see. His very manner made Ysmaine wary, and she followed his gaze, noting only now how people moved more quickly. Where the Street of Herbs merged with others to become Saint Stephen Street, leading to the city gate of the same name, there was a throng of pedestrian traffic. There were more pilgrims than usual carrying their belongings as if to leave, and all hastening to the gate.

Where would they sleep? How far could they walk this day? The ports were distant, and she doubted such a crowd could be accommodated on whatever ships might be in the harbor.

She clutched Gaston's hand in newfound fear, but he closed his own fingers over hers.

He was as steady and reliable as a rock.

"There is no cause for alarm," he said softly. "Merely caution."

"I see." Ysmaine understood that he would not tell her more of the situation when they were standing in the street. She hoped he would do so later. His gaze locked with hers once more, his intense manner sending a thrill through her. "You must trust me, my lady, though I recognize it is a bold request to make."

"And if I do not?" Ysmaine had to ask.

He bent and touched his lips to her ear, as if planting a kiss upon her cheek. "Then you may never see France again."

The situation was dire, then. Ysmaine caught her breath and closed her eyes, giving every appearance of being overwhelmed by his touch. It made sense that they would know the truth of the battle within the Temple, and that a knight like Gaston would know best what was to be done.

All the same, it was discomfiting to put her life and that of her maid into the hands of a virtual stranger.

You must trust me, my lady.

Ysmaine reminded herself that Gaston had not lied to her, but more importantly, there was that integrity in his manner. It was easy to doubt that he had ever told a falsehood in his life. He might be wrong about the outcome of whatever tidings he had heard, but he believed what he was telling her.

And she believed him, whether it was folly or not.

Aware that at least one of the sisters watched their conversation, Ysmaine straightened with a smile and a light laugh. "Your ardor, sir, is most persuasive. I, too, will be glad to have our vows exchanged."

"Now, my lady," Gaston said with heat, his hand closing around hers with possessive ease. "It must be now, at the Temple."

"But Radegunde cannot walk so far as the Temple, and I cannot leave her behind, sir."

"Of course not." Gaston lifted a finger and his squire led the palfrey out of the shadows on one side of the street. "I brought the palfrey for this very reason. Perhaps you might ride with her, to ensure she stays in the saddle."

Her intended had come prepared. Again, Ysmaine had that sense that she no longer struggled alone, and she liked Gaston's practicality very well.

"I shall fetch our belongings, sir. We have very little, and the sisters will assist Radegunde to the portal." Ysmaine spun away, but Gaston caught her elbow in his hand, tugging her to a halt. She turned to confront him, her heart leaping when he smiled. He took her hand, pressing a small stack of silver pennies into her palm and closing her fingers over it.

"One must pay one's debts, my lady, or one's name carries no honor at all."

Ysmaine stared at the coins in awe. "Sir, you spend too much in my name," she protested, for she felt she should, though she was relieved to be able to pay the sisters. She did not like to beg for charity, and she shared Gaston's view about paying one's debts.

"It is expended in my name. You will be my wife and your debts are now mine." Gaston bent and touched his lips to hers, as confident that she would accept his salute as she would take the coin. It was a kiss as practical as the man himself, firm and dry yet dispassionate in a way that seemed too cool to Ysmaine. She wanted to provoke a reaction from him, and to surprise him, to have him look at her with that admiration she had glimpsed already.

She wanted more from marriage than safety and sons, she realized.

She wanted passion and partnership. Indeed, Ysmaine wanted love, like the love her parents shared. It was Gaston's gift to her to revive her yearning for the future she had always desired but which she had lost hope of ever possessing.

Impulsively, Ysmaine curled her hand around the back of Gaston's neck and deepened their kiss. She tasted his surprise, but pressed herself against him, letting all in the street believe what they wished. His arm locked around her waist with astonishing speed and he lifted her to her toes, slanting his mouth across hers as if he could not resist the feast she offered. Their kiss sent a fire through Ysmaine's veins, and she knew with utter certainty that trusting Gaston was the right choice.

She could almost believe that he felt the same way.

Gaston fairly tore his mouth from hers and looked down at her, his eyes glittering with a desire that echoed her own. He seemed struck to silence, which Ysmaine could only assume was a good sign for their future and their match.

"My lady, we must make haste," he said, his words hoarse.

"Aye, sir, I would hasten to exchange vows with you, as well." Her own voice was husky and her chest was tight when she touched his cheek with her fingertips. A wondrous joy had unfurled within her, one that gave her hope once again.

"God in heaven, sir, I hope with all my heart that you survive our nuptial night," she whispered. Gaston blinked, clearly astonished, and Ysmaine found herself smiling as she turned back to the dormitory.

Her heart was light again, and the world filled with new promise. Perhaps it had not been a curse that had brought her all the way to Jerusalem, but destiny, driving her to the man she was fated to wed.

Ysmaine's smile broadened at the appeal of that notion.

Chapter Four

Wulfe could not believe his situation.

It was absurd that he should be compelled to wait on the command of another brother, and worse, that he should be dispatched from the Holy City when every blade was needed. An entire night had passed in idleness! He did not have the missive, which had been entrusted to the French knight, and he had no notion of what treasure they were to carry, much less where it was.

The sole advantage to the delay was that his steed was sufficiently rested. It was a significant detail, but for Wulfe, it was not enough.

He paced in the stables of the Jerusalem priory, filled with restless impatience. He had discovered the location of the stall where this French knight's horse was stabled, and at least he could acknowledge that the man had a fine dappled destrier. That Templar's horse had been groomed and nosed in the hay, a dark palfrey tethered beside him.

They were not even saddled.

And there was no sign of the man.

Perhaps he meant to depart the next day, or the one after that. Perhaps this Gaston did not share Wulfe's determination to do his part to aid the cause of the Christians in the Holy City. Wulfe paced and growled beneath his breath at the delay.

In the adjacent stall, a man who could only be a Scottish barbarian and thus the former Templar they were doomed to include in their party, sat on a barrel and sipped his ale. He would be no good to them besotted, though he might not be any good to them at all. This Fergus had a look of complacency about him, like a milk cow turned out to pasture, content to wait until coaxed back to the barn. Though Gaston has spoken long and quietly to him the night before, Wulfe had not bothered. Indeed, he could scarce understand a word the man said. If naught else, Fergus appeared to be taking half of Jerusalem home to his betrothed.

Fergus had a russet-haired squire with freckles across his nose who snored as he slept, and a slightly older blond one with eyes that darted back and forth. Wulfe would not have turned his back on the boy in a fight.

He thought little of the count who meant to accompany them, and even less of the merchant. Between the three of them, Wulfe doubted there was any token of value left in all of Outremer. They carried more trunks and bundles and saddlebags than Wulfe had owned in all of his life. Those two men sat and chatted together, evidently content to wait as long as necessary. Wulfe chafed at the delay.

That he should be sitting idle while other brethren rode to war was absurd!

Wulfe would not have believed it, had he not been living it.

"The tales are true," he muttered, confident that none other than his squires would understand his German. Every knight and lay brother he had encountered in this establishment had clearly been French.

Perhaps *that* was the problem. Certainly, Wulfe had no admiration of the French. They were too concerned with appearances and cautious to ride to battle—with the exception of the Grand Master, of course. They had a disdain for the dirty labor of war, and he regretted yet again that he had not found a welcome in the ranks of the Hospitaliers.

At least, though, the French were not Scottish. The only merit of those warriors was their bloodlust, and this Fergus looked to have none of it either.

"The Jerusalem priory rots from within," Wulfe grumbled and paced the length of the corridor again. "The brethren are comfortable and complacent, which can only diminish their effectiveness."

"Aye, sir," agreed his older squire, Stephen.

Wulfe did not believe for one moment that the preceptor had told him the truth. The King of Jerusalem err in his strategy and abandon a precious source of water? It could not be so. Wulfe slapped his gloves against his palm and gritted his teeth, snared by his sworn oath to never deny an order from a superior.

The preceptor knew it, of course. That was why he had *ordered* this mission be undertaken.

But what folly! To ride out of Jerusalem now was madness. They should stay and defend the priory, not abandon their brethren in a time of need. Or they should ride north to aid the troops led by the king. To leave the Latin Kingdoms was the worst decision possible. Wulfe paced more quickly. He did not care what they took with them, what missive or what token from the crypt. He would rather lend his sword to the fight.

The sooner they were away on this ridiculous excuse of a quest, the sooner he might return and contribute.

Even that was infuriating, for Wulfe was to answer to this knight who had clearly gone soft in the comfort of the Jerusalem priory. Teufel had been brushed down, fed and watered and saddled, and was stamping to depart with as much impatience as his master. Wulfe had eaten and refreshed himself, as had his squires.

Yet there was no sign of Gaston. The watch had changed and he knew it had to be mid-morning.

"The problem with this priory is that it is impossible to see the street," Wulfe complained to Stephen who nodded rapid agreement. "A man cannot take the mood of the city from within such stout walls. Indeed, a man might forget that the city is even beyond these walls and be oblivious when its occupants seethe in discontent. Nay, a citadel should be solid but precarious, its view sweeping, like the priory at Gaza. No man ever felt truly safe within those walls. No man ever took his survival for granted there. Such uncertainty ensures vigilance."

"Aye, sir," Stephen agreed and bowed.

"This entire building could be destroyed, and we should learn of it too late to make a difference to our own fates," Wulfe complained. "Where in the name of God has that man gone?"

He spun at the sound of the gate opening and strode toward it with purpose. He was not surprised to see Gaston returning, though he was amazed that the man led a chestnut palfrey. A younger man followed the horse, the same man who had been in the chapel the previous day. He must be Gaston's squire, although Wulfe thought him old for the task.

When Wulfe saw the occupants of the saddle, his curiosity

about the younger man was dismissed. He understood all too well the import of this errand. He could not believe the other knight's folly.

And he was not in the mood to bite his tongue.

❧

Gaston was dazzled. He had been kissed before, of course, and he had granted kisses to women in his time, but never had his blood simmered as it did after Ysmaine's kiss. She had kindled a desire within him that raged with such power that he felt he was a different man. His customary temperate manner seemed distant to him, terrifyingly so, and he could think only of a future of nights with this woman in his bed.

Gaston never forgot his duties, much less his routines. He was never late or distracted from his purpose or otherwise beguiled by the temptations of the flesh.

Was it natural for a man to feel so enflamed by his betrothed?

Was there some witchery at root?

His wits were addled, as much by Ysmaine's kiss as by her words. She challenged and provoked him, as well as sending fire through his blood. He had nigh forgotten the need for haste in speaking with her, for he had wanted to linger and watch her eyes sparkle, to reassure her and to tempt her smile. He had felt a cur for doubting her, but once they were separated even by the distance of her being in the saddle, he wondered whether she had simply persuaded him to her will.

He was not a man well accustomed to the wiles of women, after all, and that felt suddenly to be a lack. He had no sense whether Ysmaine was typical of a noblewoman or uncommon, and even less what to expect of her.

Was he a fool to choose to trust her about her herb?

Gaston hoped not. He hoped the truth was as she insisted it was, but he would be vigilant until he was sure. He was usually the one cautious to trust, but Bartholomew had learned well from his teaching. Aye, he would eat no morsel that Ysmaine had prepared for him, or drink of no cup she had seasoned. It should be simple to do while they traveled, and by the time they reached home, he would know whether his trust was misplaced.

Ysmaine made him think overmuch about their nuptial night, when he should have been thinking about their departure. He pondered her assertion that no man survived his wedding night with her, and wondered anew at it.

Had she just been unlucky?

Or was there a darker reason behind it all? When not staring into the lovely features of the lady or enchanted by her kiss, Gaston's doubts could find fertile soil.

Indeed, Ysmaine's kiss seemed to have kindled a thousand questions, and Gaston scowled, disliking the change. He was decisive. He chose justly and deliberately, which was why he was so often right. He had simply become unaccustomed to indulging the urges of his body.

That had to change if he were to have a son.

Indeed, consummating their match would see many of these uncertainties resolved. He would survive, so she would cease to fret about his fate. Her touch would undoubtedly lose its power once he had claimed her, and matters could become simple again.

There were sufficient details to be arranged to dismiss Ysmaine's past marital history. She was noble. She cared for her maid, and her eyes sparkled in a most enticing manner. He needed only a son from his wife, and she was young enough to grant him several.

All other details were irrelevant, at least for the moment.

The gate had only just closed behind them when the knight who was to be his companion on the preceptor's quest came charging toward him.

"*This* is the errand you had to undertake?" Wulfe roared without preamble. He was so furious that he apparently forgot that he was speaking in German. He flung out a hand. "You had to collect your *whores*?"

The maid caught her breath and lifted her head for a moment before she looked down at her hands again. Wulfe did not notice, but Gaston did. He glanced at his betrothed and saw Ysmaine's confusion. It was clear that the maid understood German, but his lady did not. It was perhaps just as well, given how this tirade had begun.

Although, given the bond between the women, he doubted that ignorance would last.

"This is my betrothed," Gaston interrupted firmly.

"Your betrothed?" the other knight spat. He folded his arms across his chest. "I don't recall that we brethren wed."

"I have left the order..."

"And yet you have a betrothed already." Wulfe propped his hands upon his hips. Gaston realized that other knights and brethren were watching, including Fergus who yet lingered beside his horse. "How clever of her to find a husband who will take her safely away from this city. I hope she paid you well and in advance, and that her wares were worth the price."

The maid inhaled sharply. The lady's gaze flicked between Gaston and Wulfe.

Gaston took a steadying breath and clenched his fists, reminding himself that naught would be accomplished if he followed his impulse. It was against the rules for one brother to strike another, and though his vows were behind him, he knew that a battle with Wulfe could cast a shadow over their journey.

Indeed, they were still within the Jerusalem Temple.

They had to work together, no matter how difficult that might prove to be. Gaston lifted Ysmaine from the saddle as if untroubled by Wulfe's words, ignoring the anger that simmered within him. She looked at him so keenly that he knew she discerned his mood, but he offered a hand to the maid that she might also dismount.

Aware that Wulfe fumed awaiting his reply, he nodded at Bartholomew to take the steed. "I thank you for your counsel, brother Wulfe," he said, his tone deceptively temperate. He stepped past the knight, escorting Ysmaine toward the chapel. He was immediately aware of her surprise and considered the stables with new eyes.

He had almost forgotten his first glimpse of them, years before.

The stables of the Temple were extensive and generously proportioned. The ceilings arched high overhead, all wrought of fitted stone, and the corridors extended long in either direction. The stone ensured that the stables were always cool, which was imperative for the steeds.

"This is merely the stable," she whispered in wonder and he nodded. "What splendor have you enjoyed in this abode?" she asked lightly.

Gaston smiled. "Our cells are simple enough and small."

Her eyes danced. "So it is true that the steeds of the Templars live better than most in Jerusalem?"

"It might well be so."

Wulfe exhaled noisily, and Gaston glanced back to see that the other knight had pinched the bridge of his nose. "We are *late*, sir," he said through his teeth, continuing again in German. "Time is of the essence, and the sooner we depart on this quest, the sooner we might return. A dalliance with a woman, whether she be betrothed or whore, can *wait*."

Gaston felt his jaw clench as he hid his reaction. "I am well aware of the press of time," he said with a patience he did not feel.

"And yet, you linger in the city, gathering women to accompany us. They will only slow our progress!"

"They will not."

"How can that be? Look at them! The one is pale and sickly, the other scarce better. They cannot ride hard and long and would be best left behind."

The very suggestion tightened Gaston's chest. "I will not leave Jerusalem without my betrothed."

"Perhaps you do not mean to leave Jerusalem at all," Wulfe challenged in an undertone. "Perhaps you intend to wait until there is no choice."

Gaston spun to hiss at the other knight. "Silence yourself!"

Wulfe's eyes snapped as he folded his arms across his chest. The man did not abandon a cause, that was certain. "We embark upon a quest granted by the preceptor of the Temple," he reminded Gaston tersely. "There is no place in our party for women, and you should know as much. What abomination is it that you even pollute the Temple with their presences?"

Gaston strode back to the other knight, leaving Ysmaine with her maid. "I understand full well the task I have been granted, and my responsibilities," he retorted with soft heat and the other knight took a step back. "What I also know is that the command of our mission is mine. I say my lady and her maid shall ride with us."

Wulfe bristled. "Your lady," he sneered. "You need not put a gloss on the truth of this matter for me. Look at her tawdry dress! She is not lady, nor is she your betrothed..."

"She certainly *is* my betrothed. We will wed in the chapel immediately."

"Now? And cause more delay!" the knight cried, flinging out his hands again. "For what purpose? If you mean to ensure your own comfort on this quest, you could find solace in any port. Between here and Paris, there must be a thousand whores, ten thousand whores even, any one of whom is more attractive and more likely to satisfy whatever needs you deem necessary..."

Gaston's battle was lost. He punched Wulfe so hard that the knight lost his balance and fell backward. Blood spurted from that man's nose as he lay sprawled on the floor of the stable, and more than one chuckle carried from those surreptitiously watching the exchange. Red suffused the fair knight's face, and he glared at Gaston with animosity. "I think you broke it."

"I hope so. If not, be sure to grant me the opportunity to correct my error."

Fergus, his eyes glinting, began to applaud, and Gaston felt the back of his neck heat. He had struck a brother. Though, truly, he had been so provoked that he would like to do it again.

He could not avoid the simple truth that he had never been so provoked.

At least Wulfe was silenced.

For the moment. That knight sat up, his shock clear, and lifted a hand to his injured nose. His astonishment at the sight of blood on his own fingertips prompted a giggle from Ysmaine's maid. Bartholomew ducked his head to hide his smile, and Ysmaine developed a fascination with her toes.

"You will pay for this indignity," Wulfe muttered as he rose to his feet. He strode to the stall where his horse was tethered, his two squires hastening behind him. He pivoted to shake a finger at Gaston. "I will ensure that you pay."

Gaston held the other knight's gaze. "It is my command," he reminded Wulfe softly, so softly that no other would hear his words, to show that he was not intimidated. "Ensure that you are prepared to depart at my order. It will not grieve me to leave you behind, should it come to that."

Wulfe's eyes flashed, but Gaston turned to his betrothed. He offered his hand to her even as he raised his voice. "We shall not delay the departure of the party overlong, Wulfe," he said, not turning to that man. "The priest awaits us, my lady."

Her gaze flicked to the knight then back to him. "You arranged for the exchange of our vows before you came for me."

"I spoke with the priest last night, when I knew we would depart this day."

"You prepare much in advance, sir."

"It is my nature to do as much. Does that trouble you?"

Her smile flashed. "I like it well in this instance, sir." Ysmaine placed her hand upon his elbow.

"We should be so lucky that Wulfe chooses to remain behind," Fergus drawled as they passed him. His French was difficult to follow for some, given his Gaelic accent, but Ysmaine seemed to understand him readily.

"He will not," Gaston said with conviction.

"More's the pity." Fergus bowed to Ysmaine. "And so you are to wed our Gaston. My best wishes to you, my lady."

"I thank you, sir. You are most kind." Again she showed the grace of a well-mannered noblewoman, and Gaston felt a curious surge of pride that she would be his wife.

Then he recalled that kiss and felt a prick of trepidation. What did he know of being a good husband? What did he know of ensuring the happiness of a wife? He could protect her, to be sure, but he had been a Templar for almost twenty years. He had seldom been with a woman, and only then with a whore. His wedding night seemed suddenly fraught with peril, for surely it would color their future together.

How could he fulfill his lady's expectations without knowing what they might be?

Would she see to his end if he did not?

છ

If Ysmaine had possessed any doubt in Gaston's conviction that they had to leave Jerusalem, the short journey to the Temple had banished it completely. The streets had been filled with agitated people, either carrying their worldly goods to the gates or securing their homes. The sense of desperation had grown with every passing moment, and she was glad they would be departing.

Indeed, she feared they might be too late. Ysmaine felt a

foreboding that matters moved too quickly, that events were sweeping along at a speed that threatened to leave them behind.

She had not understood the fair-haired knight but it was clear that he also chafed with impatience to be gone. She stole a glance at Gaston, who was grim, and knew he would not tell her what the knight had said to prompt his reaction. She did not doubt it had been a slight against her and Radegunde, for the knight had gestured, and the maid, who was not easily shocked, had caught her breath.

An insult then, and one Gaston had not seen fit to tolerate. Doubtless Radegunde would provide a translation later.

Even without it, Ysmaine liked that the other knight had been struck by her betrothed. It was curious to feel so relieved that she had a defender.

But not so strange to wish to keep him. Was it merely bad fortune that had seen her two former husbands die on her wedding night? Or was she cursed? Ysmaine did not want to find out the truth until the peril was far behind them.

Yet she did not know Gaston well enough to know best how to present her view.

"What did he say?" Ysmaine asked her husband quietly as he led her through a stone corridor that arched high overhead. Radegunde followed behind them, her slippers brushing softly against the stone.

"Wulfe?" Gaston shrugged at her nod, a dull flush rising on the back of his neck. "He talks overmuch. I believe he wishes to hasten our departure."

"Surely you had no argument with that?"

His sidelong glance was quick. "Your maid will undoubtedly tell you the truth of his objection."

Ysmaine guessed then that the other knight had taken issue with her presence. She also concluded that Gaston knew Radegunde had understood the knight's German. Was she imagining that Gaston now showed discomfiture? Had the sharp words found their mark? Her betrothed seemed less certain than he had, and that frightened her.

"Do you change your thinking, sir?" she asked, knowing that she should be demure but wanting to argue her own case with him.

Gaston halted and turned to face her. "Forgive my blunt

speech, my lady, but Wulfe believes that you are a whore who has made a fine bargain."

Did Gaston mean to put her aside?

Ysmaine's heart skipped though she spoke with care. "It is my experience, sir, that those who make such accusations tend to see their own truth in the choices of others. It is not in my nature to scheme so, and I must hope that you know as much."

Her words seemed to reassure him. "Indeed, the suggestion to wed was mine."

Ysmaine saw no reason to be shy, not when so much was at stake. Her cheeks burned as she continued, but she held Gaston's gaze steadily as she confessed the truth. "And I am a maiden, sir, not a whore."

An assessing glint lit his eyes. "You said you were widowed twice."

"Yet neither match was consummated. I am as yet untouched."

"But that kiss..."

Ysmaine's blush deepened for her impulsive nature had revealed itself. "I am grateful to you, sir, and I would ensure that you are not disappointed in your choice. I have been told that men prefer enthusiasm abed."

"Only if it is honest," Gaston murmured, bending down as his gaze locked with hers. "Never lie to me, my lady, and I will never betray you."

"Aye, my lord."

"Deception is my sole abhorrence," he continued with fervor, his gaze locked with hers. "Pledge to me that you will never lie."

"I will never lie to you, upon that you can rely."

"And all you have told me thus far is true?"

"All of it," Ysmaine replied. "Can the same be said of what you have told me?"

"It is true, all of it." Gaston's smile was rueful. "I have not the ability to deceive."

"Then we shall do well together, sir. You need not fear a lack of forthright speech with me."

Radegunde snorted at that, but her expression was carefully innocent when the pair turned to face her.

Gaston glanced down at Ysmaine. "I fear, sir," she admitted, "that I can be too blunt of speech."

"I am a warrior, my lady. I doubt you could be so blunt as to surprise me." He nodded once, then turned to continue, apparently not hearing Radegunde's small chuckle. Ysmaine dared to hope that she had reassured him. He did not change his course, which was a good sign.

Could she be so fortunate that her new spouse might approve of her true nature? Ysmaine let Gaston lead her and when he said no more, she asked a question. "This Wulfe will travel with us?"

Gaston nodded. "We will be a small party, for there are several leaving at the same time. It is better to travel together." He did not seem to be concerned with her curiosity, so she asked more.

"What is his destination?"

"He has been dispatched by the preceptor, and our paths lie together for some distance," Gaston said stiffly, his gaze fixed on the corridor ahead. Clearly, it was not for Ysmaine, or perhaps even for Gaston, to know the business of the Temple.

"And the others in this party?"

"I believe that Fergus, the Scotsman in the stables, will depart with us. He has completed his service and returns home to wed." Gaston glanced down at Ysmaine with sudden interest. "You understood his French well enough."

"My father hired Scottish mercenaries. He said they were loyal as well as effective."

"And so is Fergus, although he appears complacent at first. It is a guise, and one that works well."

"It is oft best to be under-estimated," Ysmaine agreed, earning a quick glance from her betrothed.

"There will be two others: a nobleman returning home to his dying father and a merchant."

"I see." They reached a doorway then and the wooden door was opened from the other side. Gaston hesitated only a moment before gesturing for Ysmaine to precede him.

It was a simple chapel, illuminated by a single candle. A priest stood at the altar and glanced up from his prayers at their arrival. A young boy closed the door behind them and waited for instruction. Ysmaine was relieved that Gaston had not changed his mind.

Yet she feared the import of exchanging these vows yet again. Here was a man she could come to rely upon. Ysmaine already liked Gaston too well to risk losing him so soon.

"I have no ring for you, my lady," Gaston said. "But that will be remedied in France. Our vows will be witnessed by God, the priest, and your maid."

"And what of the nuptial night?"

"It will have to wait until we reach this day's destination." He flicked a glance at her, his uncertainty palpable.

Did he fear the night ahead?

Ysmaine smiled with confidence she did not feel. "I think that a wise choice, sir, for it is clear that a more hasty departure would be better."

But instead of being reassured, Gaston bent his full attention upon her.

ন

Something was amiss.

Ysmaine was too relieved that they would delay the consummation of their match for Gaston to forget Wulfe's accusations. Was it possible that she saw only to her own advantage? That knight had a talent for uttering poison that found a weakness.

"You do?" he asked, watching her closely.

"Indeed, I think of practicalities, sir," Ysmaine said with a nod. "There was a restlessness in the city that troubled me this day, and I believe your desire to depart soon is a good one."

Was that the root of it?

"Speak to me bluntly, my lady," Gaston urged and she flushed. "I would know the truth of your heart."

Her lashes fluttered before she met his gaze. "I was taught a lady should not be too forthright. My mother said it was unseemly."

"That was before you vowed to be honest with me."

Ysmaine's smile was luminous then, and she leaned toward him. "I know you think it whimsy, sir, but I fear that you might share the fate of my other husbands. I would not deny you the marital debt, sir, but I am not in such a hurry to lose your protection."

Did she know that her fingers were digging into his arm?

Did she truly believe he would die on their wedding night? He

67

had not given the whimsical notion much credence the day before, but in this moment, she seemed most concerned.

Gaston covered her hand with his and loosened her grip, feeling both protective and curiously reassured. "I do not mean to die, my lady."

"Does any man mean to do so?" Ysmaine asked, her words soft.

"We ride after our vows are exchanged and will celebrate our first night together in Nablus."

"On this very night?" Ysmaine winced. "Can we not wait until we are aboard the ship, sir?" She leaned closer. "Though you likely believe me foolish, sir, I would not lose you so soon as this. I would be your wife in every way, whether my blood stains the linens here in Palestine or later, but I would beg you to delay." There was an entreaty in her eyes that made his heart thump, and Gaston dropped his gaze that he might think clearly.

Perhaps she merely gave him what he desired.

He had demanded honesty, and she had promised it. It would be churlish of him to doubt her word before they had even exchanged their vows. The sole way to build a match was with trust, and Gaston chose in that moment to trust Ysmaine.

He tightened his grip on her hand. "Your position as my wife will be better assured once the match is consummated," he said. "And the likelihood of your bearing a son sooner much improved. Nablus, it will be."

Ysmaine dropped her gaze, hiding her thoughts. "As you wish, sir." Her tone was so temperate that Gaston was uncertain.

Surely, her concern was solely as she had confessed?

Surely Wulfe was mistaken?

Father Hilaire bowed to the lady when she and Gaston stood before the altar, his pleasure more than clear. "I witness few weddings in this place," he said to Ysmaine with a smile after he had blessed them both. "And I would beg your forgiveness should I err in the vows."

Ysmaine gave him a smile so bright that the older man was left blinking. "You need not fear for the ceremony, sir. I know the vows very well and can advise upon any part you forget."

Gaston knelt beside her, favoring his injured leg only slightly in doing so. He was aware of the way that Ysmaine watched him from the corner of her eye and wondered what she thought of his wounded state.

Surely she did not pity him?

He stifled all the doubt in his mind and took the lady's hand in his. They began a future together, and he meant to ensure that this match was Ysmaine's last. Trust was the key to a solid beginning, and Gaston knew it well.

He *would* trust his lady wife.

Chapter Five

Bartholomew ran down the corridor to the stables, carrying the last of Gaston's possessions. The saddlebags were almost completely packed, and he had retrieved the last of his knight's belongings from his cell. He felt rushed, for he had not prepared as well as he might have preferred, since he had been dispatched to watch over the lady. The steeds still needed to be saddled, although they were already fed and rested. He hastened to have all prepared by the time the vows were exchanged.

Gaston never lingered once his choice was made.

Bartholomew had just dropped the saddle onto Fantôme's back when he heard his name whispered from the shadows. His heart leapt with certainty of who it must be, and he feared for her safety. He pivoted in silence, seeking Leila's presence.

She was in the corner, crouched behind the bales of hay.

"What are you doing here?" he whispered. "Your uncle will be angry that you are not home."

"My uncle means to leave the city," she confessed. "I am to wed my cousin this very night, but I will not do it." Her dark eyes flashed. "You have to help me, Bartholomew!"

"You cannot take refuge in the Temple," he argued. "We depart within moments and I will not be able to bring you food. I dare not trust any other soul here with the secret..."

"Take me with you."

"Leila! It cannot be done." Even as he spoke, Bartholomew feared for Leila's future.

"I am coming with you, or I will run away on my own," she said, showing an obstinacy he knew well. On good days, he called it persistence. She glared at him. "You can be a friend and help me, or join the ranks of those against me."

"We ride out in a party of knights..."

"I can ride as well as any of them, and you know it."

"But they are *men*, Leila. You cannot hide within the party..."

"I hide here most days," she noted.

Bartholomew's protest faded as he realized that Leila was wearing his old chausses and boots. He had given them to her when they became too small for him, because he had thought she might prefer them when she rode. More than five years his junior and a Saracen, Leila had a gift with horses that could not be denied.

"No one will be fooled," he argued, even as he wondered.

"I cut my hair," she said, pushing back her hood to show him. She did look like a boy, if a delicate one, with her hair chopped shorter. "I used dirt to hide the hue of my skin."

"You used manure," Bartholomew countered with a grimace and she grinned.

"A lot of it! No one will look twice, *if* you vouch for me." She sobered then, and he saw that her hands were shaking. "You know I can ride. You know I will not allow you to be punished for my choice. I will say I lied to you if I am caught. I will say that you showed Christian charity."

"Stop," Bartholomew said, holding up his hand. "Are you certain you cannot wed your cousin and remain here, happily?"

She shook her head, defiance bright in her eyes. "I will not do it. I despise him. My uncle thinks he does what is good and responsible for me, but he has not seen the shadow in this cousin of mine. He has not seen how he treats women." Her chin lifted. "If you deny me, I will find another way. I will *not* wed him."

Bartholomew winced. He knew enough of the world and its ways to understand that Leila would fare worse on her own. Still, what tale could he tell? "All the knights have squires," he whispered to her. "One of them will betray you to win favor with his knight. How will I disguise you? How would I explain your presence?"

"There must be a way," Leila insisted.

"There is," interjected a deep voice from the entry to the stables. Bartholomew spun to find Fergus leaning against the wall there. The Scotsman had moved so silently that Bartholomew wondered how much he had overheard. "All of it," Fergus said with a wink, showing his ability to guess the thoughts of others that so disconcerted Bartholomew. Fergus then nodded at Leila as he raised his voice. "How enterprising of you, Bartholomew. I have need of another squire on my journey home. If you vouch for this friend of yours, he will serve me well."

"I do, sir," Bartholomew said with relief. "He has the greatest skill with horses I have ever witnessed. Indeed, he has taught me much."

Leila bowed, and Fergus' eyes twinkled. "And has he a name?"

Bartholomew stammered for a moment, then Leila gave him a hard nudge. Her elbow was sharp, and he winced. Fergus' lips twisted, and he knew the former knight had seen the gesture. "Laurent," he said, on impulse.

"Laurent," Fergus echoed. "Very well, Laurent. You will tend my horses, and sleep with them to ensure their security."

"Aye, sir."

"For you smell as if you oft sleep with them."

"I do, sir."

"And once we reach Killairic, the choice of remaining in my service will be yours."

"I thank you, sir."

Fergus ducked back and eyed his other two squires who were yet a distance away. He snapped his fingers. "Come with me, Laurent. I must buy another horse and you will advise me on the purchase. Show me what you know, prove your worth, and I shall let you ride your pick of the palfreys."

"Aye, my lord." Leila did not hesitate for a moment. She ducked around Bartholomew with purpose, then scurried after Fergus, who was striding through the stables. There were always horses for sale between brethren, and he did not doubt she would pick the best mount and advise the best price.

He tightened the strap of Fantôme's saddle and dared to be relieved that Leila was not being abandoned. She was a good friend, and he had to believe that whatever fate awaited her in their party, it had to be better than the one she was so determined to leave behind.

৯♠

In one way, Ysmaine wished the exchange of their vows would last forever. It was so tranquil in the chapel, and the heat of Gaston beside her was reassuring. She could forget their departure, as well as any dangers that might confront them. She knew that once they left this haven, many challenges would be cast in their path, and she wished to savor this moment.

She hoped with all her heart that it would be the last time she wed.

In another way, Ysmaine was impatient to be gone. She could feel the tension in Gaston, confirmation that he knew more of the peril before them than she did.

Her own observations of the mood of Jerusalem made her fear it might already be too late.

She repeated her vows, liking Gaston's firm grip on her hand and the deep deliberation of his voice. The man wanted honesty of her. Ysmaine could not believe her good fortune. Could she truly be wedded, saved from peril and bound to a man who might love her for who she was? It was strange that a little sleep, a little food, and a little hope could be so potent a mix. Ysmaine felt her old spirit returning, as well as her ambition for a marriage that would fulfill her dreams.

Gaston certainly seemed like a man she could come to love. She liked his strength and his gentleness, his resolve and his integrity. She did not like that limp, not in the least. It would only worsen as he aged, particularly if he had not spared the time for it to fully recover, and she hoped that she might convince him to treat himself kindly as Fatima had not. Perhaps this departure from a warrior's life would be good for him.

She wondered what port they would sail from, and knew it could not be Jaffa, not if they would spend this night in Nablus. Acre? Tyre? Surely not Tripoli. And what would be their destination? Sicily? Crete? Venice? Farther would be better to her thinking, for her husband would be off his feet for more time if the passage by ship was longer. His hip might improve on its own with such a forced rest.

She would keep him abed, rub unguent into his hip, and perhaps conceive his son.

The prospect made Ysmaine smile in anticipation, until she recalled that he had to survive their nuptial night first.

And they had to make it to that ship safely.

When the vows were done and they were blessed again, Gaston rose to his feet. He held fast to her hands and lifted her to face him. His eyes were a vibrant blue, his resolve so clear that Ysmaine's heart thundered.

"And so we begin, lady mine," he murmured for her ears alone, then bent to capture her lips beneath his own.

Lady mine. She liked the salute well.

His was a sweet kiss, a resolute kiss, a kiss that was not exactly chaste but not scandalous either. It was potent enough to set her blood to simmering, yet subdued enough that the priest was not shocked. When Gaston lifted his head, Ysmaine found herself hungry for more. His eyes glittered as he surveyed her, then he genuflected and bowed to the altar.

"The party awaits," he said, escorting her from the chapel with purpose. All softness was dispatched from his manner, and he was both as grim and as determined as the moment she had first seen him. His limp did not slow his pace overmuch, and Ysmaine nigh had to run to keep up with him. She reached back and seized Radegunde's hand, ensuring the maid was not left behind.

It seemed that once a decision was made, Gaston did not linger over its fulfillment.

Ysmaine could admire that.

They reached the stables to find a party of horses saddled and waiting, squires holding reins and knights mounted to depart. All had been prepared during the exchange of their vows, and Ysmaine understood that the dark-haired squire had understood his knight's mind. She had best be ready for her husband's choices, too, for he might not take well to uncustomary delays. Gaston introduced the younger man as Bartholomew, even as Bartholomew offered heavy dark cloaks to both women.

That blond knight who Gaston had struck awaited them with obvious impatience. That man's expression was disparaging. Though his nose had stopped bleeding, it was reddened and swollen. It seemed he would lead the party, for he was already mounted, his black destrier tethered to his palfrey's saddle and stamping with impatience to be gone.

"He said we would slow their departure," Radegunde whispered to Ysmaine, giving her lady the determination to prove the knight's expectations wrong.

She would not disappoint her new husband.

Ysmaine counted three more destriers in the party. Those steeds were harnessed not saddled. Like the black one of the Templar, their reins were tethered to the saddles of palfreys. That detail told Ysmaine that they meant to ride with haste. The size and weight of destriers gave them sufficient burden, and their strength was usually saved for battles. In the heat of the day, they would tire quickly, so being without riders would ensure they could travel farther.

There were more than a dozen palfreys, restless as if they too knew the danger of lingering. A number of them were heavily loaded with saddlebags and small trunks, more than one with a squire atop the baggage. The men in the party wore heavy dark cloaks, like the ones brought by Bartholomew, making them indistinguishable from each other. The cloaks were tucked tightly around them, hiding the blades they must be carrying, and there were no visible insignia.

Gaston flung one cloak around Ysmaine and lifted her to the saddle of a chestnut palfrey in one smooth move. She locked her boot into the stirrup by rote, prepared to ride hard, and saw his smile as he noted the gesture.

"You can ride, lady mine?"

"Of course." Ysmaine was glad that her boots had been too well worn to fetch a good price. "If you mean to ride with haste, Radegunde should ride with me." She saw Gaston's gaze flick over the maid, who stood straight in an echo of her usual determination.

"Nay, she is too weakened for this journey," he said with a flick of his hand, and Ysmaine feared for a heartbeat that he meant to abandon her maid. "She will ride with me, for if she slumbers, she may pull you from the saddle." His gaze locked with hers and his eyes glowed sapphire. "I am not prepared to lose my wife so soon as this," he said with a thrilling heat, and Ysmaine found herself afire again.

Then Gaston was in his saddle, Radegunde before him. Bartholomew mounted last, then at Wulfe's gesture, the entire party cantered as one toward the Temple gates.

"We ride hard throughout this day and perhaps into the night," the Templar told the others.

"We should make Nablus before we rest," Gaston confirmed.

"Nablus?" that blond knight protested, glancing back at Gaston. "Why suggest that we ride north? We could ride to Jaffa and set sail this very day..."

"You should cede to the experience of Gaston," the Scotsman drawled. "For he knows these lands better than any of us."

The blond knight clearly resented the suggestion. He glared at Gaston.

"The road to Jaffa is choked with pilgrims," Gaston said, interrupting him flatly. "We would make poor time and might not find passage when we arrive. The ships will be overwhelmed. We should make for Acre."

The other knight's lips set and his eyes flashed but he did not argue. Ysmaine guessed that he wished to do so, but did not, and she wondered why. "Do not fall back, for we shall not delay," he advised.

Ysmaine took that as a warning. She gripped the reins with determination.

"We may be attacked. We may be besieged," the Templar continued. The men nodded grimly, and Ysmaine saw more than one gloved hand drop to a hidden hilt. "But we carry the blessing of the Temple and by the goodness of God, we shall do all that is possible to reach our destination. I thank you for hiding your insignia and your weapons. Remain close and ride tightly together, with the destriers in the middle so they might be less readily observed. Let us keep silent, beyond the sound of the horses' hooves, so none might readily guess our identities from our speech."

There was a murmur of assent and a jostling in the group as the warhorses, which would reveal the presence of knights, were moved into the middle so they would be less readily noted. Gaston rode at the right of the party, and the Templar led them. The Scotsman was on the left of the group and another nobleman defended the rear. He was richly dressed, that one, so must have been a secular knight well graced by Fortune. He was older than Gaston and a handsome man, with silver in his hair. In the middle were squires aplenty, a grizzled man-at-arms who rode between the Scotsman and Ysmaine, as well as a stout man directly behind the Templar who looked to be terrified.

She and Radegunde were the sole women, but Ysmaine wagered it would be the plump man who caused any delay. He already was pale with worry and fussed overmuch with his reins.

Gaston seized the palfrey's bridle and pulled Ysmaine's steed to his side. "On my left, lady mine," he said with resolve. "Be always on my left. I need to know your location without a glance."

Because he would protect her. Ysmaine guessed that her new husband favored his right hand. She nodded, knowing she would not be given this counsel twice. Gaston held Radegunde on his left, ensuring that his right hand was unobstructed, should he need to seize his blade.

That choice told her all she needed to know of the ride before them.

Indeed, she felt a quiver of fear.

The gate was opened with a creak and the party poured into the streets, keeping in formation. The city was bustling in the sunlight, and she heard the tolling of a distant church bell. The party moved steadily toward the city gates, their hoods drawn purportedly against the sun and their manner quiet. The Templar exchanged a word with the gatekeeper, who saluted them as they rode past.

All Ysmaine could see beyond the city gates was the road and the hot sunlight on the earth. Her heart skipped with fear of what laid ahead of them. Was Gaston right that they should head north? Or would the journey take too long? The king had led his army to the north, after all, and that was where the battle must be in progress.

If not already won or lost.

At the Templar's gesture, they erupted from the city, the horses thundering down the road toward whatever fate awaited them.

Ysmaine bowed her head and uttered one last prayer as she rode beneath the shadow of the gate and left the Holy City forever.

❧

It was past sunset when they reached Nablus, for even the road to the north had been busy with departing pilgrims. They rode into the bailey of the citadel with relief, their horses lathered and their cloaks choked with dust. This was not a Templar priory but a secular keep, held by a Frankish lord.

Ysmaine did not particularly care. She was glad that they had reached a haven, and could not believe how sore she was. Once she had ridden long at the hunt, and even longer on journeys with her kin, but she had walked for the past year. She felt the difference in every muscle she possessed. Radegunde had fallen asleep in Gaston's grip as they rode, but Gaston did not appear to be tired in the least.

His eyes were slightly more narrowed and his manner an increment more stern, but beyond the dust on his boots and the slight growth of stubble upon his chin, he looked much as he had when they had left Jerusalem. It was clear that he was accustomed to such long days, and even his destrier did not look to be as exhausted as she might have expected.

Ysmaine was certain that she could have eaten whatsoever was put before her.

And that she would sleep for a week afterward.

The squires bustled around the knights and their horses, and she slipped from her own saddle, wanting only to stretch her legs. She reached up to assist Radegunde to the ground and the maid yawned as she accepted Ysmaine's helping hand. Gaston lowered the maid with care, his gaze flicking to Ysmaine's in silent question.

She smiled for him. "We are both well, sir, thanks to you."

Whatever reply he might have made was not to be uttered. An ostler came out of the stables, but that man spared them no welcoming smile. "Have you heard the tidings from Nazareth?" he demanded of them, his voice rising with an urgency that did not bode well. He turned to the Templar who led their party. "A messenger came but an hour ago with news."

"What news?" the Templar demanded.

Ysmaine saw that the other knights in the company attended this conversation avidly.

The suzerain himself came to the bailey then, his manner distraught. "You will all know the truth of it soon enough," he said with dismay. "We are lost! Two hundred knights of the Temple and the Hospital have fallen to Saladin and thousands of other knights, as well."

Ysmaine saw her husband pale beneath his tan.

"But how can this be?" the Templar demanded.

"On the third, they rode to Tiberias, but were surrounded by the Saracens before even making Hattin," the lord confessed.

Gaston winced, and Ysmaine wondered why.

"They were snared, without water for the men or the horses, then the Saracens set fire to the grasses all around them. Yesterday morning, the men broke ranks and tried to run for the springs of Hattin. They were captured or slaughtered, the forces routed by the Saracens. King Guy was captured, along with the Masters of the Temple and the Hospital and more than two hundred knights of both orders."

Gaston inhaled and looked away. "All of them," he murmured under his breath.

"Surely they will be ransomed," Ysmaine whispered, but her husband shook his head.

"It is against the rule," he said through thin lips.

Consternation passed through the small party, and Ysmaine felt new fear. She clutched Radegunde's hand tightly on one side and her husband's arm on the other. She and Radegunde had watched the army ride out. There had been thousands of men, on foot and on horseback, their banners flying. Yet more were to meet them, riding from Acre and Tripoli and Tyre.

"They were so many," she whispered, unable to comprehend such a loss.

"It was rumored that Saladin led thirty thousand," Gaston said. "King Guy did not believe it."

But Gaston had. Ysmaine saw the truth of it in his expression.

"But that is not the worst of it," the lord said.

"What can be worse?" the fourth knight, the richly attired one whose name Ysmaine did not know, cried out. The others nodded.

"The True Cross, which the Bishop of Acre carried into battle, was lost to the Saracens when the bishop was killed," the lord said with despair. "Reginald of Chatîllon was cut down in Saladin's tent by Saladin's own hand. He was beheaded before them all!"

Gaston pinched the bridge of his nose at this detail.

The lord took a breath. "And those two hundred knights of the Temple and Hospital were beheaded next."

Ysmaine guessed that Gaston must have known many of them. There were lines of strain around his eyes and he looked suddenly older. The Templar raged that vengeance must be claimed, but Gaston looked down, his brow furrowed in thought.

"How do you know of this?" he asked quietly. "Is the report reliable?"

"Raymond of Tripoli broke through the ranks of the Saracens. Those in his small party were the sole ones to survive, or so he dispatched word."

"So, it is true," the Scotsman murmured, more troubled than he had been. "Twenty thousand, the largest army ever mustered in these kingdoms, and virtually all dead."

The members of the party crossed themselves at this summary.

"Yesterday?" Gaston asked of the lord of the citadel.

"Aye."

Her husband nodded once, turned, and locked his gloved fingers together. Then he lifted his gaze to Ysmaine's and bent before her. She understood immediately. "I will ride as far as you deem fitting, my lord," she said, putting her boot into his hand.

"Samaria," he murmured after he had lifted her to the saddle again. "I do not think the steeds can go farther this night."

Ysmaine considered him for a moment, for it sounded as if Gaston made the decision. She turned to the Templar, who slapped his gloves upon his palms and looked vexed.

"You speak aright," he said, as if the choice were obvious. "We must ride for Samaria."

"We will have to make Acre tomorrow," the Scotsman added with a wince.

Ysmaine felt her fear rise, despite Gaston's apparent calm. Even at Samaria, they would not be half way to the port. She looked between the two knights, realizing the import of the Scotsman's words. He believed that if they did not make Acre on the morrow, they might never make it at all.

"I follow your dictate, sir," Ysmaine said, her exhaustion banished. "I will not slow the party." She held her husband's regard, let him see her resolve, then watched him nod once in approval.

As before, there was no delay once his choice was made. Indeed, even the horses seemed to take some urgency from his manner, and the entire party rode out again as the last light of the sun dipped below the horizon.

Ysmaine struggled against a curious sense that the Templar followed her husband's dictate, though that made no sense at all. Perhaps he simply deferred to one who knew the region better.

Or perhaps she was sufficiently exhausted that she saw matters as they were not.

≿♠

They made Samaria.

Gaston was relieved about that, at least. He had seen the silhouettes of raiding parties of bandits on either side of the road, and their numbers had increased as they rode north. Their boldness had grown, too, but the size of the party had kept them at bay until they reached Samaria's gates. There was no question of riding farther this night. The horses needed rest, as did his lady and her maid, and the road would be too dangerous in darkness.

They found accommodation with welcome ease, which was one benefit of such a large host having ridden north with King Guy. There was plenty of space in the hospice for pilgrims, which was also well stocked as yet with fodder for the horses and simple fare for travelers.

Its greatest asset in Gaston's view, however, was its deep well. The water was cool and clear, and more than welcome after the day's long dusty ride.

Even if it reminded him overmuch of what had transpired at Hattin.

To Gaston's surprise, Ysmaine had not eaten or retired, but had gone to the tomb of John the Baptist to pray before even eating.

He had been praying all the day long, which he thought sufficient. There were no more tidings to be heard, for the same messenger had stopped here first with the same tidings as they had heard in Nablus.

Bartholomew and Fergus had gone with Ysmaine and Radegunde to the tomb, along with several of the other squires, and Gaston did not doubt that some of their party feared for their future.

He was fairly certain he could guess Saladin's intent. He turned the facts in his mind, reviewing all he knew, confirming his conclusions as he awaited his lady wife. He was convinced they would make Acre safely.

The remainder of the party had retired or lingered in the common room, clearly exhausted but perhaps too agitated to sleep. Gaston sat at the board in the small hospice and sipped of the cold water. He had seen to the horses but awaited his wife before eating any of the bread.

Nay, he awaited the consummation of his nuptial vows. The promise made him too restless to consider sleeping and filled him with a curious mix of excitement and anticipation. The buoyant feeling reminded him of the thrill of the holidays when he had been a mere boy, and that thought made him smile.

In but a day, his new wife made him feel young again.

"I find little amusing in our situation, or indeed, the tidings that greet us." Wulfe came to sit opposite Gaston, his manner that of a man who would have his say. Gaston did not doubt it would be provocative and yearned for once in his days to have no impetuous knights to pacify.

It was hard to ignore the fact that Wulfe's nose was swollen and red. His manner, at least, was less adversarial than it had been previously. He spoke German as he had before, probably thinking that few in the party would understand him.

Gaston was not nearly as certain of that.

The other knight exhaled when Gaston did not reply.

"I hope we do not meet the infidel army on the road," Wulfe muttered, and Gaston had naught to say to that. He studied his cup instead.

"Is this why you rode to Acre?" Wulfe's quick glance was shrewd. "Because you wanted to hear whatever tidings there were?"

"I thought there might be more news to take to Paris," Gaston admitted. "But I also believed the road would be more open."

"As it has been," Wulfe ceded, then destroyed the tentative accord between them. "We have made good time, even burdened with the women."

Gaston shook his head at that. He had seen the resolve in Ysmaine's eyes and knew she would have bound herself to the saddle rather than give substance to any charge that she had delayed them. She was stubborn, this wife of his, and he was glad of it.

Wulfe continued grimly. "Though now, we must make Acre before it is taken by Saladin. You have put us in peril by choosing this route. Had we ridden for Jaffa, we would have already been a-sail."

"Perhaps," Gaston ceded. "Perhaps not."

"But worse." Wulfe leaned closer, his eyes gleaming. "We were *followed* this day."

"I know." Gaston turned his cup in the wet ring it had made on the board. He neither knew nor trusted Wulfe sufficiently to give voice to his suspicions.

"Do you know who it was?"

Gaston shrugged.

"Infidels. Thieves who would claim the prize which has been entrusted to us." At Gaston's warning glance, Wulfe dropped his voice to a hiss. "If we are already betrayed, there can be only one culprit. Perhaps your new wife is not a whore, but a spy."

Gaston gave him a quelling look, but Wulfe did not flinch. "Perhaps I should break more than your nose," he said quietly.

Wulfe shook his head. "Leave emotion aside, Gaston. Who else could it be? We are all Templars, at least we were, and know each other's merit on that basis alone."

Gaston was not so quick to agree to that. There were men who thought solely of themselves in the ranks of every army. He had only to think of the Grand Master of the Temple, Gerard de Ridefort, to be reminded of that. He did not doubt that man had survived the slaughter at Hattin, whether he had escaped with Raymond or not. Gerard had a talent for keeping a blade from his own neck.

"There are others in the party," he noted, wanting to hear what Wulfe had observed.

"Everard de Montmorency, a knight who accompanies us on his return to his father's deathbed. If we are to be hunted for wealth en route, it will be due to him and his baggage."

"Aye. He has fared well in Outremer as a younger son." Gaston did not wonder aloud why a knight and secular lord would choose to abandon his holding and his home just when it was likely to be lost. Doubtless there was great fondness between Everard and his father, and he put aside his own concerns in an attempt to see his father one last time. He chose to see the decision as sentimental.

"You know him well?"

"He has been at the king's court for years and has a good repute."

Wulfe frowned. "The merchant Joscelin de Provins seems but a man desperate to return home with his spice and what little silk he could seize. Do you know him?"

Gaston shook his head. "Only his repute."

"I do not distrust either of them, not even the barbarian knight. You, I cannot distrust or your squire. Indeed none of the squires can have a scheme, for they rely solely upon us for their welfare. Nay, it must be the women, if not your wife then her maid."

"Who has been so ill that she has not the strength to plan beyond the taking of her next breath."

Wulfe met his gaze in challenge. "You said it, not me." He leaned closer. "Consider that your wife might have other goals beyond making a match and escaping Jerusalem. You could not have consummated the marriage for there was no time, which means the match can be annulled. At the very least, Gaston, she might find you useful. At the very worst, she might be using you for her own ends."

Gaston bristled. "Your comments are inappropriate."

"Aye? How much will you sacrifice to defend her?"

"She is my wife!"

"But what do you truly know of her?" Wulfe shook his head again. "This is folly. You have no understanding of the truth of women, and perhaps that is the result of too many years spent in our ranks."

"While you know more?"

Wulfe's smile was quick and bright. "I have not forsaken all of the pleasures of the flesh. There is a place for a whore in a man's life. Though a woman may provide relief of a kind to a warrior, she should not know his thoughts and secrets."

"You took a vow of chastity," Gaston reminded the other knight.

"I am not the sole one. Indeed, you might be the sole one who kept that vow."

Gaston shoved to his feet, impatient with Wulfe's attitude. His blood boiled, and there were more important matters to consider than how he might best silence this vexing knight. "I would excuse myself, before I do you injury again." He pivoted to march away, intending to seek out his lady wife, only to have Wulfe's words follow him.

"If you were compelled to choose between your comrades and your wife, which would it be?" that knight demanded.

Gaston could not resist. He glanced back with a confident smile, hoping to shake Wulfe's cursed confidence. "I have left the order," he said softly. "If ever you were my comrade, you are no longer. Those in this group are merely my companions."

Wulfe might have protested, but Gaston was not interested in whatever venomous words that man might utter. He strode out of the hospice, in search of his lady wife.

Surely Wulfe's suspicions could not be right?

But who *had* followed them?

Surely the treasure could not be at risk so soon as this?

Chapter Six

Ysmaine knelt at the tomb of John the Baptist in Samaria to pray, her thoughts straying to her aches and pains with a persistence that could not bode well for her prayers. She was nigh asleep on her feet. Radegunde was beside and slightly behind her, the sound of her murmured prayers doubly reassuring.

Though all seemed to improve, she still fretted. Indeed, Ysmaine had many blessings on this day thanks to her new spouse. A pang touched her heart, and she feared again for Gaston's survival, then prayed for him. She forced herself to remain on her knees until she murmured the entire *Paternoster* and the *Ave* without a single thought about her buttocks.

Then she winced as she began to rise to her feet.

She found a masculine hand beneath her elbow and recognized Gaston's scent before she turned to face him. "It seems I oft find you at prayer," he said quietly, his gaze searching. "Do you still seek divine intercession?"

"I merely give thanks for the goodness you have done for me, and for the safe journey we had on this day," she said and his glance flicked over her, as if he were uncertain whether to believe her. Curse his wretched squire! Ysmaine bit her tongue, though, knowing any protest would only add to his concerns. She had to find a better way to make the squire realize she was an ally.

Gaston guided her toward the hospice where they were quartered, and she knew he was aware of every movement on the street around them. Here there was a sense of urgency much like that in Jerusalem, if greater. The rest of the party that had gone to the shrine followed behind them, and she noticed how Bartholomew remained on her left side. She and Radegunde were between knight and squire, both men watchful. So, despite his concerns, the squire would defend her at his knight's dictate.

What was afoot?

"Have you heard more tidings?" she asked Gaston.

"I but gather impressions from others, but you need not concern yourself with such matters."

Ysmaine found a measure of her old audacity returning. "If it concerns our welfare, then I would know about it, sir."

"You need only concern yourself with conceiving an heir," Gaston countered. "I have need of a son with all haste, lady mine, and would have you round with child upon our arrival at my home estate."

Ysmaine could have taken issue with several notions in his declaration, but she chose the one that seemed of greatest import. "Surely you are as tired as I am after our ride this day..." she began but Gaston interrupted her.

"You have a chamber of your own for this night. I have arranged it. The maid can sleep with you after I leave. We will eat before retiring and ride out again before dawn."

Once again, Ysmaine was reminded of his resolve. The man would not be shaken from any objective once he had set his sights upon it.

Once he had arisen hale from their nuptial bed, she would admire that trait more fully. For the moment, she could not suppress her dread, even knowing it must be fanciful.

What if Gaston died this night? What would happen to her and Radegunde? She did not imagine for a moment that the Templar Wulfe would take compassion upon them.

In silence, they stepped into the shadowed common room of the small inn, and Gaston led Ysmaine toward a table. There could not be more than two rooms above this crowded space, and she did not doubt that all of those who traveled with them would hear whatever she and Gaston did. Still, her husband's hand was firm beneath her elbow, and she understood his resolve. Her color high, she ducked her head to avoid the knowing glances of the other knights—particularly that loathsome Templar.

Ysmaine would have had to have been witless to have missed the tension between the two knights. Gaston hid his irritation well, and another might have thought his expression impassive, but she already knew to pay heed to his eyes. They were vividly blue and flashing, though he dropped his gaze to disguise the heat of his reaction. His body was taut, too, his grip slightly tighter.

What had they said to each other?

She recalled the Templar's comments about the women delaying the party and feared that her presence was again the cause of dissent.

"I apologize for any delay, sir," she said, well aware that others listened. "I hope you refreshed yourself in my absence."

"I awaited you," he said simply and gestured to a table. The Templar rose from that table and flicked his cloak around himself, summoning his squires with a snap of his fingers, as he marched away. It was clear that he refused to eat in her presence.

It was hard to feel any Christian charity toward such a proud and irksome man, but Ysmaine strove to do so. She hoped that he was the root of her husband's annoyance, as well.

"Would you not all make the acquaintance of my lady wife?" Gaston asked the knight with a politeness that seemed forced. "There was little time to do as much this morning and we should know something of our companions."

The Templar spun, his gaze cold. "Madame," he said, and bowed.

"Brother Wulfe from the Gaza priory," Gaston said, his tone just as frosty. "My wife, Lady Ysmaine de Valeroy, who will be Baroness de Châmont-sur-Maine."

Wulfe bowed, looking as if he would have preferred not to do so.

Gaston continued, gesturing to the dark-haired man. "You know my squire, Bartholomew de Burgh, my lady."

"Indeed," Ysmaine agreed.

"And this is Fergus of Killairic, a former brother of the order like myself. You spoke to him briefly in Jerusalem, yet I was remiss in making introductions. Fergus returns home to his nuptials."

"You joined the order while betrothed, sir?"

Fergus bowed over her hand, his russet hair gleaming with copper lights. "My father and I agreed that the military training would be fitting, so I pledged three years of service." He smiled and a light dawned in his eyes that bode well for that match, to Ysmaine's thinking. "I would ride with yet more haste, were the choice mine to make, for I have missed my lady Isobel overmuch."

Ysmaine found herself warming to the Scotsman, who was clearly impassioned with his betrothed. "I am certain that you have."

Gaston guided Ysmaine to the knight who had ridden at the rear of the party, that handsome older man who now bowed low with charm and grace. "Everard de Montmorency, whose companionship we are fortunate to have."

"My lady, I wish you every good fortune on your wedding day for all your days and nights together." He was richly attired and had much baggage. Ysmaine was surprised that he had neither squire nor man-at-arms in his company.

"I thank you, sir." She dared to ask. "You journey alone?"

"Aye." Everard's response was touched with regret. "My father is ailing, and I would see him one last time, though all seemed to conspire against me. My squire was taken ill and my knights joined the army of King Guy, two even without my permission. Since I journey alone, I asked for the protection of the Temple."

"That seems a most wise choice, sir."

"And this is Joscelin de Provins, a merchant who returns also to Paris." Gaston gestured to the stout man, who nigh burst his belt as he bowed low.

"A great pleasure it is to meet you, my lady, and might I say that if you have provisions to acquire for your new household, I have a complete array of spices and herbs available..."

"I thank you for your thoughtful suggestion, sir." Ysmaine interrupted smoothly. "But surely you can understand that it is impossible for me to ascertain the requirements of my husband's home before we arrive there."

Joscelin colored and stepped back with a bow. "Of course, my lady."

"I be Duncan MacDonald, my lady," interjected the older man who had ridden beside her that day. "And sworn to the service of young Fergus, I am, by way of his father's command to ensure he returns home." He patted the scabbard on his belt. "Be not afeared that you will be undefended from my side, my lady."

"Indeed I do not," Ysmaine said. "I feel most valiantly defended in his party, to be sure."

Gaston then escorted her to the board. They broke bread

together, and she sipped of the wondrous cool water, watching him all the while.

The silence between them unnerved her, especially when she would have savored some conversation before they met abed. Her husband might have spent years living in the silence of a religious order, but she had not.

If the conversation had to be launched by someone. Ysmaine would do it.

૨**

"The other knights have many squires," Ysmaine noted quietly and Gaston nodded agreement. She was relieved when he made to answer her, and thought she had chosen a topic well.

"It is the way of knights to need many hands to aid them." He nodded at a pair of boys. "They two ride with Wulfe." One was tall and slim with fair hair while the other was shorter, more portly and had dark curly hair.

"They could not look more different from each other," she ventured.

"I know not their names, though I know those of the Scotsman." Gaston indicated Fergus with a nod. "The squire with reddish hair is Hamish, and you should entrust him with no item that would break upon hitting the ground."

Ysmaine smiled. "I will not."

"The older one with fair hair is Kerr."

Ysmaine considered the blond boy. "He looks more like an angel than a squire."

Gaston widened his eyes for a moment. "Appearances can deceive, lady mine."

Ysmaine understood, stifled a smile, then looked for the other boy. "Fergus had a dark boy with him earlier."

"Laurent," Gaston supplied. "He is good with horses and will remain with them each night. He was oft in the stables of the Temple, and Fergus chose not to be parted from him."

Fergus had saved the boy's life, Ysmaine guessed.

Gaston fell silent then, though he did not eat much. He tore the bread and when he did eat a bite. he did so absently, as if he considered greater matters.

"You are concerned," she dared to say, keeping her voice low.

"If I am, it is not of import." He averted his gaze then, as if to hide his thoughts, and Ysmaine regarded him with some vexation.

Though it might be inappropriate, it was not within her to keep silent. She hoped that her new husband would not find fault with that. She put her hand over his and made an appeal. "You wished for honesty between us, sir, and I wish for confidence. My parents always have discussed matters together, and my father says a shared burden is lighter. I would have the same comfort in our match."

He almost flinched.

What cause had he to distrust her?

When Gaston remained silent, Ysmaine could not. "Did you know any of the knights lost at Hattin?"

"There were thousands of them, but most of those from the order I would have met at least in passing." He frowned and his voice turned husky. "I knew others very well in that departing host."

Did he grieve his lost fellows? She could not imagine that he would not. Did he wish to avenge their deaths and attack the infidels?

Ysmaine studied Gaston with care and spoke with yet more. "It is a brutal way for a man to end his days."

"It is not unexpected when one earns his way with his blade," he replied with a mildness she did not share. "I would wager that to a man they had made their peace with the possibility."

She had to ask. "Had you?"

Gaston nodded then sipped of the water again. Implacable. Impassive. Impossible to read. His manner was more irksome than his words. She wished to know him, to talk to him and to understand him, but Gaston seemed to value his privacy. No doubt about it, he was more accustomed to silence than she.

Ysmaine, never one to be shy, chose to be forthright, hoping she might provoke him into a confession of some kind.

"I could never make my peace with the notion of being slaughtered by an infidel," Ysmaine said. "I admire any man who could placidly accept such a fate."

No sooner had the words crossed her lips than she knew she had her husband's attention in truth.

Gaston's gaze collided with hers, and she sensed that he would chide her. "War is war, and it is not only *infidels* who slaughter, lady mine. At least in this, there were no innocents."

Ysmaine was intrigued, not just by his response but by his vehemence. "You cannot take the Saracen side!" she protested, not really believing that he did.

She thought that Gaston would turn away and keep his secrets, but instead he leaned over the table toward her, his manner intent. "I have negotiated with the Saracens over matters large and sundry for over ten years." He tapped a heavy finger on the board as Ysmaine watched him, fascinated by this confession of his past deeds. "I have gone to their courts and they have come to me. I have negotiated the ransom of prisoners and taken treaties from kings and counts to them. I cannot fail to look for their reasoning in any conflict, for it has been my task, time and again, to find a point of agreement between us. The safe passage of religious pilgrims has been one such point, and one of easy agreement." He leaned back and quaffed his water. "Or it was, until Reginald of Chatîllon claimed Karak."

Her husband had been a diplomat as well as a fighting knight. Ysmaine was most impressed. This ability to find common ground would serve him well as a baron. "What did he do?"

"He broke his sworn oath," Gaston replied without hesitation. "Repeatedly."

Ysmaine winced. "Why?"

"Because he believed it did not matter, if it was sworn to a Saracen, I would wager," Gaston said. "The fact is that that value of a sworn oath is something many of us hold in high estimation, regardless of our religious affiliation."

"What manner of pledge was it?"

"Does it matter?"

"Only that it might reveal more of the man's nature."

Gaston regarded her, a smile lifting one corner of his mouth. "Are you a strategic thinker, lady mine?"

Ysmaine found herself blushing. "I like to understand people, and if possible, why they make the choices they do."

"As do I," Gaston agreed, his surety making her heart flutter. He took another sip of water and leaned toward her, speaking to her as if she were an equal, or another man. Ysmaine was delighted. "Reginald of Chatîllon consistently broke his pledge to allow safe passage to Saracen pilgrims. He attacked their parties, imprisoned them, and plundered their goods, over and over again. Each time, he treated with Saladin and swore that he would not repeat his crime, and each time, he broke his oath again."

Ysmaine bit her lip, understanding something of what had happened in this battle. "And so he was killed at Hattin for his own perfidy."

Gaston nodded. "I believe so. Saladin swore almost a year ago, when his own sister was a pilgrim in one of those caravans, that he would take vengeance upon Reginald with his own hand."

It did sound like a vow a knight would swear, even to Ysmaine. Just as she saw the similarity between Fatima and Mathilde, she saw similarity between Saracen and knight in Gaston's tale.

"And the Templars are sworn to the defense of pilgrims, as well," she said. "Our party from Jaffa was escorted by four Templars."

Her husband nodded vigorously. "Our order was created to ensure the safe passage of pilgrims from Jaffa to Jerusalem. It is no accident that one of our order was oft sent to repair the damage wrought by Reginald and to negotiate a new treaty, for pilgrims were at the root of it."

"You," Ysmaine concluded, seeing why Reginald's feats would anger him so much.

Gaston nodded again. "We survived here as long as we did by respecting each other in such matters as this, in areas where we might find common ground. Reginald did not care about more than his own advantage, and thus, many more will die to pay for his greed."

Ysmaine thought of all the knights said to be lost, and knew there would be many more soldiers beyond that. It seemed a horrific waste. "My mother always insists that there is good and bad in every kind."

"And she is right." Gaston finished his water and looked over the company as Ysmaine watched him. She was intrigued by this glimpse of his experience, but she could already see that the task would have suited him well. He spoke with care, told less than he knew and considered his choices well before making a decision.

Indeed, there was much in Gaston's very manner that inspired calm and confidence.

And she herself trusted his word.

"Do you speak their tongue?" Ysmaine asked, wondering about those negotiations.

Gaston gaze flicked to her and away before he shook his head with impatience. "The Temple has interpreters for such exchanges, and I was always accompanied by at least one."

It was not exactly a denial. Indeed, it seemed a diplomat's reply, for it appeared to mean one thing without stating as much. She supposed it did not precisely fail to be honest. Ysmaine had the sense that Gaston might understand the Saracen tongue, and that if he did, it would be most useful if others were unaware of that. She realized then that he had lived long in the Latin Kingdoms and had made a life for himself here. Indeed, France might be strange to him now.

"Will you miss the Holy Land?" she asked.

Gaston shrugged. "In some ways. In others, though, I will be glad to see home again." A shadow touched his features then, and she guessed he regretted the news that summoned him home. Of course, he only went because his brother had died.

Otherwise, he would have ridden in the party to Hattin.

And he likely would have died there.

Ysmaine could not bear to think of it. "Were you close to your brother?"

Gaston's eyes glittered as he eyed her anew. "You are full of questions this night, lady mine."

Ysmaine flushed. "I am intrigued by my new husband."

"I think you would delay the inevitable," he mused.

Ysmaine lifted her chin boldly and held his gaze. "I grow to admire you, sir. I believe that having you as my spouse will suit me well."

"I will not die, Ysmaine," he murmured, uttering her name aloud for the first time.

She nodded, feeling foolish, flustered and pleased. Had there ever been a man who so confused her reactions?

Gaston eyed her for a moment, then spoke quietly. "Bayard was my older brother, my mentor and my companion. I cannot truly believe that he laughs no longer, for he was always so vital."

It seemed to Ysmaine that Gaston himself was most vital. She reached and covered his hand with hers, only realizing after she had done so that she was again showing herself bold. He considered her hand atop his with a little smile, as if he truly did not mind that she was so candid, then turned his hand so that their fingers entangled. His fingers were warm, his hand strong and his grip gentle.

He lifted his gaze to hers, and she caught her breath at the vivid blue hue of his eyes. "Perhaps it is time to retire, lady mine," he murmured, his voice so low that the sound made her shiver.

Ysmaine's heart leapt. They were far from safety as yet, and she did not want to lose her defender. She wanted to entreat him, yet did not want him to have more doubts about her intent. She opened her mouth, then closed it again.

Gaston squeezed her fingers. "It will not take long, and I will rest easier knowing the obligation is fulfilled." He smiled at her. "You might rest easier knowing your fear to be groundless."

Ysmaine understood that she would not change his thinking, and it was his right to demand the marital debt. She rose to her feet and bowed, hoping the wild pace of her heart did not show.

"I shall await your pleasure, sir," she said with a little bow. There was a lump in her throat and her voice sounded strained. Certainly, her palms were damp. "And will be prepared to ride on the morrow at your earliest command."

She spun then, terrified that she would see a third husband dead this very night, then tried to climb the stairs with composure. She did not doubt the blond Templar would happily abandon her and Radegunde if Gaston could not insist upon them being in the party.

What would become of them if he was lost?

How could Ysmaine ensure he was not?

ἐ▲

Radegunde followed Ysmaine and helped her lady to unlace her kirtle. Ysmaine's hands were shaking but the maid pretended not to notice. She folded the kirtle and surcoat, then put Ysmaine's stockings atop them. She combed out Ysmaine's hair, admiring it when it was spread over her lady's shoulders.

"I wish I had hair of such a hue," she murmured. "It is like spun gold."

"Yours is like dark silk, Radegunde, and the wave of it most pretty."

"Ah, but men are said to prefer flaxen hair."

Ysmaine had not found it that much of an advantage to be considered appealing by men, but she refrained from such comment. "I hope only that my husband likes it."

A heavy foot sounded on the stair and both women glanced that way. Ysmaine's heart was thundering and it seemed she could not draw a full breath.

"You would tempt a saint, my lady," Radegunde murmured by way of encouragement, then smiled and left when Ysmaine did not reply. She heard maid and husband exchange a cursory greeting, but kept her back to the door.

The room was small and simply furnished, for there was only a straw pallet upon the floor. It had no window, and she guessed that once Gaston entered, it would seem full indeed.

The door opened, and she caught her breath.

It was warm, but she felt a shiver deep inside that she wore only her chemise. She folded her arms around herself and strove not to tremble in dread. The silence did little to reassure her. It made it far too easy to recall Richard's bulk motionless atop her, and when she inhaled, she was sure she smelled him again.

Terror unfurled in her belly.

Ysmaine did not know what to expect from real intimacy. Her mother had explained to her what happened abed between man and wife, and she had waited abed twice to experience the truth. Should she touch him first? Would he think her a harlot if she did as much? Should she obediently wait for his command? Ysmaine stood by the pallet and knotted her hands before herself as her husband closed the door with the deliberation she had come to associate with him.

Would this be a beginning of a new life together or yet another ending?

Gaston gave no evidence of having doubts. As soon as the door was secured behind them, he unfastened his belt and laid his weapons aside with care. He shrugged out of his chain mail hauberk with some effort, declining her assistance with a frown.

"It is not the labor of a lady," he chided, and Ysmaine dropped her hands.

"Why not?"

"It is an implement of war, and as such, not the concern of a noblewoman."

"It seems to me that war concerns me, especially when it threatens the survival of all of us," Ysmaine said mildly. She earned herself a very blue glance for that, but did not have the impression that Gaston disapproved of her words.

Indeed, it seemed she had surprised him and perhaps given him food for thought.

She watched as he bent over his own knees and bit back a smile as he wriggled. The mail, though, slid over his shoulders at his move, reminding her of a snake as it spilled to the floor at his feet. He straightened and rolled his shoulders, the only indication he gave of being relieved to be without its weight. His hair was disheveled and he looked large in his aketon, the quilted red garment he wore beneath the mail. He twisted and glanced over his shoulder to the ties that bound it closed, for they were on his back, then turned to her with a slight smile.

"But this I cannot contrive on my own. Would you be of aid, lady mine?"

"Is it not an implement of war?" she teased with a smile, and he had the grace to color.

"Indeed, and as such, it is unfitting to come to a lady while wearing it."

Ysmaine gestured for him to turn around and quickly untied the laces. It was clear that the aketon had been worn for many years, for there were stains upon its quilted surface. She did not doubt that the darker ones were dried blood and knew it had to be Gaston's own. There were lines of stitching on the surface, where tears in the garment had been repaired, and Ysmaine could guess what would rend such a garment.

Her husband's past trade was made most clear by this item of his garb.

She fully expected that his skin would bear a similar tale with marks of his labor.

"I know little of aketons," she said. "For I have no brothers. Are they passed from father to son, or brother to brother?"

"Some," Gaston ceded. "This one was made for me as a gift from my uncle and patron when I earned my spurs."

"At fifteen summers."

"Aye."

"So you could not defeat your weaker cousin again, and would be compelled to leave to make your way in the world." Ysmaine's tone was tart, for she disliked that Gaston had been so ill treated, but he granted her a smile.

"Aye."

Ysmaine could not hold back the words. "And so all the blood that stains it must be yours."

"It is." He reached for the hem of the garment once she stepped back and hauled it over his head, shaking it before setting it aside. Ysmaine did not fail to note how he laid his gear out in an orderly manner, arranging it so he could garb and armor himself in haste.

She also did not miss the glimpse of a scroll of parchment, much hung with ribbons, that fell out of his aketon. He hid it quickly from view, and she knew she was not to have noticed it.

But Ysmaine recognized that her husband carried a missive. It was one of import, or at least dispatched from an important individual, given the seals and ribbons upon it. She thought again of her impression that Wulfe deferred to her husband, even though Gaston said he had left the order, and wondered what secrets her husband held close.

In the meantime, Gaston shed his boots, then cast aside his chausses, as if he removed his garb in her presence all the time. Ysmaine dared to sneak a glance at him through her lashes and had to admit that he was no less fine in solely his chemise. That garment hung white and loose to his thighs, and he had pushed up the sleeves. There were intriguing shadows beneath the linen, but she could see the tanned skin of his forearms and the muscled strength of his legs.

He was wrought so differently from she, and the sight drove all other thought from her mind other than what they would soon do. She would have liked to have looked upon him fully, but his hands landed upon her shoulders. She noted now the minute scars upon his knuckles, the work-roughened strength of his hands, and wondered how many other scars he bore. Her grandfather had placed great measure in a warrior's scars. One hand fell to her unbound hair, and Gaston touched it with a reverence that surprised and touched Ysmaine.

"Like spun gold," he murmured, his voice a deep rumble close to her back. He flicked a glance her way, and she was snared by the bright blue of his eyes. "We had a cook when I was a boy who told tales of straw being spun by a fairy into strands of gold." The corner of his mouth lifted and his voice changed, as if he mimicked that cook. "And so it was that the straw was spun before their astonished gazes, the spindle spinning so fast that it could not clearly be seen. In the morn, when the fairy was gone and the bowl of milk emptied, the spindle was left filled with thread as fine as gossamer but wrought of finest gold."

Ysmaine smiled despite herself. "We had a nurse who told a similar tale."

He entwined their fingers. "It is not the sole thing we have in common, lady mine."

"Nay, sir, it is not."

"I would have you call me by my name."

Ysmaine swallowed the lump in her throat. She appreciated that he was trying to ease her trepidation and tried to meet him partway. "Aye, Gaston."

He smiled fully then and turned her in his embrace so that they faced each other fully. Ysmaine spared a quick downward glance and saw that he was more prepared for this than she.

God in heaven, she hoped the deed did not hurt so much as she had heard.

"It will be done quickly enough," Gaston murmured, which she supposed was meant to be reassuring. He tipped her chin with a fingertip and gave her a kiss.

It was the kiss that restored her confidence, its sweet languor giving her the strength to face what must be. She chose to believe that he would survive this night, for he was hale and young.

And truly Mary could not have interceded, only to abandon her again.

Chapter Seven

Ysmaine returned Gaston's caress with growing enthusiasm, recalling well enough how alluring she found him and how their kiss in Jerusalem had fueled her desire. Her body responded as it had before, a most encouraging sign, and she relaxed ever so slightly.

Gaston swept her into his arms and deepened his kiss, holding her fast against his chest with one arm. His other hand speared through her hair, the feel of his hand at her nape most enticing. Ysmaine put her arms around his neck, showing him that his touch was welcome, then found herself abruptly on her back on the pallet.

She supposed he had warned her that it would be quick, although truly, she could have savored that kiss a little longer. Gaston's dark hair fell over his brow as he smiled down at her, and clearly they did not share that desire to linger over the deed. Ysmaine smiled back at him, though she guessed her expression was tremulous, for he granted her another slow kiss.

If he intended to coax her pleasure, his kiss certainly aided in that. There was much to be said for having his strength stretched out beside her, his hand roving over her from breast to knee, his other hand cupping her head as he kissed her thoroughly. His manhood pressed against her hip, and she wished to see him fully, but his chemise hid him from view and his kiss nigh made her swoon.

Ysmaine felt that heat build, a curious pleasure sliding through her body. She had a sense that there was more to be found abed than she had yet experienced—indeed, she heartily hoped as much, and Gaston's purposeful progress was most encouraging.

As was the fire he conjured beneath her skin.

Just when she was certain she could have kissed him all the

night long, Gaston slipped his hand beneath the hem of her chemise. Ysmaine's eyes widened at the warm weight of his palm against her thigh. It felt wicked to have his skin against hers there, wicked and wonderful. Her anticipation rose, redoubling as his hand moved, sliding slowly upwards. Indeed, Ysmaine's heart skipped. She felt a most delicious desire for her spouse. She felt her skin flush, and she yearned for...something.

Gaston's strong fingers eased between her thighs then, his sure touch making her gasp, first with surprise and then with delight. The feel of his fingertip on her was beguiling indeed, and she broke their kiss, shocked by so intimate a touch.

"I would have you prepared," he said, his caress making her writhe like a wanton. Ysmaine knew from the twinkle in his eye that he realized what sweet torment he inflicted upon her. She flushed more deeply as he continued, and it seemed the room heated. That desire simmered within her and increased to a boil, advancing far beyond the quickening summoned by Gaston's kiss.

Ysmaine could not name her desire, but she knew Gaston could provide it. She pulled him closer with new hunger and opened her mouth to him, wanting more of whatever he intended to give. Ysmaine arched her back as he lowered himself over her and his kiss demanded more, for she liked both the heat of him and the strength of him. She wanted to rub herself against him, but she didn't want to move away from those beguiling fingers.

She heard herself moan, and Gaston chuckled against her throat, his satisfaction most clear.

His weight was between his thighs a moment later. To Ysmaine's relief, he showed no signs of expiring as yet. Indeed, he looked most vital and hale. Nay, he looked uncommonly roguish and alluring, for his dark hair had fallen over his brow, that smile played over his lips and his eyes sparkled like the night sky. She impulsively pushed the hair back from his brow, shoving her fingers into the thick waves, and Gaston's smile broadened with a satisfaction that thrilled her. He braced himself over her on his elbows, watching her closely as he eased himself inside her.

Ysmaine could not completely suppress her wince at the pain, but he kissed her anew and murmured an apology in her ear. She recalled her mother's counsel and parted her thighs more widely, welcoming him into her heat instead of locking her knees together as impulse demanded. Gaston shuddered in a most remarkable way and murmured her name with a fervor that thrilled her in turn.

Was it possible that she had some power to influence his desire, as well?

Gaston nuzzled her ear as he eased within her, and Ysmaine gripped his shoulders, awed by the feeling. The pain passed and there was only a strange sensation of being filled, of being surrounded by her husband. Then he was within her fully, and she felt the wild pounding of his heart where his chest pressed against her own. His eyes were that bright blue and his face so close to hers, his gaze intent in his concern.

He would await a sign from her, even when he was so bound in his own pleasure. Even when it was his right to do as he would. Ysmaine lost the last of her reservations at that, for she knew she had wed a man who would treat her well. She embraced him, welcoming him as her mother had once instructed was right and good.

The difference was that Ysmaine did not do as much out of duty, but out of desire.

"You fare well, sir, to my relief," she murmured and he grinned. He looked young and carefree then and her heart skipped.

"And I mean to finish what is begun," he whispered with resolve. "With your permission, lady mine."

Ysmaine nodded once and felt him chuckle, his satisfaction more than clear. She wanted to know where this tingling would take her, what relief would come of the ardor he had aroused, and she kissed his mouth, wanting all he would give.

Gaston moved, making her gasp again at the sensation. His nostrils flared and his eyes gleamed as he moved with greater vigor, his entire body growing taut. Ysmaine did not know what to do, so she held fast to his shoulders, her own breath coming more quickly. Her sense grew steadily that some elusive delight was just beyond reach, tantalizing her with the prospect of a new and wild pleasure she had yet to taste. Her heart pounded, her breath caught. Gaston moved more quickly, his gaze brightening. Desire coiled within her and roared for satisfaction. Her body seemed to stretch for something she could not name.

Gaston knew it. He watched her with a dangerous smile as she whispered his name. She wriggled beneath him, wanting only to be released from this escalating need. She dug her nails into his shoulders, wanting to be claimed by him in truth, and he groaned as if the sound was torn from deep within him.

He moved more and more quickly, then suddenly buried himself within her, a curiously satisfying sensation. He closed his eyes and groaned, then shuddered from head to toe, his entire body taut.

A moment later, he sagged against her, his forehead falling to her shoulder, so still that terror filled Ysmaine.

She had no time to fear his demise, for Gaston took a ragged breath and lifted his head. His eyes, if anything, were an even deeper hue of sapphire and she noted the dark thickness of his lashes. He looked sleepy, pleased, and utterly enticing.

He kissed her cheek, his gesture almost perfunctory, then rose from the pallet. "And so it is done," he said with a satisfaction Ysmaine did not share.

Done? Ysmaine blinked. Then why did she still yearn? What had she missed? What had *not* been done?

All of import was finished, by her husband's reckoning, it was clear. Ysmaine watched him, incredulous. Surely that could not be the sum of it?

Surely she had no idea what to demand of him.

Beyond *more*.

Gaston whistled under his breath as he washed himself, using the pail of water and cloth that had been provided, then donned his chausses and boots. He fastened his belt with care, checking his weapons in what she guessed was his routine, then returned to the pallet to consider her. "And so you see that I have survived after all," he said, his voice a teasing rumble.

"Indeed." Ysmaine, however, felt an unexpected annoyance with him. Surely he knew that she yet yearned for some satisfaction?

Would it be to bold to tell him as much? Even a man who desired a forthright wife might have limited expectations in that regard.

He regarded her, his expression turning quizzical. "Did it hurt overmuch?"

"Less than I had expected," Ysmaine replied, somewhat irked by his practical tone. They might have been discussing the weather. She much preferred when he overwhelmed her with sweet kisses. Indeed, she could have savored one of those kisses in this moment.

"That bodes well, then," he said, apparently content. "We shall couple daily until you conceive." He offered his hand and helped her to her feet. She watched as he removed the linen from the pallet and Ysmaine saw the red blood of her maidenhead upon it.

Of course, he would want evidence of their coupling.

Gaston folded the linen with care, bade her goodnight, gathered his garb and made to depart.

"Do you not mean to sleep here, sir?" Ysmaine asked in surprise.

Her husband looked back, his expression astonished. "I will sleep in the stables, the better to guard Fantôme."

"Your destrier?"

"And my most precious possession. We should be in a poor situation without the horses, lady mine." His tone was temperate, his gaze level, then he turned to leave the chamber.

Without so much as a parting kiss.

Ysmaine could no longer hold her tongue.

❧

"What is it?" his wife demanded with sudden fervor when Gaston's hand was on the latch of the door.

And he knew.

She had seen it.

Gaston froze a heartbeat too long before he glanced back, endeavoring to keep his manner casual. "What do you mean?"

"The missive you carry. The one I was not to glimpse. Who is it from? Who is its intended recipient?" Ysmaine took a step closer, her eyes bright with curiosity. "What does it say?"

Gaston kept his expression was impassive. "I do not know what you mean," he said with care.

His lady wife, however, rolled her eyes. "You, sir, were the one to insist upon honesty between us. If you cannot tell me, simply say as much."

"I cannot tell you."

Ysmaine regarded him. "Me or anyone?"

"Anyone," he ceded and leaned his back against the door. He folded his arms across his chest and watched her warily.

It seemed he had wed an observant woman.

Would this be his doom or his pride?

"Then you should hide it better than you have," Ysmaine said crisply. She beckoned to him. "Give me your aketon."

"Why?"

"Because it is padded and mended and no one will take note of another lump or row of stitches."

Gaston did as bidden, intrigued.

Ysmaine considered the garment, even as Gaston hovered over her, protective of his gear. "It should be in a place beneath your tabard, where you can be easily ascertained of its security," she mused. "Here. In the front." She put out her hand with obvious expectation. "Your blade is sharper than mine." She wiggled her fingers, beckoning for his blade when he did not immediately comply with her request.

"This is not your concern..." he began, but Ysmaine exhaled with what might have been frustration.

"If you do not believe that a wife can bring more to his advantage than a son, I must simply change your thinking," she said, her eyes flashing like emeralds in the sun, and beckoned again.

Gaston was curious. Nay, he was fascinated. He surrendered his blade then watched as Ysmaine cut a slit in the garment with care.

"You can slide it in from the top," she informed him, as if she hid documents all the time. "And it will be hidden against your chest, above your belt so it is not damaged." She handed him the garment then turned to her own meager possessions, seeking a needle and thread. "I will not look as you put it in its place."

Gaston turned away, then slid the rolled document into the garment. It fit well, and he did not fail to realize that she had noted the size of it quite well. He bit back a concern about what else she might have noticed.

It seemed he had not wed a foolish woman.

But still, this was most practical. He offered her the aketon again.

"It cannot even be discerned," she said with satisfaction. "I must press upon the spot to feel the vellum. Excellent."

Gaston had thought she might remove the document and satisfy her curiosity but she did not. She stitched up the slit with care, then shook out the garment to examine her work.

"Let me see," she instructed, and he tugged it on. Ysmaine laced the back, then surveyed her workmanship again before granting her husband a smile. "Secure and hidden from view," she said with undisguised satisfaction.

Gaston ran his fingertips over the concealed document. "I thank you for this, lady mine. Your solution is most practical."

"And now I will have your tabard and your purse, sir," Ysmaine demanded. His shock must have shown because she smiled up at him. "Your purse is too obviously heavy."

Gaston bristled. "I have traveled with coin in such quantity before."

"Like as not when you wore the insignia of the Temple," Ysmaine chided softly. "As a pilgrim or a traveler, such a fat purse will find you dead in a tavern."

He inhaled sharply, knowing she referred to her own experience. "What do you mean to do with it?"

She cast him a smile that was impish. "Hide it, of course."

He surrendered the tabard and his purse. She dumped half of the coins on to the floor before her and returned the purse to him. She lined them up as he watched, creating a line as long as the hem of his tabard. She then picked out the hem of his tabard and began to sew the coins into it at intervals.

"My mother bade me do this when we left on pilgrimage, for my father granted us much coin," she confided. "Although the weight is better disguised in a tabard than a bliaut, I feared to surrender it to Thibaud."

Gaston saw his lady wife's regret that her choice had cost her father's man his life. "Did it cost so much as that to travel the distance?" he asked, crouching down before her. He handed her each coin as she prepared to insert it, knowing there was little more he could do to aid in this endeavor.

"Nay, we were betrayed. One of those charged to escort us murdered Thibaud, then stole my bliaut one night. I was so innocent of the vices of inns that I did not wear it to bed." Her voice softened. "I was a fool, and Thibaud paid the price."

"I would wager that you and Radegunde also paid it."

She nodded. "The thief was gone in the morning, with one of the steeds. The keeper told me that I was fortunate, for had it been both stranger and thief, he might have simply slit my throat for the coin." She shuddered. "But he did slit the throat of Thibaud, a man in my father's service all of my life."

Gaston felt his ire rise that his lady had been so abused. "I would avenge you," he murmured, without intending to do so.

She granted him one of those beguiling smiles. "You need not, for justice was served, and the thief was rewarded for his own folly."

"He did not hide the coin."

She shook her head. "He did not, and two nights hence, when we stopped at an inn, we were warned that a guest had been killed for his coin there just the night before."

"You cannot be certain it was him."

Ysmaine lifted her gaze to his, and he was startled by the coolness in her eyes. "Aye, I can. I went to see the corpse." She finished the hem and bit the thread. "He was yet laid in the church, and I had to resist the urge to spit upon him lest the priest disapprove."

There was a resolve within her that Gaston admired, a steel to her spine that had served her well. "I might have done as much anyway," he admitted.

"Had the priest not been there, I might have done more," Ysmaine admitted. "I knew Thibaud all of my life. My parents only consented to my desire to go on pilgrimage because he offered to accompany me. They trusted him with my life."

Gaston could well understand his lady's sense of guilt. "I cannot believe he regretted the choice, lady mine."

Her tears welled. "I can," she whispered. "I can."

Gaston added to the coins on the floor, moving the bulk of them into another pile in the hope of distracting her. There was little to be gained in reviewing the troubles of the past to his thinking. "Put these in your own hem, lady mine. If we are separated, I will know that you will not be impoverished again."

She swallowed and he saw her blink back those tears. "You are most good to me, husband," she said, her voice husky. "I shall see you rewarded."

"I do not doubt it."

"Aye, you do doubt it and most heartily," she argued, softening her words with a smile. She wagged the needle at him as he stared at her, beguiled anew. "You have lived long amongst men, with no expectation of marriage. But I shall win your trust in the end."

In this moment, Gaston could well believe it. She sewed coins into the other hem of his tabard, her stitches quick and neat. "Tell me more of this thief."

"There is little more to tell, save that he granted me a gift, sir, for in his death I saw divine justice. I had prayed to Mary when we awakened to find the coin stolen, and I had continued on pilgrimage believing my own sins were the cause of our misfortunes. When we discovered that the thief had been killed by one of his own kind, I knew my choice was sound. I knew I had to finish what I had begun and go all the way to Jerusalem, thus keeping my word to Mary."

"You might have gone home," he suggested again, not surprised when she shook her head.

"I had tainted two good matches. I had despoiled the opportunities for my sisters. I had seen a loyal man die in my defense. I could not return home without knowing for certain that something had changed, that I would not be the doom of them all."

"And now? Will we halt at Valeroy?"

Ysmaine's smile was like the sun erupting from behind storm clouds. "Aye, sir, I should like to do so. I believe my parents would be well pleased with our match." Her eyes glowed as she offered him the garment. "Can you discern the coins?"

Gaston took the garment, examining her work with pleasure. "Nay. This is most artfully done. You are skilled with a needle."

She paused in picking out her own hem to grant him an intent look. "I will be a good wife to you, Gaston," she vowed softly. "I know I have failings, but I swear to do my best."

Gaston was touched by her fervor. "That is all any of us can do, lady mine."

And then, because he could do naught else, he bent and kissed her soundly once again. Indeed, his future seemed filled with more promise than ever he had expected.

Because he had taken *this* valiant lady to wife.

ε&

Gaston's kiss filled Ysmaine with anticipation all over again. Indeed, it seemed that he could summon her desire with increasing speed, each time he touched her. Her body hummed anew, a reminder that she had not yet been sated, and she lifted her hands to his shoulders.

To her dismay, he straightened. "Not twice on this night," he said, his voice husky. He held his garments and bowed to her. "Sleep well, lady mine."

And then he was gone. Ysmaine stared after him, feeling slightly annoyed. Dissatisfied. Incredulous.

Cheated.

To be sure, she was beyond glad that he had survived their nuptial night, but she could not deny a sense that she had expected more.

It did not help her mood that she did not know what exactly she had been denied. Indeed, it vexed her mightily that Gaston was sufficiently pleased to whistle as he descended the stairs, while she was still on edge, yearning.

He went to his steed.

She supposed that after she bore him a son, she might be able to contend for the place of his most valued possession. Ysmaine growled beneath her breath, dissatisfied even though she knew she should not be.

Radegunde fairly burst into the chamber, her eyes alight with curiosity. "Well?" she demanded.

Ysmaine shook her head and turned her back on her maid. "Well, he is not dead, at least," she acknowledged, hearing aggravation in her own tone. She made to wash herself, but Radegunde hastened to her side.

"Nay, my lady. Return to the pallet and lie upon your back. Raise your knees to your chest and remain there."

Ysmaine turned to her maid, incredulous. "Excuse me?"

"It is best to keep your lord's seed within you, the better than it might take root within your womb."

Ysmaine found herself heaving a sigh. It seemed a bit late for such an endeavor, but Radegunde was fussing around her, trying to coax her back to the pallet.

"I would like to wash," she muttered, keenly aware of the dust from the road upon her flesh as well as the scent of Gaston. Truly, in this moment, she would like to be scrubbed of his touch. How curious that she could be so vexed with him in this moment. He had been tender. He had spoken to her. Yet she wanted more.

"And so you shall, my lady, after you have lingered abed with your lord's seed within you..."

"The better that it might take root within my womb," Ysmaine ceded, returning to the pallet. Once she was positioned to her maid's satisfaction, she eyed the ceiling and drummed her fingers. "Your mother was a midwife, Radegunde."

"Aye, my lady."

"Then she must have known much of the creation of children as well as their arrival."

"Indeed, my lady."

Ysmaine spared a glance at the closed door, then lowered her voice. "I thought it was supposed to be pleasurable," she whispered. "I thought that was why people could not deny the temptation of meeting abed. My own mother had seven daughters, although one died in infancy. I cannot believe she would have done so had there not been some compensation in pleasure."

"As do I," Radegunde agreed. "For the bearing of a child is far from pleasurable." She glanced to the door, then leaned closer to murmur. "Was it not so?"

Ysmaine shook her head. "I had a feeling that it could be." She bit her lip, not wanting to criticize Gaston. "But in the end, it seemed a task that needed to be done."

"And so it was," Radegunde agreed cheerfully. "A match must be consummated so it cannot be annulled. A man must do his duty to bed his wife, and she must do her duty by bearing him a son."

"And once duty is done, it will be more pleasurable?"

"One can only hope, my lady."

Ysmaine most certainly did.

❦

As much as he would have liked to have been relieved of the weight of his mail for the night, Gaston knew that treachery could come in darkness. He beckoned to Bartholomew when he reached the common room and donned the hauberk again, unable to completely quell a sense that all came aright.

He had not died in Ysmaine's bed, and their coupling had been most pleasurable. He had an alluring wife who would now cease to worry about his fate. Their match could not be annulled, and they might conceive an heir with all haste. He had evidence of her virginity, and he might well arrive home with his goal of conceiving a son achieved.

All proceeded according to plan. It was unfortunate that their circumstances were not more secure. He could have savored a cup of wine or ale, for he was feeling celebratory.

But such pleasures would have to wait.

All the same, he was not in a hurry to retire to the stables.

"I thought you meant to bed your bride," Wulfe said from the board.

"I did."

The other knight blinked. "So quickly as that?"

"I saw no reason to delay."

Wulfe laughed. "I see plenty of reason to linger over a lady as alluring as your wife."

Gaston felt the back of his neck flush. "Our marital relations are not your concern."

"But they could become as much, if you do not see your lady sated." Wulfe shook a finger at Gaston. "A woman denied her due abed can be a virago, and if we are to travel together all the way to Paris, I consider it your part of the bargain to ensure your lady wife's amiability." His words made his younger squire smirk while the other giggled. Bartholomew caught his breath, annoyed for Gaston's sake.

It seemed that Wulfe would make trouble no matter what the situation. It had only been hours before that he had taken issue with Gaston's match not being consummated, and now he would criticize how it had been done.

Gaston glared at him. "I do not know what you mean. I protect and defend her, I provide for her and I shall get a son upon her. No woman could want for more."

Wulfe laughed. Indeed, Wulfe laughed so hard that he wept. Gaston regarded the other knight in astonishment, failing to see the reason for his merriment. That only prompted Wulfe to laugh harder, to laugh until he was ruddy and bent over himself, helpless in his mirth. Even Everard, reputed to be so pious, seemed to hide a knowing smile on the far side of the hall. Gaston's ears burned.

Eventually, Wulfe sobered enough to straighten and tap a finger on the board before Gaston. "Chastity," he said, his lips twitching.

"Poverty, chastity, and obedience," Gaston replied. "The core of our vows." He arched a brow. "Though I will doubt from your manner that the second is of much concern to you."

Wulfe waved off this criticism. "We are warriors, Gaston, and in need of the pleasures of the flesh. Savoring them proves to us that we are alive and makes our survival more precious."

"My oath is worth more than my pleasure."

Wulfe leaned closer. "But your lady will sleep beside you every night for the rest of your life. You need to ensure that she is your ally, as well as the mother of your sons."

"I do not believe she would betray me..." Gaston defended Ysmaine, well aware that his squire did not share his conviction of her good intentions.

"But you do not *know*." Wulfe retorted.

"You have granted this warning already..."

"But still the concern remains. You must convince her to love you, for a woman will never betray whosoever she loves."

Gaston was impatient with the notion. "I do not care whether she loves me, although I expect there will be affection between us at some point."

"You should care," Fergus contributed. "My betrothed loves me with all her heart and soul. It is a good portent for a match, and one that will ensure our married life is happy."

Gaston glanced up the stairs. Did Ysmaine possess such whimsical notions? "I cannot think this to be of import. My father wed for strategy, as did my brother..."

Wulfe shook his head. "And this is where you err. You want your wife to love you more than anything or anyone else in the world. This is how you can ensure that she is worthy of your trust." He tapped a heavy finger upon the board. "And the best way, in my experience, of winning her love is by seducing her. Give her pleasure. Teach her to welcome your touch." Wulfe nodded, so certain of himself that Gaston wondered whether his counsel might be good. "For a woman oft gives her heart where she has given her passion first."

"Her passion?" Gaston echoed.

Wulfe nodded confidently. "Make her cry out before you take your own pleasure. Make her whimper with need and beg for relief. Make her shiver and moan and whisper your name in the night. Leave her sated and sleeping each time, her skin flushed, and her perfume all over your body."

The very notion was unsettling. Nay, it was arousing. Gaston's body responded immediately to the vision of Ysmaine having such a fervor for his touch. He sat down quickly and drained a cup of water, trying to hide his reaction.

"Be the only one who sates her fully. Be the only one who can make her burn, and be the sole one who can extinguish the flame." Wulfe wagged a finger at an astonished Gaston. "Do that, and you need never doubt your wife's intent."

Was that even possible?

"I disagree," Fergus retorted from the shadows. "A man of honor courts his wife's favor and wins her heart by his deeds. That is the more enduring affection."

That sounded feasible to Gaston. He did not know whether he could win his lady's heart or her passion, but he found himself resolved to try to do both.

He also found he no longer had any taste for Wulfe's company or even for lingering in the common room. He retired to the stables, where Fantôme greeted him with a nicker and a swish of his tail. That made Gaston wish that his lady wife was as easy to read as his steed.

೪

Naught.

One soul in the party was vexed, though it was the middle of the night.

That cursed Brother Terricus had seen too much and perhaps guessed more. It was the way of the Templars to trade in treasures, and there could be no doubt that there was a valuable in the possession of this company. It made sense that Brother Terricus would dispatch a prize from the Temple in Jerusalem to Paris, but where was it?

What was it?

The imposter searched, to no avail. He could not find the treasure that he knew the party had to be carrying. All knew the Templars were rich beyond belief. All knew the Templars kept their most precious prizes in the Temple in Jerusalem. Any fool could see that Jerusalem was doomed to fall to the infidels, and surely the Templars wished to save some portion of their legendary treasure.

The imposter had diverted his course specifically to Jerusalem to take home a marvel that was better in his hands than lost to unbelievers—or buried in rubble.

Some marvel had to be entrusted to this party.

But it could not be spied.

They did not speak of it.

They were, one and all, cursed Templars with their taste for secrecy.

The sole member of the party awake at the late hour exhaled in frustration. The Templar Wulfe was most organized and deliberate: though care had been shown in disguising the investigation of his gear, he might discern it all the same. The quest was disguised with another, a rummage through the bags of a second traveler, as if a common thief had sought some coin.

Might another in the party carry either missive or treasure in trust?

There were two former Templars in their number, after all.

The search might have been extended but the smelly squire who served Fergus sneezed and clearly was awake. The Templar Gaston spoke to that boy in the stables. The hunter retired, discontent and doubly determined to find the treasure.

Regardless of the price.

Monday, July 6, 1187

Feast Day of Saint Godelva and
Saint Sexburga.

❧

Chapter Eight

Fergus was saddling his horses the next morning, certain that this Templar Wulfe would have another challenge for Gaston before they departed. It was clear that it irked the knight to have to answer to Gaston, and also that their natures were as different as could be. In truth, Fergus was glad to be under the command of Gaston, for that knight not only knew the Holy Land, its politics, feuds, and personalities better than most, but he was thoughtful in making his choices.

Wulfe reminded Fergus of Gerard de Ridefort. He seemed to be impetuous and passionate, a combination that Fergus distrusted as much as he knew Gaston did. Wulfe might fight well, but it seemed to Fergus that his survival thus far must have been more a matter of good luck than skill.

Wulfe certainly did not choose his words with care.

Fergus had risen before the dawn, checking upon his baggage. The locked trunk entrusted to them by the preceptor was hidden amongst his copious possessions. Fergus had made much of a tale that he took many gifts home for his nuptials and his bride, and had half a dozen trunks as well as bundles and saddle bags. The one from the Temple was the one that looked least rich.

The merchant Joscelin had more baggage, so much that some of it was being carried by Gaston's palfreys. Gaston and his wife had the fewest possessions of all. Everard carried a great deal, so much that Fergus wondered that the knight had no squire or servant. Perhaps he had been so long in Outremer that those in his service had been committed to remaining in these lands. Perhaps the tale he had told Gaston's lady about his deserting knights was true.

To Fergus' pleasure, his newest squire had slept with the horses and the baggage—indeed, he had found "Laurent" draped over it all. The girl looked to be asleep, but her eyes had been narrowed slits in truth. She had been aware of Fergus' presence before he had fully discerned her in the shadows.

He winked at her, then grimaced at the smell of her garb. Her smile was furtive, then she ducked her head again. He was glad he had overhead Bartholomew and been able to offer a solution to this maiden.

He hoped she found whatever she desired on their journey. All people should have their dreams come true, to the thinking of Fergus, and he smiled in anticipation of seeing his beloved Isobel again. He had done the duty demanded by his father, managed to survive his service relatively unscathed, and now could begin his life in truth.

With Isobel.

Gaston rose from where he had slept in the corner of the stables, as observant as ever, and silently began to groom his destrier. Bartholomew looked sleepy but did as his knight expected, and Fergus did not fail to note the quick glance exchanged between his new squire and that of Gaston. He was glad that Gaston knew the precise location of the treasure, and also that the knight did not challenge his own choice in granting the responsibility to "Laurent". That new squire had the most to lose if Fergus were displeased, and Fergus understood that naught could induce the newest member of his party to betray him. Another might have questioned the supposed boy's allegiance, but Fergus knew it was complete.

Gaston's new wife seemed to understand her husband well, for the stars had only begun to disappear in the east when she strode into the stable, clearly prepared to depart. Gaston's delight in her readiness was most clear, although the lady only smiled tightly in response to the kiss Gaston bestowed upon her hand.

Perhaps the knight had something to learn of seduction.

Fergus did not intend to become involved.

Everard was next to appear, and his brow was furrowed. "Did any of you seek to borrow some trinket from me last night?" he asked, and Fergus glanced over his shoulder at the nobleman.

All shook their heads, their manners alert. "Why?" Gaston asked.

Everard's frown deepened as he indicated his bags. "I admit

that I pack with great care and am perhaps overly particular about my possessions, but I am certain that items have been moved. It is as if someone looked through my baggage while I slept."

"But why?" Gaston's lady asked. "Are you known to be carrying valuables?"

Everard shook his head. "I bring much of value to myself, to be sure, but I would not expect to be targeted and make no accusation of my fellows. I thought perhaps someone sought a piece of soap or an eating knife or some other trinket to borrow."

Again, those gathered in the stables shook their heads.

"Perhaps I am mistaken, then," Everard said with such forced heartiness that Fergus knew the knight didn't believe it.

He turned so that he could see his newest squire, whose glance held his for a telling moment. Her hand was upon the bag that held the Templar treasure. Gaston examined his baggage in turn, then shook his head. "Perhaps the contents shifted during our ride," he suggested, and Everard forced a smile.

"Undoubtedly you are right."

The stables were bustling when Wulfe strode inside with a purposeful glint in his eye at the first light of dawn. The Templar's expression tightened, and Fergus swallowed a smile, knowing Wulfe had believed he would be first. Joscelin strolled into the stables behind him, looking as if he had been dragged out of bed.

Duncan entered the stables last, his expression so disgruntled that Fergus could guess who had seen fit to rouse the sleepy merchant.

"Which of you has been in my baggage?" Wulfe demanded.

That query awakened Joscelin with astonishing speed. That man hastened to his baggage and checked it with such obvious consternation that all watched him. "It appears to all be just as I left it," the merchant confessed with relief.

A comparison ensued. Those who had slept in the common room with their baggage all believed that their possessions had been examined during the night. It proved that none of them had remained awake, and so the opportunity had been created. The gates had been secured, though, which indicated it might be one of their own party.

They considered each other with suspicion.

"Perhaps it was one of those in the employ of the hospice,"

Claire Delacroix

Gaston's lady suggested. "I know I have been robbed in inns before."

"As have I," Joscelin agreed with relief.

"No doubt we shall leave the villain behind," Everard said with satisfaction.

Fergus caught Gaston's steady gaze, their gazes locking for a heartbeat.

One matter was certain: the treasure must never be left unattended.

੭੬

These were no good tidings, even if they were but suspicions. The company had been followed the day before, then the bags of some of their party examined during the night. Gaston feared that some soul knew what they carried.

Yet he did not. The precise nature of the Templar treasure was not his to know, but only to defend. The trunk surrendered to Fergus was heavy enough that it could have contained any item at all.

Gaston knew it was wise to have the trunk secured until the Grand Master in Paris opened it, but he was curious.

That someone sought the prize made him more so.

Wulfe considered the assembling company, then braced his hands upon his hips. "I have decided that we shall ride back to Jaffa," he declared, and Gaston saw Fergus duck his head. Undoubtedly he meant to hide his reaction to this defiance of Gaston's command. "It makes little sense to ride on toward an enemy army that has been triumphant and will only put our party in unnecessary peril."

Wulfe faced Gaston, his eyes bright with challenge.

Gaston would not give the other knight the satisfaction of a reaction, nor would he reveal the truth. He simmered inwardly, even as he appeared to be fixed on the challenge of adjusting the height of the stirrup for his lady. He lifted her to the palfrey's saddle and she tried it, then shook her head, bending to murmur to him that it should be a bit lower. Gaston did not fail to note how Ysmaine seemed to be agitated by his attention. He glanced up and spared her a smile, liking the flush that stained her cheeks.

There was more than one way to win a lady's favor, to be sure, and he was not so inexperienced as that.

Wulfe cleared his throat, disliking that he was being ignored.

Fergus chose to reply. "With respect, I believe there are others in our party with a deeper understanding of the region," he dared to say, earning Wulfe's obvious ire. "Perhaps we should share what we know and decide upon the better route."

Wulfe fairly crackled in his indignation.

"Indeed," Everard agreed with a nod. "These are perilous times, and more information can only improve our choice. I myself would hesitate to ride back to Jaffa. We should lose time, and as Gaston has counseled, the port might be overwhelmed."

The merchant Joscelin crossed himself and paled at the very suggestion. "I paid for protection!" he protested, but was ignored.

"Five years I have labored in these lands," Wulfe argued, folding his arms across his chest. "I know better than to put myself in proximity to infidels. We should ride *south*."

It was time to end this, that they might depart.

Gaston cleared his throat. "But if we ride back to Jaffa, we will be hard-pressed to reach the city in a day. The roads do not allow a direct course."

"It would be folly to expose our party to bandits," Everard agreed.

"And they are bolder to the south, as well as more numerous," Fergus contributed.

"We shall be equally hard-pressed to reach Acre in a day," Wulfe countered.

"But the tidings we heard last night will have reached Jerusalem by now," Gaston replied, his tone more temperate than Wulfe deserved. "Jaffa will be thick with pilgrims, desperate to depart. We may not find passage."

"We may not find passage in Acre," Wulfe retorted.

"But we will not have to compete for a place, not with the same vigor," Everard said. "Those lands were scoured clean when King Guy's party rode to war."

"Although we might have to fight infidels to gain the gates," Wulfe noted, his tone acid. He shook his head. "I will not risk it."

Gaston glared at the insubordinate knight, irked that Wulfe would compromise the preceptor's plan and defy his orders.

Fergus cleared his throat again. "Of all the men in this company, Gaston has the greatest understanding of the Saracens. I have battled them and killed them, but he has *talked* to them."

Everard and Joscelin looked up in surprise at this.

"He has negotiated with them, on the part of the Templars," Fergus supplied. "And done so with great skill. I say we are fortunate to have him in our party and that we heed his counsel."

There was a rumble of assent, one that clearly did not please Wulfe. "Is it true?" he demanded of Gaston. "Do you speak with infidels?"

"I have done so, at the command of the Grand Master," Gaston acknowledged. He secured the buckle on his lady's stirrup and spared her a glance. She tried it and smiled at him, her pleasure making his heart soar.

He took refuge in her attention to return her regard, letting all believe he was as dazzled by his wife as he was. Her eyes widened and her lips parted, her expression reminding him of what they had done the night before.

And would do again on this night. He was certain he would learn how best to give her pleasure. He put his hand on her knee and felt her shiver, liking her responsiveness well.

"What say you then?" Wulfe demanded with impatience, and Gaston savored the other knight's frustration. "If you know these Saracens so well, what will their leader Saladin do? Where will he ride? Will he retreat to the east, content with what he has done?"

Gaston shook his head. "No commander of merit retreats from such a victory as this is reputed to be."

"Merit," Wulfe echoed with disdain. "As if that trait could be associated with an infidel..."

Gaston ignored him. He abandoned his lady wife, then crouched down and drew in the dirt with a fingertip. He heard her urge the palfrey closer so she could see his work. Gaston outlined a map of the Holy Land on the ground. He drew a circle with a dot to the left of it. "The Sea of Galilee," he said to Ysmaine, glancing up to see her nod. "And the fortress of Tiberias." When she nodded again, he drew another longer lake to the south, then a jagged line down the left side that had to be the coast. "The Dead Sea, and the Mediterranean." The company gathered around as he considered his own map. He dropped a fingertip to the right of the Sea of

Galilee, making a point. "Not al-Ashtara," he murmured.

"Where?" Wulfe demanded and Gaston could not hide his disdain.

"Where Saladin mustered his troops, just over a week ago. If he retreated, it would be there, but he will not retreat. He will consolidate his victory, for it is the only sensible deed to do. The question is how." Far to the north, Gaston marked another spot then another on the coast almost alongside it. "Krak des Chevaliers," he said. "And the Latin port of Tripoli." Below Krak, he made another dot, so that the three formed a triangle. "He could attack O'Akka on the way to either."

It was distant, though, especially in the heat of this time of year. Saladin would not risk the loss of any men in such a quest.

To the left of Tiberias, on the line that indicated the coast, Gaston marked three dots.

"Tyre to the north," Ysmaine said to his pride. "And Acre in the middle, then Haifa."

"Two Latin ports and a fortress," Gaston agreed, marking a dot between them and Tiberias. "And Nazareth between." He dropped south to mark their own location with a dot, then yet further to the south to indicate Jerusalem with a cross. The port to the west of the Holy City was so clearly Jaffa that he felt no need to state as much.

"He could sweep west," Fergus suggested, hunkering down beside him to gesture. "Then down the coast, taking as many ports as possible to ensure that no more Christians could return to Europe."

Gaston nodded. "Yet that would trap many pilgrims, and it is not his way to slaughter innocents."

Wulfe snorted at that.

"Nay, he has time to claim his prize, if his goal is Jerusalem," Gaston murmured. "I believe he will grant those who are not warriors themselves the chance to leave before he does so." His finger dropped down to the east of the Dead Sea, where he made another point. "Karak," he said softly.

"Unsecured now that Reginald is dead," Wulfe noted, his eyes narrowed.

"And the root of the trouble," Ysmaine said, proving that she had listened to him. "Is that not where the Saracen pilgrims were attacked?"

"It was indeed," Gaston agreed. "For their holy cities lie far to the southeast. From Jerusalem, we look west, but they look southeast." He tapped his finger on that point in the dirt. "I believe he will secure that passage for pilgrims first, then return to claim Jerusalem."

"You believe he will take the Holy City, then?" Joscelin asked, clearly horrified by the prospect.

Gaston raised his head. "With virtually every knight in these lands dead or captive, I cannot see who will stop him. How will several hundred achieve what thousands failed to do?" There was a moment of silence as they each considered what Gaston suspected was inevitable.

"I vote for Acre," Everard said with resolve.

"I do not believe there is a vote," Wulfe protested.

"Then there should be," Fergus argued. "If I am to risk my life, I would choose when and where I make my stand." Wulfe glared at him for that, but Fergus returned the look with defiance. "Acre," he said, biting off the word.

"Acre," Ysmaine said, speaking with like a noblewoman who expected to be heard. She offered a hand to her maid. "Ride with me this day, Radegunde, in case our party has need of my husband's blade." Gaston nodded in acknowledgment of this choice, admiring his lady's practicality.

They did seem to be well matched in that.

"I guess Acre it must be," Joscelin said, his voice tremulous with fear.

Gaston glanced up at Wulfe. "Well then?" he asked quietly. "What would be your choice, brother Wulfe?"

"Acre!" Wulfe fumed, then flung himself into his saddle in poor temper. "And may all of you pray that Gaston knows his infidels well."

◆

Gaston had been certain of his choice, convinced of his understanding of Saladin, until they reached Nazareth.

It was near the end of the day, and they had ridden without cease. The horses were tired and the entire party was dusty. His wife was yet straight in the saddle, and she held fast to her maid, who had dozed often. There were shadows beneath Ysmaine's eyes, though, and Gaston knew she was exhausted.

The sun was sinking low, and he knew that over the next rise, they would be able to glimpse Nazareth. He was considering how best to suggest to Wulfe that their party pause there, that his lady might refresh herself.

Then he saw the cloud of dust in the east.

"Halt!" he roared, driving the party off the road and to one side with vigor.

"You have no right," Wulfe sputtered, but Gaston pointed. The knight removed his helm and stared, his lips thin. "You were wrong," he whispered. The horses stamped and milled as despair welled in Gaston's heart. Ysmaine gasped and turned to watch him.

"We do not know that as yet," Gaston said, his tone mild. "But we will ride past Nazareth, to the west. There is a road ahead that forks to the left. It is smaller than this one and less wide, but even so, it will save us time."

"Or keep us out of sight," Wulfe agreed. He directed the party so that the knights could best defend the rest of the party, doing so with an efficiency that showed he was decisive in battle. Gaston could admire that. Many a battle was lost due to hesitation.

They conferred briefly about changing mounts, so that the knights rode their destriers. Wulfe, Fergus and Gaston changed horses, but Everard decided to continue on his palfrey. Gaston could not ride to battle on any other steed than Fantôme. The dapple destrier tossed his head so that his black mane rippled in the wind, and Gaston chose to believe that the horse wished it to be thus as well.

Within moments, they were on the move again, a new fear forcing them onward.

Gaston kept Ysmaine's palfrey hard at his left. He wondered whether she perceived the import of his change of mount. "Are you certain it is Saracens?" she asked him in an undertone.

"A large army moves west, lady mine," he admitted grimly. "And we no longer possess one, according to the reports."

"Then he means to seal the ports," she murmured. To his relief, she did not faint or quail in fear, but gripped her reins and gave the palfrey her heels. Radegunde clung to her mistress, her eyes wide.

"We shall make it, Ysmaine," Gaston vowed. "A small party is more agile than an army."

"Truly?" She glanced at him, her eyes so clear a green that he could not lie to her.

"We shall make it," he vowed, then winced. "But not, perhaps, with much margin to spare."

Her gaze flicked to Fantôme, though she did not comment upon his choice. "You should don your helm," she said tersely.

Gaston shook his head. "It will catch the light of the sun and reveal our party to be more heavily defended. I have heard that it is oft good to be under-estimated."

Her quick smile was filled with a resolve that he could only admire.

He spurred his destrier, and Fantôme leapt forward. Ysmaine encouraged her palfrey to match the larger horse's pace, and they thundered down the path beside each other. He hoped they could reach Acre and claim that promising future together.

But he did not think it would be easily won.

In that moment, Gaston knew that he would do whatever was necessary to ensure his bride's safety.

Whatever the cost to himself

&

It was madness.

They encouraged the horses to gallop with a speed that was beyond good sense. The knights' urgency to reach Acre's gates told Ysmaine that they were not so certain of their survival as they might have the rest of the party believe. She hoped none of the horses threw a shoe or stepped into a hole. That beast and its rider might well be left behind, for the safety of the others.

The road was no better than a wide track, and she had to ride before Gaston in some places. The destriers, at least, seemed to understand the situation, for they ran full out alongside their knights. Perhaps they were accustomed to this, or perhaps they responded to the mood of their masters.

The stars were coming out when the track rejoined the road from Nazareth to Acre, and the walls of the port city loomed on the horizon. Ysmaine and Radegunde shared a smile of relief, even as Wulfe stood in his stirrups and looked back to the east.

"They set camp at Nazareth, I would wager," he said and relief rippled through the company. He nodded to Gaston. "You were right in this, at least. We shall make the gates, but barely so."

Gaston did not respond, and Ysmaine wondered what he suspected that the others did not. "The time to slow our pace is not this moment," he said tersely and slapped the rump of his destrier.

The Templar seemed to have learned his lesson, for he spurred his own destrier, setting an even quicker pace now that they had gained the main road. It was nigh deserted, for the hour was late, and Ysmaine hoped the gates of Acre were not closed against them. She watched as the walls drew larger, her heart thumping with hope that this last obstacle would be overcome.

Their assailants came out of the hills with alarming speed, a company of bandits with cloth wrapped across their faces. They seemed to appear from naught. Even in the twilight, Ysmaine could see that they were not Christians, for their steeds were saddled more simply and their garb was different. She noted that the horses were like fine palfreys, then saw the flash of blades and heard a warning shouted at them in another language.

"God in heaven," Radegunde whispered and crossed herself.

Ysmaine looked to Gaston, not surprised to find his expression grim. He seized the small pouch bound to his belt and slammed it into her hand, then slapped the rump of her steed so hard that the beast jumped.

"Ride on!" he roared and the entire company surged forward with new speed.

Gaston, though, turned his destrier to confront their attackers. He drew his blade, making himself a target, and took up position in the middle of the road.

The Saracens shouted and descended toward him like a dark cloud.

"Nay!" Ysmaine shrieked, twisting in her saddle. "Gaston!" She reached for the reins of her palfrey, but Wulfe's steed was suddenly beside her. He seized the reins and hauled the horse onward, taking command.

"Ride on!" the Templar bellowed, echoing Gaston.

"Nay!" Ysmaine cried, though less vehemently than before.

She turned back to watch, Radegunde's fingers digging into her skin.

Her husband sat proudly, his sword drawn, his reins tight in his fist, as the Saracen party surrounded him.

"He is alone!" she protested, trying to tug her horse's reins from Wulfe's iron grip.

"He has chosen for the good of us all," that knight said through gritted teeth. "Do not waste his sacrifice."

Sacrifice. The very word sickened Ysmaine. The horses galloped forward, the men grim, and Ysmaine was the only one who looked back.

Gaston was outnumbered.

He was surrounded.

She could not bear to watch him die, nor could she avert her gaze. In that moment, Ysmaine knew that the man who had taken her to wife possessed every honorable trait she had hoped to find in a husband.

And he would die.

"Gaston," she whispered, her tears rising along with a fierce hope that she already carried his son. That was the sole thing she could give him, the sole honor that he deserved, but with only one coupling, Ysmaine feared she might fail her lord husband in that task.

Her curse had claimed another husband, and it was bitter that this was the sole one she had wanted.

ਠ੍ਹ

As Gaston had told Ysmaine, he always known his life might end thus. There had been a hundred times when he had thought his days finished, that he had been sure he would die in service to the Templars, and he found it ironic that it should be so, but after he had left the order. Still he was duty-bound to see to the protection of the quest granted by Brother Terricus, and the defense of his lady wife. There was far more at stake than his own life.

He needed only to survive until the party made Acre's gates.

To Gaston's surprise, he found himself less at peace with this eventuality than he had declared himself to be.

Because of Ysmaine. He regretted only that he had not had

more time to spend with his lady wife. He had wanted to win her regard, her heart, her love, and to have had sons with her. Gaston suspected that it would have been good to grow older with his lady, to have had decades together and many sons in their hall.

But it was not God's will that his life should be so, and Gaston tried to accept that.

At least his choice should see to his lady's survival.

He wished she had not sewn half his coin into his tabard. She would have need of it, but it would be claimed by whosoever killed him instead. He regretted that even this measure of worldly gain would be denied her.

The missive would be lost as well, though he wagered that Wulfe and Bartholomew could report what they knew to the Grand Master in Paris. There was no telling whether Terricus had included some other detail in the missive itself, but Gaston could do naught about that now. The treasure was with the departing party, and he prayed that it would safely reach Paris.

At least the quest had not been compromised due to his error.

Curiously, though, it was Ysmaine's fate that troubled Gaston the most, and the promise of the future now denied to him, not the errands of the Temple. That was a new perspective for him, but it seemed he would not have the opportunity to savor it overlong.

The Saracens circled their horses around him, their faces hidden behind the scarves they wrapped around themselves to fight the dust. Their eyes glinted as did their blades, and their sleek horses stepped proudly. They did not fight but tried to provoke his response, probably intending to weaken him or make him strike out in error. They did not attack, which surprised him until he realized the truth.

They awaited the one who would choose his fate.

Or they wished to take him alive, that he might be interrogated.

Gaston was not so foolish as to try to engage when he was so outnumbered. Although the delay made him fear the end result, he knew that every moment that passed improved Ysmaine's chances of survival.

And he had no qualms in trading his life for her own.

Chapter Nine

The party rode even faster than they had before. The horses galloped wildly and any pretense at a formation was lost.

Bartholomew cried out and would have ridden to Gaston's aid, but Fergus seized his horse's reins. "You have been ordered!" he reminded the squire, who was clearly frustrated.

Ysmaine tried to tug the reins free of Wulfe's grasp that she might aid Gaston, but the Templar held fast. The palfrey might have slowed or heeded her, but Duncan rode around her to take Gaston's place and seized the palfrey's halter on that side. The horse fought the bit, not liking to be so restrained, but their choices made it run with greater vigor.

"Use your wits, my lady," Duncan growled. "You know his desire and you know it to be right."

"It is not fair!"

"Little enough is fair in this world," the older man retorted. He spared her a bright glance. "Do not compel me to answer to Gaston de Châmont-sur-Maine before St. Peter himself."

Ysmaine caught her breath, not wanting to even think of Gaston dying.

"He may escape, my lady," Radegunde whispered but Ysmaine shook her head. She twisted in the saddle to look back, her vision blurring with tears as she saw the lone knight surrounded by the enemy.

There had to be two dozen of them.

Gaston was lost.

One of the Saracens lifted a blade and it flashed against the night. Ysmaine turned back, her heart hammering, wanting to remember this husband alive. The walls of Acre rose high ahead, the gates barred, and the horses thundered toward them.

Wulfe abandoned her side, spurring his horse to race ahead of the party. "Open the gates, for the mercy of pilgrims!" he roared in French, then repeated his request in German. "The Temple rides in their defense!"

Ysmaine thought he would be declined, but evidently his tabard and insignia had been seen. One of the great wooden portals was opened slowly, the opening wide enough for two horses to ride abreast.

"Do not slacken your pace!" Wulfe bellowed, drawing his destrier to one side as he flagged the entire party into the security of the city. "They are fast behind us!" he called to the keeper.

A volley of flaming arrows were fired into the night, and Ysmaine followed their course. They struck the ground behind the last palfrey with deadly accuracy, creating a line of fire across the road. She saw the silhouettes of riders beyond them, riders dressed in flowing garments whose horses whinnied and turned back.

The front of an army? Or bandits?

Of Gaston, she could glimpse no sign.

The gate was closed behind them, the heavy wooden portal falling home with a thud that made the ground rumble. It was barred and their horses slowed their pace. A man leapt down from the gate and ran beside them, talking to Wulfe. They spoke quickly, Wulfe telling the man what he had witnessed on the road this day.

Bartholomew turned to Ysmaine. "I do not know why you weep so," he said, his tone hard. "This way you are rid of him without staining your hands."

Ysmaine was shocked, and she felt the other two knights turning to listen, along with the merchant. "I assure you I have no desire to be rid of my husband!"

"Nay? Then why did you acquire poison *for him*?"

The other men were startled by this, it was clear.

"He would not be warned against you, not Gaston. He trusted you, and now he has given his life, for *you*!"

"He sacrificed himself for all of us," Fergus corrected gently.

Ysmaine straightened in the saddle, glaring at Gaston's squire. "I acquired an herb from Fatima to aid my husband," she said coldly. "For he had shown me such kindness that I wished to repay him."

"With poison?" Bartholomew scoffed. "Remind me never to

do a kindness for you, my lady."

"If you knew any teaching about herbs, you would know that some which are fatal to eat are of benefit on the skin," Ysmaine retorted. "I was taught by my grandmother to mix a salve for my grandfather."

"God bless his soul," Radegunde whispered and crossed herself.

Ysmaine continued hotly. "I wished to help with Gaston's limp and asked Fatima whether she knew the herb. She had some but knew it not. When I told her of its use, she trusted me with a measure of its root."

"So, you have this poison?" Fergus asked quietly.

"I carry it for my lady," Radegunde said with pride, when Ysmaine might have preferred the girl keep silent.

"I wanted to help him," she continued. "I wanted to be a good wife and see to his comfort." Bartholomew looked chastened, but not entirely convinced. "And now, I shall have no chance to do so. Do not imagine that I am gladdened by this circumstance."

Indeed, she was devastated by it.

The men exchanged glances and the party continued through the city. It was impossible to miss how preparations were being made for Acre's defense. It had always been a fortress, of course, but men were storing arrows on the parapets and oil was being poured into cauldrons that could be tipped over invaders. There was a bustle and more than a tinge of desperation.

Wulfe finished confiding in the man from the gates, who ran a hand over his brow.

"They are close then," he said. "We had feared as much. The new moon is tomorrow night."

Everard inhaled sharply, glancing up at the sky. The moon was rising, and it was the barest sliver of light. Even Ysmaine knew that an attack on the darkest night of the month was the least likely to be discerned in time, but she had lost track of the days and nights of late.

"And ships?" Wulfe demanded. "We ride for Paris with urgency."

The man's eyes narrowed. "On the business of the Temple?" he asked, then nodded without waiting for a reply. "That is no surprise. Two ships are in the harbor, preparing for departure on the tide this night. One is bound for Venice and the other for Sicily."

"The Venetians," Joscelin said, surprising the men with his interjection. "I have had dealings with them in the past. I will make a wager with them for our passage."

Wulfe's skepticism showed, even to the plump merchant.

Joscelin smiled. "We all have our talents, sir. Your skill has seen us this far, but mine lies in negotiating an agreement."

"If ever men had need of one who could bargain with Venetians, we would be them," Everard said heartily.

"Both ships are hard-pressed to take as many as they can," the man from the gate warned. "And you are a large party."

"You might not succeed," Wulfe suggested to the merchant.

Joscelin smiled. "Perhaps you would like to make a small wager," he invited with a confidence that Ysmaine found reassuring.

❧

Gaston waited. The time passed with immeasurable slowness, and he could not hear the party that Wulfe led any longer. He prayed that Ysmaine would be safe.

Indeed, he prayed with a fervor he had never shown in supplication before.

When the stars were out, a lone rider galloped down the road toward them, and Gaston wondered whether these men awaited his arrival. They certainly straightened and turned their steeds to face him.

This would be scouting party, then, and intent upon capturing men upon this road to learn more of what the Christians did to retaliate. Gaston did not know whether to be glad that he had so few tidings to share. The shadows were growing alongside the road, the night sky illuminated only with myriad stars overhead.

As the horse cantered closer, Gaston watched Fantôme's ears prick. Did his destrier know this steed? He surveyed it, but it was as fine as all the others. He could distinguish little of it in the night, and less of its rider.

The Saracens rode more slender horses, most of them of a chestnut hue, some with white socks. This one had a gleaming coat and a proud glimmer in its eye, but truly, he had seen a hundred so fine in their ranks.

The men greeted the new arrival with deference, a quick patter of Arabic reporting how they had found the party and what had happened. Gaston was surprised that the man even reported Ysmaine's shout.

He, of course, gave no indication that he understood their words.

"Gaston?" the rider asked, his gruff voice more familiar than his steed. "The lady called you Gaston." His French was better than Gaston's Arabic, though he had been a diplomat in these parts too long to risk giving insult.

Particularly when he was so outnumbered.

Gaston answered in French. "For it is my name, and it is only fitting that a lady call her spouse by his name." The man rode closer and Fantôme nickered a greeting.

The man stared at the horse, then peered at Gaston. "I know this steed," he murmured in Arabic, then rode toward Gaston with boldness.

Gaston lifted his blade, determined that if he could make a single blow, it would count.

"Gaston de Châmont-sur-Maine!" the man exclaimed and tugged the scarf away to reveal his face.

"Ibrahim al Abdul al Rashid!" Gaston declared in surprise. They two had negotiated countless times over the exchange of hostages and the ransoming of captives. Indeed, he had oft requested that Ibrahim speak for the Saracen warlords, for he trusted the man to promise only what could be done, and to keep his word.

"But you are alive!" Ibrahim declared, revealing that he had expected Gaston to be with his brethren at Hattin. "Where is your Templar tabard?" that man demanded without granting Gaston a chance to reply. "Why are you not in Jerusalem? And how is it that you have a *wife*?"

"I have left the order," Gaston explained, switching to his halting Arabic, for he thought the courtesy would not be misplaced. "I return home, for my brother has died and made me heir."

Ibrahim nodded with understanding. "And so you have a wife,

for you have need of a son." He shook his head. "And you would sail from Acre, though Jaffa would have been closer?"

"The road is choked with pilgrims, who flee for fear of Saladin," Gaston said. "I wished the horses to run before being confined on the ship."

It was but part of the truth, and he saw that Ibrahim realized as much.

He knew that Ibrahim was not in this place by accident, yet would not confide that truth to him. The strength of their relationship had always been rooted in an understanding of what was too much to ask.

"And this party?" Ibrahim prompted.

"A final party of pilgrims escorted to the port, except I find myself in their number now."

Ibrahim considered this. "I had thought yours a spying party, my friend."

Gaston guessed that Ibrahim was a scout himself. Saladin was making for the port. He was surprised by the choice, but he would not declare as much aloud. The Saracen leader's patience must be fully expired.

He nodded at the eastern sky. "No man has need of a spy to guess the import of that cloud of dust." Ibrahim averted his gaze but Gaston continued softly. "Or to realize that tomorrow night will be a moonless one."

Ibrahim flicked a knowing glance at Gaston, and Gaston understood that Acre would be besieged the next night. He prayed anew that Ysmaine was on a ship that had set sail by then and hoped that Wulfe found them passage.

"Yet you came from Jerusalem?"

"Aye."

Ibrahim sidled closer, his eyes narrowed as he dropped his voice. "What do you know of a girl?"

Gaston frowned, thinking he had misunderstood. "A girl?"

"One of my kinsmen complains that his niece has been abducted by the Franj and carried from Jerusalem. She is a beauty with a high bride price and he is not pleased. Is this girl in your party, by chance?"

It would have been quite the coincidence if she had been. Yet, the party had been followed for two days, ever since they had left

Jerusalem. Was this why?

Gaston had to hope as much. Saracens in search of a missing girl were a better option than a thief seeking to claim the Templar treasure.

He shook his head, aware that Ibrahim watched him closely. "Nay, I know naught of this. We are men traveling together, with squires and horses. My wife and her maid are the sole women in our party."

"Your wife?"

"Ysmaine de Valeroy. She is the one who called my name."

Ibrahim nodded at this, his gaze flicking to the man who had made the report.

"Her hair is gold of hue. I doubt she bears any resemblance to the girl you seek."

Ibrahim cast the man a look, and he nodded.

"And the maid?"

"Radegunde. They came on pilgrimage together and the maid nigh died in the Holy City. The healer Fatima was of aid."

Ibrahim considered Gaston. "But Fatima is leagues away, and I will guess that she did not glimpse the maid. Fatima would not have been allowed into any of the places a Franj noblewoman might stay."

"She did not," Gaston agreed. "So, it is my word you must accept that the maid is not the maiden you seek. She has served my lady and her family for years."

"You vouch for her?"

"I do."

Ibrahim's gaze was unswerving. "Swear it. Swear it on the relic in your blade."

Gaston did as much without hesitation. There was a golden hair trapped between two halves of a sphere of crystal and mounted in the pommel of Gaston's sword. It was said to be one of the hairs of Saint Ursula, who had saved eleven thousand virgins. Gaston had always been glad that the relic that guided his blade was one that represented innocence and goodness. Ibrahim had been fascinated, both by the relic and Gaston's faith in its powers, and had commented upon it years before when they had admired each other's weapons.

When he was done, Ibrahim nodded with satisfaction. "It must be so," he said in Arabic to one of his companions. "This man I trust as my own brother." He then sheathed his sword, shed his glove, and offered his hand to Gaston. "I wish you well, Gaston," he said in French. "A safe journey and many sons with your new wife."

"What is this?" Gaston asked in astonishment. He was to be released?

"There will be little mercy shown in the days ahead, so let me show some now." Ibrahim smiled. "This battle is no longer yours to fight, my friend, and I shall not be the one to exact a price from you."

Gaston seized the other man's hand with gratitude. "I thank you, Ibrahim." He shook his hand heartily. "And I, too, wish you all that is good in this world, and the next." They looked into each other's eyes and Gaston knew he was not the only one with good memories to savor of their discussions and negotiations.

There was a sound of approaching hoof beats, and Ibrahim glanced over his shoulder. "Ride now!" he said in French with urgency. "Ride now, or you may not have the choice."

Gaston did not need to be told twice. He turned Fantôme, touched his spurs to the destrier's flanks and raced for Acre's gates.

ৰ

Gaston roared for entry to the city of Acre but was denied.

The keeper gave no indication that Gaston had been heard. Of course, he had been heard. The very walls were bristling with archers and sentries.

He cursed that he had put his surplice aside, for without it, he was but another desperate stranger seeking admission in the night. He spurred Fantôme and made for the Templar gate near the lighthouse. He prayed as he rode that some soul would know him there.

He had been stationed in Acre for his first two years in Outremer.

Could he be so fortunate that those on the gate this night recalled him—and would recognize him without his surplice?

The terrain grew more rough as he rode around the high

curtain walls of Acre, for he had to remain far enough away to not draw the fire of the archers already positioned on the walls. Fantôme leapt gullies and dodged rocks with such agility that Gaston did not try to guide the horse. He simply let the destrier run, trusting that the beast would see to its own survival.

"Hoy there!" came a cry from the Templar gate, and Gaston was relieved to hear the sound of a familiar voice.

"Michel de Montlhery!" Gaston bellowed. "I beg of you to admit a knight of the order!"

"Gaston?" Michel's helm gleamed as he peeked over the gate. "What, for the love of God, are you doing here?"

"Open the gate!" Gaston replied, relieved beyond belief when Michel did as much. Once he was inside, he dismounted, finding that he was shaking. He confided what he knew in Michel, whose eyes gleamed as he listened to the detail.

"A wife," Michel teased, and Gaston pointed east.

"And Saracens preparing for attack."

Michel sobered immediately. "We feared as much," he said. "If you mean to be away from here, this night will be your last chance. There are two ships in the harbor..."

"When does the tide go out?"

The other knight spared a glance to the sky. "Within the hour. I fear they will be the last to leave before we are besieged, so if you mean to go, this is the moment."

Gaston shook his head, his heart sinking. It seemed he would survive long enough to fight again, but not to share his life with Ysmaine. "The harbor is on the far side of the city," he noted. "I cannot possibly arrive in time." He considered the bailey of the fortress, which was bustling with knights and lay brothers making preparations. No man would sleep this night, he was sure of it.

He could hear similar activity in the city beyond the fortress walls and could readily imagine the congestion of the narrow streets. There had always been a problem with moving between fortress and harbor when he had served within these walls, for the way was narrow and convoluted, so that the slightest excitement in the city proper made it nigh impassible.

Or at least, very slow.

He sighed, knowing he could not do the impossible. "If the master of this priory will welcome me in your ranks again, I will defend this place to the last."

Michel, to Gaston's amazement, smiled. "You need not surrender so readily as that, Gaston. Surely your new wife deserves your every effort to be by her side."

"Surely she does, but that does not make the harbor closer or the streets less crowded." He nodded at his old companion. "I remember well enough how slow the passage to the harbor can be."

Michel seized his elbow, calling to another brother to watch the gates in his stead. He dropped his voice to a whisper. "I have a surprise for you, my friend, although it is a secret that can only be entrusted to one such as you."

"What manner of secret?"

"We have begun to dig a tunnel between our fortress and the harbor," Michel confided, his eyes shining. "It is not complete, but it can be used. You will have to lead Fantôme through the middle, but you might well make the harbor in time."

A tunnel? What a marvel!

"Truly?" Gaston eyed his old comrade as his heart leapt.

"Truly," Michel said. The master of the priory strode across the bailey to meet them, and to Gaston's delight, it was another old comrade of his who ruled this fortress now. They spoke briefly, then Michel descended into the darkness with Fantôme and Gaston.

"There!" the other knight said, gesturing to the dark space ahead of them. Gaston could scarce believe the sight. "Ride on, Gaston, with every blessing." They embraced, and Gaston led his destrier into the dark space. He carried a small torch, given to him by Michel, and he could see the light of the boy's torch far ahead.

The tunnel was wide and tall, its walls smooth and its ceiling fitted with stones. There was a bit of water gathered in the bottom of it, but the way was smooth. It appeared to be very straight.

Fantôme seemed to welcome the coolness of the air. Gaston patted the steed, vowing he would brush him thoroughly once their passage was secured, swung into the saddle and rode.

He could only hope that he would make the harbor in time.

ॐ

It seemed her curse would not be denied.

Ysmaine marveled that her reaction to losing a spouse was so different this time. Again, with regards to Gaston, she felt cheated. There had been more about him than his allure and his comparative youth, that slow smile that set her very flesh aflame. More than his kisses and his gentle strength. He was not perfect, not by any means. He had been stubborn, to be sure, and taciturn, and oblivious to any expectations a wife might have had from a spouse or a marriage, but still. He defended her. He spoke to her as if she had her wits about her. Even knowing they might have argued more than once in their stolen future, Ysmaine wished they might have had the chance. She had sensed a promise in their match, one that she had wanted very much to explore.

She found herself greedy for more than had been her lot in the past.

Though she knew Gaston had chosen the only course acceptable to him, that he should sacrifice himself for the good of the others, taking responsibility for his miscalculation, Ysmaine regretted his loss bitterly. Indeed, his choice showed the truth of his nature as nothing else could have done.

She wanted to bear his son.

She wanted to return to his holding and raise that son, to tell the boy what little she knew of his father. She wanted to ensure the future that Gaston had envisioned. She would not wed again, she knew it to her very marrow.

She prayed that she might have conceived.

And if Ysmaine did not carry Gaston's son, she resolved she would retire to a convent and be penitent for the rest of her days.

While her thoughts churned, she did as Wulfe bade, not delaying the party in any way. She would not compromise the opportunity Gaston had created.

Acre claimed a point of land that jutted into the sea. A bay curled beneath the city to the south and rose on the eastern side, making the sole approach from the north. The harbor was on the eastern side, so that it and the docked ships were sheltered in that bay. The town itself was walled on the north side and had grown beyond original expectations. The streets were narrow and crowded, and it seemed that every soul in Christendom thronged the way. They had no small challenge pushing their way through the congestion, even with the horses. The knights' squires ran ahead, shouting and trying to clear a course, and the company rode tightly packed together.

It seemed to take forever to reach the harbor itself.

Joscelin demanded that they halt before they reached the ship so he could ascertain exactly how much coin they carried between them. There was a shrewd light in his eye and his manner was quick, which made Ysmaine think he might do well in this task. Then he advised the others to put their funds away and to contrive to look as impoverished as possible.

"I doubt it will matter in the end," Joscelin said, his manner more bold than it had been. Clearly, he felt on familiar ground. "But it cannot hurt." Without another word, he strode to the ship flying the colors of Venice, leading his palfrey. The others followed him, and Ysmaine wished she could hear his words.

If he spoke in Venetian, she would not have understood him at any rate.

He saluted the man who supervised the loading of the ship, and she guessed that he asked for the captain. An argument appeared to ensue, and the horses were counted. The Venetians shook their heads but Joscelin persisted. Ysmaine was increasingly vexed by how long the exercise took.

They would never be away from Acre!

"Use the time we have, Stephen," Wulfe bade the taller of his squires. The blond boy nodded. "We shall need fodder for the steeds on the ship. The Venetians, no doubt, will sell us fodder and water at a killing price, so it would be best to provide some of our own." Stephen ducked into the crowd to do his knight's bidding.

"Aid him in this, Kerr," Fergus bade his older squire, the one who looked so angelic. The boys disappeared with purpose.

Ysmaine's heart sank as the other ship departed, the men on board shouting to people who remained on the docks. There was much well wishing and more than a few tears shed. The ship was rowed away from the harbor, and Ysmaine saw men on deck begin to unbind its sails. Those sails were unfurled moments later, snapping white against the night sky, and the ship sailed west, disappearing around the point.

"I should have negotiated," Wulfe muttered.

"They would have turned you down," Fergus replied. "The

Venetians have no fondness for the military orders." Wulfe grimaced at that, so Ysmaine supposed it was true. "At least they still talk to him."

"Why is that?" Ysmaine asked Fergus, and he smothered a smile.

"Perhaps Templars and Hospitaliers do not spend enough coin on the riches in which the Venetians trade."

Duncan scoffed. "They spend sufficient on courtesans," he muttered, and Wulfe flicked a glance his way.

"There is no need for such speech before a lady," Fergus said, and the men fell silent again.

Watching Joscelin.

"They will talk all the night," Wulfe complained moments later. "While the tide retreats."

"The man can spin a tale, that much is certain," Duncan contributed.

Ysmaine thought of the missive Gaston had secured into his aketon with her assistance and wondered anew what tidings it contained. She recalled her recurring sense that Gaston led the party, not Wulfe, and realized that they had ridden onward when *Gaston* had given the command that they do as much. She noted now the agitation amongst the knights, particularly Wulfe and Fergus, and wondered at the truth of this quest.

She bit her lip when she remembered how Everard and Wulfe had complained that very morning of their baggage being plundered while they slept and the hair pricked on the back of her neck. Had it truly been a scouting party of Saracens who surrounded and detained Gaston? Or had he been sought out deliberately?

Did someone desire the missive he carried enough to kill him?

She could not convince herself that her husband had been surprised by events. He had not hesitated to sacrifice himself for the good of all. Was it simply that he was prepared for any foul deed, or had he anticipated this particular tragedy? Had he known what the attackers wanted and offered it so that the rest of them could ride free?

Ysmaine had a hundred questions, it seemed, and few answers. She did not imagine that these knights would confide more detail in her than Gaston had done, but she wanted very much to know the truth of their mission.

Had Gaston sent them onward because the missive was only part of what they carried? Wulfe had, after all, abandoned Gaston without a moment's hesitation, as if there was more at stake than a single life or even a missive.

Or as if he had been glad to be rid of the man who commanded him.

Ysmaine frowned at that. Could a man who had left the order command a Templar knight? She had to think not. If Gaston commanded Wulfe, as it surely seemed, did that mean he had not truly left the order?

Did it mean that their nuptial vows were void? Certainly she had no evidence that they had occurred, beyond the word of Radegunde, whose motivation could and would be questioned in this matter. The priest at the Temple in Jerusalem might not be able or inclined to respond to queries on such a matter, given that the city was likely to be attacked, and its lack of knights meant almost certain capture.

Perhaps a convent loomed larger in Ysmaine's future than she had realized.

The notion made her restless. Indeed, what took so very long? Ysmaine nearly tapped her toe with impatience as time passed by and the conversation continued without resolution. Would Gaston's sacrifice be for naught in the end? Would the Saracens attack on this night? It was worrisome that the other ship was gone, especially when she saw the sailors on this one were making preparations to depart. They checked the wind and lashed items down on the deck. They shouted as the last of the provisions were hauled aboard, and she saw them cast off one of the heavy ropes tethering the ship to the dock.

She clenched her hands together tightly, closed her eyes, and prayed.

There was little else she could do, though Ysmaine despised that her choices were so few.

"We should have tried the other ship," Everard complained, echoing her thoughts, then sighed. "Perhaps we will be fighting Saracens after all."

"Impossible!" Wulfe declared and strode forward to intervene.

In that moment, Joscelin turned, his expression triumphant,

and beckoned to them. He snapped his fingers to hasten them along. "The agreement is made, but they will sail shortly, with or without us! Hasten yourselves!"

The horses were led on board one at a time, though it was clear that the destriers thought little of this choice. Wulfe's black stallion snorted and fought the bit, refusing to cross the gangplank—at least until one of the palfreys nipped him in the butt. He tossed his head and neighed outrage, so resembling his knight that Ysmaine had to bite back a smile. Once that steed was aboard, the others followed, some more meekly than others. They had to be tethered on the deck. Ysmaine and Radegunde helped Bartholomew to secure the palfreys, though he would accept no aid in brushing them down after their ride. The squires returned with fodder for all the horses, and they were watered, as well.

There was naught for her to do, so she returned to the deck to watch the preparations, Radegunde fast by her side. Joscelin was there, looking proud of himself, the knights beside him. They informed her of her contribution to the cost of their passage, and she gladly gave the coins to Joscelin, ensuring that she did not reveal the contents of the purse Gaston had given her.

It was heavier than she had realized, and she was glad of that.

The man ensured her welfare, even after his demise.

Would she be welcomed at Châmont-sur-Maine as his widow? She did not even want to think of it.

"You proved to be as good as your word," she said to the merchant. "I should not have doubted you."

He laughed. "An agreement can always be made. It merely depends upon the price, and the price is better if you know the other party's desire."

"Although the matter was closer than we might have preferred," Wulfe said, nodding at the ropes being cast off.

"All the same, I am glad I did not take a wager against him," Fergus said amiably. The others might have laughed but there was a shout from the crowd and to Ysmaine's delight, a knight upon a dapple destrier galloped through the crowd.

It could not be.

But Ysmaine knew that steed, she knew that dark hair, she knew the breadth and size of that knight...

Praise be to Mary, for Gaston survived!

Chapter Ten

"Hold the ship!" Gaston bellowed, standing in his stirrups as he waved. Ysmaine thrilled at the sight of him, more hale than she could ever have hoped. Her heart thundered, and she wanted to fling herself upon him.

Curse this crowd between them!

Gaston's tone turned imperious when the people did not move aside. "I will not be left behind!"

"Gaston!" Ysmaine cried with delight and relief.

"He is alive!" Radegunde declared, her pleasure echoed in the expressions of the entire company. She hugged Ysmaine impulsively. "You are a wedded woman yet, my lady."

Ysmaine noted that the crew were drawing up the gangplank and that her husband's survival was not yet assured. "Nay! He will be abandoned!" she cried, even as Wulfe strode to the captain with purpose. An argument ensued there, as the gangplank was stowed away, and in the meantime, Gaston gained the lip of the wharf. He dismounted and held his destrier's reins, impatience in every line of his figure. Ysmaine surveyed him greedily, then knew she should try to influence the captain's choice. She smiled when his gaze flicked to her and did not disguise her joy.

Did her taciturn husband smile? Ysmaine believed as much.

She hastened to Wulfe and produced a coin from Gaston's purse. "My husband, sir," she explained, uncertain whether she would be understood or not. "We thought him killed, but he has arrived. You must allow him aboard!"

The captain eyed her, then considered the proffered coin. He made a gesture and Ysmaine added another. His hand closed over the coins, and she had a moment's fear of his intent. "Another man might have been tempted to ensure you were at his mercy, my lady, but my own wife would think poorly of such conduct." He winked at her then, a man confident of his charms, then called to his men to replace the gangplank.

"I salute your wife then and would send her my thanks," Ysmaine said. "She, like me, is wed to a man of honor."

"And she will have a gift from him when we reach home port." The captain tucked the coins into his own purse, then bowed to her before returning to his duties.

Ysmaine spun, her heart in her throat as she watched the gangplank replaced.

"It seems Gaston chose well," Wulfe murmured. "You spend his coin to good purpose, at least."

She bit back any reply, wanting only to watch her husband's approach. She could have anticipated that he would guide the horse with gentle resolve, and that the beast would trust him completely—even though it could not like the gangplank any more than the other steeds had done. Bartholomew greeted his knight with obvious pleasure, and Gaston shook the younger man's hand before granting him the destrier's reins.

Did Ysmaine imagine that the relief of the other knights seemed greater than might have been expected?

Either way, Gaston was alive!

She had been given another chance, and she would not betray Mary's kindness. Nay, she would be the best wife in all of Christendom, the best wife a man could desire, and she would do whatsoever was necessary to see her husband well pleased.

Ysmaine stood back, heart thumping. She knew it would be inappropriate to rush toward him, though that was precisely what she wished to do. It would not be proper conduct. She should await him, be demure, offer her hand when he deigned to turn his attention upon her.

Everything within Ysmaine battled against such decorum.

Gaston, meanwhile, was embraced by the other men in their party. He shook hands and accepted their goodwill, moving through the company so slowly that she could not bear the waiting. The gangplank was stowed and the ship being pushed away from the wharf when he halted before Ysmaine. The wind was in his hair and his eyes were alight, that smile lifting one corner of his lips.

There had never been a more handsome man in all the days of

the world, Ysmaine was certain of it. Her heart pounded and she felt blessed beyond all expectation that he was her lord husband.

And that he yet drew breath.

"I regret to inform you, lady mine, that you are not again a widow," he murmured, his tone both deep and teasing. "Did I not confide that I did not intend to die as yet?" He offered his hand but a kiss on her knuckles would not suffice in this moment, not when she was fair bursting with delight.

If a woman could not greet her husband with enthusiasm when he had cheated the grave, then the world was far less just than she had previously believed it to be.

"Gaston!" Ysmaine cried and flung herself toward him, loving the way he caught her close and lifted her in his embrace. He swung her around and laughed at her enthusiasm. Even though the ship was underway and rocked slightly, his feet were planted so solidly on the deck that she knew he would not lose his footing or drop her. Her husband was a rock, a foundation upon which she could build her life. Ysmaine nigh wept at that, only realizing in the heat of his embrace how solitary and adrift she had felt.

She *would* bear him sons, as many as she could manage.

Many of those on both ship and dock cheered at their reunion, but Ysmaine did not care for their reactions.

Her husband held her close, his heart beating against her own.

Gaston was *alive*.

She framed his face in her hands, studied him for a moment, and savored the heat of his skin beneath her hands. "How did you manage this feat?" she whispered. "Have I wed a sorcerer?"

His lips quirked. "Perhaps merely a fortunate man." His eyes twinkled. "Or one destined to be wed to you."

"More than that," Ysmaine retorted, though she liked the sound of that. "Did you guess we would be assaulted?"

His eyes narrowed slightly. "Why would you imagine as much?"

"Because you did not hesitate. You had a scheme for the eventuality, in case it did occur." She smiled and saw his expression soften again. "A sound plan is often mistaken for good fortune, after all."

"Indeed. Do you regret not losing another husband?" he murmured, clearly knowing the reply.

Ysmaine shook her head, unable and unwilling to hide her relief. "Nay," she whispered, her voice husky. "I would keep this one for a few years yet. I do not doubt he has a plan to ensure that is so."

Gaston made to laugh, but Ysmaine then bent to kiss him with gusto, not caring who witnessed her relief.

ૐ

The lady dazzled him anew.

Even when Gaston was prepared for his wife's embrace, even when he glimpsed the intent in her eyes before she kissed him, her touch was nigh overwhelming in its power.

It seemed the lady had awakened a passion within him that had slumbered long, but now demanded to be sated.

Gaston broke his kiss with regret and surveyed his lady wife. Ysmaine smiled up at him. She put his purse of coins into his palm, granting him a quick accounting of what she had spent and why.

By all the saints, she was a practical wife, and a beauteous one, as well.

Gaston was thinking that a single coupling, perhaps even a daily coupling, might not suffice to control his ardor for this lady.

The others demanded the tale of his escape, and he summarized it, mentioning the mercy of his old friend and not Ibrahim's quest for a missing girl. The other men clapped him on the shoulder and congratulated him, then dispersed.

The ship had rounded the point occupied by Acre and the sea was rougher beyond the shelter of the harbor. He held Ysmaine close, aware of her curves and softness. He was cursing the lack of privacy on the ship and trying to guess how long it would be until they made port, when Ysmaine astonished him anew.

"You command this party, do you not?" she asked, her words so quietly uttered that only he would discern them.

Even so, Gaston's heart clenched. "Why would you believe as much?" he demurred, watching her lips tighten even as he tried to hide his reaction.

Her eyes flashed and she shook her head. "I am no fool, sir!" she chided. "It was you who chose our route, and you who gave the command to ride on. It is you who carry the missive, as I have seen." Gaston made to protest but Ysmaine put her fingertips over his lips to silence him. "I will guess that you have sworn an oath to keep this a secret," she murmured, with a confidence he could only admire. "Indeed, I can think of no other reason why you would break your own demand for honesty between us."

Gaston swallowed, aware again of the perceptiveness of his wife.

"But here is the nut of the matter," she continued, a small frown between her brows. "My concern is solely thus: are we wedded in truth? Because if you lead this party and command a Templar knight, then you must yet be pledged to the order, and thus our nuptial vows must be hollow." Her gaze clung to his. "I would know, sir, whether I am wedded in truth or not."

Relief flooded through Gaston that her concern was so simple. He whispered to her, hiding his action in their embrace. "I have but one task to complete, lady mine, and it is true that all is not as it might seem. I beg of you to keep such observations to yourself."

"I will," she vowed quietly, her gaze searching his. He saw that she was dissatisfied with his partial answer, but it would have to suffice. "If you pledge to tell me all of it, once we reach Châmont-sur-Maine."

Gaston smiled at the very notion. "It will not be of import then, and truly, such matters should not be of concern to a lady."

He had thought he might pacify her, but Ysmaine's gaze hardened in a way that was becoming familiar.

"Indeed?" she asked, arching a fair brow. The wind gained momentum and strands of her hair escaped her braid. "Why should that be?"

Gaston's confidence faltered. "Because ladies should not have to trouble themselves with matters of strategy and warfare, or even alliance. The courts on a holding are administered by the lord, as are the accounts..."

Ysmaine interrupted him crisply. "Perhaps it is so in the Temple, for you have no women to rely upon."

"Of course we do not," Gaston agreed. The light in his lady's eyes left him feeling that he had erred in his easy agreement.

"But what of life at Châmont-sur-Maine? Did your mother ignore all matters beyond her embroidery and her son?"

Gaston blinked. He had not considered his parents' marriage in years, if ever he had. "She kept the keys," he recalled, speaking slowly. "And was said to be sharp with the inventories."

Ysmaine smiled. "I shall like her, then."

"She took the veil upon my father's death."

His wife frowned. "But why? Was she beyond the age to remarry?"

Gaston turned to watch the port fade from view, his throat tight with the memories. "She had seen only sixteen summers when she bore me," he admitted. "She was my father's third wife, and it was said she was the one who made him feel young again. I recall the laughter from the solar in the evenings or even in the afternoons."

Ysmaine smiled a little. "Then we have this in common, sir, for my parents also laugh often in their chamber." She leaned close to him to whisper. "I believe such conviviality is rooted not only honesty but discussion and partnership."

Again, it seemed his wife had expectations of their match that exceeded his own. Gaston regarded her with some wariness. "You have said your parents confer much."

"And I would wager that yours did, as well." There was a knowing glint in the lady's eyes. "Perhaps I will visit your mother in her cloister to discover the truth. Perhaps she will convince you of the merit of my view."

It was remarkable how Ysmaine could tempt him, especially as his reaction had so little to do with her charms. She was a beautiful woman, to be sure, but what made Gaston's breath catch in his throat was the challenge in her eyes, as in this moment. Despite all he had been taught in the order about the place of women—or lack of it—she made him question his assumptions. He liked to banter with her, and he was fascinated by the way she argued with much logic. She was insightful and clever, and he was glad to have chosen her as his wife.

"I must thank Wulfe for ensuring your safety."

Ysmaine's smile turned knowing. "Or for following an order?" she asked lightly.

Gaston took warning from that. He should be more concerned that his wife understood him so well as she did. Even knowing that he was sworn to secrecy, he was tempted to trust her with the truth.

This could not be.

He excused himself without reply, knowing that she watched him depart.

As galling as the prospect was, Gaston might have to take counsel from Wulfe in the matter of earning a lady's heart. His wife, it seemed, was adept at perceiving his secrets, and Gaston wished to be able to trust her fully. Once they were home, he would join her abed, of course, and he would have need of his sleep.

He did not believe, though, that conjuring Ysmaine's passion in the way Wulfe suggested—as enticing as the prospect was— would be a successful strategy as winning her heart. Nay, Ysmaine was too practical for that. He had to convince her to love him, but he had to do so by proving the advantage of having him by her side.

Though Gaston knew little of such romantic quests, surely, the conquest of a woman's heart was much like any other siege. He would prove himself reliable and win her trust in that. He would treat her with honor. He had already shown his willingness to protect her. He cast a glance over her faded gown and resolved to indulge her, once they reached Venice. He had to believe that would win her regard.

And a son in her belly would ensure her loyalty.

That had been his father's strategy and lacking any other, Gaston was convinced of it.

To Wulfe's surprise, Gaston came to his side. They two were alone at the stern of the ship, watching Acre fade into the shadows of the horizon behind them.

"I would thank you for seeing to my wife's protection," Gaston said, his tone formal.

"I did as commanded, no more than that," Wulfe admitted.

Gaston bit back a smile, but did not reply.

"She carries poison, you know."

"Aye, I do know."

Wulfe was startled. "And you do naught about it?"

"I would see what she will do about it," Gaston replied mildly. "Possession in itself is no crime."

"It may be too late for you by the time she acts."

"Have you seen me consume any item from her hand?"

Wulfe considered the other knight. "You watch and you wait, and you risk much in this."

Gaston shrugged. "I would risk more should I make an unfounded accusation of my lady wife."

There was truth in that. Wulfe had to cede that patience had its place.

"You were fortunate at Acre," he said when the silence had stretched long.

"It was the site of my first assignment in Outremer," Gaston admitted. "Though it was luck indeed that one of my comrades armed the gates on this night."

"I am amazed that you managed to cross the city with such haste."

Gaston nodded, clearly choosing his words before he spoke. "I suppose there is little harm in confiding that they build a tunnel beneath the city, to link Temple and harbor. It is not complete, but it was passable."

Wulfe inhaled sharply. "Brilliant! It might aid them in this attack."

"It might, though they will still be susceptible to a siege."

"What else do you know that you do not confide?" Wulfe asked, not truly expecting a reply.

He did not get one.

Wulfe watched the ocean behind them, relieved that he could not discern any other ships taking the same direction. "It seems that whoever followed us has been left behind," he murmured.

Gaston frowned. "They might not have had any inclination to pursue us," he said with care. Wulfe glanced toward the former Templar, struck by his tone. He saw now that Gaston was a man of considerable experience and one who kept much in confidence. "Ibrahim told me that a Saracen girl fled from Jerusalem with the aid of Christians on the same day that we departed."

"Why would she do such a deed?"

"I will guess that she disagreed with the choice of spouse made for her. He spoke of her bride price being high and also said that she is much sought by her family." He turned a look on the other knight. "He made me swear that she was not in our party."

"A girl? But your wife and her maid are the sole women."

Gaston nodded, his manner thoughtful. "So I told him. He made me swear it upon the relic in my sword."

Wulfe turned as if in idleness and surveyed the deck of the ship. His gaze flicked over the members of their party, then he winced when he saw that the smallest of Fergus' squires was being sick over the sides of the ship. "It seems on every voyage that there must be one so afflicted."

Gaston followed his gaze, then nodded before turning back to watch Acre fade from view.

"Do you still have the missive?" Wulfe asked, impatient to know as much as possible.

"Of course."

"Have you read it?"

Gaston's quelling glance revealed that he did not share Wulfe's curiosity. "I pledged to not do so."

"Do you know what else we carry?"

Gaston shook his head. "We were sworn to defend it in ignorance, and I would keep my vow."

"Do you know where it is?"

"I can guess," the other knight admitted. He so studiously avoided scanning their party that Wulfe did as much again.

Even in sickness, that small boy kept one of Fergus' saddlebags between his ankles. Wulfe could not recall having seen the boy without it. And truly, from the stench of him, any soul who claimed it could not keep his deed hidden.

Wulfe smiled and turned back to the fading sight of the city, content that he did not travel in a company of fools. "Tell me of Acre," he invited. "I never served there."

❧

Something was afoot.

Ysmaine could fairly smell it, and the scent of intrigue grew stronger with every passing day. Gaston was evasive when she asked him questions, which meant there was something at root.

Otherwise, he would have denied it outright. She had great respect for his insistence upon honesty and knew he would never breach his own terms. Gaston, it was clear, had no intention of trusting her with the full truth. Ysmaine, on the other hand, was determined to prove to him that she was trustworthy, and that she could bring more than children to their match. She did not blame him for his skepticism about the place of women, not when he had spent nigh twenty years amongst men, but she had no doubt she could prove his assumptions wrong. He might not believe the value in partnership, but she would prove it to him.

If her strategy failed, she *would* visit his mother, no matter where that convent was located.

The ship was bigger than those Ysmaine had journeyed upon before, but not that large all the same. The horses remained tethered closely together on the deck, and a single lateen sail snapped in the wind overhead. The ship had a hold, but it was packed so tightly that she doubted even a rat could find passage there. The opening to the hold had been secured by their boarding, so they lashed their belongings to the deck and slept near them that first night. Ysmaine doubted she was the only one reminding herself that at least they were not trapped in a town destined to be besieged by Saracens.

That first night, she wrapped herself in the cloak that Gaston had provided for her back in Jerusalem and curled up with Radegunde near Gaston's saddlebags. He strode back and forth, long after the stars had come out, speaking with the men in their party and the captain. Ysmaine watched him until her eyelids drooped, guessing that he gathered information. She was vexed that he did not rest his hip, even now, but would choose her moment to make that observation.

What was her husband's quest? She knew Gaston carried a missive, but there must be more than that. She waited, wanting to ask him for details, but it seemed her husband anticipated her queries and would avoid them.

She fell asleep beneath the stars, powerless to remain awake any longer. At some point in the night, Ysmaine was dimly aware that Gaston gathered her into his lap. She knew his scent, and his heat was more than welcome.

Indeed, she slept fully in his embrace, content that she was finally safe.

Tuesday, July 7, 1187

Feast Day of Saint Ethelberga, and Saint Thomas of Canterbury.

&

Chapter Eleven

At first light, Ysmaine awakened beside Radegunde, who snored softly as always she did. Gaston was standing at the prow of the ship, watching the sea ahead. It looked as if it would be a clear day. Ysmaine rose and went to his side.

"Good morning," he said without turning, just before she reached his side.

"Did you sleep at all?"

"A little." He eyed her, his gaze slipping over her. "You?"

"I was sufficiently tired to sleep anywhere, I fear." Ysmaine smiled. "The ship is cramped with so many aboard, though I am not ungrateful for the passage. Will you tell me how all is to be managed?"

He considered her, then nodded in understanding of her question. It proved that they were to dock at several ports en route to Venice, and that the captain estimated their journey would take a fortnight. The ship was too small to carry many provisions, and on this particular trip, had less than usual. They would need fresh water for themselves and the horses, as well as food. The captain had proposed to stop at Tripoli—as much for tidings as supplies— then Cyprus, Crete, and Ragusa. At most, they would go four or five days without visiting a port. He anticipated calm seas at this time of year, although there was always a possibility of a storm.

Indeed, Ysmaine noted that Fergus' newest squire was already hanging over the side of the ship, ill even on these comparatively calm seas. It said much for that boy's dedication to his knight that he still vigilantly guarded one of the saddlebags.

There were no garderobes, which Ysmaine had noted, but

Gaston had already asked after such mundane details. It seemed the sailors used buckets that were stowed at the stern and heaved the contents over the side of the ship when necessary. Gaston had already insisted upon one bucket being designated solely for the use of herself and Radegunde and had hung a discarded sail around a small area at one side of the stern.

"As close to a garderobe as one might have in such a place," he said to her, his manner apologetic.

She smiled at him. "I thank you greatly, sir, for your foresight. I would ask another favor of you."

Gaston lifted a brow.

"Might you discover whether there is a mortar and pestle to be borrowed from the crew? Also, I have need of a small bottle of sour wine, if it can be had."

His gaze flicked over her, and she saw him decide not to ask after her reasoning. Doubtless, given their discussion of garderobes, he believed she had need of it for some delicate matter. "I am certain the loan can be arranged and the vinegar purchased."

"Thank you, sir."

"There is still bread and cheese, as well as a bit of hard sausage and some ale, if you and Radegunde would break your fast."

"We will, sir, if you will grant me but a few moments."

He bowed, and Ysmaine returned to the awakening maid to inform her of the arrangements. She saw Bartholomew rise from his makeshift bed and grant her a glance that did not bode well for tranquility in future in her husband's household.

Ysmaine was Gaston's lady wife, and she knew her role well. She had to build an alliance with all of those in his household and employ, even this squire determined to think ill of her.

Doubtless they shared a concern for the knight's wellbeing.

Doubtless she could base an alliance upon that.

ॐ

Bartholomew heard someone being sick in the night, but did not realize until the dawn that it was Leila. He had not dared to speak openly to her since their departure, but used her illness as cause to do so now.

He hoped it was but a guise to keep others away from her.

The scent of manure on her garb had matured to the point that it brought a tear to his eye when he approached. "You have a good tactic for keeping others away," he said lightly. "You need not indulge in another."

Leila turned his way, and he knew with a glance that her discomfort was not feigned. "I have never been on a boat before," she said. "And I never wish to be so again."

If she might have said more, she had no chance to do so, for she was ill yet again.

He felt badly for he was enjoying the fresh breeze and the feel of the wind.

"How can you still be voiding your stomach?" he asked, taking a place at the rail beside her. "We have not eaten so much as that these past days."

"I do not know," she said, her misery clear. "Worse, I think Kerr has discerned the truth."

Bartholomew was immediately alarmed. "Which truth?"

"Mine, you fool." Leila was disparaging as she seldom was, but then, illness could make one impatient.

"That is less of a surprise than might be, for he contrives to learn all he should not and cares not how he does it."

"I had hoped it might take longer to be revealed," Leila replied. She spat with vigor. "I had hoped to be more hale when required to defend myself."

"I will defend you."

"Should you have the chance."

Her mood was dark on this morn, to be sure. "Do you regret your choice?"

Leila shook her head emphatically. "I would endure far more than this if necessary."

"Careful of your wishes," Bartholomew teased, and she managed a smile.

"As you should have been. You wished to return to France, and look at the price."

Bartholomew was immediately glum. "I thought we would return with the order, to serve at the Temple in Paris." This time, he spat over the rail. "Not that Gaston would be compelled to *wed*."

"He was not compelled."

"He has need of a legitimate heir. How else is that contrived without a wife?"

"He looks most content, and she was clearly pleased that he survived. Perhaps their match is a good one."

Bartholomew contented himself with glowering at the horizon, for he was not pleased with this new circumstance.

"You were outspoken with your lady last evening," Leila continued, as if trying to distract herself from her discomfort.

"She is not *my* lady," Bartholomew retorted. Leila glanced his way, as if she might censure him, then her gaze flicked over his shoulder and her dark eyes widened.

When she covertly kicked him, Bartholomew knew what—or more accurately, who—he would discover behind himself when he turned.

He sighed and did as much, not at all consoled to discover that he was right. Lady Ysmaine stood but two steps away, her gaze so bright that he knew she had overheard his words.

He wondered whether she would chastise him or feign ignorance, or worse, whether she would complain to Gaston about his rudeness. Surely she would not see him cast out? He bowed, well aware that Leila was enjoying his discomfiture.

The lady stepped closer, her chin high, and dread rose within him. "Good morning to you both," she said, then nodded toward Leila before Bartholomew could do more than mumble a reply. "I could not help but note your discomfort. You might ask your knight Fergus to enquire as to whether there are any fennel seeds on board. If not, they might be acquired when we port."

"Fennel seeds, my lady?" Bartholomew echoed, knowing his suspicion was clear.

The lady eyed him coolly. "So, I *am* your lady after all. I am glad to hear it." Leila chuckled but disguised her reaction with a cough, while Bartholomew felt himself flush. "Aye, chewing upon fennel seeds is said to be good for sea sickness. When we sailed to Outremer, there was a merchant aboard selling it at high prices to those who were ill." The lady spared a glance to the merchant Joscelin, who was just rousing himself from sleep. "Indeed, the merchant in our party might have some to share, though God only knows what his price might be."

"I thank you for your counsel, my lady," Leila said, then bowed. "The relief would be most welcome."

"I expect so, particularly as my lord husband anticipates our journey will take a fortnight."

Leila moaned and bent over the rails again.

She still managed to nudge Bartholomew with her foot, and he knew she was right.

He cleared his throat, well aware that Gaston's lady was waiting for his apology. He had no idea that women were so forthright in collecting what they perceived to be their due, but he respected that trait. Indeed, that her behavior was consistent with Gaston's choices made her seem less mysterious and fearsome. "I owe you an apology, my lady, and I would offer it to you now."

"I thank you for it, Bartholomew." Lady Ysmaine smiled quickly. "Indeed, I cannot hold your reaction against you, for it is rooted in a desire to ensure my husband's welfare. We share this objective, though it may not have seemed as much to you."

"Aye, my lady." Bartholomew was not entirely convinced of her motives.

"So it is that I would show you what I mean to do with that herb, that you might learn how to prepare the liniment that will give relief to my husband. It is of use to all fighting men, for it is their fate to sustain injury and for their bodies to recall as much more heartily as they age." Her smile brightened then. "My grandfather used to say that it was a great gift for a warrior to age, even if it meant aches and pains at intervals, for the alternative was far less appealing."

Leila laughed, which prompted her to cough again. Bartholomew thumped her on the back until the fit passed, and she leaned on the rail, clearly exhausted. The lady considered the squire, and Bartholomew feared how much she might discern. When she lifted a hand in summons, he again feared the worst, and guessed that the lady noted his reaction.

Lady Ysmaine's maid came with haste.

"Radegunde, would you take word to my lord Fergus that his squire Laurent has need of fennel seeds? I have no doubt that some can be found on the ship, or acquired from Master Joscelin, or even obtained when we harbor at Tripoli. The boy is most ill."

"Of course, my lady."

Some of the tension slid out of Bartholomew's shoulders, for he could not resent her taking such an active role in seeing to Leila's relief.

"And now, Bartholomew," the lady said. "I would know from you what plans you have."

"Plans? I would serve my knight..."

"But you are old for a squire," she interrupted. "How many summers have you seen?"

"Three and twenty, my lady."

She regarded him with what seemed to be genuine curiosity. "How curious, for my lord husband confessed to earning his own spurs at fifteen summers of age. Should you not have earned spurs of your own by now?"

It was mortifying to have to admit his lack of family or wealth, but Bartholomew did as much. Within the order, his origins had not mattered, but he knew well enough that in the secular world, they did. "I have not a patron."

"No uncle?" the lady prodded and he wondered how much of his history she would compel him to confess. "No friend of your father kindly disposed to you?"

Bartholomew shook his head. "Only my lord knight."

"Yet surely you have learned much in his service?"

"Indeed! But a brother of the order cannot sponsor a squire for knighthood. It is a secular duty."

"Of course." Lady Ysmaine tilted her head to study him, as if she would miss no measure of his reaction. "But my lord husband is now a baron of his own estate. I am certain he could sponsor your dubbing as a knight."

Bartholomew shook his head, even as the notion thrilled him. He knew better than to hope for what could not be his own. "But I have no holding, my lady, so there is little point in another man making such expenditure on my behalf. I would serve my lord Gaston."

"You sell your future short, Bartholomew." Her tone was terse and her lips tight with disapproval.

Bartholomew feared then that she meant to cast him out from Châmont-sur-Maine once they arrived, and that this would be the reward for his accusation against her. "I would serve my lord Gaston," he repeated, his voice rising. "I have no taste for the life of a mercenary..."

"If you served him as a knight, your compensation would be such that you could wed," the lady replied, cutting short his protest. "You are no longer a boy, Bartholomew, and a boy's ambitions will not suffice. You should have the reward due to you for your training and service. I will speak to Gaston about this."

He blinked in amazement and uttered his fear aloud before he could halt himself. "You would not cast me out?"

The lady frowned in apparent surprise. "Cast out the one who has served my husband faithfully for years? I think not, Bartholomew. We return to a keep my husband left almost twenty years ago. Alliances in that household are by no means assured. Indeed, his return at this time may be deeply resented by those who have remained behind."

Bartholomew had never considered that any soul would be less than glad of Gaston's arrival.

The lady smiled at him. "Gaston may well have need of every ally he can find. Shall you and I be the first of that company?" She offered him the mortar and pestle, no censure in her gaze, and Bartholomew shook his head.

"Why do you forgive me so readily as this?"

"Because it is the rightful place of a lord's wife to build consensus in his household. My husband does not yet realize the import of this role, and I would teach him of it. He trusts you, thus so will I."

"And this...this liniment you would have me aid in concocting, it will not injure him?"

"It will give him relief."

Leila turned and though she was pale, her eyes were bright. "I would learn of this potion, my lady, if you would teach me."

"I would be glad to do as much."

"Can it be used upon horses, as well?"

The lady considered this, then nodded. "I cannot see why not. The liniment creates a heat on the skin and then in the muscle itself. My grandmother said it summoned healing to where it was needed, and then it grants the gift of numbness to the spot, so that the person is relieved temporarily of the burden of the pain."

"That could be most useful," Leila agreed. "Pain can keep one from sleeping, which is the best healing balm of all."

Lady Ysmaine nodded. "But this herb must be treated with respect," she continued. "It is a poison, to be sure, just as Fatima noted. My grandmother said it offered a lesson that even in the greatest of evils, some measure of good can be found."

Bartholomew accepted the mortar and pestle from her outstretched hand. "I would aid you in this, my lady, and learn of this liniment."

She smiled. "And we shall be allied in ensuring my husband's welfare."

To Bartholomew's surprise, she then offered her hand, as a knight would seal a wager. He blinked for a moment, but did not need Leila's encouragement to know what he should do. He shook hands with her, not feeling that she was so unpredictable, and liked the firmness of her grip well.

Then the maid brought the fennel seeds. Before Leila put them in her mouth, the lady showed them both how to be sure that the seeds were what was expected and taught them the look and the smell of the fennel. Once Leila was chewing upon the seeds, the lady took a dried root from a small sack, the sack Bartholomew had seen her carrying from Fatima's shop. The root looked much like other roots to him, but she showed them how to distinguish its shape, then broke it to teach them its smell.

Then Bartholomew was set to work grinding the dried root as finely as he could.

It was only then he realized that Gaston's wife instructed much as the knight himself did. She was patient and spoke clearly, explaining the matter without being either condescending or overly brief.

He thought of her scheme for his future, far beyond any plan he might have had for himself. He was alone in the world, with no surviving kin or source of wealth, and had known all of his life that his future was his own to make. Could he avenge his family's deaths and regain the legacy that once would have come to his hand, if he was knighted? The prospect made Bartholomew's thoughts spin. He had never imagined that he might return home in triumph. He had never thought that the damage of the past could be undone, or that he could aspire to more than his current circumstance. He felt blessed to be alive and safe.

Indeed, only Gaston had ever shown him kindness in his life.

But it seemed that Gaston's lady wife would do the same.
And that was too great a gift to spurn.

ॐ

His lady had a scheme. Gaston was certain of it. What
concoction would she make? He gave Bartholomew's accusations
no more credit now than he had chosen to grant them in Jerusalem.
He recalled women at home requesting soured wine for some
ministration and would not ask for indelicate details. He simply
saw his wife's requests fulfilled by the time she returned from her
preparations to greet the day and was rewarded by her thanks and
her smile.

She excused herself after her fast was broken, and to his
surprise, sought out Bartholomew. He might have followed, but
Wulfe joined him then. There was much to discuss and Gaston
welcomed the liberty of doing so when the wind was so strong.

No other soul would hear them confer.

Still he watched his wife and his squire, without giving any
indication that he did as much. He knew Bartholomew sufficiently
well to see the thaw in the younger man's manner toward Ysmaine
and wondered what she had said to him.

He could not imagine, not until Bartholomew himself sought
him out later that day.

"Your lady has made a suggestion that I find most appealing,"
Bartholomew said, the light in his eyes revealing to Gaston that the
younger man was excited.

"Indeed? Will she tell me of it?"

"She said a man should not sell himself short, and so I will
not." Bartholomew squared his shoulders as Gaston watched in
wonder. "I will ask for my desire. Would you train me for
knighthood, sir?"

Gaston gasped aloud at the perfection of the idea. He was so
accustomed to viewing the world as a brother of the Temple that
he had scarce begun to think of the new opportunities available to
him. But Ysmaine was right. As a baron, he could sponsor
Bartholomew's knighting.

The younger man took his astonishment as doubt and hastened
to fill the silence. "She noted that now you have left the order and

have all the rights of a secular lord, so you can train and dub knights..."

"Indeed, I can!" Gaston interrupted his squire with delight. "And I am grateful to the lady for the reminder of my new powers. Is this your desire, then?"

"Aye." Bartholomew met Gaston's gaze. "She said I might then seek employment from you, for you would need warriors allied with you to defend your holding."

"Indeed, I will." Gaston nodded with real pleasure. "This is a fine notion. I regret only that I did not think of it sooner."

"I will train..."

"You have trained, Bartholomew. You are as worthy of being knighted as any man I know." Gaston smiled warmly at the younger man. "And truly, there is no man with such a valiant heart."

Color touched Bartholomew's neck and he swallowed, discomfited by some part of this scheme.

"What vexes you?" Gaston asked softly.

"Though it is my heart's desire to earn my spurs, I would do more than serve you in your household. I would not abandon you..."

"What is your desire, Gaston?"

"To return home. To avenge my mother and father." A determined gleam lit Bartholomew's eyes. "I never thought to have the opportunity, and now I would seize it."

Gaston frowned, recalling the dirty urchin who had insisted upon giving aid to him in Paris. "I thought you an orphan."

"I am, but I am not common born." Bartholomew smiled. "And I am not French."

Gaston regarded his squire with wonder. "All these years and I did not know your truth."

"At first I dared not confess it, for I had been hunted by the lord who stole my father's manor." Bartholomew shrugged. "And then, it seemed not to matter. I had a life with you and with the order and so I thought it would be. I knew myself to be fortunate beyond all." He lifted his gaze, his eyes shining. "But to be knighted! I can avenge my parents, perhaps even claim what is rightfully mine own." He sobered then. "But I would not be false to you, for you have been kind to me."

Gaston smiled. "And I would not deny you your heart's desire. Come with me to Châmont-sur-Maine, so I have more opportunity to grant you counsel and fortify your training. I will dub you in the chapel there."

"Thank you, Gaston."

"You seem to grant my lady wife the opportunity to win your support."

Bartholomew frowned. "She makes a liniment, one that she says will be of aid to you. I mean to test it myself first, to ensure its safety, but I think, sir, that I might have misjudged her intent that day." He met Gaston's gaze. "I think she might make you a fine wife, sir."

Gaston clapped the younger man on the shoulder, gladdened to see him finally with purpose in his life—and that thanks to Ysmaine. "Indeed, I believe she will."

ॐ

Ysmaine thought she made progress on the journey to winning the trust of Gaston's squire. She learned much from Bartholomew of her husband's past, by asking him questions while they worked together. They seemed quite naturally to establish a balance of each answering the questions of the other and alternating opportunities to ask. Ysmaine found him a likeable young man— though in truth he was older than she, he had always been subordinate and deference showed in his manner. He possessed some uncertainty and suspicion, to be sure, which was perhaps more justified by his own history than his experience of specific people.

When he confided to her that his parents had been robbed of their holding when he was young and that he had fled the villain, she understood the root of his caution in trusting others. The villain, evidently, had been a trusted friend of his father.

To Gaston, Bartholomew's loyalty was complete. Given that they had spent eighteen years in each other's company, Ysmaine took this as an endorsement of her husband's character. That Gaston had plucked the impoverished boy from the streets of Paris and become his protector was a sign of a noble nature indeed.

The squire, Laurent, whose state improved with the fennel

seeds, was so small and finely wrought that Ysmaine knew she would have mistaken him for a girl under other circumstance. He clung to one of the saddlebags from Fergus' steeds as if his very survival depended upon its protection. Though it was the simplest of Fergus' many bags and undoubtedly the least valuable, it was heavy. The boy seemed to consider that it imperative that he not fail the knight's trust in defending it.

"Its contents are likely humble indeed, my lady," Laurent confessed. "But I see its defense as a test of my merit. My lord knight does not know me so well as would be ideal, but I will prove myself."

"It smells as if it is filled with dung," Ysmaine noted and the boy smiled.

"It might well be, my lady, but I will not fail my lord Fergus."

She could not fail to admire such resolve.

It was evident to her that Bartholomew was protective of the younger and smaller squire, another trait which showed his nature well. When he told her about the other squires, she was amused by the vehemence of his commentary and was reminded of the gossip in the kitchens at home. The servants knew far more of their masters than was oft suspected, and a great deal more about each other.

Wulfe had two squires, as she had noted, the older one being taller and blonder than the other. Stephen was an orphan, which meant that Bartholomew felt a certain bond with him, though Ysmaine had noticed that Stephen was very eager to please. She wondered whether his efforts ever satisfied Wulfe, who seemed most demanding.

Wulfe's younger squire, Simon, had been donated to a monastic order as an oblate and knew little of his family history. It was unclear how he had come to serve Wulfe, for Bartholomew made it clear that the Templars accepted no children as donations. Simon was a plumper boy with curly dark hair who always seemed to be sleepy. Perhaps his parents had thought he might become a monk or lay brother, and certainly there was a complacency about him that Ysmaine could more readily associate with a contemplative life. She did not comment about boys and men who had no experience of family or the company of women. Perhaps this too prepared them well for a life within the order.

Everard traveled with no squire, which made him unworthy of the attention of Bartholomew. Laurent shared his poor opinion of the nobleman. He noted that Everard did not feed his horse well, despite his wealth, and admitted that he had secretly fed the creature better fare.

It appeared that Laurent had an affinity with horses. He spoke with great animation of the natures of the destriers in the party, the value of the palfreys, and spoke with such enthusiasm of the proper care of horses that Ysmaine was nigh overwhelmed.

Hamish was the younger squire employed by Fergus, a boy with flaming red hair and fair skin. He was heavily freckled after his time in the east, and Bartholomew confided that although his heart was good, Hamish was clumsy beyond belief.

Laurent and Kerr were Fergus' other squires, and Ysmaine saw immediately that Laurent did not like Kerr. He was blond and blue-eyed, as sweetly faced as a cherub, but there was something about him that troubled Ysmaine as well. Bartholomew confided that Kerr had a desire to know all that was afoot and did not care what he had to do to learn it.

Ysmaine thought of her own concerns and resolved to watch Kerr.

Save Bartholomew, the squires ranged in age from ten to fourteen years of age, the oldest being just slightly younger than Radegunde. Bartholomew professed that none of them would earn their spurs soon. He declared that Stephen was not sufficiently bold, Simon had not the skill with a blade, and Hamish might never hone a blade without dropping it immediately thereafter. That boy had nicked many fine blades, to the despair of his knight. Both Bartholomew and Laurent declined to comment upon Kerr's chances.

Finally, Bartholomew had ground sufficient of the root to a fine powder. The wind was not so strong this day as to steal the result of his labor away. Under the watchful gazes of the squires, Ysmaine put the ground root into the bottle of soured wine. Radegunde had been working a piece of beeswax in her fingers, letting it warm in the sun as well, and sealed the stopper into place. Ysmaine shook it well.

"That is the sum of it?" Bartholomew asked.

"It must sit now," Ysmaine said. "For the power of the herb

must eke into the liquid to make the liniment potent." She grimaced at the bottle. "My grandmother left it six weeks to cure, but she knew the source of the herb and its strength. It is best to be cautious with an herb of this power, so I will try it in a week. Even if its potency is not fully realized, it may help Gaston."

"Nay, I will try it first," Bartholomew insisted, and Ysmaine readily agreed.

"Help Gaston?" that man enquired from behind her, and Ysmaine turned to him with a smile. His gaze flicked between her, the bottle, and his squire before he met her gaze anew.

"We concoct a liniment for your hip, sir," she said easily. "Though it would not be a bad notion for you to walk less upon it when you have the opportunity."

"And here I came to invite my wife to savor the view," he said, offering his hand. Ysmaine entrusted the bottle to Radegunde then went with her husband to the rail, where he tucked her into his embrace. His body warmed her back as he braced his hands on the rail on either side of her, and her heart skipped. She felt that wondrous warmth spreading inside her, that promise of some pleasure she had not yet savored.

And when Gaston murmured in her ear, his breath against her cheek, and told her of the places they passed, Ysmaine could not imagine a finer place to be.

She should have known that happy state could not last.

≀♠

At Ragusa, some freight had been delivered and room made available in the hold. The unloading of goods simplified matters enormously. Joscelin had stowed his baggage there, and Fergus had followed suit, the two of them certain that they carried the items of greatest value.

The imposter was not convinced of that.

Gaston carried so little that it was easy to believe him recently departed from a monastic life. Bartholomew had less. Wulfe traveled with the bags that had already been searched without result, and several other smaller ones.

The man who called himself Everard also stowed his baggage, ensuring that he knew the location of all before climbing to the deck again.

It had proven to be impossible to search the baggage of the others in the party while all was stowed on the deck of the ship, or at least to do so unobserved. They were cheek-to-jowl, and there always seemed to be some person awake. As often as not it was Gaston, always watching. Indeed, it might be construed that he and Wulfe had a scheme to ensure that one or the other was always awake.

The only accomplishment made was a through inventory of that baggage, which was far from a satisfactory achievement.

All had changed with this development, however, and the imposter was impatient for an opportunity to learn more. When most of the company were asleep, he slipped into the hold, appreciating the cover of darkness. He waited for what seemed an eternity, then struck a flint and searched the baggage with quick efficiency.

He found naught of particular interest. He certainly did not find the missive that he knew must have been entrusted to the party, the one which he most wished to read. He also did not find any token that resembled the legendary Templar treasure.

Was he wrong about this party's true quest?

Did Wulfe have the missive hidden on his person? What did it say? Though truly there were greater events to recount than the imposter's own secret, it could be argued that keeping his secret was of greatest concern to him. He feared that the Templars had discerned the truth and that they would use it against them, for he did not trust them a whit. He needed to know precisely what they knew, and he needed some advantage with which to bargain.

But again he was foiled. The imposter forced himself to think.

Wulfe led the party. In Venice, he would have to somehow contrive to search the intimate possessions of Wulfe. That knight must have secured the missive in his garments or hidden it on his own person. He might even have hidden the treasure in an intimate place. That Wulfe had learned to sleep only when his squires watched over him certainly complicated the pursuit of that objective.

When the imposter heard voices, he doused his light. He realized that the squires bickered overhead, their voices carrying through the opening to the hold, which he had not fully secured.

He should have guessed that the boys would know the secrets of their knights.

"I tell you there is treasure," insisted one in a whisper. The eavesdropper listened with interest. "They were granted it from the preceptor himself and entrusted with delivering it to the Paris Temple."

"I should think not," scoffed a second boy, also in a whisper. "I could believe a missive or a token, but not a true *treasure*."

"Why not? Jerusalem will be taken. I heard Gaston say as much, and my lord Fergus agreed."

The first boy was a squire of the Scotsman, then. The eavesdropper could not believe it was the younger boy, the red-haired squire who was so clumsy. Nay, it would be the older one, the blond one who he had already guessed was a collector of secrets. There was a slyness about that boy, however pretty his features.

That trait might prove most useful.

"And what has that to do with the matter?" protested the second. His accent convinced the eavesdropper that this was the other squire of the Scotsman, the clumsy Hamish. "You do not know that the city will be attacked, let alone that it will fall. You think you know everything..."

"They carry the Templar treasure, fool! It was hidden in the Temple in Jerusalem. They could not let the Saracens claim it!"

"But the treasure is said to be magnificent and extensive. No man has seen all of it, and we are but a small party. I think you create a tale."

"We are entrusted with the best of it," the first boy whispered in excitement. "The prize jewel of the hoard, to ensure its safety."

"I think not."

"I think so! I will find it and prove as much to you!"

"If you find it, you will sell it."

The boys argued, then shushed each other. The eavesdropper considered the contents of the hold again, knowing the Templar treasure was not in baggage in the hold.

Where then?

He would watch Kerr for the rest of this journey, in case Fergus' squire discovered the prize. And as soon as possible, he would search Wulfe's person for that missive. It was less than he had hoped to achieve on this sea journey, but it would have to suffice.

Venice might offer the opportunities he sought.

≥&

Tempers were wearing thin by the time the ship sailed toward Venice. The space was cramped, the fare was poor, and the days were hot. Ysmaine's hands had turned pink and then brown, and she did not doubt her face had done the same.

In contrast to Bartholomew, who conversed with her with ever increasing animation, her husband remained taciturn and kept his secrets close. Ysmaine supposed that another woman might have accepted his nature to be as it was, but she believed he had learned this secretive behavior from the Templars. All she could do was overwhelm his doubts with her own actions.

Fortunately, Ysmaine, had an unholy measure of persistence.

Though they had stopped repeatedly, the fare had been limited, and she was not the only one who had lost weight. The companionship of the others wore thin, as did the manners of the seamen, and Ysmaine was more than ready to find her feet on solid ground again. Gaston spent much time conferring with Wulfe, perhaps comparing their memories of battles fought in Outremer, although he was gracious to her and she was aware that he kept her warm during the night.

Bartholomew had tried the liniment, as agreed. Ysmaine tried it upon her own hand first, and then upon Bartholomew, after a mere week. It warmed the skin in a most satisfactory way, but was not yet as potent as it should be. She thought it would be of sufficient strength by the time they reached Venice.

On the day after they left Ragusa, Ysmaine awakened early. Her monthly courses, which had been unpredictable of late due to poor nutrition, had begun, and she had to tend to herself. Gaston was awake, and she pointed to indicate her need for the garderobe. Radegunde snored contentedly. He gestured that he would accompany her but Ysmaine shook her head, then gave his hand a squeeze before she made her way across the deck. She felt him watching her and was glad of his protectiveness.

She would have to tell him about her bleeding and hoped he

would not be overly disappointed.

When she left the privy Gaston had contrived for them, Ysmaine paused to look up at the stars, marveling at their numbers. A shooting star drew a pale line across the firmament, and she made a wish as she watched its progress. When it faded, she made to return to Gaston and glimpsed a shadow moving against the darkness of night and sea. There was a man near the entry to the hold, she was certain of it.

She could not spy him again and wondered whether her eyes had deceived him. Gaston welcomed her back against his side and wrapped her cloak around her. "Are you well?" he murmured, his voice a low rumble that gave her shivers.

"I have my courses," she confessed. "So, we have not yet wrought a child."

He ran his fingertips down her cheek and cupped her chin. "I cannot be so surprised, for we have met abed only the once." He sighed. "And this way, none can doubt that any child you bear is of my seed."

Ysmaine blinked. "Who would doubt our word?"

He grimaced. "Who can say? It is better to avoid any such questions." He nuzzled her ear, kissing her there in a way that sent shivers over her flesh. "And I cannot regret that we must try yet more."

Ysmaine curled in Gaston's lap, once again assaulted by that pleasurable sensation, the one that promised so much more. She tucked her feet up and felt his enthusiasm, then surrendered to a most satisfactory kiss. Her heart was thundering when Gaston lifted his head and he inhaled sharply even as his arms tightened around her.

"Do not tempt me so soon as this, lady mine," he murmured and his voice was most deliciously rough. "You shall have a chamber to call your own soon enough."

Ysmaine could not wait.

Wednesday, July 22, 1187

Feast Day of Saint Mary Magdalene and Saint Agnes.

❧

Claire Delacroix

Chapter Twelve

At morning's light, it was revealed that some argument had erupted between the squires, and Laurent had clearly been found wanting. Ysmaine had fallen back asleep, but she awakened to the sounds of a scuffle and the sight of Gaston trying to intervene. In the end, Kerr had a black eye, and Bartholomew won a scolding from Gaston so severe that his ears were red with mortification even when they sailed into port.

Hamish was missing, which was cause for some alarm, until the boy was discovered in the hold. He had been struck on the head and was not coherent, the size of the lump making Ysmaine insist that an apothecary be found as soon as they reached the port. The bags stowed there had been investigated, it proved, a revelation that prompted consternation in both Fergus and Joscelin. Ysmaine saw Gaston's eyes narrow at this.

Ysmaine noted that the dirtiest of the Fergus' saddlebags was yet in the custody of Laurent. Though he had jested about its defense being a test, she began to wonder. As far as she could recall, the boy had had that bag in his possession since they had left Jerusalem. He dragged or carried it everywhere, though it was clearly heavy.

What was in it?

Ysmaine had thought the boy's manner a case of devotion but now she wondered. It seemed that every soul in their party had discovered that their baggage had been examined without their knowledge. Ysmaine thought of the missive Gaston carried and wondered whether it was the sought prize, or whether the party had been entrusted with the delivery of more than a letter.

She did not believe that a mere piece of correspondence could encourage such persistent searching of their baggage. There was something else entrusted to the party, something Gaston knew about and for all his insistence upon honesty, refused to tell her about.

The Templars, after all, were said to hold a magnificent treasure in the Temple of Jerusalem. If they had guessed Saladin's intent, might they have wanted to ensure its safety? If she had a prize to see taken safely back to Paris, Ysmaine would have chosen Gaston for the quest.

If she was right, where might that prize be?

By her reckoning, there was only one bag that had not been searched.

But what might the Templar treasure be? The rumors she had heard were wild and varied, from heaps of gold, to mysterious tokens that could summon deities or invoke wealth upon any man. Fergus' bag was not small, but not so large that he could have been carrying a king's ransom in jewels and gold.

It was time Ysmaine discovered the truth.

After all, some soul sought to discover it, and if they succeeded, Gaston would be disgraced. She could not let her husband fail in his last, albeit secret, mission for the order.

She had to look within that bag.

៛

In the end, Ysmaine's search was contrived more readily than she might have expected. They docked in the harbor and there was much disarray as the horses were unloaded along with the rest of the party.

Then the party scattered. Bartholomew was dispatched to find accommodation for them all, while Fergus took Hamish to an apothecary. By midday, they were all installed in a small house with a pleasant courtyard, far enough away from the port to be quiet. The landlady was retained to cook for them, but she would not lay the board for dinner until the sun had set. They shared a simple meal of bread, ham, cheese and wine, the fare more than welcome after the lack of variety on the ship. It was hot already, the sunlight bright in the courtyard and more than one member of the party began to yawn.

Gaston saw the portal locked and granted the keys to Ysmaine, then took Bartholomew with him to seek out provisions for the

The Crusader's Bride

instructions that the boy not ride a horse for at least three days.
After a brief argument, Wulfe threw up his hands and left the
house in what was clearly poor temper, Stephen and Simon
running behind him.

Ysmaine guessed that he would have preferred to ride out
more quickly than that.

Everard declared himself exhausted and retired to sleep until
the next morning. Joscelin left their abode to visit some fellow
merchants in town who were friends he saw seldom. Fergus looked
to be as tired as Everard, so Ysmaine suggested he sleep until the
meal, as well. He readily agreed.

The courtyard beyond the common room must have once been
larger, but the greater part of it had been roofed. There were stalls
for the horses, though the end adjacent to the courtyard was open,
granting a view into the shadowed shelter. Ysmaine could even see
Laurent dozing atop his precious burden in the back corner. Kerr
followed Fergus up the stairs, while Hamish slept, purportedly
under Ysmaine's watchful eye.

The house fell quiet and filled with the sounds of slumber. The
landlady's activity in the kitchens could be heard at a distance, as
could the bells from the church towers. The horses stamped, as if
reassuring themselves that their hooves were on solid ground, and
gradually, Laurent fell into a deep sleep. The boy slumped over the
bag, his grip lax, then slid away from it to collapse on the floor. He
was not roused, even by this movement.

Ysmaine's heart squeezed. The poor boy must be exhausted.

But his condition created the opportunity she sought. She
roused Radegunde and insisted in a whisper that the girl watch for
any arrival, as well as tending to Hamish. She then crossed the
courtyard silently, her heart in her throat.

Gaston had declared his intention to take her to the markets
this very day.

There might not be much time.

❧

The imposter could not believe his good fortune. He turned his
cloak inside out and pulled the hood over his face, then followed

Wulfe and the squires at a distance. The knight strode through the streets of Venice with purpose and some annoyance. Irritation made him careless and confident, for he glanced back only once.

He spoke to many in the market, his Venetian so fluent that even when the imposter caught a few words, he could not understand.

When Wulfe rapped at the portal of a house, the imposter ducked into a doorway farther down the street to watch. There could be no doubt of the occupation of the woman who opened the door, nor the role that of the large male slave who stood by her side. That man looked up and down the street with suspicion, then folded his arms across his chest to glare at Wulfe.

Undaunted, Wulfe spoke to the woman.

He disappeared inside the house with the boys following, the slave surveying the street once more before following them.

The imposter smiled. Wulfe went to a courtesan. He would be both naked and occupied. Here was the opportunity the imposter needed most.

And if his search went awry, any violence would be readily explained by the location where it had occurred. He strode away, confident he could find the location again, and sought a disguise.

He would return later, when Wulfe was perhaps drunk and certainly abed.

❧

Ysmaine went directly to the bag so carefully guarded by Laurent. She stood beside the boy for a long moment, ensuring that Laurent continued to sleep. As she waited, she studied the way the bag was bound, knowing she would have to make it look exactly as it was to avoid detection.

It seemed that growing up with a number of sisters, each of whom was curious beyond compare, was good preparation for her task. She gave Laurent a minute nudge and the boy curled up in a ball to sleep, increasing the distance between himself and his precious burden.

Ysmaine did not linger. She untied the bundle with rapid fingers, then found something heavy within. It was large and hard, about the size of two hand spans in every direction. She ran her hands over the bundled shape, trying to guess its contents.

It was a box of some kind, for it had hard corners, and a box heavily wrapped. Was it fragile? Precious? Ysmaine again observed the pattern of the protective cloth, then unbound its contents.

The smell brought a tear to her eye, and she realized she would have to ensure that the cloth did not touch her own garments. Her breath caught in her throat at first glimpse of a large round gem mounted in gold, and she was glad to be in the darkness of the stables. That gem, a huge amethyst sphere was mounted in gold and affixed to the side of the box. She pushed aside the cloth to see that beside it was another gem of green and a row of large pearls.

Indeed, it *was* a box, wrought of gold and studded with gems. It was a treasure to be sure and one of a value unimaginable. Ysmaine concluded as much before she saw the inscription and realized its material value was but a fraction of its spiritual worth.

St. Euphemia.

She stared in awe. This fine box was a reliquary, containing the sacred bones of a saint. Ysmaine had heard that the Temple in Jerusalem held the relics of St. Euphemia, specifically the saint's head, but it had been but one of a thousand stories circulated about the mysteries of the order's possessions.

That she should touch such a treasure was beyond all expectation.

Ysmaine held the reliquary in her hands, only half unwrapped, and considered the shape of it, so like a small chapel. She closed her eyes and was sure she could feel the sanctity of the martyr seeping into her palms, suffusing her, healing her body and soul.

This was the prize their party defended.

And what a treasure it was!

Ysmaine thought of the baggage being explored and knew this was the reason why. Someone was prepared to steal this prize! Laurent stirred, and Ysmaine knew she dared not linger. She wrapped the reliquary again exactly as it had been, her hands shaking in her haste.

The safe delivery of this treasure was Gaston's secret mission.

And if he failed, there would be a price exacted from her new husband, to be sure. Whether it would be by the order of the Templars or by divine force, it mattered little.

Ysmaine had to figure out a way to help Gaston, to protect this prize and ensure its safe delivery to its destination. She bound the bag as it had been before and replaced it within Fergus' belongings, just as it had been. Laurent moved in his sleep, a frown marring his brow, and Ysmaine coaxed his hand to the saddlebag. The boy drew it closer, almost embracing it, and sighed with relief in his sleep.

Did he know what he protected?

Or only that Fergus had asked it of him?

Ysmaine surveyed the bag, ensuring it was exactly as she had found it, then spun at the sound of a woman's laughter. She drew back into the shadows as Radegunde laughed again at something Everard said to her. He left the common room to step into the courtyard, stretching and then drawing a cup of water from the well.

Ysmaine's heart pounded as he scanned the opening to the stables and she wondered whether she had been seen. She moved to the back of the stables and behind the horses, then strode into the last of the sunlight and feigned surprise at the sight of the knight.

"Sir! I thought you meant to sleep all the night long!" she said, as if jesting with him.

He laughed. "I have been, but am much restored. This cursed thirst will not be sated." Everard lifted his cup to her in salute. "And you?" His gaze flicked to the stables and back to her. "Surely you do not undertake the duties of a groom?" The notion seemed to amuse him.

Ysmaine laughed lightly. "Not I! Gaston summoned Bartholomew with such haste that I wanted to ensure the steeds had sufficient water. Of course, I should not have doubted that he would accomplish all before he departed with Gaston." She lifted her hands and made a face. "And now I must wash myself in truth."

The knight smiled and finished his water. Ysmaine curtseyed and returned to the common room, her heart pounding even though she was certain she had evaded detection.

Now, she simply had need of a plan to ensure Gaston's success.

❧

Ysmaine had a vague recollection that the markets of Venice were fine, but she had been without coin when last she had passed through the city and had scarce glanced at the wares. Indeed, she and Radegunde had not spent much time in the fabled city, but had secured passage on a ship as quickly as possible. It had been food that had tempted her most, she recalled.

They were to remain a few days, though, so that Hamish could recover from his blow, and Gaston, it was revealed, was determined that she should refurbish her wardrobe.

"You are my lady wife," he said firmly when she protested at this extravagance. "Your garb was once fine but has faded and worn. I would have you look your best when we arrive at Châmont-sur-Maine."

And so it was that they visited the markets together that first day, Radegunde's eyes round with wonder as she trailed behind the pair. Ysmaine waited for her husband to make the first choice, for she did not know his finances well enough.

"This hue would suit you well," he said, fingering a length of cloth the color of peridots.

"It is silk, sir, and most expensive."

"Fit for a lady," he countered with a smile.

"Wool," Ysmaine said flatly. "Wool endures best of all."

"Then wool as well," he said easily.

Ysmaine turned him into a corner, and he smiled down at her. "Sir, you must tell me of your expectations in this. I would not spend overmuch, and I suspect I shall have to bargain hard. If I know the sum and the tally, I can choose one merchant and make a better wager for all."

He nodded, seemingly impressed by this logic. "By my reckoning, you need garb for travel—a cloak, a wool kirtle, and new boots."

"This cloak will service for traveling," she replied.

"If we dine with a nobleman en route, you will need garb for that, though I know not what other feminine fripperies you might require."

Ysmaine made an inventory on her fingertips. "Boots, slippers, two pairs of stockings—one warm and one fine—two chemises—

similarly one sturdy and one fine—a plain wool kirtle and a finer bliaut. Radegunde and I will do whatever embroidery is desired. One veil will suffice, as will my plain circlet and the belt I already possess." She bit her lip. "I should like a pair of gloves for riding, as it will become colder in the mountains."

"So little as that?" Gaston asked. "What of gems and other finery?"

She met his gaze, wondering what answer would best please him. "I have become unaccustomed to such finery, sir." She smiled a little. "My mother always said it was unfitting for a woman to be lavish with her own wardrobe, though she always welcomed my father's gifts."

Gaston nodded with satisfaction. "Then I insist that you add the green silk as a third garment, lady mine, and please acquire whatever is necessary to see its hems as lavish as the hems once were on the gown you wear this day."

Ysmaine could not believe her good fortune. To have so many clothes, although far from the extent of the wardrobe she had once possessed, seemed a blessing indeed after years of wearing the same threadbare garment. She was determined that Gaston generosity should not come at too high of a price, so she visited the larger merchants each in turn. Her husband followed, listening.

And when she had bargained for all she desired, and struck the best price she could, he pressed the silver into her hand with evident satisfaction.

"I shall let you negotiate for all our acquisitions, lady mine," he murmured in her ear. "For you are most resolute in gaining your objective at a good price."

❧

Gaston climbed the stairs to the chamber he had secured for his lady, anticipation giving new haste to his step. It seemed an eternity since he had enjoyed his wife's companionship abed, yet he had been in her presence nigh every moment since. He knew the scent of her skin and was entranced by the flash of her eyes. He knew better how to prompt her smile and even what was mostly likely to vex her.

He had accompanied her on her expedition to shop on this day, her delight giving him such pleasure that he had been more indulgent than any who knew him well might have expected. Gaston was fascinated by his lady wife, and he did not care who knew it.

He was more than ready to embark upon the challenge of making that son.

He tapped at her door before opening it, and the maid bowed low before she swept past him and left the chamber. It was a room of reasonable proportions, with a large window overlooking the courtyard and a finely carved ceiling. It was three floors from the ground, neither at the summit of the building where his lady could be accosted from the roof, nor so close to the street that any villain could climb through the window. The courtyard contained a fountain, and its gate was locked as well. Gaston was convinced that his wife could sleep safely in this place.

She did not need to know that he had examined every possible choice before making his selection. It was his responsibility to ensure her security, after all.

Her hair was unbound already, and he guessed that the maid had been combing it out. Again, he was struck that it looked like spun gold, and he marveled that its length fell to her waist. Its waves snared the candlelight, just as its length would snare his fingers. She wore only her chemise, and he could discern the shadows of her curves beneath the sheer cloth. This garment was made of fine linen, a purchase newly made this day, and he was glad to see her more finely garbed. When the garments she had ordered this day were complete, she would be as resplendent as a queen.

His queen.

His pride in this was curious, for he had never anticipated that he would wed. Even so early in their match as this, Gaston could not imagine being without Ysmaine.

Her feet were bare, looking pale and elegant against the stone floor. The tie of the chemise was loose at her neck and he could see the delicate hollow of her throat. She glanced up at him, those green eyes alight with a pleasure that humbled him. Indeed, he paused on the threshold, awed that this lovely creature was his wife.

"Do you change your thinking, sir?" she teased, a twinkle

Claire Delacroix

lighting her eye. "Was I wrong in believing that you still desired me?"

"Of course I do." Gaston swallowed, feeling his lack of courtly charm most keenly in this moment. "I but appreciate how fair you are."

He meant to grant a compliment, but knew he did so poorly. All the same, Ysmaine's smile broadened. She put down the small bottle she had been holding and came toward him, reaching to unfasten the buckle of his belt.

"You are limping again," she noted, even as Gaston brushed away her busy fingers.

He unfastened the clasp himself and laid aside his belt, ensuring that his weapons were set down with care. "That is of no import. It is always thus when I walk."

"Because you walk too much, without ensuring that you rest."

"A man must walk as far as necessary." Gaston shed his tabard and his coif.

"A wise man ensures his injuries heal before he worsens them."

Gaston glanced up at that, but Ysmaine held his gaze for a telling moment. Did she chide him? She reached for the hem of his mail hauberk, but he retreated. "You should not act as my squire."

"But I will," she replied with a determination he now recognized. "For I will not couple with you when you are armed. That is the place of a whore, not a wife."

Gaston was appalled. "I would not..."

"I know and I am glad of it." She tugged and Gaston bent, accepting her aid in shedding the hauberk. As ever, he straightened and rolled his shoulders once relieved of its weight, but this time, was aware of his wife's assessing gaze upon him.

He shed his boots and chausses, folding the chausses and standing the boots with care beside his armor.

Ysmaine crossed the chamber and picked up the bottle once again. She held it before herself. "I would have you lie on the pallet, sir."

Gaston balked. Lie down, without his weapons, when he was nigh naked? It defied his every instinct—yet Ysmaine's eyes shone with challenge. She had anticipated his reaction, which meant there was no cause to pretend. "That would be the herb you acquired

186

from Fatima."

"When did Bartholomew tell you of this?"

"That very day, but I gave the tale little credence."

"Why?"

"Because you had no coin, and I did not believe that Fatima did not part with any of her cures without payment." Gaston watched his wife's features harden and assumed she had misinterpreted his words. "It is only good sense, for she has a skill," he added, his tone conciliatory. "She should not devalue it by sharing her wisdom without any exchange."

He knew immediately that he had erred.

"It would have been better if you had told your squire that your betrothed was trustworthy," Ysmaine said softly.

"But I did not know as much at the time," Gaston protested and saw that he had only compounded his error.

"Do you know that now?" Ysmaine asked.

Gaston licked his lips. "I wished to see what you would do with it."

"As with the coin."

"Indeed."

She lifted the bottle. "I wrought this. For you. For your hip. I showed Bartholomew how to make this liniment, and he insisted that I use it first upon him."

"I know."

"Yet still you doubt my intent."

There were a hundred ways the contents of the bottle could have been altered or even substituted since Bartholomew's insistence upon trying it. There were poisons that worked their evil slowly and over time. There were stories of his lady burying husbands. He knew little of her, in truth, and it was not in Gaston's nature to trust easily—particularly women, for he knew so little of them as to find them incomprehensible.

But this he understood. His lady wished evidence that he trusted her, and his choice in this moment would color much of their future together. Gaston knew what he had to do, though his instincts urged against it.

He regarded the bottle, then met his lady's gaze. "We as yet know little of each other, lady mine, but I would put my trust in you."

"Prove as much," she said quietly.

Gaston arched a brow in silent query.

Ysmaine looked at the pallet.

Naked and unarmed. At her mercy. A bead of cold sweat slid down Gaston's back. The very notion defied his every instinct.

But he understood that his marriage could be condemned forever in this moment. The match was consummated. They were bound to each other until death. Gaston deliberately recalled Ysmaine's assertion that a live husband suited her better than a dead one and nodded once curtly.

His decision made, he stretched out on the pallet. To his relief, Ysmaine's smile was not just brilliant but genuine.

"Oh, Gaston," she said as she dropped to her knees beside him. She appeared to be overwhelmed by relief, a sign that she understood his tumult. "Truly, you give me a great gift in this choice."

To Gaston's amazement, Ysmaine bent over him and brushed her lips across his own. That fleeting kiss lit a fire within him, one that he suspected could only be quenched by his lady.

For once, it seemed he did not err in this lady's presence.

He caught her nape in his hand and pulled her closer, deepening their kiss, even as he resolved to make a habit of seeing her pleased. There could be no greater reward than the marvel in her eyes when she looked upon him thus, except perhaps the sweet ardor of her kiss.

Chapter Thirteen

Ysmaine finally straightened and tugged up the hem of Gaston's chemise, intent upon the task she had assigned herself. He feared that all would be undone in this moment, for she was a noblewoman and undoubtedly had been gently reared. He was a warrior and his body revealed the truth of it.

She eyed his hip, the scar from the mail being pounded into the skin still visible, but did not recoil.

Indeed, she considered it without flinching. "Your mail broke the skin," she guessed.

"Indeed."

She pushed up the chemise, baring more of him to her view, and he forced himself to remain still, to let her look. Her gaze roved over him and she flushed. She straightened and he feared her rejection, but then her smile suddenly turned impish. "You are well wrought, husband," she whispered and brushed her fingertips down his chest, then the length of his thigh.

Naught could have fired Gaston more than that fleeting touch.

She shook whatever was in the bottle, then set it on the floor. She loosed the stopper, then poured some of the contents into her cupped palm. "Good. It warms," she said, almost to herself, then cast him a sparkling glance. "Bartholomew was most impressed, if that eases your torment."

Gaston might have replied, but she spread the substance on his hip. He gasped at the immediate sensation of heat that flowed through his skin. *Was* it poison? Surely a lotion that created such a pleasurable sensation could not do ill. The heat penetrated his muscle, seeming to touch the very bone, and for the first time in a long time, the pain in that joint faded. The relief was almost unbearable.

Gaston chose to trust his wife and closed his eyes.

He was surprised when she began to speak to him, her words soft and low, even as her hands worked the unguent into his skin. "My grandfather was a warrior and a hunter, a vigorous man who lived long and well. He was robust beyond all and had a taste for every pleasure. I think he lived each day of his life to the fullest and as a child, he fascinated me. He taught me to ride. He showed me how to shoot a crossbow, though my father disapproved of that. He never thought that I was less because I was first born but a daughter rather than a son."

"You said you had sisters."

"Six of them, one lost in infancy, but my grandfather shared his expertise with me." Gaston glanced through his lashes to see her smile. "I remember his laugh, as if it had echoed at the board this very night." She flicked a sparkling glance at Gaston. "My grandmother adored him, perhaps only slightly more than me."

Gaston chuckled at that. It was a marvel to share this intimacy with her, to listen to her tale and feel her hands upon him. He decided in that moment that married life would suit him very well.

"They had been wedded when she was widowed at twenty-five summers. My grandfather had seen forty summers then, but had never wed. He said he spied her across a crowded hall and knew she was the woman he had awaited all his life."

Gaston watched Ysmaine, intrigued both by the story and by her obvious affection for it. The unguent put a languid heat in his body, making him feel at ease as he seldom did. "I understand the sentiment well," he dared to say and his lady smiled with pleasure.

"They were happy together, I believe, and savored many years of ease." Ysmaine sobered. "And so it came one autumn that my grandmother began to cough. She knew much of herbs and of healing, though by that time, she had taught me little of it. She said it was better for a noblewoman to observe than to fix potions, that such labor should be left to the wise women like Mathilde. But that October, she entrusted me with the greatest secret of all. She taught me how to make this liniment."

When she fell silent, Gaston had to ask. "Of the herb Fatima declared to be poison."

"It *is* poison," Ysmaine said and Gaston caught his breath. "It should never be consumed or applied to an open wound." She rubbed his hip more deliberately. "But the same trait that gives it the power to kill also ensures it can ease an injury if applied to unbroken skin. It creates a quickening in all it touches, which summons a heat. My grandmother made it for my grandfather, and she knew that in February, when the wind blows cold and damp, he would ache from his old wounds. That autumn, she knew that she would not be able to tend him in all the Februaries to come, and so she taught me the cure." Ysmaine blinked and Gaston saw the tears on her lashes. "She died on Christmas night and my grandfather, whom I had never seen shed a tear, wept through Epiphany."

Gaston could only watch his wife, a lump in his throat.

After a moment, she squared her shoulders and continued her tale. "In that February, the damp winds came. I saw that my grandfather began to wince when he moved. I had mixed this on my own for the first time after Epiphany, feeling that my grandmother was at my shoulder, for she had insisted it cure for at least six weeks. I did not wish to fail her trust."

"And I wager you did not."

Ysmaine shook her head. "My grandfather was nigh overwhelmed by this unexpected gift, and so it was that I would rub this into his shoulder each time before he retired. He told me stories, stories of war and of the hunt, and of the way he had gained this injury. Years before he hunted a devious wolf that had plagued the occupants of his holding, the holding I knew as home. He told me of responsibility and of sacrifice and of determination to see an end achieved."

"You learned much from him, then," Gaston dared to say.

Ysmaine nodded. "And so it was when I saw you limp that first day, I guessed that you had a similar injury, one that had not healed, one that perhaps would never fully heal." Her gaze met his. "Here is the honesty you ask of me, husband. You speak aright that Fatima does not grant cures for no payment, but not all payment is hard coin. She knew this herb only as a poison, for that was what she was told of it. She had several times traded for cures with pilgrims and had a small collection of roots that she did not have the knowledge to use."

Understanding dawned for Gaston.

"I recognized the one I sought in that collection and shared my grandmother's instruction. In exchange for the knowledge, Fatima

divided the quantity of root in her possession between us."
Ysmaine lifted her gaze. "And so you see, husband, I had
something with which to wager other than silver."

"I confess I did not think of it. I thought your skill in healing
lay in observation."

"And so it does, save for this one liniment."

"What is the herb?"

"It has many names. The ancients called it aconite and said it
grew on the hill where the hero Hercules fought Cerberus..."

"The three-headed dog that guarded the gates of Hades,"
Gaston supplied, and she smiled.

"Indeed. In the exertion of that struggle, the saliva from the
dog's mouth fell upon the plant, turning it to a deadly poison."
Ysmaine nodded, her finger kneading his skin with marvelous
force. He wished she would never halt. "My grandmother knew all
the tales of it. It was said that Medea killed Theseus with aconite
and also rumored that certain women, fed small doses of the herb
daily from childhood, could kill a man with sexual congress."

It was not the most reassuring detail she could have provided,
given the reason that Gaston had come to her chamber. He
reminded himself that his trust was granted to his lady wife.

"My grandfather, when I tended to his shoulder, told me that
they had used it on the tips of arrows when they hunted wolves to
ensure that any blow was fatal. That is why another name for it is
wolf's bane."

"Would the poison not taint the meat?"

"Aye, he said as much, but my grandfather refused to let even
his dogs consume wolf. He had their carcasses burned, for he
believed them to be vermin."

"My father shared that view, but then, there were days within
his memory when wolves ravaged our corner of Christendom."

Ysmaine nodded. "My grandmother said also that my
grandfather had told her of invading armies tainting the water of
those territories they pillaged by putting wolf's bane into cisterns
and wells."

"Like sowing fields with salt," Gaston said. "I do not know of
the herbs used, but the strategy is a well established, if
reprehensible, one."

"Because it punishes those who work, not those who fight."

Gaston nodded agreement.

"My grandfather considered such men to be vermin, as well. He said it was sufficient to defeat an enemy, that there was no reason to condemn the people who worked the land to starvation for years in the future."

"He taught you about mercy and justice, then, too."

Ysmaine smiled and lifted her hands from his flesh. "He found it appropriate that the same poison he had used to kill that wolf gave him relief from the injury he had sustained in that hunt. He said it made a fitting tale." She considered him, her expression stern, and he knew she would chastise him. "Fatima said you did not give your injury sufficient time to heal."

Gaston smiled, liking his lady's protectiveness well. "It has not been my luxury to languish abed, lady mine."

A smile curved her lips. "You sound like my grandfather. He said a warrior of merit wears his experience on his hide."

Gaston found himself agreeing with that sentiment, for he had more than a few scars himself.

Her voice softened. "He said that a man who rides to war and returns unscathed is a coward, for any man who raises his blade with integrity will be injured unless he flees the fight."

Gaston found his wife's gaze locked upon him. This then, was why she did not recoil from the marks she had seen on his body.

Her gaze locked with his. "I believe he would approve of you, husband."

He found himself smiling, for he recognized the import of her words and like it well. "It seems I must be flattered that you make the comparison."

She nodded and continued to work the liniment into his skin. Gaston watched her as she fixed her attention upon her ministrations and knew he had to make another choice to see their match made.

Ysmaine trusted him with tales of her past, the words flowing more readily from her lips than ever they would from his own.

But he had to try. Gaston frowned slightly and chose to surrender part of his own history to his lady wife. He might not be able to offer the partnership she believed marriage should be, but he could make a step in that direction.

It might, after all, make all the difference in the world to her if he confided in her.

èa

Gaston cleared his throat. "Your grandfather spoke aright that a warrior wears his experience on his hide."

Ysmaine glanced to his face but Gaston did not falter.

"I was thrown in the battle at Montisgard, almost ten years ago." Once the first confession was made, it was easier to continue with the tale. "Odo de St. Amand was master of the Temple then, and he led us behind the banner of the King of Jerusalem, Baldwin IV, to battle Saladin at Ascalon." He had thought she might be bored, but she watched him avidly.

"How were you hurt?"

"Fantôme was young then, and not so accustomed to warfare. He shied in the midst of the fighting, for there was much blood and carnage."

Ysmaine shook her head, her golden hair catching the light. "Steeds do not like blood. I know this well."

"Or open flames," Gaston acknowledged, liking that she was so practical. "He had been well-trained, but the battle was uncommonly brutal. He stepped on a corpse, his hoof going clear through the body, and lost his wits."

Ysmaine grimaced in sympathy. "As might I. And you?"

"Cast so hard to the ground that I heard a crack, but there was no time to cede to it. I had to rise fighting, or I would not have had the opportunity to rise again."

"And so you endured the pain and compounded the injury," Ysmaine said. Gaston had to concede the truth in that. "But the king was triumphant on that day, due to the valor of you and others." Ysmaine smiled. "I remember hearing of that battle."

"Aye, he did triumph. Although outnumbered and very ill himself, he prayed before a fragment of the True Cross and led the army. It must be said that Saladin underestimated his foe, and his forces were spread too wide." Gaston nodded, his mind filled with the memory. "It was not an easy victory, and one made against formidable odds."

Ysmaine bit her lip. "Which is perhaps why this king believed he could win against Saladin, as well."

Gaston nodded. "Aye, but he was not the sole one who recalled the past, it would seem."

Ysmaine worked his muscles as he watched her. Her hair had slipped over her shoulder and hung toward him, like a curtain of gold. "This is the first time you have told me a tale of yourself, husband," she said softly, the glow in her eyes making it clear how this pleased her.

He was glad he had chosen aright.

"I wish I had finer tales to tell," Gaston admitted and reached for that tendril of hair. He wound it around his finger, marveling at its softness, and her lips curved in a smile that he found most alluring. He gave that tendril a tug, feeling uncharacteristically playful, and the lady leaned down to kiss him sweetly.

"Roll to your side, please, sir," she bade him when she lifted her lips from his. Gaston hoped she did not know that he would have followed any command she granted to him in this moment of moments. Rolling to his side was no feat at all. He felt her knees against his back, and again, the warmth of the liniment on his skin. He closed his eyes as she rubbed toward the middle of his back, easing a tension that he was so accustomed to enduring that he had nigh forgotten it.

Until Ysmaine's fingers eased it away, and he felt as hale as a pup.

"My grandfather shared few tales, as well, but he told me the full tale of the wolf not long before he died. I had asked for more detail many times, but he had declined. That winter night, though, I was rubbing the liniment into his skin and he noted that he had gained his injury on a night much like the one beyond the windows. After my grandmother's demise, his thoughts turned more frequently to the past, though on this night, he was confiding in me." She seemed pensive, and Gaston twisted so that he could see her face. "He was a scarred man, for all that he was handsome."

"A valiant warrior, then, by his own reckoning," Gaston teased and she smiled.

"Hair as white as snow, vigor in his body even at seventy summers and eyes so clear that my grandmother said they might have been gems."

"Green eyes?" Gaston guessed, unable to look away from the

lady's own fine eyes.

She smiled and flushed a little. "Aye. Mine are said to be like his."

He nodded. "They are magnificent."

His compliment seemed to fluster her and she dropped her gaze, her voice husky as she continued. "There was a deep scar on his cheek, which tugged at the corner of his eye." She indicated on her own face without touching her skin, lest she spread the unguent there. Her fingertip swept a line through the air from the corner of her eye to the middle of her chin. "I had never dared to ask after it, of course, though one of my sisters had once done so and been scolded by our mother. He told me that night, when the wind was whistling through the chinks and the snow was being hurled against the walls, that it had been the wolf who had left this mark upon him."

"On his very face?" Gaston asked. "He had been that close?"

Ysmaine nodded. "He said he had ridden to hunt the wolf that night, and that he had gone alone because of the foul weather. He said he had been too furious to show a care for his own welfare, for the wolf had taken a ewe and a lamb the night before, and done so from within the enclosure of the village. He said it grew too bold in its hunger and had to be stopped. He had his crossbow and arrows each tipped in wolf's bane, and so too had he embellished the blade of his dagger. He said the night was wild, filled with swirling white and that the forest seemed a maze of deceptive shadows. The wolf's pelt had blended into the forest as he feared he did not."

She swallowed. "And the wolf led him a merry chase. He pursued the beast with vigor, firing arrows when he could. He missed so often that he began to think the creature was enchanted, but with his last arrow, he heard a cry of pain. He found the blood in the snow and followed the trail, knowing the wolf would not fight the poison long. The wolf was vigorous, though, large and recently fed, and perhaps as cunning as my grandfather had believed it to be. It hid in the forest, doubling back upon its trail, then leapt upon him when he did not expect such an attack." Gaston caught his breath. "The horse shied in terror then threw my grandfather. The stallion fled for home and the safety of the stables, leaving my grandfather alone in the woods."

"With a wolf determined to have its due."

She nodded. "He had landed upon his shoulder and, like you, heard a bone crack. The wolf was upon him even before the sound of the horse's hoof beats had faded. It bit and tore at him, as big as a man and filled with terrifying power. My grandfather struck it in the face with all his might and it fell back snarling for only a moment, but long enough that he could draw his blade. When it leapt upon him again, he let it assail him. It bit at his face, and he said he would never forget the look of that open maw, the display of those sharp teeth, or the feel of his blade sinking into its gut." She swallowed. "He cut it from gullet to groin, then kicked it aside, watching to be sure it died. He was covered with blood, both his own and that of the wolf, shaking and alone in the forest. The snow fell quietly as the wolf's last breath left its body." She swallowed. "He skinned that one, and the cured pelt graced my grandmother's bed."

"He admired it," Gaston wagered. "It was a worthy opponent."

She shrugged, then he watched her gaze filled with resolve. "He told me that defeat comes to those who believe themselves lost. He told me that he had a choice that night, to surrender to the wolf and abandon those who trusted him to defend them, or to fight until he could fight no more, regardless of the cost. It took him months to heal from that battle, and truly it could be argued that he never did fully recover. He told me that he survived because he refused to do otherwise."

Gaston nodded understanding, knowing that this lesson was what had kept the steel in his lady's spine, despite all that had befallen her in recent years. He smiled at her and shifted his weight to his back again. He stretched, savoring the relief she had given to him. "This liniment of yours is most fine," he said and her eyes sparkled at his praise. "I thank you for preparing it and acquiring the herb."

"I thank you for trusting me enough to let me apply it."

"Again, lady mine, you not only prove suspicion unfounded but show your worth." His words pleased her mightily, it was clear.

"It should be done each night, at least for a few nights."

"Have you need of more of the root?"

"Nay, not as yet." Ysmaine frowned.

"Tell me what troubles you," he urged.

"It is not that I would hide a truth from you, sir, but more that I would not make an accusation unfounded."

"What accusation?"

"It is the most curious thing. I was certain Fatima had entrusted me with more than was in the sack when I opened it on the ship." Ysmaine shook her head. "Perhaps, though, I simply recalled the quantity wrongly. There was much afoot that morning in Jerusalem."

Gaston felt his eyes narrow. "Does anyone know you possess it?"

"Radegunde knew from the first, of course, for she carried it for me." Ysmaine sobered. "In fact, all in the party know of it, for Bartholomew made his accusation of me in Acre, when we believed you were lost."

Those were no good tidings, if she was correct about the missing root.

Gaston leaned upon his elbow. "And if someone consumes it, what symptoms would be shown?"

Ysmaine bit her lip. "It should never be eaten. It causes the same heat as on the skin, but inside, and much havoc follows. The heart leaps and the skin flushes. The body tries to void it, with vomiting or flux. Breath and pulse race, perspiration ensues, and oft numbness follows the heat. The person may see what is not there when its fire touches the mind."

"And death?"

"Quick, especially with large doses. The sole action is to assist in the vomiting of it."

This was no good news. Gaston hoped his lady wife was mistaken about the quantity of herb.

Ysmaine leaned closer. "Is it true that someone has pillaged the bags of all in the party? I know Wulfe and Everard complained of that at Samaria, but Joscelin was concerned about the same matter this very day."

Gaston's gaze flew to hers, for his bags had been investigated the night before. "Have you had this trouble?"

Ysmaine smiled. "I have few belongings, sir, and naught that any thief would find of interest."

Save the herb.

Gaston sat up, filled with new purpose. He dared not savor his lady's company and her charms overmuch as yet. He had to remain vigilant until the treasure safely reached its destination. The enticement that his lady offered, to linger and converse with her, would have to wait until they were safely returned to Châmont-sur-Maine.

On this night, he had to watch the stables, for another set of eyes upon the bag defended by Laurent would be best. "I thank you for this aid, lady mine, but I came to you to beget that son and the hour grows most late."

If she was dismayed by the change in his manner, she hid it well. Gaston saw only a quick flash of those eyes, then his wife was washing her hands.

"This will not take long," he said, meaning to reassure her.

"Of course not," she said beneath her breath. He had a moment to wonder if she were displeased with his affections before the sweet splendor of her kiss stole all other thought from his mind.

Claire Delacroix

Thursday, June 23, 1187

Feast Day of Apollinaris and of the martyrs Saint Nabor and Saint Felix.

❧

Claire Delacroix

Chapter Fourteen

Ysmaine awakened to heavy knocking upon the doors of the house.

She slept alone, of course, and refused to dwell upon the fact that she was yet of less value to her lord husband than his steed. She supposed she could have been sworn to a man who labored overlong in his passion, but Gaston, abed as in all else, was purposeful. He coaxed just enough response from her that she would not be injured, then was quick about seeing the matter done. She had fallen asleep with her knees tucked against her chest, once again fighting that strange dissatisfaction.

"I demand admission!" a man roared, and pounded yet more. Ysmaine thought it might be Wulfe and her eyes opened wide. Had he not returned the night before? Radegunde slept against the door, still snoring, showing again her remarkable ability to sleep through any disturbance.

Ysmaine hastened to the window, drawing the heavy cloak over her shoulders, only to find Wulfe confronting the other knights in the party in the courtyard below. It was just past dawn and clearly all had been roused from their sleep by his return. The Templar was flushed in his anger and his tabard appeared to be torn. He might have dressed in haste and his hair was disheveled.

He certainly appeared to be most agitated.

Ysmaine could smell smoke.

A woman was behind Wulfe, lacing her lavish kirtle as if she stood in her own chamber, not before a number of men. Her hair was the richest hue of golden red Ysmaine had ever seen, and it spilled over her shoulders like a wavy curtain wrought of richest silk. In contrast to Wulfe, her manner was so serene that Ysmaine was reminded of a cat grooming itself in the sun.

Wulfe's older squire, Stephen, was holding his knight's cloak and kneading the fabric with agitation. He looked as if he had been running hard and his hair stood up on one side of his head. The younger squire, Simon, looked between the men, his glance darting to the woman at intervals, and Ysmaine was uncertain which of them he feared the most.

"We are in peril and must ride out at once," Wulfe declared. "I have been attacked!"

Ysmaine was alarmed, but then she noticed Gaston in the shadows of the stable roof. His arms were folded across his chest and though he was listening to Wulfe, he did not seem inclined to hasten anywhere.

Perhaps he knew more of what was afoot. Ysmaine lingered in the shadows to listen. Radegunde came to the other side of the window, yawned elaborately and grimaced at the man below. Her expression portrayed her opinion of the Templar without her uttering a word. She mirrored Ysmaine's pose and remained out of sight as she watched.

"We ride out this morn!" Wulfe roared. "If not this very *moment*."

Fergus yawned and shoved his hand through his hair, before he replied to Wulfe. "What a ruckus you make for so early in the day." Duncan stood behind him, rubbing the whiskers on his chin.

"It is yet night and I was attacked while I lay abed," the Templar snapped. "It is sufficient to weary me of this city. I order our immediate departure."

Fergus shook his head. "Hamish needs more rest before he rides. So the apothecary says and so it shall be." He nodded amiably at Everard and Joscelin who had followed him from the common room, looking just as sleepy as he. "I would not answer to his mother for the boy's health." The men chuckled together, but Wulfe bristled.

Ysmaine guessed that he saw their reaction as disrespectful.

"I will *not* be delayed because of a squire, let alone one so witless that he falls into the hold of the ship when unsupervised," Wulfe replied hotly.

"I was pushed," a small voice was heard to declare.

"You tripped," scoffed another boy.

Fergus shook his head. "It matters little how the injury was inflicted. I will stay in Venice two more days."

"This party must remain together," Wulfe insisted, and Ysmaine watched Gaston consider his boots calmly. "And I am in command! I say we leave this very day. It is not safe for us to linger."

"Because you were attacked by this woman?" Duncan asked, his tone jovial. He surveyed her openly. "I wager few men would resent that assault." Fergus chuckled with him. Wulfe visibly bristled but before he could speak, Gaston stepped out of the shadows of the stable to intervene.

"What has happened?" he asked, his tone temperate. "It was only last eve that you were glad to have a night away from all of us." Gaston looked pointedly at the woman, who surveyed her garments, evidently oblivious to all of them. She tugged the hem of one sleeve, brushed a speck of something from her skirts, then straightened, her gaze surprisingly steely when she looked at Wulfe.

"I have no doubt of her trade," Radegunde murmured, and Ysmaine shot her a glance so that she would fall silent.

"Surely you wish to remain in Venice and entertain your guest," Fergus teased.

Wulfe glared at him. "She is not my *guest*. She is a whore..."

"Courtesan," the woman interrupted crisply. "And my name is Christina, as I told you."

Fergus inclined his head and might have replied, but Wulfe interrupted. "Her name is of no import. Her trade can be called whatever you desire to call it. No matter how honeyed the choice of word, it is what it is."

Christina's lips tightened slightly at this.

"I have paid her in full, but she follows me..."

"He declared himself my champion last night," Christina said, her tone both sweet and commanding. Every man turned to look at her, even Wulfe, who clearly would have preferred to have done otherwise. She smiled with a confidence in her own allure that Ysmaine found enviable. "And indeed, I owe my life to this knight. Of course, I must follow him that the debt might be repaid in kind."

"You would surrender your life for *him*?" one of the squires asked, clearly incredulous. The others snickered.

"You should not be deceived by appearances," Christina said

smoothly. "Or judge a man by your first impression of him. The lion with a thorn in his paw is yet a noble creature, though his pain may make him terrifying."

Ysmaine blinked at this comparison. It was easy to compare Wulfe to a lion—or better the predator he was named for—but she found it harder to imagine he harbored any weakness or hid any pain.

"It is easy to give credit where it is not due," Radegunde whispered and Ysmaine frowned at her.

Below them, Wulfe stood even taller than before. "You owe me no debt," he said to Christina, his manner cold. "I paid for the pleasure you granted and our agreement is fully satisfied."

Christina replied mildly. "I say it is not satisfied, and if it is an *agreement*, then the consensus of both parties is required to call it fulfilled." She smiled at Wulfe, apparently enjoying his vexation.

The knights exchanged glances of amusement, and Ysmaine saw that Wulfe did not appreciate that their humor was at his expense.

"I did *not* pay to have my life threatened, to need to defend myself in a moment of leisure or to have to flee from certain destruction."

"As bad as that?" Fergus drawled, then winked at Christina. "I would not have expected a mating with you to be so dire."

"There was an attack upon the house," she said, her manner so mild that Ysmaine wondered what she truly thought. "As can happen, when there are wealthy patrons in residence." That she could show any complacency about the circumstances of such a life told Ysmaine how different their experience had been.

Christina cleared her throat. "And brigands looted both house and patrons after setting fire to the establishment. The other women..." Her words faded and she straightened, casting a smile at Wulfe. She noted that Christina's complexion had paled even beyond its original fairness and guessed that the life of a courtesan was not so easy for her as she would have others believe. "My fate would certainly have been worse, had I not been abed with a *champion* who defended me."

"I defended myself," Wulfe argued so vehemently that Ysmaine wondered what the truth had been. "I was attacked and I ensured my own survival."

"And mine as well, to my eternal gratitude." Christina bowed deeply to the Templar.

"Your gratitude need not last so long as that. I will give you another coin, even two, that you might continue on your way as we continue on our own."

Christina lifted her chin. "And I say you shall be repaid, in kind or in trade, for saving my life. Wherever you go, sir, I will follow." Her manner was resolute. "Rely upon it."

"There are worse fates," Duncan murmured, but it was clear Wulfe did not share his view. The warrior preened a little, smoothing his hair and smiling at Christina.

She looked him up and down, but did not smile in return.

Joscelin was simply staring at Christina, his mouth open, his expression unchanged from his first glimpse of her. Ysmaine wondered whether he salivated.

"Were you injured?" Gaston asked the knight, his bright gaze so at odds with his casual manner that Ysmaine guessed he saw more of import in this incident than the others.

Wulfe gestured to his back. "It is naught, but it is naught because I was awake. Had I been asleep, the blade would have slid between my very ribs."

"I suppose such peril is a hazard of visiting such establishments," Everard mused, his tone prim.

But Ysmaine leaned back against the wall, thinking. Wulfe ostensibly led the party on a quest for the Temple. By his own account, someone had tried to kill him. Gaston truly led the party. It was not hard to conclude that her husband's life might be at risk.

After all, he did carry the missive and she knew it.

Plus there was the relic, which surely must be the treasure they guarded. Although Laurent might be devoted, he slept in the stables with all the others. The boy had been ill for two entire weeks and was worn to exhaustion. She was the sole one who had a chamber of her own, thanks to her husband's provision.

Ysmaine would use that advantage to see Gaston's mission defended.

She pulled Radegunde aside and whispered instruction to her, indicating a size with her hands, then dispatching the maid to do her bidding in secret. She then returned to the window to listen.

"It is of no matter what you believe you owe to me," Wulfe

said to Christina, clearly trying to terminate the matter. "We ride out with all haste. You have no steed, therefore you will not depart with us."

"Just because you have been routed in the midst of your pleasure by some unfortunate incident, I see no reason to hasten away," Fergus said, looking as like to move as the Temple itself. "And still Hamish requires those days of rest."

Wulfe raised his fist. "A squire will not..."

"I say we break our fast," Gaston suggested, interrupting the argument. "And review the situation after that."

Wulfe visibly ground his teeth but Gaston continued as if unaware of the knight's annoyance.

"No good decisions are made when the belly is empty," he said. "And my wife has purchases to collect on this day. Perhaps we will compromise and depart on the morrow."

"We need to reach our destination sooner rather than later, that I might return to Jerusalem to aid in its defense," Wulfe protested.

"And a delay of a day will make little difference," Gaston replied.

Again, Ysmaine saw that her husband was truly the one in charge of the party, for Wulfe inhaled sharply then spoke through clenched teeth. "Perhaps there is good sense in your advice," he said, and Ysmaine thought the admission pained him. "I will break my fast before making my decision."

"Perhaps your guest would join us," Fergus said, bowing to Christina. "Since I gather that her previous abode is no longer hospitable."

"It is not, and I should be delighted to accept your invitation," she said and put her hand on his elbow. He escorted her into the common room, Joscelin following with all the fixed attention of a dog following a roast hind. Duncan yawned again and strolled behind them, endeavoring to hide his interest in Christina without success. Everard inhaled sharply and returned to his chamber, sweeping his cloak around himself before he marched away. With a glance from Bartholomew, the squires returned to their duties, leaving the two knights alone in the courtyard.

Wulfe glared at Gaston whose expression had turned somber. Ysmaine fancied that she witnessed a battle of wills between the two knights, for the air fairly crackled between them. Abruptly

Wulfe pivoted and marched into the common room. She had thought herself unobserved all this time, but her husband looked up at the window of her room so quickly that she realized otherwise.

She held his gaze, her heart hammering, and wondered at the import of his quelling look.

≥∙

Women were incomprehensible to Gaston, but he grew to enjoy the mystery. He took Ysmaine to the market again that day to collect all she had bought the day before. He was impressed that she was frugal and glad that she had found a merchant whose daughters sewed one new kirtle for her overnight. The wool garment was of a deep emerald hue and the fabric most sturdy.

Ysmaine spun before him, her delight sufficient to push the assault upon Wulfe from his thoughts for the moment. "The hue will hide the dirt," she confided. "And the cloth is well woven. I believe I shall have this garment for a dozen years or more, sir."

"You need not justify the price," he said, enjoying that he was seen as an indulgent husband. "It suits you most well, and I was the one to suggest that you buy new garb."

The stockings she had acquired were also sensible and the new boots would keep her both warm and dry. The cloak he had chosen for her was of deepest indigo and lined with squirrel fur, a purchase she had protested, but one that favored her well. The rest was bundled up for them, as were the lady's old garments.

Gaston frowned at the sight of them. "Surely, you need not carry these home."

"They are for Radegunde," Ysmaine insisted, taking his arm with an ease that made him smile. "She is most determined to have them for her own."

"But the kirtle is faded and the boots worn to holes."

"It is her right to have them," Ysmaine said quietly. "And she is resolved to mend and even dye the kirtle anew, and to have the boots patched when we reach home."

"But to carry them all the way to France..."

Ysmaine squeezed his arm. "She will be the one burdened with them, sir, and I would not compromise her pleasure in this. She recalls the kirtle from when it was first acquired and has always admired it."

Indeed, the maid looked elated with her burden of worn garb. Between her delight and his lady's insistence, Gaston could not find it within him to argue.

In this matter also, women would remain a mystery to him, but one he was content to leave unexplored.

❧

"Mother of God," Radegunde whispered in horror when she and Ysmaine were secured in that lady's chamber again. "I feared he would compel me to discard the clothes!"

"At least they are yet clothes," Ysmaine replied. She packed away her new finery with speed, then peered out the window at the courtyard.

The house was quiet, and she guessed that their fellow travelers were either sleeping or yet abroad in the city. Ysmaine guessed that they would return within the next hour, in order to prepare for the evening meal and the camaraderie of the company.

She could already smell the food their patroness was preparing and hear the woman humming in her kitchen. That room offered no view of the courtyard. Gaston had said he had an errand to undertake. It was a rare opportunity to evade his keen eye, and Ysmaine did not intend to waste it.

"Fish stew," Radegunde noted, wrinkling her nose. "Again."

"It is better than naught at all," Ysmaine reminded her, and the maid smiled acknowledgement. She had already packed the cheap trunk she had acquired at Ysmaine's command, bundling it into the middle of the old clothes so that it looked no different than it had. It had been weighted with stones and Ysmaine verified that it had a very similar heft to the relic which she had briefly held.

"We must exchange the trunk for the reliquary," Ysmaine instructed. "And the cloth wrapping the reliquary in this moment must be placed around the stone in precisely the same pattern. Otherwise, Laurent's stench will reveal our feat."

Radegunde nodded eager agreement. "You shall do that, and I shall stand sentry." She frowned. "But how shall we distract Laurent?"

"Perhaps he sleeps as he did yesterday," Ysmaine said. "Or

perhaps he can be lured away from his prize."

"I shall go first and abandon my bundle, the better to encourage him to leave his own," Radegunde suggested. "Perhaps I will feign that Hamish needs our aid. If no knight or noblewoman is present, Laurent may abandon his assignment for a moment."

"I will need more than a moment."

"I shall contrive it, my lady," Radegunde said with resolve. "But you must not be seen entering the stables."

Ysmaine nodded and remained in the chamber. She watched, her heart thundering as Radegunde crossed the courtyard to the stables. The maid did not look to be in a rush or to be scheming any matter. She called out, as if her eyes were dazzled by the change from sunlight to shadow, demanding to know who was there. Hamish could be heard to snore, but Laurent replied.

Bartholomew, Stephen, Simon, and Kerr must be abroad with their knights or on other errands.

Ysmaine heard Radegunde's cheerful chatter as she slipped from the room, locking the portal silently behind herself. Where was the courtesan? Everard? Joscelin? To be sure, the merchant had been often about the city, for it seemed he had many friends and associates in this place. But the others? She could not say.

There was no time to look. Gaston might return at any moment.

Her palms were damp when she reached the door to the courtyard, though still Radegunde chattered merrily. She could see the maid, rubbing the nose of one of the destriers and laughing when the beast nuzzled her. Ysmaine clutched her hands together, waiting for she knew not what.

Then Radegunde cried out and dropped her bundle at her feet. "Hamish!" she exclaimed in evident terror. "Mother of God, what is amiss?" She darted into the shadows at the back right of the stables. "Laurent! Quickly! You must aid me! Oh, *Hamish!*"

Ysmaine wished with all her heart that the boy would fall for the ruse.

He did. He darted across the space toward Radegunde, his small dark figure visible for only a moment before he disappeared into the shadows after Radegunde. He carried naught at all, which was the sum of what Ysmaine needed to know.

She raced across the stable and scooped up Radegunde's

bundle, then moved with silent haste into the corner Laurent favored. She turned her back upon the courtyard, hoping her dark cloak disguised her and her deed. The smell of manure was fierce, but she fought her reaction. She again memorized the wrappings, then unfurled the relic with shaking hands.

It was even more magnificent than she recalled.

It seemed appropriate to pray for divine aid in this moment.

"He had a convulsion before my very eyes!" Radegunde exclaimed. "Mother of God, what shall we do?"

"He looks in this moment to be asleep," Laurent noted, his tone skeptical.

Ysmaine wrapped the cheap trunk in the cloths that had been around the relic. The reliquary lay gleaming in the straw on the floor of the stable, but she was intent upon making the bag Laurent defended look right.

"But this manner of illness is deceptive," Radegunde continued, her voice high with apparent fear. "I saw it once in a man brought to my mother. He twitched in his sleep, shook and thrashed, then choked on his own bile."

"Nay!"

"Aye. Hamish must not be left alone, not for a moment."

"But what shall we do?" Laurent's voice had risen as well, for he had been infected by Radegunde's fear. Ysmaine placed the bundle as it had been, then rolled the reliquary into the clothes from Radegunde's bundle. She ensured it was safely bound, then crept to the door of the stables. She placed Radegunde's bundle as it had been, then hesitated, not wanting to abandon the relic even for a moment.

She felt rather than saw Radegunde glance her way, then slipped around the edge of the portal. She crossed the courtyard with haste and leapt into the shadows at the base of the stairs. She caught her breath, tried to slow the mad pace of her heart, then began to climb the stairs silently.

"You must watch him closely," Radegunde instructed. "I will fetch my lady, for she knows something of these matters."

"But what will I do if it happens again?"

"Hold fast to his hand and speak to him."

"But I have to fetch the baggage of my lord knight. I cannot leave it unprotected."

"Fetch it now, then and I will hold his hand. Be quick!"

Ysmaine leaned her head back against the wall and strove for her usual composure. She unlocked her door quietly, then closed it loudly, turning the key in the lock so that the sound echoed in the stairwell. She hummed to herself as she descended the stairs, pretending that this was her first departure from her chamber.

Though she could see no one as yet, she feigned astonishment Radegunde assailed her in the courtyard. "My lady! Hamish has had a fit! He has need of your assistance in this very moment."

"Truly!" Ysmaine exclaimed, noting the bundle in her maid's possession. The girl's eyes danced with her success. Ysmaine pressed the key to her chamber into Radegunde's hand. "I bought some lavender this very day to soothe my own sleep. Fetch it for me, if you please, for it may be of aid to him."

"Of course, my lady." Radegunde fled up the stairs, and Ysmaine dared to be relieved. The relic was in her own possession, which could only ensure her husband's success.

Even if it had required a small falsehood to ensure the transaction was made.

❧

Gaston left his lady wife within the sanctuary of the house and strode out to confer with Wulfe. He walked toward the port first, knowing he was easily noted in the crowd because of his height. He lingered in the markets on the way, pausing to take the view from more than one bridge, certain he would spot the Templar sooner or later.

He spied Wulfe at the stall of an armorer, seeing to a repair in the hilt of one of his blades. The knight watched the craftsman closely and appeared to be pleased with that man's skill. Gaston waited until Wulfe glanced up, then looked deliberately toward the square named for St. Mark. Wulfe nodded minutely, then returned his attention to the armorer.

Gaston wandered, taking his time in getting to the square, then making a circuit of it. He spotted Wulfe at the far end and made his way toward that knight. He ducked down a side street before reaching the knight, and increased his pace, moving swiftly down the twisted way. He turned corners and crossed bridges, ducked under laundry and finally emerged in a small courtyard that faced the main canal. It was deserted, silent except for the tinkle of water in the fountain in its middle. The windows were few and high. Gaston leaned against a stone wall in the shade and waited.

Wulfe emerged from the same avenue but a moment later.

"Followed?" Gaston asked in an undertone, but the knight shook his head.

He came to stand beside Gaston and the two leaned close, speaking quietly and watching the entries to the square.

"It defies belief," Wulfe muttered. "Our party is yet followed, even though no ship departed Acre after ours."

"I am not convinced that we were followed from Acre," Gaston said. "The baggage was searched on the ship, after all."

"Do you think someone seeks the treasure entrusted to us?"

"I think someone in our own party is curious, if not more." Gaston drummed his fingers on the board. "Did you catch any glimpse of your assailant?"

Wulfe shook his head. "I was abed, asleep with the woman. We had been amorous, several times, and I dozed."

"The boys?"

"I thought them awake, but it is clear they were not so." Wulfe shook his head. "She had locked the door, but I heard the tumblers and was immediately awake. It was too close to be either of the boys." He frowned as Gaston watched. "I thought the establishment meant to rob me, as can occur, but the floor creaked as the intruder entered."

"One unfamiliar with the room, then."

Wulfe nodded. "I waited, feigning sleep, and finally saw the intruder, silhouetted against the window."

"Man? Woman?"

"Tall enough to be a man, but otherwise impossible to be sure. He or she wore a voluminous cloak."

"A thief, then."

Wulfe lifted his gaze. "A thief who went through my purse and garments, yet left the coin."

Gaston did not care for the sound of that. "And then?"

"And then, the flames. The oil from the lantern was spilled and set alight, the entire room quickly engulfed in fire."

"The intruder fled?"

Wulfe shook his head. "The intruder lingered, drawing back into the shadows of one corner."

"He or she wanted to see what you saved."

Wulfe's lips tightened. "I seized my knife and shouted to the boys. The woman made for the door as she shouted a warning, but I went after the intruder. We struggled and I felt the nick of a blade. The thief was as slippery as an eel but I struck hard."

"Did you inflict an injury?"

"My blow struck something, then I was kicked hard to the ground. A lantern was flung at me, then one at the woman, and all set afire. By the time I recovered my footing, the attacker was gone, and it was all I could do to get the four of us out of that inferno."

Gaston nodded. Though he and Wulfe had not always agreed, he appreciated that the other knight had ensured the welfare not only of his squires, but of the courtesan. He suspected that the knight felt more for Christina than desire. "You saved her life," he noted. "She speaks aright that this leaves her in your debt."

Wulfe scowled, his manner brusque. "I did what any man would have done."

"I think we both know that is not true," Gaston said gently. "More importantly, Christina knows it is not true."

"She should remain here." Wulfe flung out a hand. "There is no future for her with me."

Perhaps that was the crux of the matter. Wulfe was sworn to the Templars, quite possibly because he had few other choices. "And what makes you imagine there is a future for her in Venice?"

Wulfe looked up, visibly surprised by Gaston's words.

"Women are not born whores any more than men are born knights," Gaston said. When the other knight considered this, he turned the conversation back to more practical matters. "You smell of smoke. We must be alert to that scent on any of the others, or take note of any injury."

"You think the intruder is in our party." There was no real surprise in Wulfe's tone, and Gaston was reassured that they had come to a similar conclusion. "You believe that whoever pursued us in Outremer sought this missing girl, and not the root of our errand."

"I fear that is the only possibility that addresses all details."

Gaston met Wulfe's gaze. "And truly, what do we know of any in our party?"

"We were assembled by Brother Terricus..."

"On the basis of timing and convenience, as well as some urgency. The fact remains that we know precious little of our fellow travelers."

"I suppose this is true, but it is not unusual."

Gaston did not believe his fellow knight understood the full significance of what he was saying. "Even you and I know little of each other. To be sure, I have heard of Brother Wulfe at the Gaza Priory and his black destrier, but we have never met."

Wulfe blinked. "I could be a brigand who had assaulted him on the road and replaced him."

"Though the squires would have been difficult to find," Gaston acknowledged. He smiled. "And truly, I have heard sufficient of the Gaza brethren to doubt that you would have survived such a battle unscathed were you not the true Brother Wulfe." He did not add that any such villain would not have saved the courtesan the night before, but instead continued. "You can follow the same logic throughout out party. I first encountered Fergus a mere two years ago and have never served closely with him. The sole person in this company I can vouch for is Bartholomew, for I have known him since he was a boy."

Wulfe nodded reluctant agreement. "And we know yet less of the merchant Joscelin de Provins."

"Save his repute."

"And of your lady wife."

Gaston was forced to cede that. "At least we know Everard de Montmorency to be who he claims to be."

"Do we?" Wulfe asked.

"He has been part of the royal court at Jerusalem for at least eight years as Count of Blanche Garde . I have seen him many a time at court."

"Why did he leave Outremer, just as it faces its greatest challenge?" Wulfe asked.

"His father lies ill," Gaston replied, repeating what he had been told by Terricus. "He returns home as a dutiful son to say his farewell."

"But as Count of Blanche Garde, he has a holding, or did

before he abandoned it."

"Perhaps he did not wish to witness its loss to Saladin. Perhaps, like many others, he yearns for the familiarity of home, despite his gains in Outremer."

Wulfe's lips tightened. "Perhaps there is something amiss that he did not remain to defend it, or ride out with King Guy."

"Perhaps he has not your taste for warfare."

Wulfe sat back, his expression discontent. "A man of wealth and privilege, who rides alone. I am reminded of a thief in the night, attempting to flee detection."

"If that were so, then he would have ridden north from Blanche Garde to Jaffa, and not troubled with Jerusalem or seeking the defense of the Templars."

Wulfe shrugged, unconvinced. "I shall keep him on my list of suspects, even if you do not. Along with your lady wife."

"My wife is above reproach..."

"She acquired poison and confers often with the merchant Joscelin..."

"Who tries to gain a guarantee from her that she will buy spices from him once home in France."

Wulfe arched a brow. "And who is always missing when matters go awry."

Gaston frowned at the truth in that.

"They could be in league together, and disguising their plotting as discussions over spice."

Gaston did not believe it. He deliberately provoked his companion, for he felt some retaliation deserved. "I shall not keep a list of suspects, for I believe no one can be put upon it with surety, save perhaps your lady courtesan."

The Templar's eyes flashed. "She is not my lady courtesan..."

"She argues otherwise."

"To have a courtesan or mistress would be defy my vows!"

Gaston could not suppress his smile. "While visiting a brothel did not?'

The back of Wulfe's neck turned ruddy. "I would be gone from this place with all haste," he said, his expression yet more grim. "Tell me that we need not await the welfare of a squire."

"We must, lest *we* appear to be thieves fleeing in the night." Gaston leaned closer. "But that does not mean that our time in this city shall be wasted. Let us try to lure your assailant into making another attempt."

"Upon my life?" Wulfe asked, a thread of amusement in his tone.

"Of course. You are the one who leads this party, after all."

Wulfe grumbled a little but did not turn aside. "You have a scheme?"

"A feeble one, but it might be effective. The villain believes you to be the leader of our party and thus the one charged with possession of the item he seeks. Your baggage was searched at Samaria, that of all the others in our party searched on the ship. Last night, I suspect you were followed and your more intimate belongings searched, again in a quest for some hint of the location of the prize. It may be clear to the villain that you do not carry it."

"And so?"

"What if you acted as a man bent on collecting it?" Gaston dropped his voice, though he doubted any were close enough to hear them. "There are those in Venice oft used by the order for the safekeeping or sale of gems and precious goods. I would not threaten the security of any of them, but this practice is well known." Wulfe leaned closer. "After all retire this night, you might leave the house, as if keeping an assignation in secret. I will follow you, leaving sufficient space that the villain may lend chase."

"And that fiend will find his reckoning in the streets of Venice." Wulfe nodded with satisfaction. "I like it well, for this city is known to be violent at night."

"I will watch for your departure," Gaston said.

Wulfe and Gaston shook hands, then Wulfe left the square. Gaston waited, counting the beats of his heart to two hundred, then left the square by another avenue. He took a long and winding route back to the house, finding it all in uproar when he returned.

It seemed the apothecary had been prudent indeed in insisting that Hamish not be moved so soon.

Chapter Fifteen

Ysmaine was a wretch.

Or perhaps she was wicked.

For she failed to be satisfied with all the blessings that came to her. She had a husband, who was hale, handsome, and heir to a holding close to that of her own parents. She had food aplenty and a good palfrey to ride. Her husband was indulgent, letting her purchase whatsoever she desired in the opulent markets of Venice. Her room was comfortable and comparatively large, complete with a large window, a fine view of the building's interior courtyard, and many fat candles. She was safe and she was possessed of good health herself. She even had a priceless relic secured for its own safety.

Yet she wanted more.

On their second night since arriving in Venice, she lingered in the common room, finishing her wine. Radegunde was in her chamber already, ensuring all was prepared for Gaston's nightly visit, and also watching the relic. Ysmaine finished her wine, while Gaston checked upon Hamish. The boy was well, of course, though Ysmaine felt a twinge of guilt that Radegunde's ruse had created such an uproar. Fergus was resolved to remain with the squire this night and watch over him. The other boys chattered with excitement, and even Wulfe ceded that the apothecary must have been right.

She did not dread the inevitable coupling with Gaston, but wanted more of it than she had experienced thus far. All the same, it seemed wrong to have any complaint of a husband who defended and protected her so well. He was neither cruel nor unfair, and truly, there was much admirable in his nature. Gaston ensured that he did not injure Ysmaine, and he touched her so that she was prepared for him. She supposed he was quick about their mating because he thought it a duty best accomplished and done.

But Ysmaine could not have imagined that there had been laughter from the solar in the afternoons because her parents fulfilled a duty. She could not believe it was obligation that had her mother seizing her father's hand, her gaze dancing as she tugged him toward their bed. Nay, there was more.

And Ysmaine desired to know of it.

Indeed, it was Gaston's touch that was the root of her dissatisfaction. She liked the weight of his hand upon her, *there*, and wished he did not remove it so quickly. His touch made her yearn for something nameless that she was somehow denied.

He had demanded honesty between them, and she would gladly have told him what she desired of him.

The problem was that she did not know.

Radegunde did not know either.

Ysmaine was drumming her fingers upon the board when the night was rent with a woman's cry. Her hand stilled in her alarm.

That woman swore, calling upon several saints for relief.

Were they being attacked?

Ysmaine rose to her feet and went to the doorway to the courtyard. She saw Gaston lingering in the shadows of the stable, his gaze fixed on a window above her. It must have been the window beneath her own.

The woman cried out again, screaming Wulfe's name with abandon. Her cry ended in a moan so long and low that it gave Ysmaine gooseflesh.

Was that pain or pleasure?

Gaston bit back a smile.

It was the courtesan Christina who cried out.

And it appeared that woman knew what Ysmaine wished to learn. She noted that light spilled from a window above, casting a most intriguing shadow on to the opposite wall of the courtyard. It was evident that Wulfe and his whore were most intimately entwined and had left the lantern on the far side of the room. They were standing up, the whore balanced on the knight, her feet braced on his thighs.

Her breath caught when Gaston's gaze landed upon her. Ysmaine knew she should be modest and turn away from the silhouettes, but she could not cease to watch.

Her curiosity was too great.

And surely, it was not bad for her husband to know that she was so intrigued.

The courtesan threw back her head and wailed as Wulfe's hips pumped. She called his name again, then seized his head and bent to kiss him. The shadows disappeared, so that Ysmaine guessed they tumbled to a pallet.

She had been atop him.

Ysmaine flattened her back against the wall. She bit her lip, marveling that such options were possible. But then, why should there not be variation? The key union need not be dependent upon the pose of the couple. She felt a rising excitement at even this much of a revelation.

Then the whore wailed with such abandon that Ysmaine's gaze rose again to meet that of her lord husband. She could be heard panting, crying out for relief, and cajoling Wulfe with such volume that other lanterns were lit in the building. A fist pounded upon a floor and Ysmaine could guess whose fist it might be. She peeked into the courtyard as Gaston spared a glance to the window, then her husband crossed the courtyard with measured steps.

What did Wulfe do to Christina? Ysmaine could not help but wonder as the whore's cries grew louder. Whatever he did, Christina clearly approved. Ysmaine wanted desperately to see more and was considering the merit of going into the courtyard on some feigned mission...

Then Wulfe roared, bellowing with such vigor that it could only be one sensation causing his pleasure. Christina cried out almost in unison and at a similar volume.

She had also gained a release?

Was that possible?

If there had been any doubt that they did no violence to each other, the whore began to laugh merrily. Wulfe's throaty chuckle joined the sound. The lanterns that had been lit were extinguished and some call was heard from the street beyond the walls. This only made the whore laugh more loudly.

Ysmaine might not know exactly what she wanted from Gaston, but Wulfe's whore most certainly did. She wondered how she might enquire about such a delicate matter, when she found the heat of her husband beside her. "I apologize, lady mine, that our abode is turned into a brothel this night," he murmured, and her heart thumped at the glow of his eyes.

She felt flustered and embarrassed that they should both have witnessed the Templar's pursuit of pleasure, yet also tingled with that arousal that so beguiled her.

"I do not mind," she said, feeling herself flush at her own words.

"It seems the courtesan endeavors to change Wulfe's thinking about her place being by his side," Gaston mused.

Ysmaine looked up into her husband's eyes and her chest clenched. Was there a new heat in his eyes? Did they share their reaction to this sight?

Did she dare to ask for what she most desired.

He *had* asked her for honesty, and she hoped her granting of it did not change that.

"If she is by his side," Ysmaine added hastily, feeling most bold. "Though it looked as if she were *atop* him."

She dared to glance up at her husband again, only to find him biting back a smile. "It did, indeed."

Ysmaine took a deep breath and turned to him, placing her hands over his. "I would be atop you, sir," she whispered to Gaston, whose eyes widened slightly at her bold speech. "I would feel whatsoever makes her shout like that."

He bent his attention upon her immediately, closing his hands over hers. "Lady mine, you shall not ask this woman for instruction..."

Ysmaine put her fingertips on his lips to silence him. "You insisted upon honesty between us, sir, and here is a measure of it. I am jealous."

His astonishment was clear. "Of a whore?"

"Of a woman so well pleased that she cares not who knows of it."

Gaston shoved a hand through his hair, managing to look both exasperated and beleaguered. "You wish to be with Wulfe?"

"Nay!" Ysmaine's shock at that suggestion must have been clear, for Gaston looked reassured. She shuddered. "To couple with a man like that would not be my taste at all. I find all that is admirable in my own husband."

"Save that you do not moan abed."

She dared to smile. "It seems I am greedy for experience, sir."

Gaston watched her warily. "I thought you might find his experience alluring."

"His experience, sir, is too extensive. It suits me well that you do not share it, for I do not have to fear that my husband will give me the pox, or that when you ride to hunt, your prey is other than deer and boar."

Gaston seemed to fighting a smile. "But...?" he invited.

"But." Ysmaine took a deep breath, feeling herself flush at her audacity, and leaned close to her husband. She dropped her voice to a whisper. "I would know more of whatever it is that makes her so noisy."

His eyes twinkled, and she guessed that he meant to tease her. "So, you would have *me* enquire of the courtesan what grants her such pleasure?"

"Gaston!" Ysmaine declared and he laughed at her outrage. Her cheeks burned but she would not leave this matter be. "I would have you discover what might grant me such pleasure, as well as show me what would give you sufficient pleasure to linger over the matter."

He sobered. "You would have me render the marital debt more slowly?"

"I suspect that is part of the secret."

Gaston licked his lips and a muscle ticked in his jaw.

Ysmaine took the last step between them, her words so softly uttered that Gaston might not even be able to discern them. "I liked your hand upon my thigh," she confessed in a whisper. She swallowed and dared to look at his face. He was watching her, his eyes glittering, his manner intent. She was not even sure he breathed. "I liked it better when your hand rose even higher." She could not name the place he had touched. She swallowed. "What would ensue if you left it *there* longer? Would it be more readily achieved if I were atop you?" A fire lit in Gaston's eyes, and she had a moment to hope that he meant to do something about the matter.

"Lady mine," he murmured, his voice hoarse. He considered her for a long moment, and Ysmaine feared she had shocked him overmuch. When he inhaled sharply, pivoted and marched away from her, she knew her impulsiveness had steered her false.

She was left burning on the threshold of the common room, and it appeared her husband did not desire her honesty so much as she had hoped.

Ysmaine turned and climbed the stairs, her footfalls heavy. Would he even come to her this night? Or was he too appalled by her request?

಼

Gaston was aflame.

He could not think clearly. He could not summon a coherent course of action. He could think only of Ysmaine, of the softness of her skin, of the smoothness of her curves, of the enticing little gasp she made when he entered her. Her whispered confession of her desire to be astride him was sufficient to obliterate all other concerns. He thought of looking fully upon her, of stripping her nude and exploring her, of savoring her so that she made the same sounds of pleasure as Wulfe's whore and his mind went blank.

There was only raw need burning through his veins.

Only Ysmaine.

He had to step away from her, to collect his thoughts, and to choose the right course of action. Even putting distance between them did not help: the vision of her gasping with pleasure, her eyes alight with invitation, her lips parted, was one that would not be dislodged from his mind's eye. He could smell her perfume on his skin where she had touched him, and could not forget the press of her breast against his arm or the alluring way she had blushed when confessing her desire to him.

Gaston went into the courtyard and filled a pail with cold water from the well. He stripped down in the stables and bathed with haste, savoring the icy touch of the water upon his flesh. He hoped it might douse the fire within him, but it did not.

If anything, his ardor for his wife only grew.

What if he could give her such pleasure? What if creating heirs was not a duty, not a task to be completed but a pleasure to be savored? He thought of Wulfe's counsel that he should ensure his lady lost her heart to him and wondered whether this might be the course to ensure that end.

He scrubbed himself from head to toe, removing the muck of

the day and the weight of assumptions he had carried a long time. Why should a man and wife *not* find pleasure together abed? Why should a man *not* cultivate his lady's affection and her loyalty? Why should he *not* savor the prize of his lady wife?

Gaston washed his hair and shook out the water, reassured and resolved. He donned his chausses and boots again, then cast a glance upward to the window of Ysmaine's chamber. She stood against one edge of the window, half in shadows, just as she had that morning, her gaze fixed upon him. His blood quickened with the certainty that she had been watching him bathe and their gazes locked. She bit her lip and that ardor redoubled within him, filling him with purpose and need.

He would take her challenge. He would see his lady pleased.

And perhaps, he might set them upon a good course for the future. Gaston donned his chemise, then filled another bucket with water, taking the stairs three at a time to his lady's chamber.

≈

Ysmaine turned away from the window, flattening her back against the wall. Gaston had seen her looking, and she had been too foolish to draw back. Was he insulted? Was he dismayed? She exhaled, fearing that again she had showed her earthy interests too plainly. She knew he had not been at ease the night before when she had lifted his chemise and seen the scar on his hip.

He left the courtyard in haste, on some quest or another, while she was still simmering with desire for him.

To make matters worse, the courtesan began to moan anew.

It was as if that pair would torment Ysmaine with the knowledge of what was not to be her own. She began to list again the advantages she had that Christina did not, even as she paced her chamber.

She froze when she heard the sound of a footstep on the landing. Radegunde straightened and glanced at the door.

There came a solid rap upon the portal, one that made Ysmaine's pulse flutter.

"Lady mine?" Gaston said, and she could not believe her good fortune.

Still fearing that he meant to chastise her, Ysmaine hastened to the door, and unlocked it to him. It made no sense but he seemed larger without his armor, or perhaps he was just more vibrantly male. There was no mistaking the muscled breadth of him when his chemise stuck to his damp chest and shoulders, much less the way her mouth went dry when she met the vivid blue of his eyes. His hair was wet, his sleeves rolled up to reveal his tanned forearms, and he was more disheveled than ever she had seen him.

Could it be that there was some impulsiveness in her methodical husband?

Gaston carried a brimming bucket of water and a sponge bobbed within it. She had a fleeting thought that he meant to douse her to quench her passion, but then he spoke.

"I would take your challenge," he said, his voice husky and his eyes dark. "If still you desire it."

"I do," she admitted softly, then took a step back. She dismissed Radegunde with a gesture and the girl left the room. Gaston strode into the chamber, and Ysmaine turned the key in the lock behind him.

He hesitated in the middle of the chamber, as if uncertain how to proceed. Ysmaine swallowed, then laid a hand upon his arm. "I apologize for looking so openly upon you just now. I have never seen you fully," she admitted. "Nor indeed, have I seen any man nude."

"Nor have I looked fully upon you," Gaston replied. "It seems there is much we must see achieved." He lifted her hand to his lips and pressed a kiss to her palm. His gaze burned brightly into hers and his voice was low when he continued. "I thought we might explore each other, the better to discover what gives pleasure."

Ysmaine could not bite back her smile. "Does it vex you to have a wanton wife, sir?"

"It enchants me," Gaston confessed in a rush, then dropped her hand. With uncharacteristic haste, he speared his fingers into her hair and drew her to her toes. His touch was both resolute and gentle, all the more thrilling for the pulse she spied at his throat. He looked at her as if she were a marvel, then slanted his mouth across hers in a kiss that set her very soul aflame.

Ysmaine knotted her hands around his neck and kissed him back, liking her sense that she could provoke this very deliberate man to be impetuous. He seemed to need no more encouragement than that, for he put down the bucket from such a height that the water splashed over the rim. He framed her head between his hands and backed her into the wall, trapping her there with his hips as he kissed her deeply.

Ysmaine was flooded with pleasure. She closed her eyes and surrendered to him, her fingers knotted in his hair, her back arched so that her breasts rubbed against his chest. He kissed her with a passion that left her gasping, then eased his knee between her thighs. When Gaston lifted his head, he arched a brow. "Tell me what you like, lady mine," he invited, his voice a low rumble.

"I like when you kiss me like that," she confessed. "I like when it seems you cannot resist me. When you seem to hunger for me."

His smile was fleeting, then he kissed her again, if anything more fervidly than before. The fingers of one hand speared into her hair, and he lifted his other hand away, only to lift the hem of her chemise. She felt the warmth of his palm upon her thigh, even as his tongue dueled with hers. He laid it flat then slid it slowly upward. He spared her a simmering glance, then bent to tug the tie of her chemise loose with his teeth. His lips were on her ear, her throat, beneath her chin, his fingertips easing toward the place that burned for his intimate touch. Her very flesh seemed alive, and yet she wanted more.

Ysmaine gasped for breath, then braced her hands upon his shoulders. She spared him a quelling look then hauled her chemise over her head and cast it across the room, letting him look upon her fully. Gaston's eyes widened in a most satisfactory way.

"Tell me what you like, sir," she invited, echoing his words and her husband chuckled.

"This," he growled. He bent and flicked his tongue across her nipple, which tightened in response to his touch. "This." He cupped her breast in one hand, kissing the nipple then drawing that tight bead between his teeth in sweet torment.

Ysmaine found the fire inside her was coaxed to an inferno, and she ground her hips against him, not knowing how to find relief. "Sir!" she gasped.

"*This.*" Gaston's hand slipped between her thighs, his gaze intent as he touched her there. Ysmaine flushed, she caught her breath, framed his face in her hands, and kissed him full on the

Claire Delacroix

mouth. Gaston's fingers moved against her, summoning her passion with skill, even as she fair devoured his mouth. He moaned into her kiss, and Ysmaine was delighted that she should have some power over his passion, as he did over hers.

She plucked at his chemise, and they parted panting, smiling at each other as he echoed her move. He tugged his chemise over his head and cast it after her own, looking even more wicked and passionate than he had before. He was muscled and tanned, scarred yet healed. She thought him beautiful.

Ysmaine's fingers dropped to the lace of his chausses and he lifted her high, holding her captive against his chest with one arm around her waist. He discarded his boots and then his chausses, meeting her gaze when he was just as nude as she.

"A noble warrior," she said with a smile, tracing the line of an old scar on his shoulder. She could not believe the power of his body, the heat of him, the desire she saw in his eyes for her.

"You might have found a prettier one," he teased.

"But not a better one," Ysmaine replied, seeing how her words pleased him. He held her captive, her feet above the ground and her hair unfurled down her back, his hands locked around her waist. She kept her hands upon his shoulders and watched him with fascination. Again he backed her into the wall, purpose in his expression.

"Tell me what you like, lady mine," he invited again, then kissed the other nipple to a turgid peak.

"I like you," she admitted in a rush. "I like when you desire me." Ysmaine swallowed and met his intent gaze. "I like when you fill me." She bit her lip, then dared to say it aloud. "When you stretch me."

Gaston inhaled sharply and spun her around. He crouched so that she was sitting across his thighs. His hand landed on the inside of her thigh, awakening that tremor again. "Let us find out first what happens when my hand lingers," he murmured in a low growl.

Ysmaine smiled at him and parted her thighs in invitation. His fingers were warm and they moved slowly, his touch once again proving to be both gentle and resolute. He caressed her so that she gasped aloud, and yet he did not halt. His gaze was locked upon her, his other arm around her waist. He watched her as his caress grew more demanding, more firm, more exhilarating.

Ysmaine felt her pulse race and her breath come quickly. Shivers raced over her flesh, and heat seemed to course through her body. She found herself twisting against his finger, increasing the sweet torment of his touch. Gaston smiled as she murmured incoherently, and he chuckled when she moaned. He eased a finger inside her and then another, and she was suffused with pleasure.

She kissed him greedily, wanting his body pressed against his. Her hand fell on his throat, and she savored the wild leap of his pulse, and the evidence that she was not impassioned alone. His fingers moved against her with persuasive ease, and she was certain she could bear no more. Her lips parted in entreaty, but she made no sound before Gaston spun her around.

"I believe this was the posture," he said, lifting her above him and lowering her onto himself. He was more than ready for her. Indeed, Ysmaine believed he filled her more than he had those other nights. The sensation made her moan with pleasure and summoned a quiver deep within her. She smiled at him, much pleased with the pose, then he gripped her buttocks and moved within her.

Ysmaine smiled at her husband and wrapped her legs around his waist. "Like this?" she asked playfully, knowing she had seen the courtesan do exactly thus.

Gaston did not seem to be able to reply. He whispered her name, then again backed her into the wall. His one hand dove between them again, caressing her once more, and Ysmaine realized there was something she liked much, much more than her husband filling her.

She wriggled against him, a movement that he seemed to enjoy. She locked her legs around him and rocked, savoring how sharply he inhaled. His eyes glittered and his skin flushed. He moved deliberately and powerfully, coaxing the tumult within her to increase beyond belief. She was about to beg him for some manner of release, when his finger and thumb closed abruptly in a sensual pinch.

Ysmaine screamed in pleasure. She was caught in a maelstrom that might well shake her to pieces—save that Gaston held her fast. She clutched his shoulders and locked her legs around him, riding the wave of her release even as he roared and drove deeper inside her. He shook with the power of his own release and his teeth grazed her skin as he growled with a satisfaction that pleased her mightily. She tumbled against his chest with a shudder and held him fast, loving the sound of his galloping heart beneath her ear.

"I like *that*, sir," she whispered, and he laughed.

"As do I, lady mine," he murmured, his words making his chest vibrate beneath her ear. "As do I."

He pressed a kiss to her temple, and Ysmaine lifted her head, stretching to kiss him. This was a sweet kiss, a triumphant kiss, and one that filled her with a satisfaction beyond all expectation.

Who might have guessed that bold speech would have won her a prize such as this?

❧

Ysmaine was a madness in his blood.

Gaston had been unable to think of anything other than possessing her, yet now that she clung to him sweetly, sated and soft, he could think of naught other than having her again. He was a man of moderation and reserve, but his new wife pushed him beyond that.

He supposed he should be troubled that he did not mind.

"The liniment," she recalled, but Gaston was dismissive of such ministrations.

"I feel sufficiently hale without it this night," he growled.

Ysmaine laughed up at him, so well contented that he had to kiss her anew. When he broke their kiss, he could only admired her visible satisfaction.

She sighed contentment. "I must lie on the pallet, if you please, sir."

Uncertain why this might be, Gaston reluctantly set her down. She immediately rolled to her back and drew her knees up to her chest. Gaston could make no sense of her posture, and his confusion must have shown.

Ysmaine granted him one of those potent smiles. "Radegunde says that the longer I hold your seed within me, the more likely it is to take root."

"Truly?" Gaston doubted he needed to confess that he knew little of such matters.

"Her mother was a midwife, so it might be true." She wrinkled her nose. "I suppose it cannot hurt."

"How long do you lie thus?"

"Until I become cold."

Gaston considered her as he washed himself. "I might be of aid in that."

Again, she smiled, but her voice softened. "I should like that, husband."

There was much to be said for encouraging the lady to tell him of her preferences. Gaston seized the fur-lined cloak he had bought her that very day and joined her on the pallet, gathering her into his arms and tucking the cloak about them both. He sat with his back to the wall and his wife in his lap and liked how she smiled up at him.

"It is much better this way," she said, leaning her cheek against his chest. "As I slept on the ship."

"You knew I joined you?"

He felt her smile against his skin. "I knew I was safe and warm, and already I know that means my husband ensures my welfare." She sighed with a satisfaction Gaston shared. He found himself pressing a kiss to the top of her head and savored that strange mix he so often felt in Ysmaine's presence of excitement and contentment.

If this was how he would feel for the rest of his days and nights, wedded life would suit Gaston well indeed.

"You did not let me sit atop you," she complained easily, her words revealing that she was becoming drowsy.

"I had not the opportunity."

She glanced up at him, her expression mischievous. "We could do it again."

"But once a night is sufficient, lady mine," Gaston replied, though he knew it was not true. He could have taken her a dozen times, so great was his desire, but she was new to such pleasures and he did not wish to injure her.

"Then I have a new objective," she said, nestling against him. "I fear you have taken a greedy woman to wife, sir."

"Indeed?" He heard the thread of humor in his own tone.

"Indeed. No sooner do I have a yearning fulfilled, then I develop another. I fear that I shall never be truly sated."

"I cannot believe it. You seem quite content to me."

Ysmaine shook a finger at him. "Ah, but you do not know the truth of it. You see, when I came on pilgrimage to Palestine, I yearned for a husband and a home. But by the time I met you in Jerusalem, I yearned only for Radegunde to be cured."

"And so she was."

"With your aid, to be sure. And you ensured that there was a hot meal in my belly before I could yearn for that. Which meant that I soon recalled my desire for a husband and a home."

"And now you have both."

"Although I feared for your fate when we met abed. I wished from our nuptial vows that you would survive our first coupling."

"And I did."

"Which meant only that I wished for more couplings," Ysmaine said, feigning distress at her own greedy nature. Gaston chuckled but she looked up at him with concern and her voice softened. "Then I feared you would be lost to the Saracens, so I wished fervently for your survival."

He did not want her to dwell upon that incident. "Your wishing seems to be most effective."

"But when you survived, even that was not sufficient. I wished for pleasure abed."

"I can only hope that this dream, too, has been fulfilled."

Ysmaine sighed. "It has been, which only means that I now desire to conceive a son."

He pressed a kiss to her hair. "That may take some time. Your desire for more might be checked for a while."

"I doubt it," Ysmaine admitted. "In the meantime, I shall yearn to meet you twice abed each day."

"And thence thrice?" he guessed, winning a brilliant smile.

She made a mock frown. "You have wed a greedy woman, sir. Make no mistake."

"Then you must tell me of your each and every desire, and I shall labor to satisfy you. It is the only way a man of merit might serve his lady wife."

Her eyes sparkled with anticipation, and Gaston could not resist her allure. He kissed her then, a slow hot kiss that left his own toes curling, then reluctantly put her aside.

"Surely you do not mean to leave?"

"Surely I do," Gaston replied.

Ysmaine rolled over and propped herself on her elbows. She could not know what a tempting vision she created, with her hair cast over her shoulders and her lips swollen from his kisses. "Because Fantôme is your most valuable possession, so you must ensure his health and security."

"You know of this already."

Ysmaine watched him for a long moment and he wondered what she was thinking. He had little doubt that she would soon tell him. "Will he remain so, when I have borne you a son?"

"You have not yet done so, my lady, so on this night, I need not be compelled to choose." He fastened his belt, checked his weapons, then bent to kiss her quickly. "Sleep well, lady mine," he murmured, surveying her one last time before he strode to the door.

That last sight of her would keep him warm all the night, no matter how far he had to follow Wulfe in this city.

Indeed, it was all Gaston could do to keep himself from whistling.

Friday, June 24, 1187

*Feast Day of
Saint Lupus, Saint Wulfhade
and Saint Ruffinus of Mercia.*

Chapter Sixteen

It was past midnight when the villain fled down the crooked streets of Venice, returning to the house in haste. He soundly cursed the entire order of Templar knights beneath his breath, along with all men of supposed honor, blaming them for his failure.

He dodged down an alley and climbed to the roof of a kitchen, sneaking along the roof to the corner where this house abutted the one they had rented. The rope ladder he had lowered from his window earlier was in place as it should be. He climbed quickly to his room, pulled in the ladder and hid it behind the curtains. He washed in haste, disliking that the water took the tinge of his victim's blood.

He quaffed the remainder of the wine he had brought to his chamber and poured the red water into the decanter. He shed his garments quickly, knowing there was not a moment to be wasted, and reclined on his pallet. He willed his heart to slow its pace, even as he strained his ears for the sound of the returning knights.

Would they bring a corpse?

Or would they abandon his victim to Venice's fetid canals?

The villain knew which option he preferred. He breathed deeply and steadily, managing even to summon a small snore. He would be able to interrupt the sound when he heard the knights' return and none would doubt that he had been in this chamber, slumbering all the while.

Though he had not witnessed the collection of whatever treasure Wulfe was charged to deliver to the Paris Temple, it was clear the Templar intended to collect it in Venice. He would remain vigilant, but even if he did not observe the collection of the prize, he would know it to be in this company's possession when they departed the city.

The road was sufficiently long and lonely to Paris that opportunity would be found.

૨**

It was clear that there was merit to be found in bold speech.

And Ysmaine had no complaint with Gaston's reward for her honesty. She could scarce think of sleeping, she was so pleased with the change in their marriage. Her thoughts flew as she envisioned a joyous future together, including many afternoons abed in the solar of Châmont-sur-Maine. She nestled deeper into her new cloak as Radegunde bustled about the chamber and relished the prospect of her future with Gaston.

She must have slept, for she awakened yet again to disarray in the house.

It was nigh the middle of the night, but Wulfe was shouting in the courtyard for aid. Some soul knocked with force on the door to her chamber, and Radegunde leapt to her feet. Ysmaine seized her small eating knife.

"Who is it?" Radegunde demanded. "My lady is asleep."

"I beg leave to bring my lord knight to the lady's chamber," Bartholomew said, his voice high with agitation. "For he has been attacked."

"Nay!" Ysmaine cried and flung herself from her bed.

But it was true. Wulfe and Fergus carried Gaston up the stairs toward her chamber, his limp form telling her more than she wished to know.

The trail of blood left on the steps behind them made Ysmaine fear the worst.

Most of their group climbed the stairs behind the small party, looking as if they had been roused from sleep by the noise. She was Gaston's lady wife. His welfare in this moment was her responsibility. Ysmaine recalled every time her mother had taken charge of a situation and endeavored to do the same.

First, she had need of her most commanding tone.

"Radegunde, please put every blanket upon the pallet and fetch water for my husband. If he is injured, the wounds will need to be cleaned."

"I can do as much, my lady," Bartholomew protested.

"You may aid me in removing his armor." Ysmaine pointed at Wulfe. "And you will tell me how this transpired." She drew herself up to her full height, unaware of how much she resembled her mother. "The rest of you may retire again. We shall confer in the morning, when there is less to be done."

Radegunde raced down the steps with the bucket to the well, and Ysmaine gestured that Gaston should be laid on her pallet. He was pale and he was wet, the smell of unclean water rising from his garb.

God in Heaven but she did not want to be this man's widow.

The terror of what appeared to be a very real possibility made Ysmaine summon every scrap of strength within her and accommodate every detail.

Gaston needed her, as he never had before.

❧

"He was in one of these filthy canals," Ysmaine guessed, tugging off Gaston's boots and emptying the water inside them out the window. She stood the boots to one side of the room, showing all the care for them that Gaston always did. She turned to find Wulfe removing Gaston's tabard and thought of the coins hidden in its hems.

She recalled the missive hidden in his aketon, and knew she had to defend her husband's secrets as well as his life.

"I will send for an apothecary," Bartholomew said, but Ysmaine thought immediately of more eyes in this chamber.

"I would see the extent of his injuries first," she said with resolve. "There might be no need to expend extra coin to summon an apothecary at this hour of the night."

She felt the shock of the others, but ignored it. She did not doubt that her reaction would spark speculation but she did not care. She moved between Wulfe and her husband.

"Sir, that is not a fitting task for you," she said to him, summoning as imperious a tone as she could manage. "You are neither squire nor servant." Ysmaine moved quickly, brushing Wulfe aside along with his protests. "Your service is better needed in telling us what transpired. How was he so injured in the stables?"

There was a pause, only the sound of Bartholomew unbuckling Gaston's belt in the chamber. The squire set aside Gaston's weapons and his gloves with a care that knight would have shown himself.

Ysmaine glanced up to see that Wulfe's expression had set.

Still neither man replied.

"He was not in the stables," she concluded, and neither man argued with her. Her temper rose. "Indeed, you were abroad in this perilous town, long after the hour when all sensible men are locked into their homes, and so my husband paid the price."

"It was his idea," Wulfe said through gritted teeth.

Again, Ysmaine had the sense that matters were far from what they appeared to be. It seemed also that she was not the only one who had discerned that Gaston knew more than he admitted. That the target had moved to her husband made her all the more determined to defend him.

"I do not believe it," she retorted. "My lord husband has more sense than that."

She wanted these men out of her chamber, so that she could bar the door to all but herself and Radegunde, but she dared not arouse their suspicions. She had the relic, though they did not know as much. At best, she would feign shyness to be rid of them, and insist upon decorum.

Though that would only succeed if Gaston's injury were minor. She removed his tabard and set it aside, rolling him to his belly with Bartholomew's aid that his aketon might be removed. She wondered how to contrive that it remained in this room, for a squire was responsible for his knight's weaponry. She wondered how she would ensure that the missive was not found, but in the end, it was accomplished so easily that she might not have feared.

Bartholomew unlaced the back of the aketon and pushed it from Gaston's shoulders. Ysmaine gasped at the blood upon his shoulder and the back of his head. His pulse was yet strong though, and he breathed steadily. She examined the wounds and was relieved that they were not deeper.

"He must have sunk."

"Indeed, my lady," Bartholomew agreed. "He was struck from behind and pushed into the canal." Ysmaine thought of the squire Hamish and wondered whether the others did, as well. "He is not small and the weight of his armor is considerable."

"Fiends and thieves," she fumed. "They wished to ensure that he could not stand witness to their crime."

"Undoubtedly so, my lady," Wulfe agreed.

It was only then that Ysmaine realized Bartholomew was wet. "You pulled him out?"

"I had to dive in after him, my lady," he admitted, his consternation most clear. "I thought...I feared..."

She laid a hand over his, not surprised to find him trembling. "My lord husband is fortunate indeed to have such a loyal man in his service. I thank you, Bartholomew."

He swallowed and nodded.

"Now, let us see him dry and warm. I think that will aid him as much as any other cure. Feel the strength of his pulse." That seemed to reassure the squire. Ysmaine tugged the aketon from beneath Gaston, even as Bartholomew worked the mail hauberk over his knight's head. Wulfe was required to lift Gaston's weight to aid in the task, and Ysmaine whisked both tabard and aketon away.

Radegunde returned then and fell to her knees beside Gaston, the water spilling over the edge of the bucket in her haste to do her lady's bidding. "What shall I do, my lady?"

"Squeeze the water from his tabard and hang it to dry," Ysmaine instructed. "Then I would ask you to attempt to draw the blood out of his aketon." She cast a look at Bartholomew, who might have protested. "Radegunde is very skilled with textiles, and I would ensure that all meets Gaston's approval. Could you ensure that his mail and weapons are undamaged by this drenching?"

"Indeed, my lady."

Ysmaine looked down at her husband, now wearing solely his chemise and cursedly pale. "I will wash the wounds. Is there a brazier to be had in this establishment? A warm beverage would serve him well. Perhaps a cup of mulled wine."

"I will see to that," a woman said from the portal, and Ysmaine realized that the courtesan had not returned to her chamber. She looked frightened, though she composed her expression when she found Ysmaine's gaze upon her. She spun and hastened down the stairs, her footfalls fading from earshot.

Wulfe looked after her with a frown.

Ysmaine chose to find a mundane explanation for this event, although she guessed the truth was far from it. "I do not blame her for being distressed," she said softly, even as she washed Gaston's shoulder. "Given where you have been."

"Do you address me?" Wulfe asked coolly.

"Indeed. What other man's actions would concern Christina, at least of the company in this chamber?"

His lips tightened. "My affairs are not your concern."

"My husband's situation is. Will you grant me an explanation for this?"

"I need not do so."

"Then I will make a guess." Ysmaine surveyed Gaston. "She is dismayed because you had need of a second whore," she said tightly. "Yet you could not indulge in such vice without leaving my husband to sleep as he desired. You had to draw him into your scheme, and doubtless lured him to some part of the city of ill repute where you were assaulted. Were you both robbed? Or only my lord husband?" She let disdain fill her tone. "Praise be that you did not leave him to rot in the streets. Praise be that his squire saw fit to follow you both, that he might defend my lord husband in such peril as you invited with your sinful urges."

Wulfe hung his head, accepting her version of matters so readily that she knew it could not be true. If it had been the case, this proud knight would have argued the matter most heatedly with her. Bartholomew shifted his weight from foot to foot, uneasy beyond belief.

Aye, they had a secret these three. Had Wulfe not muttered that it had been Gaston's idea? Gaston led them in some quest which had gone awry, and his role had been discovered. If they could not protect her husband, then Ysmaine would do so.

"Leave this chamber, sir," she said to Wulfe, ensuring that her tone was proud and haughty. "I have no more to say to you, although your courtesan may no longer believe you to be her champion." She bent over Gaston, then glanced up at the Templar. "But then, perhaps that was the root of your scheme this night."

Wulfe's lips tightened. "My lady," he began, but Ysmaine rose to her feet again.

"Leave us, sir. I will bar my door against men of such base desires as yours."

Christina returned with one of Wulfe's squires, directing him to place the brazier he carried in the corner of the chamber. He lit the coal within it. It was the older boy, Stephen, and his dismay at the sight in her chamber was most clear. Christina gave the wine to Radegunde, then departed, sparing a glance from the threshold back at Wulfe.

That knight lingered, his manner grim. "He is not so badly injured, is he?"

"I suspect not, but if so, I will send Radegunde to tell you of it."

He bowed then and departed, striding past Christina with nary a word as he descended the stairs. His knavery was of no concern to Ysmaine.

She turned a quelling look upon the gaping Stephen, who accepted Gaston's boots from Bartholomew and scurried out the door.

Bartholomew gathered the rest of the armor, bowing before Ysmaine. "If I can be of any aid, my lady, no matter the hour, I would beg of you to summon me," he said. "And if my lord knight is more ill than you believe, again, I would ask to know of it."

"Bartholomew, I thank you again for your assistance. If I or my lord husband has need of your aid, you can be sure I will ask for it. I beg of you to see yourself warmed before you fall ill." Ysmaine forced a smile. "I imagine my husband will soon have need of you."

"I pray it will be so, my lady," Bartholomew said. He granted Gaston one last glance, then departed with obvious reluctance.

It was only when she was alone with Radegunde and the portal was locked behind them that Ysmaine could fall to her knees beside her injured husband and give way to the fear that clutched at her heart.

She could not lose him, not at any price.

❧

Ysmaine only breathed a sigh of relief hours later.

Finally, Gaston stirred, frowned and rolled to his side.

She might have wept in her relief.

She had cleaned and stitched the wound in his shoulder and

bathed the back of his head where he had been struck. His pulse had remained steady and strong, though she disliked the measure of blood in his aketon and tabard.

"He seems to sleep normally," Radegunde dared to suggest, and Ysmaine nodded agreement. She was exhausted suddenly, her fears having abandoned her.

The portal was locked against the others and it was yet night, although she heard a cock crow at close proximity. The house was comparatively silent, though she heard the rumble of men's voices in the common room below. Doubtless Wulfe and Fergus conferred over their course.

Now that Gaston slept, she could tend to his secrets. Ysmaine tested the spot on the front of Gaston's aketon and was relieved to feel the vellum of that missive yet in place. The padded garment was sodden, though, and she had a sudden fear for the ink of the missive. As Gaston had not read it, he could not deliver its message by memory. She picked out the stitches and removed the missive, seeing the ink leaking from one side of it.

She hesitated only a moment before breaking the seal and unfurling the document. To her relief, the ink had only run at one margin and the majority of the script could yet be read. She denied temptation and did not read it, merely weighed down the corners before leaving the document to dry.

She and Radegunde rolled the aketon and walked upon it, forcing out the water as well as they could. The maid had already done the same to Gaston's tabard and hung it near the lit brazier in the hope that it might dry by morning.

Ysmaine's gaze fell anew upon the bundle where the relic was hidden. It seemed most vulnerable to her, no matter how they managed to carry it, and she feared that the villain responsible for Gaston's injury would yet manage to seize it.

She would not see her husband dishonored.

But how could she aid him? She could not consult with him, not on this night when he lay injured. Indeed, she had not been able to confer with him otherwise, for he believed his secrets should not be her own.

"What vexes you, my lady?"

"We will leave Venice in a day or so," Ysmaine admitted quietly. She gestured to the bundle containing the relic. "How shall we best disguise it?"

Radegunde sat close by her mistress, frowning a little. "There is one place no man would deign to examine."

Ysmaine glanced up with curiosity.

"My mother did this once, when your father's holding was besieged. She smuggled a message from him to an ally through the ranks of his attackers."

Ysmaine's excitement rose. "I remember this feat! They let her pass because she was a woman and so evidently close to her time."

The women's gazes met and held. Radegunde's mother had *not* been with child, but the strangers who held the gate had not known as much. The belly that the attackers believed to her unborn child had been a bundle, one that included a missive to the ally and several jewels to prove the identity of the sender.

Radegunde dropped her voice. "You do try to conceive your lord husband's son. Who is to say when you will succeed?"

"It is too big," Ysmaine protested. "I could not be so large so soon, and they have seen me since Jerusalem. If it appears suddenly, the truth will be evident to all."

"Then disguise yourself from this day forward."

"Still, we would be in Paris before I could carry so large a child."

"Only if it was wrought of your husband's seed."

Ysmaine gasped, then met the confident gaze of her maid. "But that should mean that I had deceived him, that I had lied to him."

"You might confide in him," Radegunde suggested but Ysmaine shook her head.

"Nay, it would not do. He is a man of such virtue and integrity that he would not be able to deceive his fellows. They would spy the ruse immediately."

"Do you not trust them?"

"I trust few souls in this party: you and my husband and perhaps his squire." Ysmaine chewed her lip, thinking furiously. What if she deceived Gaston only for a few moments? When her state was revealed, she could contrive that they argued before the entire company. Then once he had reacted with outrage at her 'deception,' she could confide in him the truth in privacy.

Surely, he would recognize that she had acted for the greater good?

Surely, he would be grateful that the relic was defended?

Surely, her action would convince him of the merit of a marriage based on partnership and discussion?

She bent beside him, encouraged that he was both warm and seemed to be sleeping easily. A scab was already forming on his wound and she was glad of his vitality. No doubt they would depart soon, which meant she had to choose her course.

Ysmaine watched her husband sleep until the dawn, then made her choice. She bent to kiss his cheek when sounds of the awakening household rose from the courtyard and whispered to him. "Forgive me, sir, for what I must do. Forgive me and trust in the greater good."

❧

Forgive me.

Gaston heard Ysmaine's entreaty in his dreams, a whisper from miles away that yet managed to prick his attention.

Forgive her for what?

What did she intend to do?

The question roused him from sleep, though his body was sore and his head was pounding. He awakened to find himself in his lady's chamber yet, in her pallet, and doubted his own memory when she threw herself upon him with evident relief.

"Sir! You awaken!"

Gaston sat up, undaunted by the thudding in his skull. He could not lie abed. He had to speak to Wulfe about the night before. He had to discover what that knight had witnessed, and if possible, identify who had been absent from the house.

"What happened?" Ysmaine demanded. "What do you recall?"

"I will speak to the other knights of it," Gaston said, fearing he would distress her. "You need not know of it."

"Sir." She fixed him with a determined look and he knew that he had again offended her. "May I at least listen to the accounting of your misfortune?"

He rose to his feet, spying his chausses and chemise by the window. He could defend himself better when garbed, to be sure. Gaston took a step toward the garments, then halted to stare at what could only be the missive from Brother Terricus.

Unfurled and spread upon the table.

The seal broken.

He spun to face Ysmaine, who had wrapped herself in her cloak. She eyed him with a familiar defiance in her eyes. "I feared the ink would run," she said, anticipating his objection. "And so it had begun. Look at the margin."

Gaston looked and could not deny it. "Did you read it?"

"Nay. I was more concerned with you than the missive."

Gaston knew only that he had been sworn to secrecy, and he feared to have the contents of the missive revealed to any other soul than its intended recipient. "Swear it to me."

Ysmaine's lips tightened. "I swear as much," she said with reassuring alacrity, evidently vexed that he demanded this of her. "But *you* should read it."

"I pledged..."

"Aye, I know. And that was why I had to ensure it remained legible. If it had been destroyed, whatever message it carried would be lost forever." She shrugged and turned her back to him to don her kirtle. "I can only assume its contents have some import. Why else would it have been dispatched?"

Gaston eyed the smeared ink. Though his head ached, he knew she spoke aright. He could not have delivered the missive if all the ink had run, or indeed, if the document had been stolen. He had given his word, but he believed that even Terricus would cede to the logic in this.

He donned his chemise and chausses, but could see no sign of his boots.

"Sodden," Ysmaine supplied, evidently guessing what he sought. "Bartholomew took them, along with your belt, hauberk and weapons. I bade him ensure they were in suitable repair for you this morning." She crossed the floor before him, fully dressed, and examined his tabard. "It is dry enough, thanks to Radegunde's labor."

"Bartholomew could have tended to it, as well."

Ysmaine lifted her chin and there was a flash in her eyes that Gaston took as a warning. "I kept your treasures close, sir, as is the duty of your wife."

"There was no need for you to do such labor."

"I say there is. People would think ill of a wife who did not attend her husband's needs."

Gaston realized he had granted offense when he had not meant to do so. Truly, he was accustomed to relying upon his squire and no other! "I apologize," he said with a slight bow. "I am less familiar with the rightful obligations of a wife than you. I meant only that you could have trusted Bartholomew."

To his relief, Ysmaine smiled a little. "Ah, I understand and I believe you are right. Bartholomew saved your life at the risk of his own." Ysmaine touched him fleetingly and her voice faltered. "Some soul tried to do you injury, sir, if not to kill you." Gaston saw her concern and claimed her hand, intent upon reassuring her. Her question surprised him. "Is this missive why?"

Gaston frowned and dropped his gaze. "It was but a thief, I am certain, seizing an opportunity." It was strange how he found it increasingly unpalatable to keep matters from his wife. The night before, their mating had been both magical and potent, and he had dared to believe their future assured. On this morn, there seemed new obstacles between them and he could not help but think that the assault upon him was less at root than her perceptive nature.

Indeed, Ysmaine's lips tightened at his reply and Gaston wondered how much she had discerned of the truth.

He was the one who had insisted upon honesty, but he guessed that his lady was no less fond of truth than he. He wished this quest were behind him that he might speak to her plainly, and not feel his loyalties were divided.

To his surprise, she accepted his explanation easily.

Perhaps too easily.

"Bad fortune, then," she said lightly, turning away from him again. "But still, you might have lost the missive, sir. It would be most unfortunate if you could not deliver it or share its tidings."

"You speak aright," Gaston acknowledged, then sat to read it in full. There was naught within it that truly surprised him, though he had not known the fullness of the tidings Terricus had clearly received. He read it twice, checked that the vellum and ink were dry, then heated the wax seal slightly at the brazier. He sealed the document anew, catching Ysmaine's gaze upon him. "I shall tell the Master of the Temple that I have read it," he said, wanting to ensure she did not believe he intended any deceit. "But this will ensure that I know if any other soul does so."

Her brows rose, though she said naught.

He reached for the aketon, only to find that it was yet wet.

"It will take at least this day to dry, sir," the maid informed him. "I shall put it in the sun and turn it often to hasten the process."

Gaston considered the missive, then secreted it in his sleeve. He would hide it beneath his tabard once he had his belt again. Ysmaine watched him in silence and he knew he yet owed her an apology.

"Your counsel was wise, lady mine," he admitted. "I thank you for it, and for whatever assistance you granted to me last night."

"Will you tell me what occurred?"

Gaston smiled. "I will tell Wulfe what I recall, for he shall have to decide what best to do."

He had a fleeting glimpse of her displeasure, then she cast her new cloak over her shoulders. Gaston had a fleeting sense that his wife made some decision, or closed some portal against him.

Forgive me. Her murmured words echoed again in his thoughts.

He stepped toward her, wanting to recover the ease that had been between them the night before. "You will be overwarm," he advised, reaching to lift her cloak.

Ysmaine merely cast him a smile and stepped beyond his reach. "I think not. I find myself chilled in this city, sir." She shivered elaborately, then strode to the door. The maid turned the key in the lock, even as her lady glanced over her shoulder. "Would you clean the chamber, please, Radegunde? I will bring you something to break your fast, if you might see it done sooner."

"Of course, my lady. I shall be glad to do it."

Gaston looked between the women, fighting a sense that they knew something he did not, then winced at the pounding in his head. Indeed, the incident of the night before left him seeing peril where there was none.

If naught else, he could trust Ysmaine.

At least he believed as much until he spoke to Wulfe.

Chapter Seventeen

"Did you see him?" Gaston asked Wulfe in an undertone. The two men were in the stables, purportedly checking their steeds. Ysmaine was in the common room, breaking her fast, and Fergus brushed his own steed. His presence was apparently a coincidence, but he watched the courtyard.

"No more than a shadow," Wulfe acknowledged.

"The ploy failed, then."

"We drew the villain out, that much is certain." The portal to the street was opened, and Joscelin returned, his manner jovial. He waved farewell to an acquaintance and hummed to himself as he crossed the courtyard to the common room. He looked well pleased and had been clearly absent all the night long.

To Gaston's dismay, he made directly for Ysmaine, who smiled thinly. Her gaze flicked to the stables, then back to the merchant. Everard lounged at the other end of the board and Wulfe's courtesan sat alone in the courtyard, dipping bread into honey then eating it with languor.

"Has your wife not been widowed twice?" Wulfe asked.

Gaston glared at the Templar. "Of what import is that?"

Wulfe shrugged. "We were not followed to Venice. The treasure is yet secure, according to Fergus. Perhaps there was another reason you were attacked."

"You cannot still suspect my lady wife."

Wulfe's gaze was knowing. "She refused to summon an apothecary for you last night."

Gaston felt his own eyes narrow, but he argued for his lady. Twice before, circumstance had cast her in poor light, and in both cases, there had been a reasonable explanation—and one that proved her innocence. He would not doubt her again. "She was merely optimistic."

"It was before we knew the extent of your injury." Wulfe leaned closer. "Then she cast every soul but her maid from the chamber." He shook his head. "In truth, if I did not know you to be too cursed stubborn to die, I might have feared you would not survive the night."

Gaston did not believe the other knight truly perceived a threat to his survival. This man, he knew well, liked to sow doubt about Ysmaine and her intentions. Gaston would not be swayed. Still he noted how Joscelin and his lady conferred on the far side of the courtyard with some uneasiness. "Yet you did not intervene or protest?"

"What protest could I have made? I but watched and listened as well I could."

"She knows of healing. Perhaps she perceived more than you did, and more quickly."

Wulfe shrugged, unconvinced.

Gaston frowned, considering his wife's manner of this morn. "I fear she may have guessed more than I would prefer of our errand."

"I think not," the Templar scoffed. "Her assumption was faulty, though I saw no reason to correct it for it was useful."

Gaston was confused. "How so?"

"She was quick to accuse me of enticing you to seek out whores."

Gaston was dismayed that his wife should have any reason to think him guilty of such a deed. "Ysmaine said as much?"

"Aye, she was heartily vexed with me. I did tell her that our errand had been your idea, but she did not believe me."

Gaston was somewhat mollified by that, but still troubled by Ysmaine's accusation. She had not spoken highly of Wulfe and his inclinations, and Gaston did not want her to see him in similar light.

Wulfe evidently took his silence as annoyance. "I was so relieved that she concocted a plausible tale that I dared not argue with her." He grimaced. "To my own discomfort."

"How so?"

"Christina believed her."

Gaston might have been amused by the other knight's chagrin had he not been concerned. He was amazed that Ysmaine believed he had gone to a whore, after the interval they had shared.

Was vexation the root of her strange mood this morn?

How could he defend himself without revealing the truth of his quest to her?

"Well, you have naught to fear in that," he retorted. "You have told me repeatedly that Christina is not your courtesan or companion. Doubtless, she will be left behind on our departure and her conclusions will be of no relevance." He leaned closer to the other knight and dropped his voice to a whisper. "I would thank you, though, to refrain from tarnishing my repute with my lady wife. She and I are bound until death us do part."

Wulfe snorted. "Given last night's incident, death may come sooner than you had planned. I suggest this tactic: that you and I both avoid our respective women. Let the villain believe that dissent has been sown between us."

Gaston considered this for only a moment before he discerned the merit of the plan. The villain evidently targeted the knights, undoubtedly seeking the treasure. Were he to feign a disagreement with Ysmaine, she would not be perceived to be allied with him, or to know any detail that could make her a victim of this fiend's scheme. It would draw all the violence to himself and Wulfe.

Gaston did not like that he would have to trick his lady, but her conviction in his disapproval must be complete. She had no ability to deceive.

They would reach Paris in a matter of weeks, the treasure would be delivered, and he could spend the remainder of his life regaining her good will.

"Agreed," he said with a terse nod. "But let us ride out as soon as may be." The knights exchanged a look of resolve. "Now let us argue loudly about our departure and our route. I will insist upon granting you advice you do not desire, as has happened before."

❧

Ysmaine wished that Gaston did not confer so long in the stables with the Templar Wulfe. She sat in the common room, awaiting her spouse's company. Duncan, the man at arms who traveled with Fergus sat in the opposite corner. Evidently he intended to blend with the shadows, for he was yet furled in his cloak and said naught at all.

Ysmaine yearned to know what Wulfe and Gaston discussed.

Joscelin the merchant returned to the house, thumping on the door for admission, then fairly capering across the courtyard. Clearly he was in a merry mood. His eyes lit when he spied Ysmaine at the board, and he immediately came to sit opposite her. Ysmaine wished he would leave her be.

She was far more interested in trying to hear what passed between Gaston and Wulfe. She did not like her husband's pallor, or that he had insisted upon leaving her chamber to check upon his steed. To her thinking, he should have slept the day away, or at least lounged abed with her.

"My lady, you are clearly a noblewoman of great discernment, and one who appreciates the value of fine spices," Joscelin began. He placed a small trunk upon the table, holding it as if it were made of gold. "And so I would offer this prize to you first of all, for I have seldom seen frankincense of such quality..."

"I thank you but I have little use for frankincense," Ysmaine replied sweetly.

"Is it not used for the preparation of corpses for burial?" Everard contributed, taking the seat beside the merchant. Duncan snorted in laughter at that. "Given that the lady's husband was so recently assaulted, your appeal is somewhat poorly timed, Joscelin."

The merchant flushed. "You think of myrrh, sir, which also dulls pain. Frankincense is burned to scent the air in both sacred spaces and fine homes, such as the one Lady Ysmaine will soon occupy."

The knight feigned surprise in a way that made Ysmaine fight a smile. "Sacred spaces? Does the lady intend to live in a church? Or join a convent? I suspect her husband would take issue with either plan."

Ysmaine intervened then, not wanting the merchant to be insulted. "I thank you for this courtesy, Joscelin. You honor me by showing me such fine wares." She let her tone become more firm. "However, as I have told you before, it is not fitting for me to make acquisitions for my husband's manor before I have seen it or reviewed its inventories."

"Of course, of course, my lady." Joscelin packed away his

little trunk, then regarded her with hope. "But might I suggest that I visit you at Châmont-sur-Maine, perhaps before the Yule, to better learn of any lack in your inventories?"

"Again, I thank you for such consideration. You be sure, sir, that if I have need of provisions you can supply, I will send word to you in Provins."

The little man was delighted by this thin promise and proceeded to give Ysmaine elaborate directions to his shop, that he might be located readily in this circumstance. She glanced toward the stables as Wulfe raised his voice.

Joscelin noted her disinterest and excused himself elaborately before scurrying away.

"The tolls on the Saint Bernard Pass are well known to be expensive beyond belief, and there are thieves, to be sure," Wulfe said. "That is why I suggest the alternate route to the southwest that the merchants use, through the Mont Cenis Pass..."

"Which will leave us much farther south than Paris," Gaston interrupted calmly. "And is a longer journey from Venice. I thought you were the one who wished to reach Paris with all haste?"

Wulfe made an exclamation that expressed his frustration clearly even though the word could not be heard. "The road may be longer but it is said to be in better repair. We shall make better time."

Gaston shook his head, unconvinced, then argued for the welfare of the squire, Hamish. Ysmaine wished he would argue for his own welfare as well.

After all, he had been assaulted just the night before.

"I thought the road through the Saint Bernard Pass most excellent," Ysmaine said to Everard, agreeing with her husband.

"It has been years since I traveled either," Everard said with a smile. "I shall leave the argument to those who know more of the roads in question."

Ysmaine thought he might have lingered to converse more, but Christina rose to enter the common room, a smile playing over her full lips. The knight averted his gaze, clearly disapproving of her occupation, and strode from the room. He, too, went to check upon his horse.

"Who is he?" Christina asked, settling onto the bench opposite

Ysmaine. Again, her leisurely movements reminded Ysmaine of a contented cat, although her eyes were bright as she watched Everard's departure. "He seems most pleased with himself."

"I suppose his pride is not undeserved," Ysmaine replied. "He is Everard de Montmorency."

Christina visibly started at this. "Truly?"

"And the Count of Blanche Garde, besides," Duncan contributed. "A man whose piety is well known in Outremer." He unfolded himself from his corner and claimed a piece of bread, dipping it into the honey beside Christina. "I doubt he would savor your wares."

Christina blinked then seemed to fight a smile.

"Do you know him?" Ysmaine asked.

The courtesan shook her head hastily. "I have merely heard his name. As this man notes, his piety is well known." Her gaze trailed after the nobleman. Her lips quirked, her expression mischievous. "To even be in the same abode as such a man is most amusing. Perhaps I should try to seduce him, to see whether his deeds are as lofty as his words."

She unfastened her girdle and pooled it upon the table, her expression unreadable. Ysmaine had glimpsed the belt before, but saw now that it was a far more vulgar item than she had realized. The supposed gold already chipped from the links and the supposed gems were so vivid an orange that they could not be any true gem Ysmaine could name. Christina grimaced and began to break it apart, evidently sharing Ysmaine's view.

Had it been a gift from Wulfe? From another lover? Ysmaine saw the resolve in the other woman's gestures and did not dare to ask. Why would she break it apart? It was useful, if not elegant.

"You might try to seduce me," Duncan suggested, then took a place on the bench beside the courtesan. The roughened warrior gave Christina an appreciative smile. "Though you might find it more of an easy victory than you seem to prefer."

"And what is that to mean?" Christina asked idly.

"Only that you seem to like a challenge. It is a rare courtesan who would seek an enduring alliance with a knight like Wulfe. I cannot imagine that you will succeed in that, though I enjoy watching your attempt."

Christina granted him a cold glare. "I am gratified to know that someone finds amusement in my situation," she said, then bent over her task.

Duncan was untroubled by her dismissal, merely raising his cup of wine in salute to Christina's rigid spine.

"What will you do with it?" Ysmaine asked, genuinely curious and unable to remain silent.

Christina smiled. "Destroy it." She lifted those magnificent eyes to meet Ysmaine's gaze. "It marks me as chattel, and I would be chattel no longer."

"Has it any value?"

"Its destruction will bring satisfaction, which might be value enough."

Ysmaine watched her for a few moments, noting how quickly the pile of cut glass tokens grew. "Will you discard them?"

"Not yet. I will keep them, in case there is a purpose to be wrung from it."

"Have you a sack for the pieces?"

"Nay. Why?"

"I will give you one," Ysmaine offered. "There is one in my belongings for which I have no use." She rose to her feet even as Christina regarded her with surprise. "It is only a plain cloth bag," she said with a smile.

"Yet more than any soul has given to me in a very long time." Christina blinked quickly. "I thank you for this courtesy, Lady Ysmaine. Your kindness is much appreciated."

Ysmaine retreated to her chamber to fetch the sack and check upon Radegunde's progress, well pleased that her impulse had steered her true.

❧

Boys, the villain concluded. The boys were the key.

The knights revealed no detail of their quest or their secret, and indeed, one would never have guessed by their manner that they were entrusted even with the missive that they must carry. The Templars, truly, were skilled in subterfuge.

But boys, in the villain's estimation, were cursedly curious and most adept at discovering what they should not know. There was always the potential of using one of the squires to nefarious purpose, but then the villain recalled the incident on the ship.

Kerr had been accosted by Bartholomew.

Perhaps it had not been a minor squabble between boys. Perhaps they had argued over some matter of import.

Like the respective roles of their knights.

Or the importance of a burden entrusted to one of them.

Or even, its location.

The villain watched both squires with greater care after this realization and came to the conclusion that Kerr *had* learned some detail of import. The boy's gaze darted over the company, and he seemed to hold a secret close. He appeared to be the manner of person who gathered information, perhaps even one who would barter over either his silence or the price of sharing a secret.

The villain believed they might have much to discuss.

Though the ultimate terms would not be to the boy's liking, there was no reason to reveal all too soon.

The villain would wait until they were upon the road, the better to have the party isolated and at his mercy.

๚

Ysmaine might have lost her resolve, if Gaston had touched her.

But there was to be no risk of that. Indeed, he spent nigh all of their remaining time in Venice in either the stables or the common room of the house. He allowed himself to be examined by the apothecary when that man came to see about Hamish again, but he did not confide whatever was said in Ysmaine. Neither did they ride out with the haste Wulfe had recommended, so she guessed the apothecary had advised rest.

Yet Gaston did not rest. He was always up, always pacing, always active. That the man showed such disregard for his own welfare made her wish to strike sense into him. Yet she could not reason with him if he did not speak to her.

Ysmaine did not wish to leave the chamber lest the relic be unattended, so she feigned an illness. She hoped her husband might come to her and they might talk then, but Gaston sent word by Radegunde to ask after her recovery.

He did not even come to her bed that night.

Ysmaine tried to convince herself that it was for the best. She realized belatedly that Gaston only confided in her reluctantly, and when he came to her bed. Evidently, if he did not seduce her, they would not talk at all.

That he appeared to be unconcerned by this lack of communication was not reassuring in the least. Was this how he imagined their future life together?

It was far less than Ysmaine desired of him and of marriage. Indeed, she nigh wore a trough in the floor of her chamber, so agitatedly did she pace.

Two nights passed without her husband's companionship, and Ysmaine found the change deeply troubling. Even in the common room when she descended to eat, he avoided her so consistently that it could not be coincidence. He was departing when she arrived or in the stables, conferring with squires or arguing with Wulfe. He did not abandon these activities to join her.

Did Gaston no longer desire a son? Did he distrust her? Was he more ill than she had believed? She could think of no good reason for his absence and found herself increasingly sleepless.

On the third night, Radegunde was combing out Ysmaine's hair when a familiar knock sounded at the door. Ysmaine pulled her cloak about herself, hiding her stomach from view. The maid put down the comb and opened the door, and Ysmaine felt her heart clench at the sight of Gaston. He leaned in the doorway to consider her, even as Radegunde stood waiting.

"And how do you fare?" he asked and Ysmaine nigh flinched at the disinterest in his tone.

"Still cold," she said and shivered to punctuate the lie. She thought for a moment that he would question her, but he said naught. "And you?"

"As hale as ever," he said with a crooked smile, one that made her heart skip. "It has oft been said that my head is as hard as a rock."

"And your shoulder?"

"Much improved." He straightened then, his manner purposeful. Ysmaine thought she might have imagined that his expression had lightened, for he was cool and distant yet again. "The apothecary has declared all fit to ride, and Wulfe would leave on the morrow. Do you think you are sufficiently hale?"

"I would not delay the party, sir."

Gaston nodded once, again looked as if he might say more, then stepped back. "At dawn, then, madame."

"Will you not linger, sir?" Ysmaine asked.

"Not this night. I would not trouble you when you feel unwell."

It was on Ysmaine's lips to protest that he would not soon have a son if he abandoned the marital bed, then she recalled her ruse and bit her lip. "You limp again," she said. "Would you allow me to give you relief with the liniment?"

His gaze hardened. "No longer." He put out a hand. "In fact, I would ask you for it and the remaining herb, that both might be destroyed."

Ysmaine was startled that his trust in her should have eroded so much. But his gaze was so hard that there could be no doubt of his suspicion. What manner of marriage would they have if he refused to trust her? She fetched both root and bottle, though, for only quick compliance would show her in favorable light, and surrendered both to him.

Their fingers brushed in the transaction, and Ysmaine longed to touch him more fully. Gaston eyed the bottle and root, then lifted his gaze to hers. His eyes were vividly blue and she sensed a tumult within him.

But he said naught. He gave no explanation. He merely bent and kissed her so sweetly that she burned for more. "I am sorry," he murmured, his words so low and husky that only she could discern them.

Gaston pivoted and strode away, leaving Ysmaine filled with a curious mix of disappointment and relief. She hated to deceive him at all, but knew that if he caressed her as he had that last time, she would have confessed every truth she knew to him.

Why was he sorry? What had he done?

What did he mean to do?

"And so we depart," Radegunde murmured. She had wrapped the relic with care and sewn a pocket into Ysmaine's chemise. It would be bound to her belly as well, as secure as it could be.

What if Ysmaine's ploy was found out?

What if it was not discovered and Gaston believed her lie?

She could not sleep that night, though in truth, her pallor and the shadows beneath her eyes only gave credence to the first of her lies to her husband.

ᵈ℗

Gaston descended the stairs to the common room, much troubled by the change in his lady wife. She was pale and looked as if she had not slept. He feared that she had contracted some illness, though she did not confide as much in him. He wished he could spend time in her close company, but he had himself insisted to Wulfe that they keep a watch each night.

He had a sense that some threat grew and he feared the long, lonely distance to Paris. He knew that Wulfe would ride as hard as possible, and given the circumstances, he agreed.

But he was concerned for Ysmaine.

On his return to the stables, he paused to look up at the darkened window of her chamber for the merest heartbeat, then continued to Fantôme's stall. He passed Duncan on his way, that man wrapped tightly in his cloak and disguised by the shadows. They shared the first watch, the man-at-arms watching the common room. A light burned brightly there, as Everard and Joscelin played at dice, the courtesan looking on with boredom.

"He wins a great deal for a pious man," Duncan noted but Gaston did not care for Everard's vices.

"I would ask you to befriend my wife," he murmured softly then continued past the other man.

Duncan nodded but once, his gaze unwavering from the activities in the common room. "Aye, sir," he agreed, understanding that it was an order. Doubtless, he also guessed the reasoning behind it.

Bartholomew was already asleep, as were the other squires. Gaston thought that Laurent watched him from the far end of the stables, but when he glanced at the boy, he was clearly asleep. His mind played tricks upon him, and he saw threats where there were none. The saddlebag was hugged so close by the boy that he might have been a limpet grown upon it.

No one would ever separate the two. Reassured, Gaston wrapped his cloak around himself and settled into the darkness at the back of the stables, taking his turn at keeping a vigilant watch on the portal.

Only once the true threat was revealed and purged would he sleep in truth.

Only when his duty was complete could he bend his full attention on seducing his lady wife. Though Gaston chafed at the delay, he reasoned their ride to Paris would be fast and hard. Ysmaine would not complain, for it was not in her nature to do so, but Duncan would let him know if she ailed overmuch.

It was a poor situation, but a temporary one, and Gaston was well used to making do with what was less than ideal.

The sole consolation was that he was certain his lady had learned similar tolerance.

Monday, July 28, 1187

Feast Day of Saint Samson
and the Apostle,
Saint James the Great.

❦

Claire Delacroix

Chapter Eighteen

The company departed from Venice, the rain beating down on their shoulders. It seemed a despondent party to Ysmaine, with only Wulfe seeming glad to depart. She was surprised to see Christina in their company, riding one of Wulfe's palfreys. Though knight and courtesan exchanged a hot glare, Wulfe did not protest her presence, and Christina rode at the back of the party.

Gaston had handed Ysmaine into her saddle, but had frowned when she had refused to let him lift her. She knew that if he locked his hands around her waist, her subterfuge would be revealed too soon. She felt rather than saw the other knights note the discord between herself and her husband. She flushed but held her head high when they set out.

She made no comment when they passed through the city walls, and Gaston eased his destrier forward. It appeared that he merely conferred with Wulfe about the route, but he remained at the lead of the party.

Instead of by her side.

Radegunde urged her palfrey forward, to ride on Ysmaine's right hand. Everard spurred his horse to join Wulfe and Gaston, eagerly participating in the conference about their route. Joscelin dropped back to speak with Christina, who replied tersely to his queries, while Fergus conferred with Bartholomew about the best defense of the group. The road was yet busy, but Ysmaine knew that by afternoon, they would likely be alone upon its length and vulnerable to bandits. The knights wore their armor openly, their scabbards bared to view. She did not doubt this was intended to defer the interest of villains.

The older Scottish warrior was on her left, as he had been before, but Ysmaine jumped when he spoke to her. "It is the curse of these Templars at root, lass," he confided, his manner confidential. Ysmaine flicked a glance his way, uncertain he addressed her. His eyes gleamed, though, and he smiled. "They gain a lofty view of the world, particularly of women, and can be harsh judges upon leaving the confines of the order."

"I do not know what you mean," Ysmaine said, more for the sake of appearances than any truth. She could not guess how many listened to their conversation, though they seemed to be indifferent. Her hand, hidden beneath her cloak, stole over her supposed belly once more.

"A high moral code means that it is easy for another to fall short of the measure," Duncan continued with a nod. "I see it time and again in these men. Their hearts are valiant, to be sure. Their shortcoming is a failure to see that others must often make choices from a poor array of options, though they do so without hesitation themselves." He glanced back toward Christina. "As with this one. As your husband has noted, women are not born whores any more than men are born knights. I cannot believe one of such birth would have chosen that occupation either."

"Such birth?" Ysmaine echoed.

Duncan chuckled. "No one looks truly at a whore, lass. Have you seen how she eats? How she carries herself? How she speaks?" He shook his head. "This one was wrought in no hovel."

Ysmaine could say nothing in response to that. Could Christina have been nobly born? She reviewed what she had noted of the other woman and saw the merit of Duncan's reasoning

"I have seen it time and again, lass." Duncan shook his head. "Few women manage a pilgrimage to Jerusalem and back without incident, if their husband or defender is lost on the way. There is a reason why the Holy City has an unholy number of prostitutes. To be sure, each one rode out in pursuit of a far more lofty goal than such degradation."

Ysmaine swallowed, aware of how close she herself had come to such a fate. Her gaze rose to Gaston's broad shoulders, and again she felt gratitude toward him for his intervention.

Duncan nodded at her, his manner genial. "You are a woman of good fortune, to be sure, and the man you have wed is an honorable one. Do not blame him overmuch if he has a doubt now and then. They will pass, as he sees the truth of your measure."

"I thank you, Duncan," Ysmaine said, appreciating that he had troubled to reassure her. "You undoubtedly know more of such knights than I do."

Indeed, she felt more than gratitude toward Gaston, though Ysmaine realized only the fullness of it now. Had that been the limit of her regard, she would not be so dismayed to withhold the truth from him. She would not have missed his touch so keenly. She would not have been so devastated when she thought him lost in Acre. Her heart would not have leapt with such vigor when he granted her the favor of a smile.

She would not be imagining the joy of their lives together and be so upset by the prospect of disappointing him.

She loved him.

But if Gaston was a man of such high moral code as the warrior suggested, her choice not only to deceive him but to choose this way to do so, could only turn him against her forever.

Would she defend her husband's honor at the price of losing his good will forever?

If only he would speak to her, she would confess all!

But that situation was not to be.

ॐ

It was a miserable day, for the rain grew colder and fell with greater force with every passing hour. They were all soaked to the skin and the horses were mired to their bellies. Wulfe would have pressed onward, but Gaston was keenly aware of the pallor of his lady wife.

When darkness fell, he insisted that they halt at the first light they spied.

Wulfe agreed only with reluctance. To Gaston's dismay, that first light shone from an inn so humble that it was impoverished and mean. There was only space in the barn for them, which might have been a blessing given the raucous sounds of merriment carrying from the common room.

"We take shelter in a warren frequented by thieves," Wulfe grumbled, but Gaston felt Ysmaine shivering when he handed her down from the saddle. He was adamant that they remain, for she had to have shelter and rest.

The barn was so filthy that the squires had to muck it out.

There was a scurry of activity, as various members used the latrines and professed them disgusting. Garments were wrung out, horses brushed down, boots emptied of water. They worked in unison and grim silence to improve their situation for the night.

They hung sodden cloaks over the beams and paid an outrageous price for the loan of two lanterns, neither of which were full of oil. Wulfe was disgruntled by their circumstance and the others tight-lipped, but Gaston watched Ysmaine.

To his relief and with Radegunde's encouragement, she retreated to a stall and returned in the finer of her new kirtles. He caught a glimpse only of its hem, for she kept that wet cloak wrapped around herself. He was glad that her kirtle and chemise were dry and hoped that the fur lining of the cloak was as well. Duncan encouraged her to sit close to one of the lanterns, and Radegunde fetched her a bowl of stew. Both of them were granted a luminous smile of gratitude that filled Gaston with unfamiliar envy.

Indeed, they could not reach Paris soon enough for his taste.

He had no sooner had the thought than all went awry.

The villain had struck.

ঌ

The stew had to be wrought of goat meat and that of a beast dead of old age, for it was sinewy and strongly flavored. The sauce was thin and the wine had nigh turned to vinegar. Ysmaine could not fathom why the knights had called a halt in this poor excuse for an inn. The sound of gambling in the common room of the tavern was loud, and she did not doubt that there would be a fight there before the dawn. Joscelin and Everard were drawn to the sound of dice rolling and did not return with Fergus when he brought the pot of stew and the wine.

For a man said to be pious, Everard had a fondness for gambling, to be sure.

The bread was hard and for lack of plate or trencher, they each dipped bread into the stew to eat. The knights insisted that she and Christina eat first, and Ysmaine noted that the other woman ate as little as she. Radegunde had only a small measure herself.

Sometimes hunger was the better choice.

The knights returned from the tending of their steeds and squatted in the light of the lanterns as the rain pummeled the roof of the barn. Ysmaine noted their grim moods and guessed that Gaston and Wulfe had disagreed again. A stream of water came through some hole in the roof, splashing into a puddle in the corner and strengthening the scent of manure. Even Laurent did not seem so fragrant in this wretched place.

"At least we are out of the rain," she said, trying to lighten the mood of the party. Gaston flicked a very blue glance in her direction. Wulfe grimaced, though that might have been because he had taken his first bite of the stew.

"You speak aright, my lady," Duncan agreed, and Ysmaine realized she had a new ally. "There are worse places to spend the night. Our garb might be dry by the morning."

Bartholomew joined them then, his expression one of disgust. "They doubled their price for the fodder," he confided in Gaston, whose lips tightened. He granted the younger man some more coin from his purse, which Ysmaine noted was emptying rapidly. Had he taken the coin from his tabard hem as yet? She should grant him the coin sewn into her own hem and resolved to remove it this night.

If her husband would not accept it from her, she would give it to his squire. Bartholomew left again, and the horses stamped, one drinking noisily in its stall.

"Kerr! Hamish! Laurent!" Fergus said, raising his voice. "Come and eat of the meat." He made a face. "Such as it is."

Wulfe called to Stephen and Simon, who stopped brushing his black destrier and came to accept a measure of bread. They squatted down beside him and ate quickly. Hamish did the same, accepting a measure of food from Fergus, which disappeared with speed.

Of course, they were of an age when boys eat mightily. Ysmaine gave the last portion of her bread to Simon, who started before accepting it, then bowed low to her. It, too, was devoured in a heartbeat, as if she had fed a hungry hound.

Fergus frowned into the shadows. "Laurent, come and eat."

"I would not offend the party with my smell, sir."

Fergus laughed. "No soul will even discern it in this hovel. Come."

Ysmaine watched the boy hesitate. He still clung to that bundle as if it were the key to his life.

"Leave it," Fergus instructed. "You can watch it from here."

Reluctantly, Laurent did as he was bidden, his features looking sharp and thin when he stepped into the lantern's light. He ate rapidly as well, and Ysmaine was struck by the boy's small size. His hands were so slender that they could have been those of a girl. He was filthy, though, and despite Fergus' assurances, she did smell the muck of the boy.

"Where is Kerr?" Fergus demanded.

"He went to the latrine, sir," Hamish replied, then heaved a sigh. "In truth, I thought he took overlong to ensure that me and Laurent completed the brushing of all the horses."

Fergus spared a look at Laurent. "He seems to believe my joining your employ puts him above such tasks, sir," the boy confided.

Duncan hid a smile behind a mouthful of stew. "He schemes, that one, to be sure."

Fergus was clearly displeased. "I will not have it. He still rides by my side and is in my service." He pointed at the other boys. "Whatever is not yet done will be left for him to complete." Then he raised his voice. "Kerr! Come eat before you must go without!"

It was an empty threat, though, for when the boy did not respond or appear, Fergus granted Duncan a look. "Save him a measure," he muttered. "He will be glad of it after I find him." He strode from the stables then, pulling up the hood of his cloak as he stepped into the onslaught of the rain.

"I daresay my lord Fergus is more tolerant than I should be in his place," Duncan murmured to Ysmaine.

Glad of any conversation, she turned to him. "Indeed?"

"Indeed. That boy has been trouble since the day he gave his first yell. Even with the entreaty of the lady Isobel, I should not have willingly taken him on such a journey."

"Is the lady Isobel not the knight's betrothed?"

"She is indeed, and a more beauteous maiden has never been seen." Duncan stretched and heaved a sigh, suppressing a small burp. "If you put measure in such matters." He looked suddenly alarmed, then bowed to herself and Christina. "Present company excluded, of course."

Ysmaine smile. "But why would she care to instruct her betrothed on the choice of his squires?"

"Kerr is her nephew. I daresay some fool thought the voyage would put some sense into him. It was a lofty scheme, to be sure." Duncan's manner revealed that the boy had not changed. He forced a smile for her. "But it shall all be behind us soon enough."

Ysmaine might have made some polite reply, but Fergus gave a sudden yell from the direction of the latrines.

"Zounds!" he bellowed, such dismay in his tone that all in the stables rose to their feet. "Help me!"

Gaston swore and strode from the barn, Bartholomew, Wulfe, and Duncan fast behind him. The boys raced after their knights and Christina followed them all. Ysmaine waited in the portal, her heart racing and Radegunde close behind her, until Bartholomew came to her. "My lady, my lord seeks your counsel."

She knew from the squire's expression that something had gone terribly awry.

※

Gaston strode through the mud and rain to Fergus, who was behind the latrines in the darkness on the edge of the forest. He could hear a stream and the mud was so heavy underfoot that it sucked at his boots. Gaston feared he would be drawn down into it, but it only slowed his progress as he made his way to Fergus.

Fergus looked dismayed, and he held something above the mud. That something thrashed and shuddered. To Gaston's horror, it was the boy Kerr.

The squire's features were contorted and his color was bad.

"His heart races then nigh stops," Fergus said.

"He spoke of knowing," Bartholomew murmured and alarm shot through Gaston.

What had the boy known?

And in whom had he confided it?

"Has he spoken to you?" he demanded of Fergus who shook his head.

"What he said made little sense. I no sooner reached him then he staggered and fainted. He has been like this since."

Gaston put his fingers to the boy's throat and felt his erratic pulse. From the smell of his garb, Kerr had been sweating profusely, and it was clear his state was not natural. "Fetch my lady wife," he bade Bartholomew, hoping Ysmaine might have some insight into what plagued the boy.

It seemed, though, that whatever ailed him would be of short duration. He had another convulsion, shuddering mightily, then voided his stomach into the mud.

Gaston seized the boy's head and forced his fingers down his throat, compelling him to vomit again. "The impulse of his body must be right," he informed Fergus, who nodded, and held Kerr.

He bent over the unconscious boy, compelling him to be ill once again. "There is only bile."

"You cannot be certain. Try again." Gaston frowned, thinking of Ysmaine's counsel in treating those who had consumed wolf's bane.

Surely that could not be what ailed the boy? Who would be so cruel as to inflict this fate upon him?

Surely no villain intended to implicate his wife in such a deed?

Ysmaine came through the mud, clinging to Bartholomew's arm. The squire held a lantern aloft and there was a cry from the inn itself. More lanterns spilled out of the building as the gamblers evidently became curious.

Gaston watched his wife closely and did not miss how the blood drained from her face. "Who did this to him?" she whispered. Without awaiting a reply, she stumbled forward, abandoning Bartholomew and miring her gown as she hastened to Fergus. He found it admirable that she had such compassion, but knew her move could be misconstrued. "Did he speak nonsense? Did he convulse? What of his pulse?"

"Erratic," Gaston replied. "Very fast then so slow as to be almost stopped."

"And was he ill?"

"He vomited once and was encouraged to do so thrice more."

"And is there improvement?" she asked, her eyes filled with hope.

Gaston shook his head and saw her posture droop. At that, he knew. He dropped a hand on Fergus' shoulder even as Kerr gave a mighty shudder.

The boy then stilled. Fergus shook him and tried to revive him, but Kerr was limp. There was no doubt that he had expired, and Gaston watched Ysmaine look away. She seemed smaller and more vulnerable, as well as cold, and he wished to comfort her.

"What will I tell Isobel?" Fergus demanded of Kerr. "How will I explain to her that you do not come home with me?" He looked up at Duncan, his agitation clear. "We will take him home! She would want it thus."

The older man shook his head. "We are months away from Scotland. The boy should be laid to his rest here, before we continue."

"But Isobel..."

"Take a lock of his hair for her to remember him by." Duncan's advice was sensible, and Fergus nodded with reluctance. He lifted Kerr and carried him back to the barn, and Gaston did not have the heart to dissuade him. His dismay would only be worse if animals ravaged the boy's body in the night.

Who had done this vile thing? Gaston recalled Ysmaine's suspicion that some of the root had been missing from the sack granted to her by Fatima. He knew that his wife did not have either liniment or root now, although only her maid might be aware of that fact. He had shattered the bottle of liniment on Venice's docks and let its small quantity be diluted in the waters of the Adriatic. The portion of root he had discarded in the same place, tying the small sack to a rock before casting it into the sea.

Only he knew of this, and he wished now that he had made his deed known.

He eyed the others as they returned to the barn, all clearly shocked by the boy's demise. Someone wanted it to appear that his wife was responsible for Kerr's death. As much as he wished to console Ysmaine, he had to consider the consequences.

If he appeared to be skeptical of her apparent role, what would the villain do next? That fiend had already attacked Wulfe and himself, and Gaston would not give any cause for his wife to be assaulted.

It would be better for her to appear to be discredited in his eyes.

That might draw the villain's ire back to himself.

And truly, if they survived this journey and this quest, he would spend the rest of his life ensuring his lady knew that he had never truly doubted her. There was no malice within her. He had seen her compassion and concern.

And he loved her. There was the most compelling argument at all, for Gaston knew his own nature well enough to be certain that he could never have admired, much less loved, a woman whose character was any less noble than his own. He had no doubt that he and Ysmaine were two of a kind.

He despised that he had to pretend to be convinced otherwise, even until they reached Paris. In better circumstance, he might have been amused that he and Wulfe were in agreement on the need to complete their journey with all haste.

When they were back in the barn and Kerr's inert body laid on the floor, Fergus shoved a hand through his wet hair. He turned on Ysmaine, anger in his eyes. "How did you know his symptoms so well?" he demanded. "You did not witness them."

Ysmaine lifted her chin. "They are the signs of poisoning by wolf's bane, which is the sole toxin that is known to be carried by our company." She eyed the boy and shook her head sadly. "You cannot imagine that his demise was in any way natural."

"You say he was poisoned?" Duncan asked.

"I suspect you all believe as much already."

Bartholomew started. "The root is as potent as that?"

"Depending how much is consumed, yes." Ysmaine bit her lip. "How long ago did the signs begin?"

"We do not know," Bartholomew admitted.

"When was he last seen and hale?"

"When we arrived here." Fergus shrugged. "Hours ago. He wished to watch the men playing at dice so I left him there. I did not see him until I went in search of him." He eyed Hamish, who shook his head.

"He did not come back from the inn, sir. He said he would go to the latrine, then I was busy with the steeds."

"As was I," Laurent agreed, then that boy's eyes widened in alarm. Gaston watched as he eased to the back of the group, then darted toward the parcel he had guarded so diligently all this journey. He watched Laurent open the saddlebag and unwrap its contents, expecting to see relief light the boy's features.

Instead, he saw horror.

An answering terror shot through Gaston, and he had to turn

away with a frown to compose himself. He wanted no one to note that he had seen Laurent's reaction.

Kerr had known something.

Kerr had been compelled to confide it in someone.

Kerr had been killed and the treasure they carried in trust had been stolen while they attended the dying boy. Every soul had left the stables in pursuit of Fergus' cry, Gaston was certain of it. He did not think any had had time to seize the prize from the baggage Laurent carried, but Everard and Joscelin were still in the inn.

Who would have noticed if one of them had left for a moment? Indeed, a man could have made an excuse of visiting the latrines, and none of that drunken lot would even remember.

As if summoned by his thoughts, both Joscelin and Everard returned in that moment, laughing together at some jest. They halted on the threshold and sobered at the silence within the barn, then gaped at the boy on the ground.

"Is he...?" Joscelin asked, his voice trembling.

"He is dead," Wulfe supplied flatly. "Of poisoning by wolf's bane, according to the lady who knows so much of that toxin." He nodded at Ysmaine who did not cower.

Indeed, she straightened and locked her hands together. Gaston spared a sidelong glance her way and could see her trembling. He admired that she did not flinch from the truth. "He consumed much of it, I fear, for the action was quick. I doubt he could have been saved, which was in all probability his assailant's intent."

Fergus swore softly.

"It is unlikely that he consumed such a quantity willingly," Ysmaine added. "For it is said to burn on the tongue on first touch and enflame the lips."

"Someone compelled him to take it," Fergus guessed, anger in his tone. "He was murdered by someone in this party." All looked around the company, suspicion in their eyes.

All but Ysmaine, who stared back at Fergus.

"Aye." She stood tall. "And I do not doubt that you all believe it must have been me." She turned to Gaston, a fire in her eyes, and he hated what he had to do. "But my husband can clear me of this accusation."

Gaston frowned. He rubbed his chin, and shook his head. "I cannot tell a lie," he said quietly, though he would do precisely that. "I do not understand your meaning, my lady. You alone carry the toxin in this company."

Twin spots of color burned hot in Ysmaine's cheeks. "You know..." she began furiously, but Gaston lifted a finger.

"Do not challenge me before an entire company, madame. A woman has her place to be sure, but it is not in challenging the word of a man of honor. You will not stain my repute to save my own."

Ysmaine gasped. Ysmaine glared.

Then she spun on her heel and left the party, marching to some back corner of the stables to make her bed.

"Radegunde," Gaston called after the maid who followed her mistress. "Bring to me all the possessions of my lady wife, if you please. I will not see her lacking the use of any item, but all will remain in my trust. The safety of the company must come first."

Radegunde was nigh as furious as her mistress, and rightly so, for Ysmaine was innocent.

"Indeed, sir," she replied, her tone scathing, then stomped to do his bidding.

"We shall make arrangements for Kerr's funeral in the morning," Wulfe said, pushing a hand through his hair. "I recommend that all of you seize whatever rest you can."

"Perhaps we should set a watch," Gaston suggested. "Two men awake at all times, to better ensure the safety of those who sleep."

Wulfe cast him a look, then nodded. "A sound suggestion. Would you take the first watch with Fergus, Gaston?"

The men agreed and all settled to sleep. One lantern was extinguished, the other set to burn low and kept near the portal. Gaston did not doubt that Wulfe would rise to confer with him when the watch changed and all were asleep. He needed to decide what they would do.

"We must search the boy," he advised Fergus in an undertone. "Under guise of preparing him for the grave. I will do it."

Fergus' lips tightened. "He was consigned to my responsibility. I will do it."

Gaston sat beside the other knight and watched, his thoughts churning. The rain was slowing and the boy was dressed for burial as well as could be managed under the circumstances when he had a realization.

If the thief was in the party, then the treasure would remain with the party. It made no sense that the villain would abandon it at any point on the road and then return for it. Gaston had until Provins, where Joscelin would leave them, to find the treasure and secure it again.

And that was an encouraging realization, to be sure.

ૐ

Ysmaine could not believe it. Gaston had discredited her, before the entire party. He had not defended her by recounting that he had taken the poison in trust before they left Venice. He could have easily seen her cleared of any accusation, but he had not.

Worse, he had *lied*! She was appalled that he had done as much so well. She never would have imagined he had the capacity to do as much. It was an unsettling thing to realize about her husband.

Gaston could deceive. Perhaps it was best that she had not guessed as much earlier, for then he would have known all of her secrets.

Who was this man who so looked like her husband? She knew Gaston to be a man of integrity. She knew he had no talent for deception. She knew he would not behave without gallantry, or treat her so churlishly.

Had she misunderstood his true nature? Ysmaine could not believe it.

Why would he not defend her?

She laid in the darkness and could think of only one reason. He was the guilty party himself. Nay. Her mind refused to accept such a possibility as fact, even if Kerr had known something that might compromise the safety of all. Gaston would have ensured the boy's silence, but not with death. He would not be so base and so dishonorable. He would not have inflicted the pain and agony of such a demise upon any soul.

Though she had to admit that he had probably killed men in battle, that was a different matter. Men rode to battle expecting to kill or be killed. A squire did not go to the latrines expecting to meet his death. Kerr might not have been innocent, but he had been unarmed and thus vulnerable.

She stared at the roof of the barn and tried to account for every soul since their arrival at this hovel, but the fact remained that most had had the opportunity to do this deed. The boys had been scattered and busy, so lost in the shadows that the departure of one would not be missed. Bartholomew had blackened Kerr's eye on the ship, she recalled, so there was no love lost between them. The men had come and gone, fetching provisions, tending their steeds or playing at dice as Joscelin and Everard had done.

The only persons she knew without doubt to be innocent were herself and Radegunde.

The only person beyond that she believed to be innocent was Gaston.

Why then had he not corroborated her tale?

Ysmaine could not understand his choice, not after the wondrous night they had shared in Venice. There had been such promise for their shared future then. Who might have imagined that all the promise would be stolen away but days later?

Not Ysmaine, but she could find no other explanation.

It was late when the notion came to her, one that resonated with all the facts and made sense as nothing else did. Her husband had meant only to see her saved from her situation in the Holy Land. He did not mean to truly keep her as his wife. There was no document proving the exchange of their vows, and she knew she did not bear his son. Did he mean to demand an annulment once they reached the Paris Temple and continue to serve the order?

She had thought of this before, when she had discerned that he truly was the one leading their party, but only now Ysmaine saw that Gaston had not answered her charge.

He had avoided the question with diplomacy, instead of reassuring her that their vows were valid. He led the party. He made the choices. He must not have left the order, and thus he had no need of a wife. Doubtless he believed that saving her from a dire fate in Outremer was sufficient compensation for her.

It was too clear in hindsight. They were not wed in truth and she could not prove it. What evidence had she that he had left the order, save Gaston's own claim to that effect? He might lead the party because he was still a Templar, and he meant to remain so after they reached Paris. Perhaps he did not intend to accept the legacy of his brother's estate. Perhaps he had not truly inherited it! Châmont-sur-Maine was but a tale to draw a villain's eye away from him and she was but a disguise.

It all made a precarious sense.

Even if it made Ysmaine's heart ache.

She thought at first that he could not be so deceptive, but then she recalled how his gaze had slid from hers, how he had prevaricated in his replies, how he had declined to speak with her in privacy. He made choices to accommodate his dislike of moral compromise.

Then why had he touched her with such abandon? Clearly she had tempted him, but Ysmaine could not evade the fact that their merry time abed had been their last coupling. She feared Gaston regretted what they had done.

Indeed, it explained why he refused to speak with her.

Still she loved him. She adored his honor and sense of purpose. She could never betray him, even if it meant she would lose him forever. She would not allow his quest to fail either, not if his choice was to remain in the order. But she would not cling to him or compel him to force her from his side. Nay, she would willingly give Gaston the freedom he desired, as if their marriage was of no consequence to her.

It was, but he need never know as much. She would spurn him, then retire to a convent.

For there could be no other man for Ysmaine than Gaston. If he did not desire her, it was clear her sins were too great even for Mary to intercede successfully on her behalf, and her life would be more productively spent in prayer.

Even if she wept in the night for what had so nearly been her own. Ysmaine told herself that it was better, much better, to have tasted the promise of love and then be denied the feast, than never to have known love at all.

Claire Delacroix

Wednesday, August 12, 1187

Feast day of the martyrs, Saint Andeolus and Saint Tiburtius, and of the virgin Saint Waldetrudis.

❧

Claire Delacroix

Chapter Nineteen

They raced onward from that day forth. The weather turned fair after Kerr's funeral and the party rode hard each day, as if they would leave doubt and danger behind them. There was little discussion between the members of the party, and none that Ysmaine witnessed regarding any plan. They seemed all to be filled with a desire to reach Paris as soon as possible and had come to a consensus without exchanging a word. The wind turned colder each day and the road sloped ever upward, the trees turning to pines on either side of them.

They reached the Saint Bernard Pass after more than a fortnight. They had ridden as long each day as possible, only seeking shelter when they could go no farther. They had slept in inns and barns, once at the side of the road for lack of a better choice. They had endured rain and cold nights, hot days and stretches without bread or meat.

Ysmaine did not care. She had not slept well, burdened as she was with her secret and her fear of discovery, and it did not help that Gaston scarce spent a moment with her. He saw to her comfort and her defense, but clearly he did not miss her companionship as she missed his. There was no question of intimacy or even private discussion at night, given the places they had to stay, and so Ysmaine was not tempted to confess all to him. That he did not seek her out, or even watch her as closely as once he had, was the confirmation she needed that her fears were right.

She had no doubt that all was exactly as he desired it to be.

Her own heart was breaking. Indeed, that wondrous night of pleasure seemed a distant dream, or perhaps an incident she had imagined. Gaston was stern and vigilant over the party, and though her heart quailed when he left the party for any reason, he was not threatened again.

At the end of another long day, they halted at an inn just before the summit of the pass. This place was more cheerful than many of the others, though that might have been the influence of the crisp wind and the beauteous sunset. An alpine meadow spread at their feet, and the first of the stars were coming out.

Ysmaine dismounted with a sigh, tired in mind as well as body. The relic hung heavily against her belly and though it was padded, still it had chafed her skin. She would be glad to loosen the bonds that held it fast against her, if only for the night. Without doubt, they would head out by dawn. Ysmaine wished they were not racing with such speed toward her final parting from Gaston. She wished there was some word or sign she could give him, but was aware that all would note it.

And so it was that she erred, for her emotions were in such turmoil.

Ysmaine knew that Gaston was behind her. She knew that the light of the inn spilled through the open door ahead of her, but she was too tired to think of the result of the combination. Bartholomew spoke to her about her steed, and she spun around to reply, forgetting for a heartbeat to hold her cloak shut.

It was a heartbeat too long.

Her cloak flared, revealing the apparent curve of her belly to all. That it was silhouetted by the light from the inn made it impossible to miss.

She saw Gaston's stare, his gaze fixed on her belly, and realized her mistake.

Ysmaine pulled her cloak about herself as her color rose and pivoted to walk to the inn. Surely, he would not challenge her before the entire company?

But her husband's hand closed around her elbow, his grip so resolute that she knew he meant to have the tale here and now.

God in Heaven. As much as Ysmaine wished to speak to Gaston, this was neither the time nor the place to confide the truth.

But the choice was simple—the defense of his mission or of herself.

She had already discerned that he did not desire her as his wife. If he meant to remain with the order, his integrity must not be questioned.

There was then no real choice but to lie.

"My lady," Gaston said, his voice tight. That he no longer called her 'lady mine' seemed to Ysmaine to be of great import. "I would have a word, if you please."

?▲

Gaston was more furious than ever he had been.

He could scarce put two coherent thoughts together. Ysmaine was with child. How could this be so? It made no sense. Indeed, his shock was such that he could even ignore his concerns about the missing treasure, a fact that told him much of his lady's influence upon his thoughts. He was incredulous, even with the evidence before his eyes, and could not let the revelation pass.

Indeed, the entire company watched for his reaction. They all had seen, and the silence revealed that he was not the sole one surprised.

Ysmaine lifted her gaze to his, unflinching. "Aye, sir?" There was a challenge in her tone that Gaston could not explain.

"You bear a child."

"Indeed, sir. I understood you desired a son."

She was so calm that Gaston's fury faltered. "It seems of robust size to have been conceived in Venice less than a month ago."

"Perhaps I erred and he was conceived in Samaria."

"Still, to be so round in but a month." Gaston frowned. He knew little of such matters, but it seemed to him that babes were nigh invisible for months.

"Perhaps he is tall, like his father."

Christina snorted. At Gaston's glance, she shrugged. "That babe was conceived three months ago, at least," she supplied, and Gaston glared at Ysmaine in time to see her flush crimson. "You must have bound it down to disguise it thus far," the courtesan said.

"Aye," Ysmaine agreed hastily. "But I could bear it no longer, and I feared for the child."

"As indeed you should," Wulfe muttered, his disdain clear.

"Three months?" Gaston demanded of his wife. "*Three* months!"

"It cannot be so long as that," she said, her cheeks afire. "Not

285

quite."

"I should say not nearly. We have been wedded only *one* month." Gaston was on the verge of losing his temper when he recalled that he had touched Ysmaine in Venice but a fortnight before. He had seen her nude and caressed the smooth skin of her flat belly. There had been naught to bind down. She had been as slender as a maiden.

Indeed, he had taken her maidenhead but a month before, for he had the proof of it in his baggage. He could not comprehend how she could carry a child.

Unless she did not. The truth of it came to him like a bolt of lightning.

Ysmaine did not carry a babe.

She carried a prize.

Indeed, she had ensured that the treasure entrusted to him was hidden in the one location where it would neither be perceived nor stolen. Here was the treasure, safely defended due to his wife's initiative and not lost at all!

Gaston's heart leapt at the keen wit of his lady wife, and he yearned to sweep her into his arms and kiss her senseless. But the success of her ploy was keyed to his public acceptance of the lie. He scowled at her, trying to muster his anger anew.

"Did you never see her nude?" Wulfe asked in an undertone. He granted Ysmaine a scathing glance.

"She kept herself covered, always," Gaston lied, then let his lip curl with disdain. "I thought her modest."

Wulfe laughed. "Manipulative, perhaps, is a better choice of word."

Ysmaine's entire face was crimson with apparent mortification.

"And what other opportunity to ensure her own salvation would she have had?" Christina demanded of the Templar. "You behave as if women have all the choices that men do in this world, and I assure you, that is not the case."

"She could have told him!" Wulfe insisted.

"And lost the aid of the sole person who had offered to assist her? Aye, there is a good way to starve." Christina's expression was grim. "Or to end up in my trade."

"Did you sell yourself like a whore?" Everard asked Ysmaine, his disdain for such choices clear.

"I prayed," Ysmaine asserted. "But it is said that God helps those who help themselves."

Everard shook his head and walked away in disgust. "I am glad indeed that I have never seen reason to wed. It is true that women are the source of all perfidy."

"You said neither of your husbands had consummated the match," Gaston said, as if trying to find some excuse for his wife's state.

"They did not." Ysmaine could not meet his gaze. She plucked at her sleeve, then swallowed. "I am sorry, my lord," she said quietly. "We had to eat."

"There are alms for the poor."

Her eyes flashed. "Not so many as one might hope. The sisters gave us shelter, but little more."

Gaston summoned a thrum of outrage to his voice. "Confess the truth now, with all this company as witnesses. Did you lie to me, Ysmaine of Valeroy?"

Ysmaine sighed, then nodded. "I knew not what else I might do, sir. I entreat you..."

"I shall hear none of your entreaties!" Gaston bellowed, then shook a finger before her. "I demanded but one thing of you."

"Honesty," Ysmaine asserted softly, then lifted her chin. "But I can explain, sir, if you but grant me the opportunity..."

He could not grant her the chance to appeal to him. In this moment, he could publically spurn her with justification, which was necessary for the success of her ploy. "But one request I made of you and that one thing you could not supply!" he roared. "There is but one explanation I would have from you in this moment, and it requires only a single word in reply to my query." Gaston pivoted to face his wife, apparently livid. She blanched but held her ground. "Do not be so fool as to lie this time," he growled.

"I would not, sir."

Gaston pointed a shaking finger at her belly and ground out the words. "Do you bear *my* child?"

Ysmaine bit her lip. Her tears rose, and she glanced away before she turned back to him. "I fear I do not, sir."

It was artful, truly, that her confession *was* the truth, though Gaston would never have spoken to her thus save to preserve her own scheme. He spun to stride away from her, knowing that if he lingered by her side, he would not be able to keep himself from gathering her close.

Zounds, but he despised deceit. His guts writhed to treat his lady wife thus, even though she had compelled the situation.

"Gaston!" she cried and his pulse leapt. "Gaston, I can explain!" She raced after him, even the sound of her footfalls making his innards clench. She seized his arm, and he was tempted to cast all aside simply to have matters right between them again. "If you would but grant me a moment of privacy..."

"Madame." Gaston interrupted her in the most icy tone he could summon. She flinched, and he felt her trembling when he lifted her hand from his arm and cast off her touch. "There is not a single word you could utter to me that I would care to hear."

Her first tear fell then, her expression so devastated that he could not look upon her. He felt a cur and a fiend.

Though the scheme was her own.

Gaston left the company, abandoning his wife to the whispers and speculation of their fellow travelers. He would spend the rest of his life atoning for this exchange, ensuring that she knew he did not truly doubt her.

He had to tell Wulfe of his realization and reassure both Laurent and Fergus that their prize was safe. He would only confide its location to Wulfe, the better that they two could ensure Ysmaine's defense.

How quickly could they reach Paris?

How soon could he ensure the felicity of their match was restored? Gaston clung to the memory of that single night, the one that promised so much for their future, and was determined to claim that promise with all possible haste.

❧

It was no consolation that Ysmaine had named the price of saving Gaston's honor aright. She wept that night, which did not surprise any of the company, giving vent all the desolation within her heart.

Duncan granted her a word of encouragement, but Ysmaine knew he was in error. This man of honor would never forgive her.

Indeed, Gaston must be glad of this good reason to annul their match.

She kept away from the company, sleeping only when she was guarded by Radegunde. Who was the villain? Who had killed Kerr? She had to think it was Joscelin, the merry merchant, for he might understand the value of such a prize. Indeed, he might have the connections to see it sold quietly. He had joined the party late in Jerusalem, and he would not be the first man whose cheerful nature hid a black heart. Indeed, there was something disarming in his manner that prompted people to dismiss him as a threat to any cause.

Ysmaine nibbled her lip. Joscelin would leave the party in Provins, and indeed, Wulfe had set their route that they would pass through the city to the southeast of Paris for precisely that reason. If he was the villain, he would surely trail the party from Provins and try to claim the prize before it was delivered to the Temple. Undoubtedly, he had identified the saddlebag guarded by Laurent as the likely location of the prize. The boy was small and could be injured in a fight. Nay, if Ysmaine meant to ensure that the relic was safely delivered to the Temple in Paris and no more lives were lost, she had to draw the villain's eye to herself.

She would reveal the truth of her burden the night before they reached Provins. She would guard it closely until the night before they entered Paris, then she would exchange it with Radegunde, putting the bundle of clothes beneath her kirtle. If she left the party when they were close to the Temple, purportedly parting from Gaston, the villain would be seduced into following her to claim the prize. There would be time for Gaston to deliver the true relic to its rightful place before the villain learned that he had been deceived.

Aye, it would work. Ysmaine did not care what price she paid in this matter. She had little future, save that of a sister in a convent, and did not believe her nature well suited to that life. What was of import was ensuring Gaston's future, and she would readily do whatever was necessary to achieve that end.

It was bittersweet to realize the depth of her love for him and to know it unreturned, to suspect that he would never even guess what she had done, but Ysmaine would not regret her choice.

It must be so, for the greater good.

Nay, for the good of her beloved.

Monday, August 24, 1187

Feast Day of Saint Ouen and
Saint Bartholomew.

❧

Claire Delacroix

Chapter Twenty

They reached Paris in the last week of August, on the feast of both Saint Bartholomew the apostle and Saint Ouen, Bishop of Rouen. Despite the pouring rain and the resulting mud, the city was thick with revelers. The progress of their party was slow indeed. Ysmaine found that the weather affected her mood more than the celebrants thronging to church.

Or perhaps her mood was due to the inescapable fact that her bond with Gaston would shortly come to an end.

Their party was smaller than it had been, for Joscelin had left them in Provins, albeit with many promises to contact her in her new home at Châmont-sur-Maine in the hope that he might be of assistance to her. Everard had left them as they approached the city, stating his intent of riding directly north to Champagne to his family abode. It was clear that some argument had occurred between Wulfe and Christina for she seemed intent on remaining as far from him as possible. He led the party on his black destrier, while she trailed further and further back on her palfrey.

They entered the city from the southeast, passing the abbey and entering the city through the Porte Saint Victor. No sooner had they ridden through the gates than Ysmaine noted that Christina had abandoned them.

She met Radegunde's gaze and the maid grimaced. Ysmaine had no doubt that their thoughts were as one. Trade was good for whores in Paris, perhaps even better than in Venice, and it appeared that Wulfe had served his purpose. If he had noted Christina's departure, he gave no sign of it.

Though Ysmaine thought he sat a little taller in the saddle and glared more determinedly ahead.

She cupped her hand over her belly as if protecting her unborn child in the throng. Radegunde clung tightly to her bundle of used clothes, the two women ensuring that it never left their watchful gaze. They had switched the burdens this morn and had done so unobserved. Ysmaine felt as taut as a bow string with uncertainty and wanted only to have this day behind her. In mere hours the reliquary would be safely delivered.

She was certain she had revealed the truth of her prize, as planned, on the last night that the entire company was together in Provins. She had feared that the villain would attempt to seize the prize immediately, but all had continued without incident. Had she failed to make the location of the treasure clear? Or did the villain simply wait for opportunity?

She had been certain that Joscelin or Everard had been the culprit, yet both had apparently left the party forever. Surely, the villain could not be one of the other knights? It could not be the man-at-arms Duncan, who had been kind to her. She refused to believe it. It was not Gaston. She did not believe it could be either Fergus or Wulfe, much less one of the squires, but she must be wrong.

She would have to take the last step and draw out the villain. Ysmaine tightened her grip on her reins, her body taut with fear.

Their progress was slow to Place Maubert and slower yet as they drew nearer to the Petit Pont. Wulfe began to point out again that they would have been better to circumvent the city entirely, as the Temple was outside the walls on the north side. Gaston did not argue with him any longer, but rode in silence. Fergus expressed pleasure that they would truly see the city.

They crossed to the island, and Ysmaine watched the boys gawk at the peddlers and moneylenders doing business on the bridge. The Ile de la Cité always seemed to be the source of the city's pulse, and Ysmaine smiled in recollection of her parents' ongoing dispute as to why that should be. Her father insisted it was because the king's courts were located on the island, so from this point, law and order flowed through his demesne. Her mother, however, insisted that it was the cathedral of Notre Dame, also on this isle, that was the source of all power and goodness emanating through the kingdom. Ysmaine thought of Mary's intercession in her own life in Jerusalem and fortified her will to do what had to be done.

It would be soon now. Radegunde gave her a solemn glance.

Where the road branched and Wulfe would lead the party to the left, toward the Pont aux Changeurs on the other side of the island and the north bank, Ysmaine would take the other road, to the cathedral.

She would draw the villain to pursue her, and the apparent treasure, while the genuine reliquary was delivered to the Temple.

All too soon, they reached the branch in the road.

"Sir!" Ysmaine called and was gratified that Gaston immediately glanced back. "I would have a word with you, if you would so indulge me."

He spoke quickly to Wulfe, urging the party to continue onward, then let the company flow around him until Fantôme was beside her. "Aye? Are you ill, madame?"

She could see that he did not like the interruption and spoke quickly. "I will not delay you overlong, sir. I know your quest is of greatest import."

Gaston made to reply, but Ysmaine lifted a hand to silence him. "I left France a pilgrim and a penitent, sir, and I would return as one. I also left as a widow twice over, and to be sure, there is no one of my acquaintance who knows my situation to be otherwise, save myself and my maid Radegunde."

Gaston's eyes narrowed, the intensity of his attention making Ysmaine's heart skip.

Still she carried on, for she knew she was right. "I recognize that you do not truly wish me to be your wife, and I see no reason to burden you with my presence or my child. There is no cause for you to be kept from wedding a maiden who can grant you the sons you require, and who will not vex you overmuch."

Gaston's voice rose, as seldom it did. "You vex me in this moment, my lady, for there is no cause for this discussion..."

"There is *every* cause, sir. Our match has survived its tenure."

He appeared to be dismayed by this claim, but Ysmaine would hear no pretty words. There was an opportunity in this moment for both of them to achieve their desired ends, and if it was not seized, it would slip away forever.

"There is no record of our match, not even a ring upon a finger. I say we forget that ever we pledged our troth and call this match annulled. May you find a wife who suits you, sir, as I know I do not. Or may you live out your days in the order, as has suited you well thus far."

"Ysmaine!" he protested, but she continued in haste.

"You have been kind to me. I cannot argue that. You saved my life in Jerusalem, and for this, I know I have been blessed. Indeed, I am sufficiently grateful that I would grant you the opportunity to gain your own heart's desire." She smiled thinly. "You need not be compelled to acknowledge a bastard as your own."

Gaston shook his head and frowned. "My lady," he entreated in a low voice, his gaze searching hers. "Simply come with me to the Temple, where all will be resolved."

"Nay, sir," Ysmaine said with resolve. "It must be thus."

Gaston glanced after the party destined for the Temple, a kind of desperation affecting his manner. He leaned close to her, his tone urgent and his eyes dark. "Ysmaine, I have but one task to complete. *One!* We must talk of this matter before we part."

"You do not talk, sir, unless compelled to do so."

"And if this is a means to compel me to do so, consider your argument made. I will confer with you, but *after* this mission is completed. You cannot simply make this choice alone, and I am not convinced of your argument..."

"You must be," Ysmaine interrupted him flatly. If he appealed to her, she would be lost. "I will not be wed to you," she said and he blinked in surprise.

"But why ever not?" He seemed to be so astounded by this that Ysmaine knew she had to lie.

"I thought I could love you but I was wrong. I have been wedded twice for duty and the third time will be for love."

He met her gaze, a question in his blue eyes.

"I ask only that you escort my maid to her family, who abide in the village of my father's manor. You need not mention me to him, or even speak with him, if it is not your desire. Radegunde will tell my parents of my choice to take the veil." She took a quick breath. "I believe they might be relieved."

Gaston inhaled sharply and his eyes flashed. "You would act as if we never were wed! You would behave as if the words that passed between us never occurred! I do not believe this necessary, Ysmaine, and I will not willingly cede to you."

God in Heaven, the man was going to argue with her. Ysmaine knew what she had to do. Gaston was stubborn, and she had not the time to dispute this with him. "Your party leaves you behind," she noted, and he swore with a vigor that astonished her.

"Ysmaine! You will not do this! When this quest is complete, we shall discuss the matter...."

Ysmaine slid from the saddle even as he spoke. Gaston snatched for the reins of the palfrey but she was already on the ground. He roared her name again, but Ysmaine slipped into the crowd and ran as fast as she could. There was mud and manure underfoot, and she nigh slipped several times, but she kept running. The crowds were thick in the square before the cathedral and no man could have forced a horse through their ranks.

Although Gaston did try.

Only when she had ducked beneath the porch of the great cathedral did Ysmaine look back. Her gaze fell immediately on the dappled destrier and the proud knight who rode him. She saw that Radegunde remained close to Gaston. She saw that he had pursued her, despite the throngs of people, and had made more progress than she might have expected.

Because she was his possession?

Because she defied him?

Because he knew his duty?

Ysmaine did not know which compelled him to follow her, but she knew it was not love. Gaston lifted a hand as she watched and pointed, bellowing after her. "This is not done, lady mine!"

Lady mine. Why did Gaston address her thus in this moment? It brought tears to her eyes. Ysmaine ducked into the church and took a deep breath of the sanctity within. She was a sinner who had tried to do right. She had saved Gaston and his mission and thus his honor.

The price to herself was not of import.

She bought a candle and lit it, dropping to her knees before the Virgin to say a prayer for her husband and his success. Her heart was racing and her palms were damp, and there were tears upon her cheeks.

She jumped when the man's hand landed upon her shoulder, though she was not truly surprised. She was less surprised to feel the prick of a knife in her back and the heat of a man behind her, his position disguising his weapon. "I fear your prayers must be cut short, my lady fair," Everard murmured. "We are too late to linger here."

Ysmaine glanced up to his eyes and her spirit quailed at the warning she found there. He threatened her in the sanctuary of a church, which told her all she needed to know of his nature. She had to get him as far from Gaston as possible before he killed her, as far from all these innocent people.

"Of course, my lord," she said sweetly and rose to her feet, placing her hand in his elbow. "I wished only to pray for the child's welfare," she explained for the benefit of the any who watched them. She caressed her belly with one hand.

"And so you should," Everard agreed smoothly, then hastened her out of the church. He fairly dragged her through the crowd, making for an alley, and Ysmaine knew she would never leave that dark space alive.

She tugged her hand free, scratched his face when he turned upon her, then picked up her skirts and ran. He roared in frustration even as the crowd laughed at him, then she heard him give chase.

God in Heaven, he was so much taller than she. He would catch her before she even left the square! Ysmaine stumbled, then found her footing, hoping against all hope that Gaston was far away.

And that Radegunde was fast beside him. Everard seized her and she felt the knife against her ribs again, his breath upon her throat.

"Silently now," he whispered, punctuating his command with a poke of the blade.

Ysmaine nodded as if compliant. She had to survive until the party was safely within the confines of the Temple itself.

ža

Gaston was livid.

There was little that infuriated him, as a rule. Indeed, he could not recall the last time he had been so vexed. But for Ysmaine to flee him in this moment was beyond all expectation. That she should so imperil herself was beyond all expectation. She had the reliquary and she abandoned all protection! She ensured he could not pursue her. What folly was this?

Wulfe shouted to him, but Gaston did not turn back. He tried to force Fantôme through the crowd. But the streets were so filled with people that he made excruciatingly slow progress. He knew he would not be able to find his wife again should he leave her behind, yet he could not reach her either.

Even though Ysmaine had contrived that he had little choice. He ground his teeth and gave Fantôme a touch of his heels, then froze in sudden realization.

Ysmaine had contrived that he had little choice.

Gaston spun to face the maid, whose hand fell to the bundle of old clothing she had been carrying since Venice. Gaston blinked. The maid held his gaze unflinchingly and he understood.

They had moved the treasure.

Ysmaine's flight was a feint, intended to ensure that his mission was successfully completed.

But the price, the price might be his wife's life! The villain had killed once already, and the prospect of Ysmaine suffering any injury turned Gaston's blood to ice. He turned Fantôme, giving every indication of rejoining the party to ride toward the Temple.

He dared not reveal her, for he did not know who watched.

He had to save her, but he did not know how to do as much.

He could not wait until the mission was completed, yet he had to fulfill his assignment. It was unlike him to be caught between two options, much less to be indecisive as to the better path, but Gaston was torn between following Ysmaine's scheme to success, and casting it aside to ensure her welfare.

They crossed the bridge to the north bank and the crowds thinned ahead. Gaston could see that the road that led to the Temple was less and less congested as it progressed.

With that glimpse of a clear path to their destination, his choice was made. He seized the reins of the palfrey the maid rode and urged the steed closer to Wulfe. He shoved the palfrey's reins into that astonished man's grasp.

"Ride!" he ordered in a grim undertone. "Ride for the Temple and let none stand in your path! Ensure that she is with you to the last."

Wulfe nodded without understanding, then a light dawned in his eyes. His gaze dropped to the bundle of clothes, but before he could speak, Gaston slapped the rump of Wulfe's black stallion.

The horse gave a cry and broke into a gallop, the palfrey carrying the maid fast beside him. Fergus shouted and lent chase. Gaston granted Fantôme's reins to Bartholomew, then leapt from the saddle, knowing he would make better time on foot.

"Ride," he ordered the squire. "Ensure that all arrive together. I will follow as soon as might be."

Gaston darted into the crowd without waiting for a reply. He heard the thunder of the horses' hooves and Wulfe's shout for people to make way. They would be within the walls of the Temple within moments, and their quest would be achieved. Though it was true that Gaston should have ensured its success himself and witnessed the delivery with his own eyes, naught could compete with the importance of seeing his lady wife safe.

He raced for the square before the cathedral, the place where he had last seen his lady wife, shoving his way through the crowd.

Gaston only hoped that he found her in time.

Was the villain Everard or Joscelin? In truth, Gaston cared not who his opponent might be, only that his wife survived. But where had she fled? There was nary a sign of her, though he looked. Gaston felt a rare panic rise within him.

How would he find her?

How might he do so in time to ensure her welfare?

Gaston surveyed the area in desperation, seeking some hint of her passage. That was when he spotted the gem on the porch of the cathedral where he had last seen Ysmaine. It was cut glass of little value at all, but of a familiar hue.

He bent and picked it up, turning it in his grip. Aye, Christina had worn a belt wrought of these cheap stones when first she had come to the house with Wulfe. The color revealed that it could not be a gem, but it sparkled prettily. Gaston supposed there were many similar girdles and might have cast it aside.

But he saw another exactly the same, not three steps away. Another was beyond it and the light caught a fourth. He recalled Christina sitting in the common room of the house in Venice, picking apart the girdle so she had a pile of individual stones. Ysmaine had given her a small sack for them, though he had thought little of the exchange at the time.

A fifth stone glinted just beyond the fourth.

And Gaston understood that he had been left a trail.

Someone pursued them.

Ysmaine heard the footsteps, as stealthy as they were. Was it friend or foe? She could not imagine who would give chase to aid her and feared it to be an accomplice of Everard who defended his back. He certainly gave no indication that he heard the sounds of pursuit.

He fairly drove Ysmaine down one street, then another. He took a circuitous path, ducking through a privy to emerge in another alley, then pushed her into a courtyard that was strangely still. He flung the gate closed behind them, the sound of the latch echoing loudly.

The sounds of the city were muffled and the rain fell steadily in this place. It was empty, save for his chestnut destrier, which was tethered beneath an angled roof on the far side. The steed snorted at the sight of him, then nosed in his feed.

Ysmaine had time to think that none would witness whatever he planned to do to her, to feel her heart tremble, then the hinges on the gate squeaked and a woman spoke.

"At least some soul is gratified by your presence."

Christina!

She spoke from behind them. Everard spun, hauling Ysmaine before him and holding the point of his knife at her throat. "What are you doing here?"

Christina leaned against the gate, the latch behind her back. Her expression was assessing. "Let us say that I wished to ensure the welfare of another woman."

Everard snorted. "Whores care only for their own advantage."

"You might be surprised to learn what whores care about." She eyed the blade he held against Ysmaine. "Is it the mark of a pious man to abduct another man's wife?"

Everard ignored her query. "Doubtless you want a reward of your own. Is it not all about the coin for your kind?"

Christina glanced idly over the courtyard. "I fail to see any chance of reward in this place." She fixed a shrewd look on Everard. "Unless your desire is for the lady's charms."

"In which case you would offer your own instead?"

Christina smiled. "You might find me more to your liking as a partner." She crossed the courtyard with measured steps, her smile unswerving and confident. Ysmaine felt Everard stiffen and knew he was not so at ease as Christina appeared. "Do you think I failed to note how you watched me when you thought yourself unobserved?" She paused before him. "For a pious man, you showed a very earthy interest in my wares."

He scoffed. "I merely disapprove of you and your trade."

"Because you are a man above reproach," Ysmaine said, drawing strength from the other woman's confidence. "Abduction and assault are fair play."

"And murder," Christina added. "Do not forget murder, my lady."

"I do not know what you mean..."

Christina's gaze dropped to the knife at Ysmaine's throat. She reached out a finger and collected blood upon it, then held it before his face. "Your manners are lacking, sir. This lady is nobly born and wed to a knight. What cause have you to threaten her life?"

"This is a private matter. She holds property of mine."

"One you own or one you would claim?"

"How dare you speak thus to me?" Everard snarled.

"I have seen you look," Christina purred. She began to unfasten her kirtle, drawing the laces from one side with methodical gestures. She turned so that the ripe curve of her breast was visible, then lifted the wool away, revealing the nipple to view. "Would you like a closer look? Perhaps in exchange for the lady's freedom?"

"Whore," Everard muttered, but his interest was clear to Ysmaine. "I will not barter with you..."

"Vermin," Ysmaine charged, drawing away from him and he swore.

Christina unlaced the other side of her kirtle, a choice that did little to improve his mood. "I am Everard de Montmorency," he declared hotly. "Count of Blanche Garde and heir to Château Montmorency and I will not tolerate..."

"*Are* you?" Christina impaled him with a glance, the sharpness of her tone halting his tirade.

Everard caught his breath. "What do you insinuate?"

"Only that I know you are not Everard de Montmorency."

He sputtered, clearly astonished. Ysmaine was shocked by the charge but guessed by Everard's response that Christina was right. Then who was he?

And what had happened to the real Everard?

Christina was confident. "How exactly do you plan to convince them at Château Montmorency that you are Everard in truth?" she asked, her eyes glinting. "It was simple to take his place in Outremer, where he was known only by repute, but it will be more difficult to trick his own blood."

Everard stiffened.

Christina tilted her head to study him. "Is that why it took so very long for the duke's faithful and pious son to embark on the journey home to say a final farewell to his father?" she demanded, her tone harsh. "Did you hope the father might die before you arrived? As a dead man himself, Everard could not have managed the journey at all, but it would have been folly for the imposter who had stolen his name and his purse to reveal his own lie."

"You lying whore!" Everard flung Ysmaine aside and snatched for Christina, who kicked him hard in the crotch. He fell to his knees, astounded, and she kicked him in the head. He touched his own temple and stared at the blood on his fingertips, but Ysmaine felt his fury rising.

"No one truly looks at a whore," Christina spat. "We are breasts, at best. But I invite you to look again, to look at my face this time. I was in the party of noble pilgrims who traveled east with you and Everard. I was with my husband then, but perhaps you never look at noblewomen, either. The fact is that I *know* that you are not Everard."

Everard rose with a growl and lunged after her. "You lie!" he cried and seized her by the hair, slamming her back into the wall of the house. Christina gave Ysmaine the barest glance and she understood that the other woman wanted her to run.

But Ysmaine would not abandon her.

Christina slumped, and Everard raised his hand to strike her again. Ysmaine saw the courtesan move quickly and glimpsed the flash of a knife. Everard darted aside, flinging her to the ground, and she grunted as the blade missed him.

"I do not lie!" Christina declared with a bold laugh. "We meet again, Helmut."

Everard blanched at the sound of this name.

Christina advanced upon him with the blade before herself. "You were the mercenary assigned to defend your lord and employer, and I remember you well. My husband noted then that you were lying and lustful, and you are still vermin, if better garbed." She spat at him and he lunged at her, trying to seize the knife. They struggled over it, and Ysmaine realized that Christina was stronger than she appeared.

"Run, my lady!" the courtesan cried, and Ysmaine pretended to do as much. She feigned a stumble and picked up a rock from the ground. She spun around to see that Everard had grasped a fistful of Christina's hair, pulling it back so he could look at her face.

Ysmaine sidled closer silently, taking advantage of his distraction.

"You!" Everard whispered to Christina. "You are Juliana, the wife of Gunther, who remained in Venice..."

"And was slaughtered for the seven pennies in his purse." Christina's voice shook, and Ysmaine realized that their circumstance had not been that different. "Did you take his life, as well as his purse? I would not put it past a man of your ilk."

"I am no thief."

Christina laughed harshly. Everard struck her, and she fell to the ground. He might have fallen on her, but Ysmaine hastened forward and brought the rock down on his head as hard as she could. There was a loud crack, but he did not stumble. Indeed, he turned on her like a mad beast.

"Run, Christina!" Ysmaine cried, even as Everard backhanded her so that she stumbled. He seized the bundle that was disguised as her belly. He tore it away with a savage gesture, then flung her aside so that she fell heavily against the stone wall.

Ysmaine tried to halt her fall and heard a crack on impact. Pain shot up her arm and she knew it was her wrist that was injured. Christina lay in a heap, blood pooling beneath her, and she feared for that woman's fate. The courtesan's lashes fluttered, though, as if she battled to remain conscious.

Everard held the bundle against his chest, as yet unaware that he clutched a rock and an old kirtle. He flung dry straw from the makeshift stable onto the ground, ensuring that it fell generously on both women. He worked quickly, clearly having a scheme. He then struck a flint and lit numerous lengths of straw, tossing them into the others. The straw ignited immediately, filling the courtyard with smoke and flames, even as he grabbed the reins of his destrier and made for the gate.

"Farewell, ladies," he sneered as he lifted the latch. "Is it not said that witches should be burned alive?" He did not wait for a reply, but flung open the portal. The waft of air fanned the flames so that they burned higher and the smoke roiled in great dark clouds.

Ysmaine coughed and dragged herself to Christina. How would she carry Christina with only one arm? She felt the other woman's pulse with relief in the same moment that she heard the destrier stamp in impatience again.

Everard had not departed.

She looked up to see him backing into the courtyard instead of leaving it, the point of a sword at his chest. Gaston followed him into the courtyard. Her husband looked resolute and grim, so powerful and welcome that Ysmaine nigh wept at the sight of him.

"I believe we have unfinished business, sir," Gaston said, his voice low with threat, and Ysmaine had never been so glad to see another soul in all her life.

Her husband had not only come for her, but he had abandoned his quest to pursue her instead. Was her welfare an obligation he would fulfill?

Or did she dare to hope for more?

❧

Only vermin assaulted women.

Only a fool touched Gaston's lady wife. One look at Ysmaine, pale with blood on her hands, was enough to set his blood aflame. That this fiend had intended for her to be burned alive, that he would abandon her in such circumstance, made Gaston want to kill him slowly. He had never been filled with such a desire for vengeance.

But the lady he loved had never been so threatened before.

He assessed the flames and saw that Ysmaine bent over Christina. She might have fled and saved herself, but that was not her nature. Rather than his wife perishing in this fire, he would see

Everard left to die in flames.

Gaston stepped back and lifted his sword from Everard's chest. *"En garde,"* he murmured, and the words had barely crossed his lips before the villain lunged at him. Their swords clashed hard and Gaston felt his cheek nicked. He parried hard, driving Everard back against the wall with a flurry of blows. He forced that man away from the gate and was aware that Ysmaine tried to rouse Christina. He wished the women were safe, but he knew enough of his lady to guess that she would not abandon her companion.

He sliced down hard, compelling Everard to drop the reins, then slapped the horse. The beast fled the fire, darting through the gate to the street.

One life was saved. He had three yet to ensure.

"You attack the wrong person!" Everard protested. "The whore means to injure your wife."

"I heard only you strike my lady wife," Gaston growled and moved quickly, his blade slicing Everard's shoulder. "Wulfe was right to doubt your intent from the outset. What man of merit abandons a holding when it is about to be besieged?"

"You know naught of my intent..."

They battled, moving back and forth, almost evenly matched. When Gaston landed a blow, it was because Everard did not relinquish his grip on his burden.

"You speak aright," he replied, wanting to provoke his opponent. If the man who called himself Everard was angered, he might make a mistake. "All these years I have believed you to be Everard de Montmorency, for I had no reason to doubt the tale you told. Now I learn that this is a lie."

"The whore lies!"

"You lie," Gaston countered and saw his opponent's eyes flash. "Why did you not return to France to visit your ailing father sooner?"

"I had a holding to defend."

"But you left it unprotected in the end."

"I saw that it was doomed."

Gaston scoffed. "Your tale makes little sense, unless you are a coward. Why did you leave Outremer by coming to Jerusalem first?"

"I sought the aid of the Templars! It is your sworn task to

accompany pilgrims on the road..."

"You were nigh at the port of Jaffa in Blanche Garde. Had it been your desire to leave Outremer in haste, you could have been a-sail before we even left Jerusalem." Gaston shook his head. "Nay, the reason is in your grasp. You came seeking a prize to steal."

A partial roof on the opposite side of the courtyard fell in then, tumbling to the ground in a flurry of sparks. The flames burned higher as the wood caught and more dark smoke filled the air. Christina coughed and Gaston saw Ysmaine coax the other woman to her feet. There was something amiss with Ysmaine's hand, but he would see to that later. He willed them to move more quickly.

"I am not on trial!" Everard retorted. "I need not explain my choices to any man..."

"Nay, you are condemned, by the burden in your own grasp."

"But..."

"All you must do to prove your innocence is surrender it to me," Gaston invited. He lowered his sword and stretched out his left hand, knowing full well what his opponent would do. The women were passing through the gate, and the fire had nearly turned the courtyard into an inferno.

The man who called himself Everard attacked. "I owe naught to you!" he roared even as their blades clashed hard. "I will not answer to a monk who breaks his vows by taking a wife!" He battled hard against Gaston and jabbed suddenly. Gaston stepped back and only then saw the peril he had not realized.

Ysmaine had returned to the portal, doubtless seeking him. He could not warn her to retreat, not without calling his opponent's attention to her presence. He felt his lips thin to a grim line when she pulled her eating knife and sidled along the wall behind the villain.

The woman had too much valor, to be sure.

"You will die here, and the tale with you," Everard sneered. "I will sell this prize to see my own future secured."

"Someone else will recognize you."

"Silence can be bought, and I will have the funds."

"You did not silence Christina."

"Not yet," Everard replied grimly. "I shall see to that." He kicked a barrel toward Gaston with savage force. "And you will not survive this day to share the tale." Ysmaine eased toward the villain, though Gaston did not reveal her presence. He jumped over the barrel and attacked Everard, hoping to distract him from any sign of the lady's presence behind.

But Everard leapt aside so that Gaston's blow missed. He seized Ysmaine, spun her and flung her toward the brightest blaze of the fire. She stumbled and cried out, but Gaston did not wait to see his lady fall into the flames. He lunged after her and caught her against his chest. Unable to keep from tumbling after her, he cradled her from the force of their landing, then rolled her beneath himself to shelter her from the flames.

By the time he rolled to his feet, Everard was through the gate. Gaston heard the other man slam and lock it from the other side. He hauled Ysmaine to her feet beside him and they raced to the gate as one. He fought against the latch, but to no avail.

He spared a glance to the flames, then caught her around the waist. He fairly flung her to the top of the courtyard wall. "Jump, lady mine!" he commanded when she hesitated atop the wall.

"Aye, jump," Everard purred from the other side of the wall, the sound of his voice sending a chill through Gaston. "Grant me another pretty prize."

Ysmaine hesitated. Gaston heard a cry that he thought might have come from Christina. Ysmaine danced backward as the other man evidently lunged at her. Gaston heard the imposter laugh, then the clatter of hoof beats.

Ysmaine leapt down from the top of the wall on to the other side.

Gaston watched the flames come closer. The summit of the wall was too high for him to heft his own weight there. Indeed, he could not even brush the summit with his fingertips. There was naught in the courtyard to climb upon, for all was aflame. He shouted but there seemed no one to hear his cries. The smoke was thick, and he began to cough, fearing that Everard had called his fate aright.

At least Ysmaine was safe.

Gaston heard her swear, then the latch rattled. "It is so hot!" she complained, and he heard her kick the gate. To his relief, she unfastened the latch from the other side, and fresh air billowed into the courtyard.

"He has seized Christina and ridden that way," Ysmaine declared as Gaston stumbled into the alley. He grabbed her hand and led her away from the foul place, coughing to clear his lungs. To his relief, Wulfe was in the square before the cathedral, astride his black destrier.

He made his way to his fellow knight and told him what had transpired. "Christina left a trail of these gems," he told the Templar, whose manner was most severe. Wulfe took one of the stones and studied it, then placed it in his purse. "Ysmaine says the villain rode that way with her, and I will wager you will find a trail."

Wulfe nodded curtly and gathered his reins. "I thank you, Gaston, on behalf of the order. Know that the treasure is safely delivered." Gaston closed his eyes in relief. "May your new life suit you well." Wulfe offered his hand and the pair shook hands. Then the Templar then was gone, bending from the saddle in search of the glinting orange glass. His squires broke free of the crowd and raced their palfreys in pursuit.

Ysmaine looked between Wulfe and Gaston, her astonishment clear. "Do you not go with him?"

Gaston shook his head. "My contribution is done."

"But this matter is not completed..."

"It is for me. The treasure is delivered and the missive will be so shortly. My obligations are nigh complete, lady mine."

Still Ysmaine stared at him.

Gaston realized to his horror that his wife had not feigned her fear that he meant to return to the order and abandon her. He caught her close, compelling her to meet his gaze and willing her to see his conviction. "I am a secular lord, lady mine, with a loyal wife to my hand," he murmured to her. "It is not for me to follow the command of the order of the Temple, for I have more worldly concerns to mind."

He waited for pleasure to light her features, then he ducked his head and kissed her so thoroughly that only a witless woman could doubt his word.

And his beloved bride, Gaston knew well enough, had wits enough for three.

ᘒ

It seemed that all went aright and so readily that Ysmaine feared she had misunderstood.

Perhaps ill fortune had been her companion for so long that she dared not trust her happy circumstance.

Gaston carried her down the street, his expression resolute.

"You need not carry me, sir," she protested and he spared her an amused glance. "It is my wrist that is injured. I can walk."

"I dare not trust that you will accompany me otherwise," he murmured, stealing a kiss before he smiled anew. "For I owe you much explanation. And truly, I like this well."

"How so?"

"It grants us time to talk, as you so suggested." He shouldered his way through the crowds before Notre Dame. "And to be honest with each other, as I would prefer."

"I did not wish to deceive you..." Ysmaine began to protest but Gaston halted and silenced her with a thorough kiss, right there in the street. Passersby hooted and shouted encouragement so that Ysmaine was flushed crimson when he lifted his head. He regarded her with sparkling eyes. "I mean to explain, sir," she tried again, only to be soundly kissed once more.

"No explanation is necessary," Gaston murmured when he broke their kiss again. "All has come aright, thanks to your cleverness, and I am indebted to you. I regret only that you believed even for a moment that I wished our match annulled."

"You do not, then?"

"No man finds a treasure unexpected and casts it aside." He was so dismissive that Ysmaine smiled. Gaston continued through the square, and Ysmaine nestled against him, well pleased indeed. "I would suggest we visit the Temple, for the horses and Bartholomew are there and we might best see for ourselves that the treasure has been secured. I have also the missive to the Grand Master to deliver, and doubtless he will have questions for me as to what transpired in Jerusalem." He spared her a glance and Ysmaine nodded.

"That makes good sense, sir. And then?"

"And then." Gaston nodded. "And then I have a boon to ask of my lady wife. I would entreat her that we recall a certain night in Venice, when we both spoke and loved with vigor, when honesty was between us and much more."

"Before you were assaulted."

"That very night." Gaston smiled at her. "I would continue from the promise of that night, casting aside this last month of subterfuge, even though it was done for good cause."

"Your boon is readily won, sir."

His smile flashed. "Excellent. Then we shall have need of baths, stabling for the horses and a good inn. We will all savor a hot meal and a glass of wine, then I shall, with permission, spend a night abed with my lady wife."

"Surely you mean an interval, before you retire to the stables," Ysmaine said, but to her delight, her husband shook his head.

"An interval will no longer suffice. I will spend the entire night in my lady's bed, from this night forward."

"What of the stables? What of your steed?"

"He is of import to me, of course, but not the key treasure in my life. And truly, there is solely one prize to defend from this point onward." His eyes shone with affection as he considered her and he dropped his voice to a murmur. "My priorities have changed, lady mine."

"Gaston!" Ysmaine pulled his head down to kiss him with sufficient enthusiasm to show her approval of that notion. He crushed her against him, and Ysmaine was dizzy when he lifted his head.

"Curse responsibility," he muttered. "I would find an inn immediately."

Ysmaine laughed, happier than she had ever imagined she might be. She kicked her feet as he crossed the bridge to the north bank and could not keep herself from smiling.

"And now we come to a matter worthy of discussion," Gaston said. "I have thought often of your insistence that your parents consult upon the administration of the estate."

"Amongst other matters."

"So I would ask your counsel." Gaston shifted Ysmaine's weight, reached into the pouch at his belt and removed a missive. "From my brother's widow," he said. "I had thought little of the manner of my return, but now I wonder if I miss something of import in her words. Perhaps I see shadows where there are none, but I would ask your advice."

"You would have me read her missive?"

Gaston nodded, and Ysmaine unfurled the vellum with delight. "I know what it says, but it is possible that you will see more meaning than I have."

"She is frugal," Ysmaine said immediately. The script was crowded, cramped so that more tidings fit in less space, and the vellum had been washed of script at least twice before.

"Aye, her family considered the match to be most fortunate, as I recall."

Ysmaine nodded, reading quickly. Her gaze lingered on the last passages. "How curious that her older daughter was wed so close to her husband's funeral."

Gaston flicked a glance at her. "Coincidence? Or detail of import?" He sighed. "Will I arrive home to find my holding claimed by another?"

"Do you know this Millard?"

She watched as he pursed his lips. "It is long since I left France, remember." Ysmaine nodded agreement. "But he is of an age with me. We trained for our spurs around the same time, and encountered each other then."

"Then you know something of his nature." She saw that Gaston was choosing his words and tried to help him bypass his usual tact. "Did he ride to crusade?"

Gaston laughed aloud. "He? Nay! War might have soiled his tabard."

Ysmaine was enormously relieved. "Then he is not a knight who wears the scars of battle on his hide?"

"Unless he has changed much, I would guess not."

"Yet it has been months since your brother's demise. He might have gained allies within the hall already." Ysmaine nibbled her lip. "What if we stop at my father's abode en route to your home? My father might know more of events at Châmont-sur-Maine."

"Will your parents be pleased that you have wed a warrior such as me?"

Ysmaine smiled. "It was my father's father who taught him the merit of a warrior's scar. My father wears his with pride." She saw the Temple's high walls appearing ahead of him and had an idea. "And if you were to invite a company of your fellow knights to escort you to your new home, perhaps to linger and celebrate your good fortune, my mother might be indebted to you forevermore."

"How so?"

"I have five younger sisters, Gaston. My mother always hoped that my marriage would facilitate at least several of theirs." She smiled up at him. "And if you arrived at Châmont-sur-Maine with a company of warriors, perhaps Fergus and Duncan and Bartholomew, I doubt a man who preferred to keep his tabard unsoiled would protest your claiming of your legacy."

Gaston grinned. "Lady mine, you are a treasure to be sure," he murmured, then kissed her with such surety that her breath was stolen away.

Ysmaine twined her arms around his neck and kissed him back, her heart thundering with such vigor that she thought it might burst. "I love you, Gaston," she confessed when she was able to speak.

"Then all is aright, for I love you, as well, lady mine," Gaston confessed. Another kiss punctuated their confessions, and he looked positively disheveled as he approached the gates of the Temple.

His pleasure in their future gave her an idea. "We should not linger long at my parents' abode, for I would see you arrived at your home estate by September 16."

Gaston frowned slightly. "I have no objections, but why so precise a date, lady mine?" He nodded to the porter at the Temple gates, who waved them onward.

"That is the feast day of Saint Euphemia, who I believe has cast her favor over this journey and our match."

Gaston halted in the courtyard to look down at her, his wonder clear. "The relic of Saint Euphemia?" he asked, then shook his head. "Was that the treasure?" At Ysmaine's nod, he looked awed. "We carried a precious burden, indeed."

"You did not know?"

"It is not uncommon to know only part of a tale, lady mine."

"Do you not wish to see it?"

"I pledged to restrain my curiosity."

"But your quest is complete, and it is most beautiful. I think you should have the chance to look at least once upon such a marvel, after you have defended it."

Gaston's gaze flicked to hers. "We should petition the Grand Master to see the relic, that we might pray for Saint Euphemia's blessing."

Though Ysmaine thought it already granted, she could not protest the perfection of that scheme. She doubted the Grand Master would refuse him, and she was right.

Her heart was singing when they entered the chapel of the Temple to pray, her hand held fast within Gaston's own. So much had come aright, and she had many thanks to give. Indeed, Ysmaine had only one request to make when she touched her fingertips to the glorious reliquary of Saint Euphemia, and that was for the prompt conception of his son.

Little did she know that she would bear him a daughter before the first of their three sons arrived.

Tuesday, September 1, 1187

Feast Day of Saint Drithelm
and Saint Giles of Provence.

❧

Claire Delacroix

Epilogue

By the time Gaston's party crossed the boundaries of Valeroy, he had a veritable list of concerns about his new life. The last deed he wished to do was to disappoint Ysmaine, but he feared his lack of experience would cause him to err.

They were numerous, due to Ysmaine's suggestion. Fergus had joined their party, along with Duncan and the two squires in his service. That knight had been long in discussion with the Grand Master at Paris, and Gaston did not doubt that the Scotsman carried some missive to London on his behalf. The boy Laurent had been compelled to bathe, which made him look both younger and more delicate. Gaston hoped the boy survived the winters in Scotland.

Bartholomew also rode with them, along with four of the knights from the Temple who rode to London with Fergus. They had another six squires, and along with the palfreys burdened with Fergus' gifts for his betrothed, the party was of considerable size.

There was a balance to be struck between appearing resolute and aggressive, and Gaston believed he had struck the balance right. The Grand Master had offered as many men as Gaston wished, but he had selected only the four. He would not have minded to have Wulfe in the party, but there had been no word from that knight after he had ridden in pursuit of Christina. Gaston wondered if they would ever meet again.

He had endeavored to gather as much information about his future holding and local politics as possible while in Paris, but still he felt poorly equipped for the responsibilities ahead of him. He was blessed indeed to have Ysmaine at his side, for she had a knowledge of secular matters beyond his own.

The appearance of the keep of Valeroy on the horizon made Gaston think of his lady's parents and their reaction to her nuptials.

They had not chosen him, and indeed, they might not approve.

He considered the appearance of his party and decided upon a change. "Ride in pairs," he instructed the others. "We approach as visitors not invaders."

"That is good thinking," Ysmaine said softly, her eyes shining. Indeed, he could not miss the delight in her expression as she surveyed her home. "Is it not beautiful?"

Valeroy *was* beautiful, prosperous, and so clearly well administered that Gaston felt his lack of experience more keenly. He tried to hide his trepidation, but his perceptive wife reached to touch the back of his gloved hand.

"Fear not, Gaston. They will approve of you most heartily." She had recalled his hope that she arrive at his holding richly garbed without him making any reminder. In Paris, she had sewn the green silk into a wondrous garment with Radegunde's help. The pair of them had worked long hours upon the embroidery and though she vowed there would yet be more, even now, Ysmaine looked like a queen. He was beyond glad that she had chosen this garb for this day, but still feared their reception.

"They did not choose me."

"They had no such opportunity."

"I did not ask your father's permission to take your hand."

"There was scarce a chance to do so."

"Your wrist is broken," he reminded her, suspecting that he as a protective father might find that a sign of disregard or at least carelessness.

She smiled. "I would never have seen this place again save for you, and they will not forget it."

Gaston swallowed as the gates drew nearer.

"Gaston, I am hale, I am richly garbed, I am escorted, and I have a ring upon my finger," Ysmaine said, her voice soft but scolding all the same. Gaston glanced at her and she smiled. "It is likely that my father remembers you, as well."

That was not reassuring in the least, not when returning to France put Gaston in mind of his uncle's desire to be rid of him. He did not know Amaury's alliances or friendships and felt that he entered an uncharted realm. What man could negotiate his way without surety of alliances, both spoken and unspoken, in his fellows?

He hoped he did not err at Valeroy out of his ignorance. There was but one opportunity to make a first impression, and he would have Ysmaine's parents think well of him from the outset.

The porter hailed them and Gaston made a decision. "You speak for us first," he bade Ysmaine. "For this is your home."

She smiled, clearly thrilled that he granted her this responsibility. "Good day!" she cried, raising her voice as she addressed the porter merrily. "Is that yet you at the gates of Valeroy, Odo of Brittany? If so, my father is fortunate to yet be so well served."

An older man stepped out of the gatehouse, his astonishment clear. "Lady Ysmaine? You are returned! Praise be to God!"

"Praise be to Mary," Ysmaine corrected with a smile. "For I return with a husband and defender, who has ensured my safe journey from Jerusalem itself."

This Odo looked between Gaston and Ysmaine with wonder. "Many feared you dead, my lady."

"And I was nearly so." She spoke with a crisp authority that was not displeasing. "Please send word to my parents that we arrive, Odo."

The porter bowed and retreated, shouting for a boy to run to the hall ahead of them. He opened the gates, beckoned to the ostler, and walked beside Ysmaine. Gaston liked well this balance between deference and conviviality and pledged to learn more of how it was encouraged from his wife. "All are well here, my lady, but your sister, the lady Jehanne, was wed in April."

"Truly?" Ysmaine's pleasure was clear. "And the match is good?"

"Your father was most satisfied with it, and he seemed an amiable knight. His repute is excellent."

"That is most pleasing to know. I thank you for these tidings, Odo." Ysmaine halted her horse and addressed. "I fear you wish to ask me of Thibaud, but do not wish to be bold, so I will tell you the worst of it. I know you were good friends and long comrades."

Odo dropped his gaze, evidently guessing what she would say. "He will not return, then."

Ysmaine spoke gently. "I fear not. He died in my defense and is laid to his rest in Ornans, outside Besançon."

Odo crossed himself, his grief clear, then looked up at

Ysmaine again. "Thibaud told me before your party left that he would willingly die to ensure your welfare, my lady. He would be joyous to see you returned to Valeroy."

"He made it possible, and leaves me forever in his debt," Ysmaine acknowledged. "I will ask my father to order a mass for Thibaud here and will have one said weekly at my new abode on his behalf."

"You are most kind, my lady," Odo said and kissed the hem of her kirtle.

Gaston took note of the devotion of her father's men. He should be so fortunate as to have men sworn to his hand who would lay down their lives in defense of his own children.

"You must teach me how this balance is struck," he said to his wife when they rode on. "For his deference is as clear as his affection."

Again, Ysmaine touched Gaston's hand. "My father is fair but firm, a man who keeps his word and protects his own. His courts give timely justice at a fair price, and he is generous with those on his holding." She met his gaze. "You will strike this balance readily, Gaston, for you have much in common with him."

Gaston could not reply for they reached the portal to the hall itself. An older man and woman stood together in the bailey, their hands clasped. He recalled his father's counsel that a man should look to the mother of his bride to see the future, and so he studied Richildis. She was slender and elegant, and her gaze was direct. She was an attractive woman, and a regal one.

"Ysmaine!" she cried and his wife slipped from the saddle to run to her mother. They embraced tightly as her father looked on, and tears were shed by all three of them.

"You are home," Amaury whispered, his hand upon his eldest daughter's shoulder.

"You are too thin," Richildis scolded, but Ysmaine only laughed.

He bit back a smile at the realization that Ysmaine had already taught him something of women for he could read her mother's thoughts clearly. She surveyed her daughter, clicking her tongue that she was so thin then she surveyed him openly. Gaston did not doubt that she estimated his wealth and endeavored to guess his character. Her gaze fell to the silk bliaut, and he would have wagered she put its value within a penny. Richildis then looked at her daughter's left hand, and Gaston was glad he had seen fit to buy a gold wedding ring in Paris.

The parents turned to him expectantly but he had already dismounted.

"My husband," Ysmaine said, and Gaston knew he had her parents' attention fully.

He bowed low. "I am Gaston de Châmont-sur-Maine," he said, then offered his hand.

Richildis could not hide her delight. "So close as that?" she whispered, then hugged her daughter again. Indeed, the love within this family could not be disguised.

Amaury's grip was firm and his gaze steady. "I see Fulk in your eyes and in your stature," he said with satisfaction and Gaston felt relief. "Doubtless I should taste it in the bite of your blade should we meet in battle. No man could look upon you and doubt your father's name."

"I am glad to know of this, sir. I have been gone many years, after all."

"And much has changed in your absence," Amaury agreed easily.

Gaston realized that the information he sought might be gained from his lady's family. "I fear I have lost track of those who will be my neighbors, and hope I do not give offense where none is due."

Amaury considered him, but said naught.

"Do you know if my mother is still at the same foundation?" Gaston asked. "Neither she nor I have been permitted private correspondence, but Ysmaine would like to meet her. I, too, would be glad to see her again."

"I am not certain," Amaury said. "Richildis may know more, or at least who best to ask."

Gaston inclined his head in thanks.

Amaury continued, apparently making conversation. "There were those who said you would not leave the Templars even for the prize of a holding."

Gaston was certain Ysmaine's father sought to warn him of his reception. "I understand my niece is lately wed, to Millard de St. Roux," he said, keeping his tone mild.

Amaury's gaze flicked over Gaston's party. "And so she is. You knew of this?"

"Marie wrote to advise me of Bayard's death and mentioned the marriage. I was permitted to receive a missive of such import."

Amaury nodded, his gaze trailing over the group. "You must come into the hall and refresh yourselves."

Gaston chose to misinterpret that man's glance. "I apologize that our party is so large, sir, and would not expect your hospitality to extend to those knights who accompany us. My comrades travel to London and beyond and would readily take their relief at an inn." He knew how he might reassure his wife's father. "We travel together at Ysmaine's suggestion that our parties be joined. I thought her counsel most sensible for the road can be dangerous."

Amaury's eyes lit. "You confer with my daughter, then?"

"Of course, sir. It is long since I left these parts and her knowledge is invaluable."

Amaury smiled and beckoned to the rest of the party. "I welcome you and all of your comrades to Valeroy. There is a hind for the midday meal, and more than sufficient for all." His voice dropped. "Indeed, the hunting is most fine this year. I wonder whether you might linger a day or two here that we might ride out to hunt together."

Gaston understood that Ysmaine's father would grant him advice and news of his neighbors in the forest, where they could not be overheard. Indeed, here was a familiar technique as well as the information he sought. "I am honored by the invitation, sir, and pleased to accept."

"And I am equally pleased by the opportunity to spend time with my daughter's new husband." Amaury granted Gaston a sidelong glance that he understood well. "Indeed, I think I may feel compelled to accompany you to your holding, the better to see where my daughter will make her home." He smiled. "You will indulge a father, I hope."

"Of course."

"Ah, I remember Fulk well, and his pride in his estate. It will be good to see that place again."

"I hope you will give me the opportunity to return your hospitality," Gaston said. "And bring as large a party as you choose."

Amaury laughed and clapped Gaston on the shoulder. His eyes gleamed and Gaston knew they understood each other. "Indeed, I could do no less, for I see that my daughter has chosen well." He sobered and met Gaston's gaze steadily. "Fulk would be proud of you, make no mistake in that. And I am glad of my daughter's choice."

"I am honored by it," Gaston agreed.

They shook hands again, then Gaston led Ysmaine to the high table in her father's hall. Her sisters greeted her with delight, as did many of the servants, and he was pleased to see her joy. She brought so much advantage to him already, and he knew they would meet the challenges of the future together—as well as savor its joys. Ysmaine was radiant, as brilliant as a well-cut gem, and Gaston was resolved that his home would be the setting that would favor her best.

Indeed, he would make it so.

The lady who had claimed his wary heart deserved no less.

*Ready for more of the
Champions of Saint Euphemia?*

Read on for an excerpt from the next book in the series

The Crusader's Heart

A company of Templar knights, chosen by the Grand Master of the Temple in Jerusalem to deliver a sealed trunk to the Temple in Paris. A group of pilgrims seeking the protection of the Templars to return home as the Muslims prepare to besiege the city. A mysterious treasure that someone will even kill to possess...

A valiant warrior sworn to the order of the Knights Templar for life, Wulfe resents being dispatched to Paris just when the Latin Kingdoms are at their most vulnerable. He is determined to fulfill his duty as quickly as possible and return to fight for justice—but the courtesan he defends in Venice is resolved to remain at his side until she saves his life in return. The alluring and perceptive Christina will not be left behind, and soon Wulfe finds himself forced to choose between his vows and his heart...

Venice—July, 1187

Wulfe could not believe his ill fortune. The list of his woes was long indeed, and he ground his teeth as he marched through the twisted streets of Venice in search of relief.

First, he had been compelled to leave Jerusalem just when that city was doomed to face a challenge to its survival as a crusader holding. As a knight and a Templar, he knew his blade should be raised in defense of the Temple, not undertaking some errand that could have been managed by a clerk or lay brother.

Worse, this duty demanded that he ride all the way to Paris to deliver said missive, which meant that by the time he returned to Outremer, any battle might be completed. He might miss the opportunity to defend what he loved best, which was an abomination by any accounting.

Thirdly, he had only the appearance of leadership of the party that traveled with him. In reality, he had to cede to the dictate of Gaston, a former brother of the Temple who secretly was in command of this quest. That a knight who had left the order was more trusted than Wulfe was salt in the wound.

That Gaston made choices Wulfe would never have made, and Wulfe had to present them as his own notions, was galling. It was Gaston's fault that the mission had so nearly failed at Acre, for Gaston had insisted upon riding for that port instead of departing more quickly from the closer port of Jaffa. Wulfe snarled that he should be blamed for such a close call.

Though it was somewhat mollifying that Gaston had defended the party alone when they had been attacked and might have paid for his error with his own life.

Still, had the choice been Wulfe's, no one would have been compelled to render any price at Acre.

The final straw was that Wulfe had been saddled with the most vexing company imaginable for the journey to Paris. A fortnight trapped on a ship with them all had left him nigh murderous.

There was Gaston, so calm and deliberate, so unshakeable in

his confidence, that Wulfe was tempted to challenge him to a fight. He wanted to see Gaston riled over some matter or another. There was Gaston's wife, Ysmaine, a beauty who, like all women, should neither be trusted nor riding with knights on an errand. Indeed, she had evidently acquired toxins and brought them along. Such irresponsibility was yet another source of annoyance to Wulfe.

There was Gaston's squire, Bartholomew, a man of such an age that he should long ago have been knighted himself. Wulfe had no patience for men with little ambition. Although the younger man did not appear to be lazy, Wulfe could not understand why he did not aspire for more. It was unnatural to be content with one's lot.

Another former Templar, Fergus, had completed his military service and returned to Scotland to wed his betrothed. Wulfe could not comprehend why he would stick to the date of his planned departure when the Holy City was likely to be besieged. Indeed, he could make no sense in the decision of any of these men to abandon Jerusalem in its moment of need.

That the secret treasure they carried in trust for the Temple in Jerusalem was entrusted to the care of Fergus, another brother who had left the order, and not himself, made Wulfe's blood fairly boil. He did not even know what the prize was!

There was also the merchant, Joscelin de Provins, as soft as a grub and rightly fearful of his survival in any trouble. It was perfectly reasonable that such a plump man, so concerned with the value of his goods, would wish to be away from war. Wulfe neither liked nor respected Joscelin, but it was the sworn task of the order to defend pilgrims and he would do as much.

There was the knight, Everard, who apparently abandoned a holding in the Latin Kingdoms to visit the deathbed of his father in France. Wulfe was incredulous that any man would abandon his wealth over sentimentality. He had little patience for men who squandered the gifts granted to them, and less for those who forsook opportunity, as this one surely did. It seemed to him that Everard made a poor choice in leaving Outremer and his holding. Perhaps he was a coward.

As a man who had been given few gifts in this life, and who had labored hard for all he had won to his own hand, Wulfe knew he was a harsh judge of others. He found much of mankind wanting, but was protective of those for whom he took responsibility. He would have laid down his own life in defense of either of his squires, for example, and had taken blows intended for his destrier. In return, the loyalty of those beings—Stephen, Simon, and Teufel—was complete.

He also was a man who knew how best to manage his own passions. By the time the party reached Venice, disembarked, saw to the care of an injured squire, and found accommodation, he knew his temper was incendiary. How could such simple feats consume so much time? Contrary to his expectation that they would take a single night to fortify themselves before riding out, Gaston was resolved to await the three days decreed by the apothecary as being necessary rest for the injured squire.

For a squire, who was sufficiently clumsy to have inflicted his own injury.

Wulfe could bear their company no longer. He had left the rented house, knowing that he had need of a war or a whore. The only way to control his escalating frustration was to expend passion in one feat or the other. Venice was at peace, its laws against violence and its courts known to be harsh.

Its courtesans were also highly reputed.

The choice was an easy one.

Stephen and Simon hastened behind him, undoubtedly guessing his intent. They would ensure that he was neither robbed nor injured on this quest, though more than once a whore had found their presence unsettling. Wulfe did not care what such women thought. They were paid and paid well, and he knew himself to be a considerate lover, if a passionate one.

He was demanding in this pursuit as in all others.

He would choose a young and vigorous woman on this night.

Doubtless she would never forget him. The prospect made Wulfe smile.

る。

The best house of courtesans was located with relative ease, for Wulfe asked in the marketplace. The boys, too, sought information, and by the time they conferred in the mid-afternoon, one answer was clear.

The canals and bridges were confounding, and the directions less clear than might have been ideal. Wulfe became convinced that Venice was a burg designed to aid the trade of thieves, for it seemed a warren of crooked streets that ended abruptly with a wall or a canal. The houses were shuttered tightly on the street level, and he glimpsed that the lowest floor of the richest ones sheltered docks on the bigger canals. They all had at least two stories overhead, often with high arching windows, and he imagined that people preferred to be away from the water.

It did have a foul smell when the breeze stilled.

They finally located the house in question and were questioned before the heavy door was unbolted. The patroness came halfway down the flight of stairs on the far side of the foyer, her garb appearing as rich as the men in her employ looked dangerous. She was shrewd-eyed but well-mannered, and the house was in good repair. Wulfe could see that once she had been a beauty and wondered whether she had labored upon her back in this house in her youth. She certainly was direct. A short conversation ensured his preferences were made clear, then the patroness gestured that he should follow her up the stairs.

Wulfe was astounded by the generous proportions and richness of the room that filled second floor of the house. Sunlight shone through high arched windows and there was a view of the harbor, the sea sparkling blue. A long table was laid with fine clothes and rich fare, and boys poured generous goblets of wine. The women were both numerous and beautiful. They did not look to be starved or bruised, and he decided that, in this case, rumor had provided the truth.

Indeed, his mood improved by the moment.

"A maiden?" the patroness suggested, gesturing to a pair of young girls. Wulfe did not doubt that their maidenhead had already been sold at least once.

"I have little fondness for innocence," he said, for it was true. He liked to be with a woman who knew her body and her desires, as well as one who could anticipate his own. "Teaching is not a pastime I care to pursue abed," he clarified, and the patroness gave a throaty chuckle.

"Ah! A tigress, then," she countered, gesturing to a woman who might have seen thirty summers. There was a slyness in her expression that Wulfe did not find alluring. The patroness noted how his gaze slid past her suggestion and snapped her fingers for other women to come forward. "You are early this day, sir, which gives you the finest choice. Of course, given the time, I must assume that you desire companionship only for the afternoon." She clapped her hands when the women did not move quickly enough for her taste, and Wulfe caught a glimpse of one at the far end of the room.

She was exquisitely beautiful, her hair like russet silk. She wore it loose and the length of it gleamed, falling as it did to her hips. The color of her hair was rare in this city, where most of the other women had tresses of dark brown or black. She was taller than the other women, as well, slender and elegant in the way that Wulfe preferred. She was dressed in gold and green, the richness of her garb not unlike that of a noblewoman. Wulfe knew that the neckline was more revealing than would have been the choice of any aristocrat, but as she walked toward him, he could imagine that a queen approached him.

There was a reluctance in her manner that he admired as well. Not for him the harlot who threw herself at his feet, willing and eager for his touch and his coin. Perhaps she merely took her time. Perhaps she had the confidence that once a man looked upon her, he would wait. Wulfe did not care. He was entranced by her grace, by her wariness, by his own impression that she might have been a noblewoman.

He supposed the rich garb revealed that she earned well for her patroness, but preferred to not consider that. Her full lips tightened slightly, as she followed the other women. He thought he spied both defiance and resignation in her expression, but then she lifted her head and smiled.

And there was the key. Hers was not a genuine smile, for its light did not reach her eyes. Her lips curved in sensuous welcome, but her gaze remained wary, another hint of that reluctance.

Wulfe understood immediately that this life was not her choice, and his decision was made. He knew what it was to put aside one's own desires to serve those of another. He knew what it was to feel trapped, and to have few choices. He knew what it was to make the best of one's circumstance, regardless of the price.

And he knew what it was to await a better choice, with as

much patience as could be mustered.

"This one," he said, gesturing to the temptress who had claimed his attention. He did not care that he was interrupting the patroness as she listed the charms of her women.

"Ah, Christina is a popular choice," she acknowledged, even as the woman's gaze rose to meet Wulfe's own. Her eyes were a bewitching shade of green, thickly lashed and not without intelligence. At the impatient summons of her patroness, she halted before him, more gracious and lovely than any woman he had ever seen. The old woman looked between them, and Wulfe thought she smiled. "You may find her price high," she warned.

Christina held his gaze boldly, knowing her own worth and perhaps not expecting him to pay it. Aye, there were shadows in those wondrous eyes, shadows that told of disappointment.

Perhaps from men.

Perhaps from a man.

Wulfe felt an unexpected valor rise within him and heighten his need.

"Name it," he said, unable to imagine what she had seen of men. He doubted it had all been good and wished to surprise her.

If only to see the resignation leave her gaze.

The patroness did as much, clearly expecting Wulfe to haggle. He did not, though, for he never tainted the acquisition of any desire with such mean bargaining. He earned a good wage at the Temple, even as his basic needs were supplied.

"That, of course, is only for the afternoon," the patroness added slyly.

"And for the night as well?"

A flicker of interest made Christina consider him anew. When their gazes locked and held, he felt they shared a secret.

"Triple," the older woman said crisply. "For there are ships in the harbor."

Christina lowered her gaze, evidently anticipating his refusal.

"Triple," Wulfe agreed so readily that he was certain the patroness regretted not asking for more. He cared only for the way Christina's gaze flew to his face again. She was surprised, and he was glad. He smiled outright at her, paid the patroness, then offered his hand to the lady he so desired. He kissed her hand and saw her eyes narrow slightly. "I assume you have a private chamber where our pleasure might be pursued?"

"Of course, sir," she said, and he liked that her voice was both rich and husky. She spoke in the same Venetian dialect as her patroness, but not so fluidly as one born in this city of cities. Where was she from? What had brought her to this house? Wulfe was surprised by how much he wished to know.

Indeed, his frustrations faded already, and the pursuit of pleasure had not yet begun.

Christina did not believe for a moment that the Templar was truly different from any of the other men who visited Costanzia's house, but it was harmless to imagine otherwise. She had not yet bedded a Templar, after all, and there was something intriguing about his determination to have her for both day and night. He had no shortage of coin—at least, he had not before his arrival in this place—and there was a resolve about him that she admired. He was easy to look upon, a man who clearly earned his way with hard labor. He was broad and tall, fair of hair and resolute in every way. His manner was crisp and he did not linger over his choices. Christina admired decisive men.

Indeed, if either her father or her husband had been more decisive, she might not have found herself in her current circumstance.

But there was naught to be gained by regret, or by bitterness.

"Would you not partake of a meal?" she asked, guiding him to the table as she had been instructed. "Some wine? Or ale? Meat and bread?" Perhaps she could see him drunken in the passing of a day and a night, then slip out of the house with his fat purse. It would be a poor reward for him, but what manner of Templar frequented brothels?

He could not have as much merit as she could hope.

"I have only the appetite for one feast in this moment," he said smoothly, and Christina forced herself to smile. She was always fearful at first, for one never knew what to expect of a man. It was easier if they had at least one cup of wine, for it evened the odds should she have to fight for her survival.

Two boys followed behind them, and she guessed they were

his squires.

"At least savor one cup of wine," she urged. "My patroness is most proud of the vintages she acquires."

He accepted a cup then and let her fill it, but barely let the wine touch his lips when he sipped. "The room?" he asked, evidently determined to have his desire sooner rather than later.

Christina beckoned to a servant, but one of the knight's squires took the chalice and pitcher. She eyed the boys, wondering whether the knight meant for them to watch. There was a flutter within her, for the oldest boy was not so small as that. They would be three. "The boys can remain here in the hall..."

The knight shook his head with such resolve that she fell silent. "They will accompany me. You need not fear their intervention. They merely protect me and my purse." He smiled. "They will practice their chess."

Christina glanced toward the boys, not at all reassured.

Costanzia gave her a hard look from the far side of the chamber, and Christina bit back any argument she might have made. In this moment, the streets seemed meaner than the knight before her.

Although she might be mistaken about that.

"Have you been long sworn to the order, then?" she asked, dutifully turning her steps toward the stairs. The boys followed.

She saw his fleeting frown. "Of what import is that?"

"I thought perhaps your appetite was whetted by a hunger unsatisfied."

The knight laughed then, and it was not forced. Indeed, his eyes twinkled. "It is my challenge to uphold the pledge of chastity," he admitted.

Christina did not like the sound of that. "Then you often pay for satisfaction?"

"Not often," he said. "But there are times when a man has need of a woman's caress."

"And you find yourself in such a time," she said. It was easier if they talked about themselves, if she learned more of their needs and desires before reaching the bed. "Are such times predictable?"

"Only in their link with frustration in other arenas." He grimaced when she glanced his way. "I endeavor to be temperate. You need not fear you will be granted a pox by me. I am not so lusty as to have earned that doom." Christina was relieved and hoped he told the truth. "But there are moments when I know myself to be vexed. If I cannot change my situation, I must endeavor to find release in other ways, lest my abilities be compromised by my mood." He flicked her an intent glance. "I will not permit annoyance to compromise my fighting skills, and so, the lesser evil must have its day."

Christina could understand that well enough. "What manner of situation could cause such a state?" They reached the next floor, and she guided him toward the end of the corridor.

"An assignment that proves annoying to fulfill." He heaved a sigh. "Indeed, I fear this one may not be completed with anything like timeliness, and that vexes me beyond all."

"Why? Surely the Temple ensures your comfort regardless of your task?"

Consideration and perhaps humor lit his eyes. "As this place ensures yours?"

Christina found herself flushing. "There is food and a roof."

"Aye, there is food and a roof. Do you not ever aspire to more?"

"Do you?"

"Of course." He shook his head. "But aspirations do not ensure food and a roof, so choices must be made. Perhaps compromises must be made." Christina was shocked that his reasoning was so close to her own. He flicked a glance over her and his eyes narrowed slightly. "How came you to this place?"

"Does it matter?"

"Nay, save that I would wager that you made a similar choice."

"You would win that wager," she admitted, then wished she had not. He watched her more closely, curious, but Christina dared not confide any more.

Would he help her if she asked him to do so? Nay, he could not. Costanzia would empty his purse and demand yet more. And he was a knight sworn to the service of an order, not a man who could wed—or even keep a mistress.

Nay, she would have to trick him, or find another way.

The silence between them seemed fraught as she led him to the richest of the rooms reserved for clients. It boasted a pillared bed draped in red silk, the dark wood gilded splendidly. It was the largest room, with the finest view over the Adriatic. Also, the bed was curtained and the door could be locked.

She was not truly surprised when the knight locked the portal. Indeed, she felt a little frisson of fear. To her amazement, he surrendered the key to her with a gallant bow.

While she struggled to think of something to say, he gestured the boys toward a low divan on the far side of the room. "I would see a fire lit for the lady's comfort," he instructed. "Then the two of you will watch it closely and tend it while you play chess."

"Aye, sir," the boys agreed in unison, hastening to do his bidding.

The knight pulled the curtains on the bed on the side of the door, then across the foot. His choice would ensure that the boys could not see them coupling, and that they would have a view only of the sea. Christina dared to be relieved.

He faced her, his gaze assessing. "And so they call you Christina?"

She nodded. "They do."

"They call me Wulfe," he said. "Sometimes even Wulfe Stürmer."

"Fighting wolf," she translated easily, believing he likely was a fearsome foe.

"Just so." He leaned closer and lowered his voice, amusement lifting the corner of his lips. "But neither is really my name." His eyes sparkled in a most enticing way. "Do we have something else in common?"

Christina fought the urge to smile. Instead she held his gaze and lied. "I am Christina." She was Christina, now, and in this place.

"I do not believe you were always Christina," Wulfe said, his hands dropping to the fastening of her girdle. "Just as I do not believe that Venetian is your mother tongue."

Christina dropped her gaze to his hands, fighting the urge to step away. "Why ever not?" she asked, trying to keep her tone light. He had fine strong hands, tanned hands, and though he could have overwhelmed her readily, he untied the knot slowly.

"You understood my nickname."

"Many women in my trade understand more than one

language."

"And many were not born in this city. Where did your journey begin, Christina?"

This would not do. She owed him no tales of her past and no confessions. Her body might have been sold, but her thoughts and her history were her own. She met his gaze steadily, intent on halting his questions but doubting he would be easily deterred. "Of what import is that?" She smiled, seeing how he watched her mouth. "I am here now, as are you." She ran a hand across his chest, hoping that a caress would distract him from such queries.

Christina touched her lips to this throat, for good measure. He had shaved, which she liked well. He smelled clean, and as a man should. Not perfumed or touched with the scent of another woman. She heard him catch his breath as she let her lips linger against his skin and felt him swallow. When she might have drawn back, he bent and pressed a kiss to her neck below her ear. His lips were warm, his kiss gentle, and Christina was startled that he should be so gentle.

Tender, even.

He pulled back slightly and considered her, his eyes glinting. "Not always Christina and not always a whore," he said with resolve.

She shook her head. "You mistake my history, sir."

But Wulfe only smiled and kissed her earlobe, his hands locking around her waist. When he whispered in her ear, Christina shivered, both at his touch and his pledge. "Let us see if I can convince you to confide the truth in me," he murmured. "I have all the day and all the night to win this challenge. I assure you that I shall make the quest worth your while."

Before she could protest or reply, Wulfe cupped her nape in one hand, pulled her closer and kissed her fully. It was a sweet potent kiss, one intended to make her lose her reservations and her restraint, and it came very close to succeeding.

Of course, it was only the beginning of Wulfe's amorous assault.

❧

ᘒ

The Crusader's Heart

is the second book in Claire Delacroix's
Champions of Saint Euphemia series.

Coming October 20, 2015!

Available for pre-order at some online portals.

ᘒ

*Bestselling author Deborah Cooke sold her first romance novel in 1992 – that medieval romance, **The Romance of the Rose**, was published by Harlequin Historicals in 1993 under the pseudonym Claire Delacroix. Since then, she has published more than fifty romance novels and numerous novellas in a wide variety of sub-genres under the names Claire Delacroix, Claire Cross and Deborah Cooke. **The Beauty** by Claire Delacroix, part of her successful Bride Quest series, was her first novel to land on the New York Times' List of Bestselling Books. In 2009, Deborah was the writer in residence at the Toronto Public Library, the first time they have hosted a residency focused on the romance genre. In 2012, she was honored with RWA's Mentor of the Year Award.*

*In addition to writing the **Champions of Saint Euphemia Series** of medieval romances as Claire Delacroix, Deborah also writes contemporary romance and paranormal romance as Deborah Cooke. She lives in Canada with her husband and far too many books.*

Learn more about Deborah's books and follow her blog at her website:
http://deborahcooke.com

Subscribe to Deborah's monthly newsletter for updates on new releases:
http://eepurl.com/UCUdf

෪

CPSIA information can be obtained at www.ICGtesting.com
Printed in the USA
LVOW10s1529270915

455916LV00026B/883/P